ORDINARY PEOPLE

BY THE SAME AUTHOR

26a
The Wonder

Ordinary People

a novel

DIANA EVANS

LIVERIGHT PUBLISHING CORPORATION
A division of W. W. Norton & Company
Independent Publishers Since 1923
New York London

For information about permission to reproduce selections from this book,
write to Permissions, Liveright Publishing Corporation, a division of
W. W. Norton & Company, Inc., 500 Fifth Avenue, New York, NY 10110

For information about special discounts for bulk purchases, please contact
W. W. Norton Special Sales at specialsales@wwnorton.com or 800-233-4830

Manufacturing by LSC Communications, Harrisonburg

Library of Congress Cataloging-in-Publication Data

Names: Evans, Diana, 1971– author.
Title: Ordinary people : a novel / Diana Evans.
Description: First American edition. | New York : Liveright Publishing Corporation,
a division of W. W. Norton & Company, [2018]
Identifiers: LCCN 2018013299 | ISBN 9781631494819 (hardcover)
Subjects: LCSH: Married people—Fiction. | Marriage—Fiction. | Domestic fiction.
Classification: LCC PR6105.V345 O73 2017 | DDC 823/.92—dc23
LC record available at https://lccn.loc.gov/2018013299

Liveright Publishing Corporation, 500 Fifth Avenue, New York, N.Y. 10110
www.wwnorton.com

W. W. Norton & Company Ltd., 15 Carlisle Street, London W1D 3BS

1 2 3 4 5 6 7 8 9 0

I built myself a house of glass:
It took me years to make it:
And I was proud. But now, alas,
Would God someone would break it.

But it looks too magnificent.
No neighbour casts a stone
From where he dwells, in tenement
Or palace of glass, alone.

                    Edward Thomas

M&M

To celebrate Obama's election, the Wiley brothers threw a party at their house in Crystal Palace. They lived near the park, where the transmitting tower loomed up towards the heavens like a lesser Eiffel, stern and metallic by day, red and lit up by night, overlooking the surrounding London boroughs and the home counties beyond, and harbouring in the green land at its feet the remains of the former glass kingdom – the lake, the maze, the broken Greek statues, the eroded stone lions, and the dinosaurs made of old science.

The Wileys were originally from north of the river and had moved to the south for its creative energy and the charisma of its poverty (they were conscious of their privilege and wanted to be seen as having survived it spiritually). Bruce, the older, was a well-known photographer, his studio a labyrinth of lights and darkness at the rear of the house. Gabriele was an economist. They were opposites in all things – Bruce was large, Gabriele was thin, Bruce drank, Gabriele did not, Bruce did not own a suit, Gabriele was a suit – but they threw a party with shared commitment and singular intent. First they decided on their guest list, which featured all the important, successful and beautiful people they knew, such as lawyers, journalists, actors and politicians. Depending on the size of the event, less eminent guests were chosen on a sliding scale according to rank, connections, looks and personality, which the brothers went through in their conservatory where they had most of their evening discussions. On this occasion they invited more people than usual, as they wanted it to be bombastic. When the list was finalised Gabriele sent round a text.

Next they arranged for the three essential ingredients, drinks, food and music. The party was scheduled for the Saturday immediately following the election so they didn't have much time. They bought bottles of champagne and maca-damias and chicken wings and pimento olives, all the while going over the highlights of their sleepless Tuesday night when they had watched the blue states eating up the red states and Jesse Jackson's tears in Grant Park and the four Obamas strolling out victorious on to the bullet-proofed stage – then the weather the next day, so bright and blue for November, and people, strangers, open and smiling and saying good morning to one another, in London! They imagined, as they planned their playlist to pass on to the DJ, Jill Scott, Al Green, Jay Z, wafting out of the windows of the White House. For the purposes of insulation and protection, they covered the metallic book-shelves in the living room with sheets of chipboard and laid disused mats over the walnut floors. They left the Chris Ofili on the centre wall, a sofa below and some scattered cushions, but most of the furniture was removed. Gabriele placed a note on the bathroom mirror asking people to respect that this was someone's house and not a nightclub.

Then the people came. They came from all over, from the towns across the river and the blocks off the A205, from the outer suburbs and the neighbouring streets. They came wearing faux fur coats with skinny jeans, shiny glinting Oxford Circus sandals and flashy shirts. They too had stayed up on Tuesday night watching blue eat red, and the Obama daughters walking on to the stage in their small, well-tailored dresses and their excited shoes had reminded many of them of the four little girls bombed forty-five years before in the church in Alabama by the Ku Klux Klan. That, perhaps, was what made Jesse Jackson cry, that they walked in their flames, and it was impossible to look at this new advancement of history without also seeing the older, more terrible one, and thus the celebration was at the same time a mighty lament. There were parties all over the city that night, in Dalston, Kilburn, Brixton and Bow. Traffic sped back and forth over the Thames so that from far above the river was blackness crossed by dashing streams of light. Afros were glossed and goatees were snipped. Diminishing clouds of body spray and hairspray hung deserted near bedroom ceilings as they came, as they parked their cars in the shadows of the tower, slammed their Oyster cards through the Crystal Palace ticket barriers and meandered to the house, bearing bottles of Malbec, Merlot, whiskey and rum, which Gabriele, in the spotlit hive of the kitchen, accepted with both his slender hands. It was Bruce's job to keep the door, which he did until giving himself to the joys of drink. They kept on coming, men in good moods and just-so trainers, women with varying degrees of fake hair, their curls, their tresses, their long straight manes trailing down their backs as they walked into the music, like so many Beyoncés.

Among them were a couple, Melissa and Michael, who arrived in a red Toyota saloon. They were acquaintances of the brothers, from the media crowd, Michael had known Bruce at SOAS. He was tall and broad, with a thin, stubbled jaw and pretty eyes, the hair shaved close to the skull so as to almost disappear was naturally thick and glossy given to a distant trace of India in his ancestry. He wore loose black jeans with a sleek grey shirt, a pair of smart trainers whose white soles came and went as he walked with a hint of a skip, and a leather jacket the colour of chestnuts. Melissa was wearing a mauve silk dress with flashing boho hem, lime-green lattice wedge sandals, a black corduroy coat with a flyaway collar, and her afro was arranged in a sequence of diagonal cornrows at the front with the rest left free though tamed with a palmful of S-Curl gel. Framed within this her expression was childlike, a high forehead and slyly vulnerable eyes. Together they displayed an ordinary, transient beauty – they were a pair to turn a head, though in close proximity their faces revealed shadows, dulled, imperfect teeth and the first lines. They were on the far side of youth, at a moment in their lives when the gradual descent into age was beginning to appear, the quickening of time, the mounting of the years. They were insisting on their youth. They were carrying it with both hands.

Into the Wiley throng they stepped, where their coats were taken by Gabriele's fiancée Helen, who was pregnant, and transferred via two teenage nephews wearing trousers with creases down the front to an upstairs bedroom. The Obamas had reinforced the value of the high five so the atmosphere was slappy. There was shoulder-knocking and cheek-cheek kissing, multiple recountings of the Tuesday night and the days since, how the world was different now but just the same. Meanwhile the music thumped loudly from the dance floor, Love Like This by Faith Evans, Breathe and Stop by Q-Tip. The success of a party can often be measured according to the impact of Jump, by Kris Kross, on whether there is jumping during the chorus and for how long. Here it went all the way through, the DJ encouraged people to jump when the song said jump, or to flash a lighter when another song said do that, every once in a while exclaiming 'Obama!', sometimes in rhythm with the beat. This turned into a call-and-response pattern so that the name, whenever it was heard, was repeated by the crowd, and if the DJ was so taken he might then say it again, or instead simply 'Barack!', bringing on another collective response from the floor. Beneath it all there was a faint air of anticlimax, a contrast between the glory of the moment and the problems of reality, for there were boys outside who might have been Obamas somewhere else but here were shooting each other, and girls who might also have been Michelles.

The heat soared as the night wore on. Bodies leaned against each other helplessly hot, and all that seemed to exist was this moving darkness, this music. A song started with a laugh from Mariah Carey and some discussion with Jay Z about where to begin, another conversation followed between Amy Winehouse and Mark Ronson in which she apologised for being late. Then came Michael Jackson, his shrieking riffs in Thriller, his honeyed tones in P.Y.T., at which point the dancing synchronised into a two-step that changed direction three times before returning with a lift of the left foot to the first position. This was the climax of the night. Eventually the music would shift gear, the pace would slow, the crowd would begin to thin, making room for a more spacious dancing, for inner rhythms at the wall. Now the nephews went up and down the stairs carrying coats in the other direction. In a long nocturnal exodus the people went back out into the city, their voices hoarse from shouting, their skin damp from sweating, their ears muffled with bass. Slowly the house would empty again, and Bruce would keep on drinking until at some point near dawn he would suddenly feel that he needed immediately to lie down, so he would fall asleep on the kitchen floor or on the sofa beneath the Ofili, and Gabriele, if he came downstairs in the early morning to get a glass of water for Helen, would put a pillow under his head and a blanket over him and give him a little kick, and he would look forward to discussing the highlights of their party, and who would definitely be staying on the list of invitees.

*

What is a good rave if not an opportunity for love in the early hours? Overdue love. Kissing, touching that has been all but abandoned amid the duties of parenting, the frequent waking of a baby boy and unreasonable requests at dawn for Cheerios from a little girl. What other more pressing obligation is there, when the house is at last empty, for a whole entire night, courtesy of kindly grandparents all the way on the other side of the river, than to fiercely and deliriously copulate, to remind each other that you are more than just partners in the very tedious sense of that word, but lovers, sweethearts, even still, possibly? The urgency of this requirement weighed significantly in the atmosphere of the red Toyota saloon as it journeyed away from the tower, away from the Obama jubilation, down Westwood Hill towards Bell Green. Melissa was driving. Michael was in the passenger seat slightly drunk, his knees touching the bottom of the dashboard and his right hand placed hopefully on Melissa's thigh. She allowed him to keep it there, even though he hadn't danced with her at the party and habitually failed to clear the draining rack before washing up, leaving the dry things to get wet again; it drove her crazy. Along the sides of the car's interior were the telltale remains of a horrible upholstery of dull green and purple leaves that they had compromised on when they had bought it, for it was cheap. Only the seats themselves had been saved from their ugliness, with a grey Type R makeover set, now faded and worn by the regular pressure of Melissa and Michael's travelling side-by-side backs.

In this car, in the spring of that year, the sweet deliverance of April spilling down through the open sunroof, they had crossed the River Thames from north to south via Vauxhall Bridge, headed for their first house. Melissa was six months pregnant, and then also was driving, for she loved to drive, the thrill of the open road, the speed of the air, and anyway there was nowhere else to put the enormous peace lily that had grown with a beanstalk craze in the living room of the flat they were leaving but on Michael's lap, unhindered as it was by a bump. He held it steady to stop it from toppling, its big green leaves and tall white teardrop flowers touching the ceiling, the windows, his face. Every available chasm was taken up with their belongings, the boxes of books, the cassette tapes and vinyl, the clothes, the Cuban moka pot and the Czech marionette, an indigo painting of dancers at twilight, another of birds in Tanzania, the ebony mask from

Lekki Market in Lagos, the Russian dolls, the Dutch pot, the papasan, the framed photographs of Cassandra Wilson, Erykah Badu, Fela Kuti and other heroes, the zigzag table lamp, the kitchenware, and also their daughter Ria, who was sleeping as diamonds skipped over the river, oblivious to this momentary watery transience in their lives. Over the river they flew, listening to a long song by Isaac Hayes. The water swayed and tossed beneath their loaded red wings, turned and tumbled in the troubles of its tide, shook its silver shoulders and trembled through the quiet arches of the bridges.

And approximately one hundred and fifty-six years before that, not in a car but by a multitude of horses and carts, the Crystal Palace and the things inside it were likewise transported across the river from Hyde Park to their new home in a wilderness of oak trees on the panoramic summit of Sydenham Hill. The Great Exhibition of 1851 was over. There was no more need for that showy glass kingdom in the heart of central London's prime green space, so south it went, to shine and show off at a margin, where people would come from miles and miles and even across oceans to see such things as the colossi of Abu Simbel and the tomb of Beni Hassan, the air gymnastics of Leona Dare as she hung from her hot-air balloon, and the exotic wares of distant lands. Over the river came mummies. There was velvet, hemp and Belgian lace. There were bedsteads from Vienna, and majolica and terracotta, and awesome blocks of Welsh gold. Also warships, military rifles, interesting shackles and manacles and rhubarb champagne. All of it came slowly over the water at the pull of the horses, down they went through Lambeth and into Lewisham, up the southern slopes they climbed, coming to a stop in the vast expanse of edgy green that came to be known as Crystal Palace Park, the distant peaks of which were now disappearing in the back windscreen of the red Toyota saloon.

Michael was hoping that tonight would be similar to a night of around thirteen years ago, in his and Melissa's first months together, when they had returned home from some other party, and oblivious to the new day beginning, the requirement for sleep, had continued the music in the soft silence of the sheets with the mist receding and the light rising and the calling of the birds outside. They would let themselves into the empty house. They would take off their coats and shoes and perhaps talk a little, then they would go upstairs to their bedroom with their hands interlocked, and there they would resume, cautious at first, questioning, then speeding up. Gemstones and diamonds do not lose their shine. It would be just like unwrapping a dusty, neglected jewel and finding that it still glowed. He kept his hand on Melissa's thigh to help them hold on to this glow, though it was dimmed by the fact that they could not seem to find anything to talk about ('Did you have a good time?' 'Yeah, did you?' 'Yeah, cool. Are you tired?' 'Yeah, are you?' 'No.'). Melissa kept her thigh very still, neither encouraging nor rejecting. Down Westwood Hill she drove towards the Cobb's Corner roundabout at the helm of the high street, where immediately in front of them was the wedding shop, leering out in the dark with its weedy mannequins in their old-fashioned dresses, offering yet more pressure for a long-awaited union. In those first months thirteen years ago, Michael had proposed to Melissa in a surge of euphoria and she had said yes, but as yet there had been no wedding. The wedding was lost somewhere, first in an apathy of implementation, then in a cooling of euphoria which happens generally after three years, according to research, and later in the rubble of domesticity that mounts at the door of passion when a child has come and adult life has fully revealed itself, wearing a limp, grey dressing-gown. Perhaps there might still be a wedding, Melissa sometimes imagined. If there was it would happen in a vaulted room in the old colonial buildings of the University of Greenwich, she in a strapless electric-blue dress with a train, he in a white suit, and afterwards, they would walk out to the river as man and wife, and stand at the railing watching the water as it danced with the sun. At this moment, though, it did not seem likely.

Down they went that spring day with all of their things and the baby kicking and a peace lily leaf toying with Michael's nostril. Past the wedding shop, over the roundabout, past Station Approach, through a barrage of more shops, where they were continually brought to a halt by traffic. On the high street there were six hairdressers, five chicken takeaways, four pound shops, five charity shops, three West Indian takeaways, two pawnbrokers, a tattooist, a Nigerian printers, and a selection of dingy workman's cafés. Starbucks and Caffè Nero had not yet arrived and possibly never would, though there was an air of aspiration. One of the Indian takeaways, for example, had printed across its faded fabric awning,

THE TAJ
NEW YORK LONDON DELHI

with the intention that the existence of these other distant branches, in other cities of lights, might draw people to their burgundy tikkas and reheated kormas. Near the bottom of the high street was a library which still adhered to dated Wednesday closing, refusing to accept that words had relinquished their midweek sleep. Next to that was a siren-abused children's playground in a park lined by tower blocks, then finally, upon a five-way gyratory encrusted with the worst of the traffic, a supermarket a little bit smaller than Japan. No matter where you were, in the Japan car park or standing next to a silver birch tree in one of the back streets, or even in the surrounding areas of Beckenham, Catford or Penge, it was possible to see the Crystal Palace tower, soaring over the landscape, appearing and disappearing in the gaps between the buildings. There were in fact two towers – another, lesser than the lesser Eiffel, stood further out at the top of Beulah Hill, mimicking the first. Together they were a tall, far reminder of that long-ago glass kingdom, which was rebuilt on the south side of the Thames after its arduous horse-drawn journey.

The glass itself was bought anew. It arrived at the site in wooden crates lined with straw. Three hundred thousand panes. Two hundred acres of space. This palace would be three times larger than its original self. The land sloped down in the east so a basement storey was added. The central transept was expanded and needed two new wings for balance. There were several courts, Byzantine, Egyptian, Alhambra and Renaissance. The tomb of Beni Hassan was placed in the Egyptian Court. The statues of the lions were arranged in the Alhambra Court. After ninety days of crossings, the velvet, the Welsh gold, the shackles and the rhubarb champagne all found their places. There were birds in the aviaries and lilies in the flower temples. In the gardens the renditions of the dinosaurs were established in the shrubs overlooking the lake. When everything was done the wide staircase to the entrance was swept, the fountains and the water towers were switched on, the kingdom rose again, a palace on the hill, a sprawling house of glass, with a shining, see-through, ferro-vitreous roof.

At the bottom of the high street, a few blocks past the library, Melissa turned left, and parked halfway up Paradise Row, on the right-hand side.

The house was thirteenth along a terrace of its siblings; they were numbered consecutively, odd and even together. It was a slim, white Victorian, with a skinny front door and twins of windows. Inside, at the top of the narrow staircase, there was a skylight, through which on clear nights distant stars could be seen. The rooms were bright though small, and had a slight crooked quality. The path to the front door was very brief. The hallway was not wide enough for two people to walk along side by side.

It was owned previously by a now-divorced couple and their daughter, and over the years had undergone various alterations and modifications leaving an awkwardness of structure, particularly of doors. Someone had wanted to move the bathroom downstairs so a flat-roofed extension had been added past the kitchen, enabling a third bedroom upstairs. Someone else had felt that the front room was lonely and pokey in its separation from the dining room, so had removed the connecting wall during the trend for open-plan living, leaving a wide ecclesiastical arch below the ceiling. And the previous owner Brigitte's ex-husband Alan (before he became her ex) had felt that a set of double doors would be so much nicer to separate the kitchen from the bathroom than the sliding broken pleated thing that Brigitte had asked him to replace. He had wanted, of a magnificent sun-stroked morning, say, to come downstairs in his silky dressing-gown and stride through into the kitchen en route to the bathroom, and instead of hauling open another awkward and unro-mantic plastic pleated thing, he had imagined throwing open a pair of stylish white hardwood double doors with his chest full and his head up and his heart open, ready to face another day of his marriage. So he had gone to Homebase, situated a short drive away in a ferro-vitreous building. Although he hated Homebase, he had walked committedly up and down the aisles looking for his materials, then spent the next four weekends installing his doors. He had sawed and sanded. He had squatted for long periods making his thighs ache. He missed a date with his mistress. He injured his wrist. And on the fourth Sunday, as evening was falling, a beautiful, pink-flecked dusk, it was done. Double doors. Majestic, grand double doors, tastefully demarcating consumption from digestion. Brigitte would be pleased. Their love would be rekindled. He would never again have to sleep in his car. But what Alan had not duly considered in the making of this dream was that there was not really enough space for it here.

There were already too many doorways in this small passage. The throwing open was therefore not as magnificent or uplifting as he had imagined, the stepping through was disappointing. What he had created instead was a jumble of doors of which his were the most crooked, and which caused morning congestion and the annoying catching of dressing-gown belt loops on brass handles. Brigitte was not impressed. Not long after that, Alan moved out.

Melissa had met Brigitte, along with her daughter, on her second, lone visit to the house (she had not been completely sure, there was 'a feeling', as she had put it to Michael, that worried her, more than just the number). She was a gloomy brunette in office clothes, standing rigidly next to the dining table, close to the bottom of the stairs, while Melissa asked her questions about mice and neighbours and burglaries. Only when she was about to leave, having been told by Brigitte not to go into the second bedroom upstairs as her daughter was sleeping in there, had she moved away from the table into the hall. There had been a sound from above, the sound of someone moving. Melissa looked up, and there at the top of the stairs, directly beneath the skylight, was a little girl. She was seven or eight years old, wearing blue pyjamas and a yellow dressing-gown. She was unnaturally pale, especially her hands. A piece of cool winter sunlight from the glass above was balancing on the helm of her white-blonde hair.

'Lily,' Brigitte said with anger in her voice, 'you're not supposed to be out of bed.'

'I'm not tired,' the girl replied.

'Go on, go back up. I'll be there in a minute.'

But Lily didn't move. Brigitte turned, remembering Melissa's presence. 'Sorry . . . my daughter. She's not very well.'

'Not very well,' Lily said, in exactly the same tone. She began to descend the stairs. She was limping, and on her face was a small, mischievous smile, a faint wickedness. Brigitte backed away from her. When Lily reached the fifth stair up, she sat down and said to Melissa, 'Are you the lady who's finally going to buy this house?'

Despite which, all of it, the 'feeling', the number, they did buy it. The ceilings were high. The light was good. That charming butler sink in the kitchen, the persuasive under-floor heating. The garden was nothing more than a paved cubic courtyard a little bit bigger than a stamp, but they needed a house, they needed upstairs and downstairs so that dreaming could have a floor of its own and breakfast and new days could be descended into. By then they had been searching for over a year. They had looked in the north – too pricey. They had looked in the east (the darkness of Walthamstow, the barren lawns of Chingford), and it was only here, on this sloping street in Bell Green, in the deep deep south, that they could picture and also afford this upstairs dreaming and downstairs breakfasting, Ria sleeping in a room of her own, bookshelves in the alcoves, the birds and dancers on the walls, the heroes in the passage of too many doors, the peace lily in the light of a window twin.

So four months later the saloon was unloaded to form a bewildering mountain of things on the new through-lounge floor. The old laminate had been replaced by a buttery varnished oak flecked with the inner blackness of its trees. The walls had been washed down with extreme bicarbonate to eliminate the traces of Brigitte's cat. Further feline toxins were tossed out with the blue carpet on the stairs and landing, and in its place came a warm paprika similar to the kitchen and bathroom tiles. Ria's room, her court, where Lily used to sleep, was painted yellow. This room would eventually also belong to the baby, who kicked and kicked, whose feet-shape could be seen on the surface of Melissa's skin. And the master court, at the front of the house overlooking the street, became a rich, dark, husky red, the colour of enduring love, the colour of passion. Raffia blinds were draped across its three windows. The twilight dancers were hung on the wall

13

opposite and the birds of Tanzania on the landing outside. A king-size bed, bought new from a Camden boutique, was placed in the centre of the room, like an enormous hulking ship, and one night when all of this was done, when the mountain was gone and all that was left was the gradual arranging of the smaller things that make a house a home – the positioning of ornaments, the erecting of tea-towel hooks – Melissa was lying beached on her side in a black cotton slip in the heat of July, unable to sleep, when she felt a large, grasping wave move up and down her body, more grasping and more commanding than all the others before, a pair of big phantom hands gripping her stomach as if about to throw it, and she flicked open her restless eyes and stared wide at the dark and quiet night. She had arrived at the precipice. She was thoroughly alone. Nativity was nigh.

Melissa came from a family of women who handled childbirth with warm and willing stoicism and natural might. Her mother had delivered three girls and a stillborn boy in the screaming days before the mass use of the epidural. Her sisters, Carol and Adel, had survived on only basic pain relief, refusing to pollute their babies' birth canals with unnecessary drugs. They were earth mothers. The child was the leader, the body was the ship, the pain was the sea, a beauty, a giving, an embrace by the universe, embrace it back. Melissa was not an earth mother. This had been confirmed at the arrival of Ria, who after three days of beautiful embracing pain was cut from her stomach like Macduff. She had been fully intent, this time round, on not visiting at all the house of horror, the cruel sea, and heading directly to the cutting room, until around the fifth month of incubation when it had occurred to her while practising pregnancy yoga to wonder what it would actually be like to witness the mighty movements of the canal, the emptying of the swollen womb, the crowning of the head. The wondering had increased, until she had announced to the midwife that she wanted a VBAC, the term referring to the category of women who are stupid enough to try it again the natural way, to return to the vagina, to risk the rupturing of the caesarean scar in order to know what it feels like to experience the profound and ultimate summit of womanhood.

Standing the next morning then in the cubic courtyard after another grasping phantom wave, she gathered in her brain all that she had been told by the earth mothers, her VBAC hypnosis CD, her antenatal classes, the pregnancy yoga book Carol had given her, and let the *sensations* – not pain, they were *sensations* – lead her gently to (the house of horror), which the hypnosis CD had not quite succeeded in persuading her to think of as a benign and relaxing shore, a *nice . . . gentle stroll . . . by the calm . . . water's edge.* She swayed and hummed and breathed in the magnitude of what was about to happen to her, each phantom grasping a low song, each rise and fall a misty climbing up and down with her breath, picturing in her mind the helpless, harmless little cub who was also terrified. Imagine what it must be like, an earth mother had written in the sleeve notes of the CD, to be a floating small thing in a warm, protecting darkness, and all of a sudden the waters start to tremble and judder and you're faced with this colossal, difficult upheaval into the *world*, the noisy, tumultuous, sharp-edged *world*. Wouldn't *you* be terrified? Wouldn't *you* want to stay right where you were and put up every possible resistance you could? If the mother and child are together in one mind, if there is an emotive connection and sympathy between them, the passage will be easier, she had said. So Melissa held it firmly in her mind and in her heart, the fear and the dilemma of her defenceless cub, as the *sensations* travelled outwards from the centre towards every part of her, down her legs and around her hips, most sensationally of all into her back, where a hard metal plate was forming. She hummed and she blew. She walked elephantine up and down listening to Jeb Loy Nichols, thinking of the good things ahead such as when she could go back to zumba and when she could resume size eight. The plan was that she would accommodate the sensations herself, in the comfort of her own home, until they became 'over-challenging' and she required hospital assistance. Babies, the earth mothers opined, do not like hospitals. They are full of forceps, unhelpful stress and premature interventions, and they should be avoided for as long as possible.

By lunchtime, though, Melissa was thinking that maybe they weren't so bad. Surely she was close, surely she had made centimetres, what sensations! Michael was home from work, giving her humble, loving looks and gathering bags. He was on the other side of the canyon, a distant friend, necessary but also useless. From where he was standing he could see her magnificence and her great bloom. She was the house that held their future, she was giver of life, an avalanching force. He was frightened of her and pitied her at the same time.

'Remind me not to get into a car with *you* the next time I'm having contractions!' He was taking speed bumps like a drunk. He was nervous as hell, and he hated driving even when he wasn't nervous. Melissa was leaning far back in the passenger seat as another wave took surge. She held on to the window frame, breezy summer air rushing by, the southern sirens of the afternoon, the towers in the far distance behind. They parked on a back street in Camberwell because the hospital car park was full, and she waded, she waddled, Michael holding her arm, into the foreboding building with its reflective windows and sliding doors, where a sad-eyed Indian doctor told them it was time to go to the labour ward. She sent them up in a lift to the third floor, where they sat in the waiting area with two other avalanching women. Strange that waiting rooms are simply waiting rooms at a time like this, a vending machine, magazines, posters on domestic violence and breastfeeding, that women wait together in such extremity of circumstance, in a normal, angular room, not womb-shaped, with uncomfortable chairs.

'I want to go home,' Melissa said to Michael.

'Melissa Pitt?' a voice called.

A woman in a blue cloth hat and white overalls emerged from the corridor that led within. She appeared as a fixture of a nightmare, white hairs flailing out of her hat, a pink, tired face with one eye higher than the other and a cruel walk, a careless stomping, as if in the many years of her midwifery she had used up all of her sympathy and now it was just plain old work. 'Come on through,' she said. Michael was told to stay in the waiting area as if he had nothing to do with any of this, while Melissa went reluctantly with the white-haired witch, who stomped next to her down the hall into a ward and deposited her behind a pale-blue curtain next to a stretcher, an aluminium sink and a wiry machine. 'Someone will be with you shortly,' she said, and left.

Shortly was five minutes, then ten minutes. Meanwhile sensations mounted. Out in the corridor two overly relaxed women were talking among themselves. 'Is anyone coming?' Melissa asked them. 'Is someone coming? I was told someone would come soon and no one has come. I'm having contractions?'

These two NHS labour ward administrators were used to such rambling and moodiness. Between them they tried to decipher who it was who was going to come. They were bored, underpaid women. They were continuing with indignation the long affiliation between the West Indian immigrant and the National Health Service. 'We're very busy today,' one said. 'Someone is coming soon, don't worry.'

So she went back to her corner, and found that it was less sensational to bend over the stretcher with her head in her hands during the surges. They were getting more violent, more difficult to ride. In another ten minutes, a hand gently, finally, pulled back the curtain, and a pretty, kindly-looking woman in an NHS-blue smock appeared.

'Hello,' she said softly. 'I'm Pamela. How are you?'

This came across as an absurd question. Melissa repeated that she wanted to go home. Pamela smiled, pulled out the wiry machine from the end of the stretcher and began to unravel it. 'Well,' she said, 'first let's check if it's safe for you to go home.' She looked at her folder. 'Oh. You're a VBAC. I don't think you'll be able to go home if you're VBAC. It's dangerous.' She measured dilation at just one and a half centimetres. So it was true, Melissa thought. It was going to be Macduff all over again. She wanted to cry.

'Just lie back now,' Pamela said, lifting the ends of the wires and taking hold of the rubber pads used for monitoring the waves. Lying down was the worst thing. Lying flat on your back with the waves raging up and down, yet Pamela insisted, and Melissa let her place the rubber pads on her stomach as another surge began. They were coming faster and faster. She concentrated on trying to be an earth mother but it was becoming increasingly unfeasible, especially in this position. Pamela said she would be back soon, and for a while Melissa lay there as surges came and went, making spectacles of themselves, happy on their new supine stage, singing gloriously, swirling in deepening currents. During this time she forgot all about the feelings of the cub. The earth mothers went up in flames. A giant wave came up that she was unable to accommodate, and she hauled herself off the stretcher and began tearing at the wires. Pamela reappeared.

'What are you doing?'

'I'm going home. That's it. No more. This is unbearable.'

'Look, why do you want to go home so much?' Pamela said. 'Most women, we have trouble sending them home, they want to stay in the hospital where it's safe, but you, you want to go home. Why?'

'Because I'm more *comfortable* there. Oh please, just get this thing off me!'

Melissa tugged at the wires, almost knocking the machine over. Another sensation came and she leaned forward, groaning. That was when Pamela got tough with her. She was no more sweet. She came down on her with a frowning, matronly authority.

'Listen,' she said, 'let me explain something to you, right? The reason why it's dangerous for you to go home is that you could rupture and bleed to death. Do you understand what I'm saying? We couldn't save you if there was an emergency. We had a woman in here last week who ruptured in the waiting area. If she'd been at home, she would probably have died. Another woman ruptured while she was at home, and the *baby* died. Yes, it did. But if you really want to go home, I can sign you out now and discharge you – if that's what you really want. I would strongly advise you to stay here, but it's up to you.'

In the dawn of this new reason, Melissa acquiesced. She let go of the dream of slow dilation in the little crooked house. The night was spent in the dim pool of a curtained antenatal bed, in long pulls on a cylinder of gas and air, in wretched holdings on to Michael's neck. How she needed him then. How she loved him. He was all strength, all rescue, his warm chest and his sturdy length. Over and over again inhaling the medicine mist she told him that she loved him, drunkenly, insisting, the clearest thing she felt. By 4 a.m. she had said goodbye to VBAC altogether. She wanted to be cut. The summit was no longer of interest to her, and later that morning she was wheeled to the operating theatre on a stretcher.

Michael walked beside her in blue hospital overalls, a sea of attendants surrounding. They wore green hats.

In the theatre they erected a makeshift tent between the almost-mother and her stomach so that she couldn't see. She only saw the snipping tops of the utensils.

The sound of knives, scissors. Silver blades flashed in the light and cut across.

Then a child, like a wet bag being lifted by a sudden hand, rose.

'He's a big boy,' someone said.

Michael brought him over so that Melissa could look at him. A tiny face wrapped in white. Luscious and beige. Beneath the blanket he was hot-pink and jaundiced, pinkest in the cove of his shoulder blades, yellowest on the soles of his feet, which were long, long-toed, one of them turned inwards from compression in the final months. A bow leg. A club foot. Long arms also, slithering, dancing arms, as if intended first as wings. He had shiny black hair with a patch of gold at the back above the neck. Sliding navy eyes that went from side to side like water collected in marbles. A worried stare. A hexagon mouth when he cried. He was her offshoot, her extension. She looked at him, and everything went but love.

They took him home on a Sunday morning, the grey day stretched low and mute over Camberwell. There were shreds of clouds leaning towards the west. The air was silk to the cheeks, and Melissa cried then on the wide steps of the hospital, because she understood that this was the life she would live now, this man, this boy, this girl, it was no more subject to fundamental change, and because she was bringing this new breath, this small heart, into this large unsafety. They took him back to the skinny house on Paradise Row. In the master court she placed a small red wooden heart on the wall above the Moses basket and that was where he lay. Two weeks followed containing the singular magic that surrounds the newborn. Two otherworldly weeks, in which the air sings lullabies, and you stare and stare into the crevices and the movements of the little face, fall asleep together around your sleeping cub, like curlicues, like a treble clef. 'I feel as if I've entered another stage of my life,' Melissa said to Michael, standing by the window. 'Yes, I know,' Michael said. Then the following week, like a crucial protagonist extracted from a play, he went back to work.

★

Now it was a few hours before dawn. They entered through the front gate and went inside. After the opulence of the party, the house seemed smaller and narrower than usual. Melissa went in first, along the hallway that was not wide enough for two people to walk side by side, and took off her lime-green shoes. She wanted to sleep. She did not want to continue the music in the soft silence of the sheets with the light rising and the calling of the birds outside. But she could feel Michael's wanting, his earnestness. He drifted after her as she went to the kitchen to make tea. Chamomile, for sleeping. 'Do you want some?' she said.

'No thanks.' He would rather have a brandy, a late, sweet celebration – the empty house, no toss or turn of little limb, no early requests for Cheerios. He poured himself one from the drinks rack that only he ever used and offered her one in return. She shook her head, yawning, and he leaned against the butler sink disliking her for it. The paprika floor was warm beneath their feet. The Obamas were on the fridge, in magnet, taunting them with their outrageous perfection and success, Michelle's long arms across her girls, Barack smiling victoriously. Around this magnet there were other, lowlier magnets, such as Ria's lunchtime star award, a handmade silver Santa, and a lighthearted complaint in capitals, YESTERDAY WAS HELL, AND IT'S ALREADY TODAY!, which Michael agreed with every morning before going to work. He had a firm, recession-proof job as a corporate responsibility coordinator for a management company, having intended originally to be a radio presenter. He had been talented, meant for it, with his good wit and smooth tone. He had got as far as the pirate stations, but then there had come the need for money. Sometimes he was envious of Melissa for being freelance, doing something creative (she wrote for a fashion magazine). He took a wonderful, warm swig of the brandy and offered her a massage instead.

'Um, maybe,' she said. But Melissa wasn't much of a

massage person, he knew. That and reflexology and jacuzzis, they did nothing for her. She was a doer; a runner, a swimmer, a yogi. Her physical strength was clandestine beneath the narrow shoulders and thin neck. Underneath she was all power, in sinew and in spirit, whereas Michael was quintessentially laid back and sloping. He was a sitter, a receiver. He liked jacuzzis. It was one of the fundamental differences between them.

When the tea was made she went through the failed double doors into the bathroom. It was freezing in there, even with the paprika heating, and there was a loud extractor fan that gave the feeling of being inside a generator. The panel along the side of the bath was loose and beginning to sag. As Melissa was drying her face, just as she opened her eyes and took the towel away, she saw something crawling along this panel, up the vertical edge against the wall. A wriggling, a strange brown lightening, moving and then disappearing into a crack at the top of the panel. It was a mouse, a big mouse. 'Shit!' she said.

'What?'

'There's a mouse under the bath.'

'What?'

'I'm serious, I saw it. It went in there.' She pointed.

'Are you sure?' Michael said.

She was stepping from one foot to the other, having retreated to the dining area. 'That woman said there were no mice.' She was referring to Brigitte. 'I asked her. She said there were no mice.'

'We'll have to call someone.' Michael felt irritated by the timing of this intrusion and also deeply disturbed, but was determined not to show it. He hated vermin of any kind. They were dirty. 'Anyway, I thought women weren't supposed to be scared of mice any more,' he joked as she scuttled to the stairs. 'Call yourself a feminist.'

'I'm not a feminist. I'm a woman.'

'I know you are.' And he looked at her with a shy, private

questioning, forlorn and determined at once. 'Don't go,' he said. 'Wait for me.'

But she went, with her tea, all furry and jumpy inside, and once upstairs proceeded to change into the long-sleeved white cotton nightdress that her mother Alice had given her for her thirty-eighth birthday. It was comfortable. She liked the feel of the cool cotton against her skin. Meanwhile Michael remained downstairs for as little time as possible as it took to perform his nightly checks. This involved staring at the cooker for exactly ten seconds to make sure it was off, turning the bathroom taps to absolute infallible closure to obliterate any chances of flood, pulling the window handles to ensure that they too were closed, and finally re-chaining and latching the front door. Only then could he mount the stairs to bed, often with a heavy, celibacy-weary tread but tonight a sprightly pace in which he hoped she would detect his virility and, waiting for him, perhaps in the cappuccino slip he had once given her, be excited by it. He was thoroughly disappointed, passing beneath the skylight and turning towards the bedroom, to catch a glimpse of her nakedness, a flash of sweet brown thigh, disappearing beneath the stiff, long nightdress.

'Please don't wear that,' he said.

'Why not?'

Don't you know why? he wanted to shout. Don't you understand that we have something important and pressing to do? Aren't you with me on this?

'Because it hides your beauty.'

'No it doesn't.' She put on her doo-rag and tied the strings. It would be her, she knew, who would end up being the one to do something about the mouse, to call someone. It was always her who called the people. When Michael left the house in the mornings he forgot all about the workings and the health of this kingdom and she became its lone minister. 'It hides *your* version of my beauty,' she added, a little spitefully, 'which is basic compared to my version of it. You don't like me how I like me.'

This was followed by a silence.

'Will you definitely call someone?'

'Yes, OK.'

'And we need to fix that window, it's so cold in here.'

The window furthest to the left in this court was prone to a piercing winter's draught – its frame was dislodged. The rich red walls, the soft light coming from the lampshades, the moon leaking through the raffia on to the mocha bedspread, all of it called for a warmer atmosphere, so the room seemed not quite settled in itself. Beneath their feet the hundred-year-old floorboards creaked as they moved from bed to wardrobe, making an ugly accompaniment to the cold. And the absence of Blake, the cub, on this his first night away, exacerbated Melissa's discomfort. She missed him, his tiny presence, his small brief breathing.

'I hope he's all right,' she said.

'Who?'

'Who d'you think? Blake.'

Fuck Blake, thought Michael's penis. Fuck the window. Fuck the mouse.

'He's fine.'

'How do you know?'

Melissa had not told Michael about the time she had been woken in the night by the sound of shuffling, three months ago, when Blake was six weeks old. A muffled moving had fractured her sleep. She had opened her eyes, looked over at the Moses basket, and Blake's feet and knees were thrashing against his blanket, which had ridden up over his face. She had sprung out of bed in a panic and ripped the blanket away. She'd taken it as a bad omen.

Michael said, 'You worry too much. Chill out, man. Don't you think this is nice, just us? Can't we just forget about the kids for tonight? This is our time. Let's enjoy it.'

He had taken off his shirt and she watched him, discreetly. He had wide, basketball-player shoulders and thin arms. Inside him next to his heart was a light the shape of a boomerang that made the skin a touch yellower there, he glowed from within; and then, across the small of his back, were lines of a similar paler tone against the dark background, as though perhaps, in a former life, he had been whipped. Michael's beauty was a question. It was secretive. It posed itself to her like dappled light through trees, in sudden moments, the lamplight in the pool of his collarbones as he unbuckled his belt by the wardrobe, his arms braced, head down, just there. The brilliant whiteness of his matching boomerang smile when she had met him. And the thick eyebrows, those still young eyes, only a little hurt by life. It continued to surprise her, this eventual beauty, which was extreme and hid behind his boyishness. It was there now as he leaned forward on to the bed folding his jeans, his shoulders ready to clutch, to crush around her. She felt a snatch of old feeling, a visceral pull towards him. A hot bolt of love went through her.

'It's Sunday tomorrow,' he smiled. 'We can sleep all day if we want to.'

He took a hanger out of the wardrobe and flipped the jeans on to it, encouraged by the softening in Melissa's face, that look in her eyes just now. She lay back, half waiting. He put the hanger on the rail. It was a weak rail, something else that needed fixing. Twice already it had collapsed, bringing all his clothes to a pile on the floor, and as he turned back to his fine, supine woman now ready to ravish her, it chose to do so again, with tactless and unkind calamity, his trousers, shirts, jackets and jeans came toppling out on to the floor, making him swear.

'Why now?' he said. 'Why fucking now?'

'It needs *fixing*.'

'I can't fix it now!'

'I don't mean now, I mean just some *time*.'

Melissa felt sorry for him as he came towards the big bed annoyed with the floorboards groaning beneath him. He hated the mess of clothes there, the disorderly heap waiting for the morning, but distracted and pissed off as he was, he was not going to let a wardrobe, an alleged mouse or a draught spoil his chances. Naked except for his underwear, which had been carefully chosen earlier that evening for tightness and flattery, he lifted the covers on his side of the bed and got in next to her. The moment was ruined, they both sensed, it would take a lot to get it back, and it was so late now, the birds were actually singing, but the last thing that dies in mankind is hope.

'Just come here,' he said, and smelt her neck. Her neck had stopped smelling of chicken around seven years ago. Now it just smelt of her shea butter. Still he searched for it, sniffing at her, his stubble making her itch. She scratched. He tried to ignore that she was scratching. She wrenched her neck away from him cat-like and he moved downwards to the vicinity of her milk-designated chest, which he could not really suck with any degree of self-respect but what the hell.

'I'd rather you didn't do that,' she said.

She felt his hardness against her leg and resented the obligation that she should do something for it. She just didn't feel like it now. And it bothered her not just that he had proposed to lap at her shore of milk, but that he had started on the left. He always started on the left. The monotony and the lazy lack of adventure in it distressed her.

'I'm tired, Michael.'

'Oh, don't be tired,' he said.

She lay back, her arm flailed limply around his neck. He kissed her stomach. But he could feel her retreating from him. She was not with him. He tried for a little longer to see if he could call her to him, then unwilling to make love alone, he also retreated. No, there would be no love tonight.

He stilled his hands and sadly drifted. A helicopter was circling in the skies over Bell Green. A lone siren went by. From the wide stretch of land at the top of Westwood Hill, the Crystal tower loomed and shone red.

The palace was no longer standing. It had burnt to the ground in 1936, after a long and steady decline.

2

DAMIAN

'Damian?' Stephanie called from the landing. 'Do you know where the purple fitted sheet is?'

Damian was in the kitchen, wearing his pyjamas and dressing-gown, in the pocket of which was a single decrepit Marlboro Light that he had found with an un-non-smokerly joy at the very back of the vase cupboard above the fridge about fifteen minutes ago. He was on the verge of smoking it, having persuaded himself that after eleven months of abstinence it would be OK. His one regret about giving up smoking was that he had not consciously enjoyed, that New Year's Eve night out, his LAST ONE EVER. He had been too drunk. The only and proper way to refrain from this filthy luxurious habit was to smoke a tonne of them to the point of nausea, which he had, and then smoke the last one with ceremony, with grave and grieving concentration, gathering strength and determination, so that the final puff was a full stop, which he hadn't. There had been no goodbye, no bow, no final nicotine curtain, and this was what was holding him back in his life as a non-smoker. So he was going to allow himself to have that last one now. It was meant to be. It had been waiting for him all this time behind the vases, for a morning like this when he woke up desperate and needing and weak and depressed. The only problem was that he couldn't find a light. After much hungry and irritated searching he had resolved to use the cooker (risky), and had just opened the back door in preparation for his flight out into the garden when this was done. It was raining outside but he was undeterred.

'Damian?'

With great reluctance, he went in the opposite direction towards the hall, returning the Marlboro to his pocket and continuing to fondle it. Why did she have to pick this moment to ask about a sheet? Why did he marry her? Why did he live on the outskirts of Dorking?

'What?' he snapped.

Stephanie was standing at the top of the stairs wearing Saturday-morning cleaning clothes – tracksuit bottoms, an I LOVE MADRID T-shirt with no bra underneath, a navy-blue and white bandana from which splayed wispy chestnut hairs, moccasins, and no make-up. It often struck him in moments like these how willingly she was colluding in her fading, and it briefly crossed his mind, for some freakish unknown reason, taking him by surprise, in fact, that when Melissa cleaned *her* house she probably wore lip gloss and perhaps some nice earrings or a nice top, and that should Michael come across her in this way he probably experienced a mild and enduring satisfaction.

'I bought a purple sheet last week from BHS and put it in the trunk and now it's gone,' she said. 'It was fitted. It moulds around the corners of the mattress through a clever elasti-cated system so that I don't have to break my back folding the flaps under.' The tone of peevishness in her voice was down to a few things. First of all, she did not like *his* tone, and it annoyed her that she was being made to feel like a pest in going about the general and necessary maintenance of their domestic existence. Second of all, this tone was becoming indicative of his behaviour towards her as a whole – irritability, indifference, neglect, even – which she admitted to herself must be linked to the recent death of his father. The funeral was only a month ago. She was trying to be patient and understanding but it was getting to be a strain, his moping around the house and practically ignoring the children and going to bed deliberately much later than she did and getting up earlier, like last night and this morning, for instance, so that they wouldn't have to actually *communicate* with each other, and when asked what was wrong and whether he wanted to talk about it just saying that he was fine, when clearly he wasn't. And third of all, she hated it when people moved things around without telling her. And fourth of all she really did hate folding sheet flaps, especially under their ridiculously heavy mattress that Damian had insisted on buying because it was cheaper than the memory foam that she had wanted. She was in the process of conducting a gradual sheet overhaul, soon every mattress in the house would wear fitted only, and if she was going to be snapped at in trying to achieve this small utopia then, well, fatherless or not, she had no sympathy for him.

'I haven't *seen* a purple sheet,' he said. 'I don't even know what you're talking about.'

'This house,' Stephanie said sharply, raising her arm in a grand gesture to their ceilings, their walls and cupboards and UPVC windows and generous lawn and to the Surrey Hills beyond, 'is a communal space, Damian. Do you know what *that* means? As in, we all live here *together*, you and me and our *children*? You have three of them. Their names are Jerry, Avril and Summer. My name is Stephanie, and we are married, and married people talk to each other and tell each other their problems if something is troubling them.' As she proceeded with this speech, Stephanie could feel herself becoming upset. She had acquired her sarcastic tongue from witnessing her older sister Charlotte's vituperative exchanges with their mother during adolescence, and she had only discovered that she had it in quite such a large proportion since being married to Damian. But it was wrong for him. It was too cruel. He was looking up at her with a sad, hostile, slightly baffled expression. She felt pity for him, but she continued. 'And if there *is* something troubling you, which I know there is, well, now is the time to spit it out and weep on my shoulder, Mister, because if you carry on moping around the house like this I'm frankly going to lose it. It's hard losing a parent. I know it is. I know I'll feel just the same when, if, when, my dad, well, I don't even want to think about it, but . . . Oh, Damian, I wish you'd just *talk* to me!'

Now she was crying, not copiously weeping, which would be unlike her, but there were tears in her eyes and her shoulders were fallen in pleading. Damian sensed that he should comfort her, which irritated him even more. He was still thinking about the Marlboro, still held in that moment of being about to smoke it. He could hear the rain on the other side of the front door and was imagining it also falling on the other side of the back door, where it was waiting for him, the last one. He would look out at the sky, and blow the smoke up to the water, and feel washed away for a little while of all feeling, all obligation and emptiness, become the embodiment of emptiness itself. In an attempt to return to this brief, interrupted paradise, he placed one foot up on the first stair in a gesture of empathy, at which Stephanie took two steps down, more generous than him in her comparative psychological good health. He was supposed to say something.

'Look, Steph, I'm fine.' (Vituperation rose again within her but she bore with him.) 'Don't be upset. I'm sorry. I guess I am a bit distant. It's just work, stuff, you know. I'm fine about Laurence, honestly. It's really not a big deal.'

'Do you know how crazy that sounds? How can it not be a big deal?'

It still seemed strange and dysfunctional to Stephanie that Damian called his father by his first name. She had never heard him refer to him in the usual way. She had only met 'Laurence' a few times, once at the Southbank Centre in London for dinner with Damian when they were first together, another

31

time at the wedding. She had found him rather stiff and abrupt, a bit condescending, not a happy man.

'It's just not,' Damian said, again in that snappy tone. 'We weren't close. I'm not devastated. You know we weren't that close.'

'Yes I *know* I know you weren't that close, but he was your *dad*.'

Stephanie stared at her husband for a second as if she were looking at something in a fish tank and realised that there was going to be no emotionally intelligent conclusion to this conversation. She would just have to give him time. She had said what needed to be said and felt some relief, and now she was going to carry on with her Saturday, which after the cleaning would be spent in the rich and all-consuming company of her children. There was a toffee ship to make, a Buckingham Palace puzzle to complete, a swimming lesson to be attended, and – oh, she now remembered – dinner at Michael and Melissa's to meet the new baby. The thought of a tense drive up to London with Damian did not fill her with joy. She had bought a gift already, a packet of 100% cotton 6-9 month babygros, but maybe it should wait.

'Are you sure you're up to going to dinner later?' she said. 'Do you want to cancel?'

'No.'

'No you're not sure you want to go or no you don't want to cancel? They're your friends, I'm not bothered.'

'No, we're going,' he said. 'I'm fine.'

'You're fine.'

'Yes. I'm fine.'

'OK. Fine. Whatever.' Stephanie turned, raising her eyebrows and her hands in exasperation, and started back upstairs. She was not going to let him ruin her day. Happiness was a human right. 'Just remember I'm here if you need me, don't shut me out, blah blah blah. I'm going to find that sheet. And please don't forget to clean the bathrooms today.'

Damian watched her disappear, feeling shitty. The excitement of the Marlboro was somewhat dampened but he was going to smoke it anyway. He returned to the kitchen and ignited the cooker, only to discover on retrieving the cigarette from his pocket that he had broken it in his fondling. There was a slit right near the butt, in the most terminal and irreparable place. He didn't even have a Rizla to fix it with. The vase cupboard had been cleared of all traces, all temptation, apart from this one accidental omission. The chance for nicotine closure was ruined. He held Stephanie personally responsible.

Damian met Stephanie fifteen and a half years ago at a fundraisers' conference in Islington when they were both living in London. He was working as a housing officer in Edgware, his first job after leaving university, and she was at the NSPCC, in their fundraising department. She was tall, sturdy and humble, not specifically his type in that she did not look like Lisa Bonet, Chilli from TLC or Toni Braxton, but she was wholesome and attractive in a Kate Moss-meets-Alison Moyet kind of way, and she possessed something that Damian did not possess: an aptitude for contentment, which he found reassuring. She hailed from Leatherhead, a small town in north Surrey. Her father Patrick, a former transport manager, owned a garden and outdoor furniture centre along the A24 towards Horsham which he ran with his wife Verena, Stephanie's mother, who was half Italian. Verena did the accounts and admin, Patrick did the marketing and customer relations. He was very big on advertising. Approximately three minutes past the garden centre on the A24 was an enormous sign stating: YOU HAVE JUST MISSED BRITAIN'S LARGEST GARDEN CENTRE – LARGEST SELECTION OF UK AND EXOTIC BUDS, CANE AND GARDEN FURNITURE. Whether it was true that Patrick's garden centre really was the largest in Britain was a marginal issue for him, because it *was* very large, and it probably was the largest *independent* garden centre, definitely along a major A road, in this country. There were all kinds of loopholes in advertising that meant you could claim practically anything you wanted, he was always telling people. Patrick had worked in advertising during his youth, before the transport managing. He often told the story, urged on by a weak, defeated look on his son-in-law's face that made him want to kick him in the teeth and say BUCK UP, MATE!, but instead he told the story: 'I worked in advertising for years, went straight into it from college, thought, this is a load of, excuse my language, tripe. But then I got into it, you know? There's a lot you can do to influence people. Signs and symbols, they're all around us. We're being coaxed, nudged and seduced by them every minute, only we don't know it. We think we're cleverer than that but we're not. I've said this many times to Vera – haven't I, V? – what makes people unhappy a lot of the time is that they think they should live outside the box. They think they're better than their lot. But really, we arrive where we arrive in accordance with our abilities and potential. I was actually a damn good advertising man, as I'm sure you're a damn good housing officer . . .' This was last Sunday in the living room, the monthly in-lawed roast. 'Research manager,' Damian had clarified, as he had many times before. 'I'm researching the effects of solar heat on large glass areas in multistorey blocks of flats.' (He could never seem to abbreviate this description, every word seemed essential.) 'I started out as a housing officer.'

'And worked your way up. Good. Yes. That's good. And it sounds very interesting, doesn't it, V?'

'*Really* interesting. Ecological. Important,' Verena said.

'It *is*. Very important work,' Stephanie said. 'That's what I'm always telling him.'

'I'm sure it is. I'm sure it is.' Patrick redid a button that had come loose on his pink shirt. 'And I bet you're really good at it too, as I was at advertising. But,' he went on, 'I *had* always wanted my own business, to be my own boss, master of my own kingdom an' all that. But if I hadn't spent all those years in advertising, and in transport also – that was useful too – well, to use a cliché, I wouldn't be where I am today. Would I, V?' 'No, he wouldn't, would he, Steph?' 'No, Dad, you wouldn't.' 'That's right, my princess.'

'Mum, Dad, can I get you anything? Do you want more crisps? More cashews? The lamb's not quite ready yet.'

'I wouldn't mind some more of those crisps. What flavour were they?'

'Thai sweet chilli and sour cream.'

'Wow. The things they do to crisps these days!' Patrick said. 'When I was a kid there was just ready salted, cheese and onion, and salt and vinegar. When they brought in beef and onion it was like caviar or something. It's like extraterrestrial television. The entrance of Channel Four into the picture was enormous, wasn't it, V?'

'Oh yes, massive.' Verena was on her third glass of wine. 'Do you remember that, Steph?'

'Kind of . . . vaguely. Do you, Damian?'

'Yep.'

'Well, because before that there were only the three channels, BBC1, BBC2 and ITV. Remember *Family Fortunes*?'

'I used to love *Family Fortunes*!'

'You did, Steph. They had all the great shows on ITV – *Benny Hill*, *Minder*. It's gone downhill a bit now.'

'*Everything*'s gone downhill, because everyone's competing with everyone.'

'Yes, V! Exactly my point. Now that's not a bad thing with crisps, not if you get – what did you say the flavour was, princess?'

'Thai sweet chilli and sour cream.'

'Yes. There's nothing wrong with a bit of healthy competition if you get amazing concoctions like that out of it. But when it means that people are making TV shows that they just know are, excuse my language, utter tripe, then it's just bad for entertainment, isn't it? I mean, what was wrong with *Grandstand*? Do you remember *Grandstand*?'

'How could I forget, Dad. You used to subject us to it every Saturday without fail.'

'Yes, Damian. He did. If any of us ever disturbed him he'd get really, really annoyed.'

'I would. I would. I loved that show. And they've got rid of it. I just don't understand it. And now there's *Football Focus* instead, which is just not of the same calibre, in my opinion. Gary Lineker is a pillock, excuse my language. He's all about the cool shirts and the baby face and the ladies love him, but he's not a commentator. He's got nothing on Don Leatherman. He may be a better-looking chap but he hasn't got half the brains Don's got.'

'He's done a lot for crisps, though,' Verena said. 'Those adverts he did . . .'

'Only Walkers, though. They don't do all the new flavours,' said Stephanie.

'There you go,' Patrick said, taking another crisp, 'a footballer turned ad man turned commentator. Brings me nicely back round to my point. Damian,' he said, 'just remember this, you can be whatever you want to be, but it's important to appreciate and learn from the roles we find ourselves in. One day when the solar heat gets too much, well, it might be time to get out of the kitchen, so to speak. But for now, you have a very precious wife and two precious princesses, as well as this little prince here – come 'ere you! – to look after. You've got to bring home that bacon, fella, and for now that is your focus – hah, football, focus, get it? Who knows what all this is leading towards, eh? The sky's the limit.'

They were all looking sympathetically at Damian, while being duly impressed by Patrick's masterful cascade of puns.

'OK . . . thanks, Patrick,' Damian said.

'You're a brilliant researcher into the effects of solar heat on large glass areas in multistorey blocks of flats,' Stephanie said.

'I bet he is,' said Verena. 'Steph, do you need any help in the kitchen?'

'No thanks, Mum. Everything's under control. You just sit back and relax. Do you want some more wine?'

It may partly be due to the long-lasting effects of these monthly in-lawed roasts that Damian woke up this morning feeling weak and needing and depressed. They always left him with the sense that his life was wrong, Stephanie was wrong, this house was wrong, everything was wrong. In the presence of her family, Stephanie seemed to revert to an earlier, more provincial, more sheltered self, a self raised on horse-riding lessons and country hikes and stoic matrimony, a playroom looking out on the Surrey Hills, much like the one she had made in this house, in fact, and he found it difficult to extricate her from this peachy daddy's princess back into the bold, forthright, somehow cooler woman he had fallen in love with and married. Or had he really fallen in love at all? Was it just that she had made him feel adequate and dynamic, that she was focused and forthright in her plans for her life when he was not, so he just went along with her? All she really wanted, she had told him very early on in a pub, was a family. 'I want children and a home and a husband. I'll work as well but my job will be secondary. My children will be my work. I want to look after them. I'm not going to shove them in a nursery when they're three months old. I'm going to teach them their alphabet and take them to the park and help them paint pictures. I'm going to feed them. I'm old-fashioned, right? But I'm allowed to want those things.'

And so it was. A warm, gravel-fronted semi on a safe and quiet street. Swings in the back. Lawn, stripy. A bamboo gazebo donated by Patrick, from which of a summer's evening the children appeared, and peeked, their silk cheeks and soft hair. They adored their mother like the sun rising, they filled her up. She taught them to identify trees and see the good in each other and be possessing of themselves. The school they attended was high-achieving and highly endorsed by the state. Jerry went to a good, bright nursery three mornings a week while Stephanie worked at a local charity. There was a country park nearby, and two leisure centres, and they were spoilt for choice in their supply of warehouse DIY shops, economy global clothing brands and chain eateries within driving distance, always returning to this big, warm and sturdy house, with its pale-blue front door and the pale-blue calico sofa in the living room where you could sit and look out at the light and the leaves of the sessile oaks through the window opposite. Stephanie loved this house. She loved its neatness and thick upstairs carpets and old wooden surfaces. She loved how the neatness met with the chaos of children – their shoes, their felt tips, their plastic microphones, their dolls, their animal puzzles, their Lego – yet was never completely overcome by it, for she had developed an efficient system of storage around the house so that everything knew where it belonged, even if did not always find itself there. The teddies, dolls and soft animals lived in an orange IKEA compartmentalised hanging basket on the landing, the hook for which Damian had erected with some difficulty given his limited DIY skills (another reason why Patrick found him unimpressive). The other, smaller objects representing any kind of human or animal life were kept in a plastic tray marked CREATURES, which could be slid in and out of a bulky pine holding frame in the playroom, also containing several further trays – PAPER, for paper, colouring books, stickers and postcards, NOISES, for rattles, musical instruments, whistles, etc., OBJECTS, for inanimate toys, miniature furniture, shells, marbles, and so on. Stephanie had applied these labels during her free time between the school run, work, housework and general household admin, as she had put up photographs of her, Damian and the children around the rooms. It was indeed a house very similar to that in which she had grown up. Her childhood had been relatively happy and she was brought easily to repeat it. She was content here. Contentment was simple.

This was all a far stretch from where Damian had begun. He was not from Surrey but from London, south London, he was a child of the Stockwell tenements. The lawn, if it was ever stripy, was communal. The staircases were outside rather than in. Four flights had led up to the front door which was painted one of four state-offered colours, red, black, blue or green (Laurence had chosen black). Alternatively you could take the lift but they were often used as toilets by dogs or drunks, only the culprits knew the truth. Once you reached your floor you waved your plastic fob key over the censor and a heavy metal-edged door released, opening on to a cold, narrow walkway. Inside each flat was a small bathroom, a small windowless toilet, a small kitchen, a medium-sized living room, and one, two or three bedrooms, depending on the size of the party (Laurence and Damian's had two). There was also a balcony, which the tenants adorned according to their taste. Some were left bare or used only for hanging out washing, then some people really went to town, displaying hanging baskets and patio tables and potted trees and lanterns, showing real pride and aspiration in their outdoor space, throwing in a little flora, a little slice of Chelsea. Laurence and Damian's balcony was mostly bare apart from a bench and an ashtray on the windowsill, and stretched across the squared air was a sheet of tough green government netting to stop the pigeons from excreting on their turf. This was where Laurence had done a lot of his thinking, evening, night, morning and afternoon. He was not green-fingered or house-proud. Thinking was everything.

Laurence Hope was a political activist and writer who had come to England from Trinidad as a teen and made a career of his outrage. He was one among the crusaders, who had witnessed personally the landlords who would not give them rooms and the police who would not let them go and the thugs who would not let them be, and retaliated. He had rioted, organised and campaigned. He wrote articles about the pernicious violations of racism, gave speeches in dim community halls about the need for action and the importance of black unity. 'Without unity we're lost,' he would say to Damian, over breakfast or while watching the evening news or on a Saturday night in the smoky living room in the company of fellow crusaders. The community halls had eventually advanced into lecture theatres and the articles were picked up by the newspapers. Laurence Hope's book of essays on the struggle for racial equality in Britain was considered a notable volume in academia and was still a set text on some university courses. He had never published another book, and he never managed to secure a permanent university post, but he had carried on writing, in the corner of his bedroom which he used as a study, even when the commissions faded and the requests for speeches dwindled, when the movement, as he saw it, crumbled, and the world turned away and turned in on itself and the legacies of Thatcher made people selfish. He carried on working and thinking until this outrage became the only world he had left, and he shrunk with it, became thin and alone. 'We're still not free,' he would tell Damian. 'They think they're free, but they're not. There's still lots of work to be done.' Damian would be haunted, worried by this work that still had to be done. He would look at the bookshelves lining the walls in his father's room, bearing Fanon, Baldwin, Wright and Du Bois, those haloed, courageous men who had spent their lives doing this very important work, and he would wonder how he was going to continue this very important work, when all he wanted to do some days was just come home from school and watch *Neighbours* and not think about how and why there were no black people in *Neighbours*, and eat shepherd's pie, or lasagne, or something that people ate in happy homes where there was someone around who cooked.

A woman's touch. That thing. That bright, tender and colourful thing. A woman's presence. The lack of it made him sexist. He wanted a woman to come and put flowers on the windowsill and make the balcony like Chelsea. Wash curtains, change sheets. He fantasised, coming up the stairs to the fourth floor, that he could smell not the clinical funk of a government stairway, but spices, marinades, tomatoes, chicken, wafting out from underneath the black door, the braising of his supper, the hot food of her love. This woman that Damian longed for was not his mother. His mother had left and gone to Canada when Damian was five and had never returned, and he practically forgot her. The woman he longed for, after she too had left, was named Joyce, an ex-girlfriend of his father's, who had come for a while and made it nice.

Joyce was also from Trinidad, though more recently arrived. She was lighter, breezy. She still held the whisper of the island. She wore colourful skirts that swayed in the air, in the winter months a purple cardigan with gold buttons down the front, and she had wonderfully soft hands. She cooked the best food Damian had ever tasted, better than the takeaway on Brixton Road where he and his father were regular customers. Her marinades were high on pepper, her rice and peas was flaky. She made ginger cake and bought pineapples and sliced them from their cores. They all ate together around the folding table in the living room, previously a dusty surface for stray folders and empty glasses, now permanently opened out, bearing a bowl of fruit and, yes, flowers. She said that men were boys and boys were men and both of them needed women to help them live. 'Damian,' she would say, 'wipe your mouth with the napkin when you finish.' 'Damian,' she would say, 'I see you have on that same shirt from yesterday, you must change it.' And they talked around the table about their days and their lives. Laurence was loosened, he was laughing. Damian discovered things about him that he had not known before, things about his child-hood in Trinidad which he hardly ever talked about, as if it were not significant, as if it were only England that had made him who he was, as if he did not exist before he became angry. The call of the crusade backed away in the light of Joyce's presence, and his father also, for a while, became light.

But the relationship did not last. Laurence eventually got tired of sharing his room with someone else and complained that he couldn't think. Joyce began to accuse him of the same things Damian's mother had once accused him of, that he was cold, blinkered, selfish, arrogant, that he didn't take her out, he didn't make her feel good any more, he didn't appreciate her. The smell of marinade became less frequent as Damian climbed the four flights of stairs, and one evening as he unlocked the front door, he heard them arguing. Joyce said to his father that he did not know how to be with a black woman. She said he could only be with white women because white women did not need to be respected in the way that black women did. Laurence told her to get out. He was angrier than Damian had ever seen him. Late that night, in the darkness of his bedroom, Damian felt her soft form sitting close by him, a soft hand brushing the side of his face. He did not open his eyes because he knew that she was going and he did not want to say goodbye. The sway of her fabric as she stood, the tread of her feet across the floor, followed by a complete silence as she paused by the door. The next morning she was gone. The flat returned to its original austerity, Laurence returned with greater doggedness to his gloomy desk, the treatment of black people by the police, the handling of the Brixton riots, the disproportionate number of black men in mental hospitals and in prison.

All of this had left Damian with a sense of obligation to do something important with his life. Like a Marley or a Kuti, he should continue his father's work, accept his position in the social strata as a vessel of ongoing change. But on trying to decide what degree to take at university in the inception of this vocation, he came up against a wall. Deep in his heart he wanted to take English, but he felt he should choose Politics, or Sociology, and rebelling against this feeling of what he should do, he chose instead to do Philosophy, and spent three years adding doubtful theoretical and literary scaffolding to the very large question of what everything meant – why do we exist? do we actually exist? what is the meaning of human life? what is the purpose of religion? He left university with a deeper vagueness about the future and allowed himself to be commissioned, through Laurence's contacts, to write occasional book reviews and to help with research for a documentary he had been working on for twelve years about the legacies of the slave trade. Meanwhile he considered postgraduate degrees in English, as a way of backtracking to the original impulse, but by then the sensation had already arrived that it was too late. He turned to the job market, that Situations Vacant that represented the safe dead end of dangerous dreaming, and after several interviews found himself in a communal office in Edgware, drafting tenancy agreements and writing eviction letters and coordinating claims for housing benefit. It was not what he had imagined for himself, but he saw it as a stopgap until he discovered what he really wanted. He read books. He read Shakespeare, Kafka and Flannery O'Connor. He read Raymond Carver and yearned to capture the piercing moments of lives. And he began, in the evenings, sitting in his room in Kennington at an old school desk he had found in a junk shop (the kind that lifts up to reveal a compartment underneath) to write a novel. It was a coming-of-age story about a man in his twenties trying to find himself. He worked on it for a year, smoking cigarette after cigarette, wearing short socks and long shorts so that only his calves were bare – this was very important, the draft around the shins, it helped him concentrate – making copious notes and reading relevant-seeming books on psychology and identity. At some point, though, he came up against another wall. He became confused. The words tripped over one another. Every time he tried to write a sentence the idea of it in his head shrivelled and turned to ash, a kind of impotency, and he could not go on with it. It was around this time that he met Stephanie.

Standing there, next to him in her red shoes, aisle 3 of the Islington Business Design Centre, red-brown hair, clear pale skin, a little bit taller than him, frank brown eyes and a gentle way of watching, she asked him if he knew, according to this over-complicated conference map, where she would find the seminar room, and they went on a friendly mission to find it together. It was clear from the beginning that she liked him. She was direct about it, she was focused. He looked, she thought, and later revealed to him, exactly like a man she had seen in a recent dream, a little stocky, going towards chubby, large hands, close dark curls and light-brown skin, charging suddenly into her dream as if he were looking for something. Maybe, he told her, I was looking for you. Maybe you were, she said, as they lay in his room with Bobby McFerrin playing on the turntable, vinyl sleeves spread across the floor, her red shoes touching toes, discarded beneath the school desk. They walked all over the city together with her in those shoes, gigs, pubs, restaurants, movies, mulled wine in a Camden twilight, the river from the banks of Hammersmith; the city which for her was temporary, she would go back to the hills, she said, with this family, these children she knew that she would have, and they would run across the fields making flying shapes and flying kites, they would ride horses, they would know the woods and the meadows. There are woods and meadows in London, Damian had said, but no they are not the same, she said, you hear traffic still, and sirens, and helicopters hover, I hate hovering helicopters they make me think of air raids. The argument continued as they rented a flat together in Dulwich, where they frequented the woods, became married people, and walked in the woods now with Summer strapped to Stephanie's torso in a Mamas & Papas baby carrier, until one day while driving through the back streets of Forest Hill with Summer peacefully asleep in the Mamas & Papas car seat, Stephanie saw three men walking along the pavement in broad daylight towards the mini-roundabout, one of them holding a rock the size of Summer's head, which he was aiming at the head of one of the other men, while the third man was trying to stop him from throwing it. Stephanie did not stop to see whether the man actually threw the rock, but the murderousness in his face was terrifying, and she went home and told Damian that very evening that she was moving back to Surrey whether he liked it or not, and had no ears when Damian tried to argue that people in the home counties probably also got their heads smashed in sometimes with large rocks.

Patrick and Verena were pleased. They helped them out with a deposit on a starter house in Dorking, three miles east from the town centre, then again on this bigger house, this final house on Rally Road when Stephanie was pregnant with Avril. Damian was adamant that they would pay them back but so far they had not. He had changed jobs twice since meeting Stephanie but had still not managed to get out of housing, only to a higher echelon of it, at a residential research consultancy in Croydon. On his journey into work now he hardly even needed to touch the surface of London. He could avoid the tube completely. He could join the other commuters flocking into East Croydon station at 5.20 p.m. with the steely office blocks and tall silver scrapers of that strange spaceship town looming above them, and board a crowded train bound on smooth, efficient rail tracks out towards the countryside, the crowd gradually decreasing, the green increasing, the city long gone, arriving home in time to help Stephanie put the children to bed. Sometimes he got home early enough to eat dinner with them and listen to them recounting their days: the times tables beat-the-clock scores, the trip to the farm, the Christmas carol concert, Stephanie's updates on insurance renewals and swimming-lesson bookings and forthcoming local funfairs or circuses they might attend. There was so much to think about and so much to do with all this activity and responsibility that he hardly had time to really consider how he missed London, the hum of it, the Brixton roar and the beloved river, the West Indian takeaways, the glittering of the tower blocks at night, the mobile phone shacks, the Africans in Peckham, the common proximity of plantain, the stern beauty of church women on Sunday mornings, the West End, the art in the air, the music in the air, the sense of possibility. He missed the tube, the telephone boxes. He even missed, deep down, the wicked parking inspectors and the heartless bus drivers who flew past queues of freezing pedestrians out of spite. He missed riding from Loughborough to Surrey Quays on his bike with the plane trees whizzing by, the sight of some long-weaved woman walking along in tight jeans and a studded belt and look-at-me boots and maybe a little boy holding her hand. The skylines, the alleyways, and yes, the *sirens* and helicopters and the hit of life, all these things he knew so well. And the fact, most of all, that he belonged there in a way that he would never, could never, belong in Dorking. He was outside, displaced. He was off the *A-Z*. He felt, in a very fundamental way, that he was living outside of his life, outside of himself. And the problem was, if indeed it was a problem – how could you call something like this a problem when there were bills to pay and children to feed and a house to maintain? – the problem was that he did not know what to do about it, how to get rid of this *feeling*, how to get to a place where he felt that he was in the *right* place. And this not being such a serious problem, not really a problem at all, he had suppressed it and accepted things as they were. He rode his bike to the station in the mornings (though lately he had stopped this and was becoming chubby, as Stephanie had predicted). He boarded the train and entered the spaceship town and re-emerged from it and came home and talked about pressing domesticities while all of his doubts, worries, yearnings and melancholic nigglings were stored away in a cupboard with his unfinished novel, where they had remained quiet, neat and generally manageable – until around about now.

Laurence died of congestive heart failure in a hospice on the north side of Clapham Common. He retreated, to a no-way-back place. His breath gave up on infinity. Damian was with him in the final days, as he sank into the sheets, as his skin became ashen, his eyes yellow, as he turned his face to the left and stopped, right there, in the deep of a September night. It was strange, when it happened, because Damian had felt almost nothing. He watched him die. He'd fallen asleep in the chair next to the bed and he woke up suddenly, at just the right time, as if Laurence had called to him with his small, awful cough, as if he did not want him to miss it. He knew straight away that something had changed, that his father was going, that this was the moment. So he watched it, this man passing into dust, receding into immediate history, his vanishing, this old man from whom he came – but apart from a faint reaching inside of him, a faint call with the arms of his heart, he felt nothing. He stood there for a while afterwards, looking just to the left of Laurence's face at the white pillow, then back at the face. Then he went out of the hospice and walked in the surrounding streets, sensing that the world was different now but not quite being able to feel it. He had expected to feel lonely in a new way, to begin a process of reconstruction in which Laurence would walk out into a chamber of his mind white-robed and holy, ennobled by his pain and glittering with a wisdom from the other side. He had expected to cry, or to be angry, or in some way ethereal and connected to heaven, but nothing happened. The clouds did not change. There was no message in the trees. He returned home, and in the following days went about the busy administration of death. Laurence died on a Thursday just after midnight. On the Monday morning, Damian went back to work.

What he did feel was something else, something specific yet ambiguous that came to him the morning after the funeral as a seventeen-word question. There was no voice attached to the question. It was very faint, an accumulation of yearnings, and once it had been asked it would not go away. The question was this: *How long will you go on living your life as if you were balancing on a ribbon?* He did not quite understand what it meant. It was teasing, flimsy yet urgent, like a trick. It followed him everywhere he went. It was in his head now as he emerged from the cleaning of the downstairs toilet, still wearing his dressing-gown, as he came through the kitchen, whose gangway was presently taken up with the Homebase extra-large ironing board and a pile of washing, as he wandered through into the dining room, tired of this house, its daytime gloom, its demeaning regularity, the frivolous, frankly tacky gazebo, he hated that gazebo. *How long?* it said. *How long will you go on living your life, as if you were balancing on a ribbon?*

Contrary to Stephanie's assumption, Damian was actually looking forward to going to Michael's place that afternoon. He and Michael went back a long way. They had been at university together. They used to have deep discussions about Franz Fanon and race and black music in the student-union bar, and Damian had come to feel that he owned these things for himself, not just through his father. Once Michael got together with Melissa they had made the effort to keep in touch, meeting for drinks or having dinner together as a foursome. Damian always enjoyed these dinners, the sharing of food, the playing of music. They always talked about the music, and films, and books, he would come away feeling happier and reconnected to the floundering artistic side of himself. At times, on returning home, after Stephanie had gone upstairs to bed and the house was still, he would even go to the cupboard in the dining room where he kept his old folders and papers, and take out the unfinished novel and look at it. He would just sit on the floor and look at it, and it would seem possible again. He would read some of the sentences and think about how they could be improved, how the whole thing could be massaged and rearranged to become a rich, complete thing. Then he would put it back in the cupboard with a firm intention to work on it the following evening – except that he never did. He blamed this, also, on Stephanie.

In the dining room, he came across a girl sitting at the table. She was holding a wafer and dipping it into a pot full of thick rust-brown liquid. She was softly auburn-haired and concentrating, she did not raise her eyes, a slice of pale and sudden sun, a respite from the rain, fell to the left of her into which she seemed to look, as if it contained the instructions to her activity. Damian often came across his children like this, like droplets of light, appearing suddenly. Their purity kept breaking his heart. The newness of their lives startled him, that he was responsible for carrying them, that whatever he did, whoever he was, would shape them. It was Avril, the middle child, six years old.

'Hi, darling,' he said. 'What are you doing?'

'I'm making a toffee ship.'

'Wow.'

'And afterwards,' she said in amazement, 'we're going to eat it!'

'Who is?'

'All of us! You, me, Summer, Jerry and Mummy! The whole family!'

3

MRS JACKSON

In Bell Green also there was cleaning. The windowsills, the shelves, the side tables, the floors. That life-usurping, burdensome act of servitude and futility that returned week after week to remind you of your never-ending domestic obligation and hopeless mundanity. Melissa despised cleaning. It was not therapeutic, refreshing or creatively stimulating, as some people liked to argue. It was just dust in your face, and she went about it with huge reluctance and discontent, wearing faded, paint-splashed dungarees and a top with holes in it, and a look on her face that gave vivid indication of what she would look like as an old woman. Now that there was a whole house to clean her misery was intensified, and dragging her cloth around the living room, halls and bedrooms she could hear millions of tiny dust particles laughing at her from their swirling microscopic freedom, screaming hilariously as she approached the static black sheen of the TV stand where dust settled even as she wiped, and dancing and tittering in the light from the skylight as she clattered over the stairs with the Hoover. Usher and Beres Hammond provided some comfort – music was power – but nothing could appease her until it was over.

It was unfortunate, then, that 13 Paradise Row was an especially dusty house. It was built circa 1900 upon a gently sloping plot of shrinkable clay sub-soil typical to much of south London and requiring homeowners to have insurance policies in place against subsidence. Because of this sloping, this possible shrinking and sinking, there was that sense of crookedness and a damp close to the ground, a feeling almost nautical. The floors tipped down in a faint eastward direction. Corners were not quite, skirting boards were jagged, struggling to sit fast against the walls in a mutual failure to make right angles. The dust nestled easily into the cracks of these failures. It settled on top of the dado rail along the upward tunnel of the staircase. It clung, through this moistness, this dampness in the air, inside the grooves of the wood-panelled wall in the dining area, where a row of kid-height hooks held the children's coats. There was dust atop the door frames, the picture frames, the lamp shades. In the master court it was worst of all, the headboard of Camden was afflicted, the upper edge of the dancers at twilight. There was mildew in the wardrobes, which gave off a musty, ancient smell, and while Melissa bent to neaten the line of shoes between the two, she found for the second time a moist, white film of something on their soles, which came off on her fingertip.

Michael was out walking Blake. Ria was in the next room doing something with a cardboard box and muttering to herself, as she often did. The muttering stopped, she called out with a high-pitched urgency, 'Mummy!' Footsteps followed, she appeared at the door, hand on hip. 'Mummy, why do you always throw away my things?'

'I don't always throw away your things.' Melissa turned to look at her. She was a long-limbed, big-eyed seven-year-old, with coming and going teeth. The front top-left was missing, giving her a hag-like grin, usually quick to explode in her face though at this moment withheld. She had Michael's rich, sharply defined lips, his long, slim, cumbersome feet, and a hint of her maternal grandmother's Nigerian nose. She liked to wear one white glove, as she was now, on her left hand, and it still bothered her slightly that some things had two names, such as pasta and spaghetti and trousers and pyjamas. It was just quite confusing.

'Yes you do,' she said back. 'Whenever I get something like a card or a leaflet or something I always try and find it and it's gone because you threw it away.'

'Well how am I supposed to know what's rubbish and what's not? We can't keep *everything* you bring into this house.' The twigs, the travelcards, the miniature London Underground maps, the double-glazing flyers, the stones, the leaves, the dirty hair clips, the coins, the badges, the flags, the fans, the bookmarks, the decrepit elastic bands, the soil. It was unbearable, the sheer avalanche and paraphernalia of object. 'I'm just trying to keep the place tidy.'

'My lottery tickets weren't rubbish. I was going to use those.'

'But you're too young to play the lottery. You have to be sixteen.'

'Oh, do you? I didn't know that. Anyway I was *collecting* them. And they were *mine*. I *needed* them. I don't throw *your* things away. If I threw something of *yours* away you'd shout at me and confuscate —'

'Confiscate.'

'Yes, confiscate, and so why can you throw *my* things away, but I can't throw *your* things away?' Ria waited for an answer, which Melissa was trying to arrange into a calm, authoritative diplomacy but she was taking too long. 'Oh just forget it,' she said, and stomped back to her room.

We have to remember that children are human beings too, so advised the parenting spokeswriter of *Raise Them Right*, which Melissa had bought one day in the throes of frustration about how she was going to manage the bringing up of a child without exercising corporal punishment, which she fundamentally did not agree with and anyway it didn't work. The one time she had smacked Ria was when she had lain down on a zebra crossing when she was three because she didn't want to walk any more, and it had not made the slightest bit of difference, she had continued to lie down on the zebra crossing and Melissa had dragged her across it. She had bought *Raise Them Right* shortly after that. It is destructive and unkind to impose our own tensions and personalities on to the lives of our children, it declared, who are engaged in the difficult task of trying to carve out their identities. They deserve patience. They deserve the space to be themselves. Avoid conflict. Praise them often. These fragments of considerate wisdom surfaced in Melissa's brain, against a background of general resentment towards their presence, and she went next door to Ria's room in the spirit of understanding and reconciliation.

Whatever it was that was in the next room, however, had lifted Ria from her grievance and she was again muttering to herself, in a busy, accelerated tone, the throwing away of important things apparently forgotten. She was kneeling on the vermilion rug in front of her cardboard box, around which were smaller cardboard boxes, bits of paper, Sellotape, scissors, foil, string, pencils, an old toothbrush, parking tickets. This room still made Melissa think of Lily, Brigitte's daughter, lying hidden away while strangers looked around the house. She wondered sometimes if there was something wrong with it. It was rectangular, with a shaded, northern aspect. Ria's bed was in the same place Lily's had been, alongside the wall to the left of the window, Blake's cot in the opposite corner.

'What are you doing?' she said.

'I'm making a house. It's for when I shrink. I have to finish it today otherwise I might not get to shrink. Today only is shrinking day.' Ria did not look up as she was talking but carried on arranging the flaps of the box into a roof.

'Can't you shrink another day? You know we've got people coming round soon. I don't think they'd like it if you shrank. They might find it disturbing, antisocial even. Don't you want to play with the other kids?'

'What other kids?'

'Jerry, Summer, Avril. They're all coming.'

Ria paused to think. 'That's OK,' she concluded. 'They can shrink with me. That's what I was going to use the lottery tickets for, for other people to get into the house. I'm the only person who doesn't need a ticket. But I'm going to use these parking tickets now instead.'

'I'm sorry I threw your lottery tickets away.'

'It's OK, Mummy.'

'Next time I'll ask you first.'

'Thank you.'

As an afterthought, Melissa added, 'Make sure you ask their parents before you shrink them. And ask them if they actually *want* to shrink.'

Damian and Stephanie arrived as the afternoon sun was abating and the morning's rain returning, bringing with it a freezing wind to the east, Stephanie having endured the exact tense drive she had anticipated, with Damian reading the literary section of the Saturday *Guardian* and hardly saying a word to anyone. His mood seemed to lift, though, as they unloaded themselves from the huge decuma-grey estate and herded down Paradise Row, Jerry running ahead, always a difficult passenger now unleashed on to the wind, the girls following behind him. It was in such moments, beholding her family in some outside, neutral place away from home, that Stephanie experienced a broad and satisfying existential rightness. There was her gang, her team. They would withstand anything and none of it mattered, moods, grievances, sheets. They were going to have a nice time.

Michael answered the door singing 'Hey!', and they crowded into the little hallway, taking off shoes and coats, stuffing gloves inside hats and pockets. 'God,' Stephanie said, unwrapping her long, long scarf, 'this city is getting more and more congested! We were stuck in traffic for ages, weren't we?'

This was directed towards Damian but he didn't respond, feeling that it wasn't strictly a question but rather that jarring, needy conversational punctuation that Patrick used. Also, Melissa had just appeared at the top of the stairs, wearing an interesting black top with shiny tassels hanging off it. Her fro was a halo. Her muscular arms were bare. She was coming down, swaying, swinging in the tassels. 'Hi all,' she said.

'Hi,' he said, only to her. Then the outside forces pressed back in, Michael said it was probably the rain causing the traffic, Stephanie said 'Whenever I come to London these days I just feel potty.'

'Have some wine, it'll chill you out,' Melissa said. 'Red or white?'

'Well, I would like white, but I think everybody's going to be drinking red, aren't they? I was just saying this to someone the other day – no one drinks white wine any more. What's wrong with it? I love white wine! But look, we brought red.' Damian handed the bottle to Melissa with gravitas in a blue plastic bag. 'Have you got any white?' Stephanie asked.

'Yeah, I like white too.'

There was Philadelphia soul playing on the system. The air smelt of nag champa joss sticks, which Michael had lit after his cleaning of the living room, celebrating its spotlessness. Jerry and Summer were towering over Blake, who was sitting in his recliner by the sofa clutching a rattle and beginning to whimper at the sudden influx of people. Ria asked Avril if she wanted to come upstairs and shrink, then remembering that she was supposed to ask first asked Stephanie if Avril could come and shrink with her. 'Shrink? What? Shrink? Oh, *shrink*. Of course, go and shrink,' Stephanie said, understanding Melissa's explanatory look. Jerry cried, 'Wait for me!' and ran up after them. Summer was instructed to go as well to keep an eye on them all, which she did, sauntering, nonchalant.

'As for you,' Stephanie knelt before Blake as if he were a shrine. '*Look* at you. Oh, he's gorgeous. He's scrumptious.

Can I hold him? . . . Look what we brought you,' she said, full of a merry empathy, handing him the babygros, which he grasped and brought to his mouth. 'It's for you to *wear*, as you're *growing* . . . as you get bigger and bigger and *bigger*, OK? That's all you have to do, you lucky thing.'

'Oop, someone's broody,' Michael said.

'She's always broody,' said Damian.

'I'm not broody! I just love babies, that's all. So tell me, how was the birth, Melissa? Did it go well? I want to hear the whole thing.'

Blake was held in Stephanie's lap at one end of the sofa, his club foot still pointing inwards though loosening with the months, while the nativity story was told for the fifteenth time, Michael joining in to make various exaggerations and elaborations. Stephanie listened with relish. It was her favourite subject, and she offered authoritative interjections about what should have been done at this or that point from an earth-mother perspective. Meanwhile Damian listened to the music and looked at book spines along the white shelves, spotting Carver and Hemingway, Tolstoy, Langston Hughes, getting that wakening feeling in the pit of him. In an attempt to bring him into the conversation, bored with retelling the story, Melissa broke off and asked him how life was, how was work, etcetera.

'You know, same old grind.'

'What was it you do again?'

And he told her, about the researching of the effects of solar heat on large glass areas in multistorey blocks of flats, also for the fifteenth time. There were no follow-up questions.

'What about you?' he asked, enjoying, while Stephanie and Michael carried on talking in the background, this private chat, which felt somehow special, meaningful.

'It's . . . um . . . precarious,' she said, her tassels glinting in the light of the zigzag lamp next to her. 'I'm freelancing now.' Melissa had been the fashion and lifestyle editor at *Open* magazine, a glossy for urban women, for five years, but had decided while pregnant with Blake to 'change her life' and take full maternity leave. When Ria was born she had gone back to work after two months, leaving the baby with her mother. 'It's very different,' she said. 'I miss the buzz.'

'You're lucky. I'd love to stay at home and write,' Damian said. 'That's my dream.'

'What would you write?'

'I'm not sure, whatever came to me.' He dared not tell her about his novel, at least not here, not like this.

'Dreams are meant for making,' Melissa said, drawing from her ever-ready store of positive affirmations and wise poets, among them Paulo Coelho, Alice Walker, the Dalai Lama, and a few other random Buddhists via her sister Carol, who taught yoga. 'I have been reading more, though,' she went on, 'which is one thing I planned to do when I left *Open*. I'm trying to read all the books I lost during my English degree – all that analysing them to death, having to write essays about them. It stopped me actually *reading* them, just reading, purely, you know, for pleasure's sake. I'm reclaiming my literary innocence.'

Damian thought about this, inspired. 'I've never looked at it that way before. I always wish I'd studied English . . . maybe it's a good thing I didn't.'

'That's how I ended up in fashion. I was basically fleeing from sentences.'

'But you still have to write sentences.'

'Yes, but they're fabric sentences. Buttonholes. Thread. Tangible things . . .' She embarked on a lengthy explanation about the distinction between Japanese denim and American denim, that while American denim gave that classic fade and vintage colour over an extended period of time, Japanese denim offered more varieties and textures, her point being that denim itself was a tangible thing, non-esoteric, non-invasive to creative whim. She read poetry sometimes after writing about clothes. There was space left in her head.

The music came to an end and Michael went to change it. There was an awkward moment when Stephanie and Damian both started saying something to Melissa at the same time, offering compliments about the house. They had always seemed to her a mismatched kind of couple, Stephanie being taller than him in the first place, but sometimes that could work, no, it was more than that, Damian so uncertain and introverted and floundering, then Stephanie so fixed and bold, sitting there in the pool of her long green cardigan, as if she never thought too deeply about anything. They were living in the shade of each other.

'Sorry to hear about your dad, by the way,' she said to Damian, at which Stephanie glanced at him, a kind, unsmiling look on her face, before returning to straightening Blake's club foot with repeated downward strokes as Melissa's midwife had advised.

From the kitchen drifted an aroma of curried chicken and fried plantain, rice and peas and scotch bonnet peppers. The chicken had been seasoned with Dunn's River All Purpose, the rice with coconut milk and thyme. There were mango and halloumi strips as hors d'oeuvres, which Summer passed round, wanting to help, while Michael topped up Malbec and the glasses of white. The evening was thick and solid at the window twins. The wind was blowing harder, bending the birch trees backwards and forwards. There was even a clap of thunder. 'Wow, this weather's adverse, man,' Michael said.

Gradually, as always, they drifted into their constraints of twoness. The men talked of sport (the boxing, the football), the women of Blake and his sleeping and eating habits. Melissa found herself going into lengthy detail about the difficulties of weaning, which Stephanie enthusiastically responded to ('what I used to do was give them bits of food while I was cooking, some broccoli or carrot or something, so that they'd be having their lunch without even realising it,' 'yeah, I've started doing that too,' Melissa said, 'but as soon as I put him in his chair he won't touch it, just sits there sucking his thumb. I say to him look, you were just *eating* this, just a minute ago. What's changed?', to which Stephanie replied, 'Oh he's just testing the boundaries. That's what they do. They have to feel like they've got some control. Everything's new and fascinating to them. And actually, if you look at the world through a baby's eyes, it *is* fascinating. It *is* fascinating whether this pan will fit into that bigger pan, or whether this little pesto jar will fit into that big Thornton's tub, and how wet water is, and just, you know, all of it!').

Then the conversations joined again and they discussed together the things they all had in common, their fixed-rate mortgage packages and primary schools and home improvements, frequently using 'we' instead of 'I' to refer to themselves as individuals. 'I' was the lost pronoun in the language of the couple. They spoke queenly of themselves, including the other and undervaluing the self, so that they all became diluted. To escape, Melissa kept checking on the food and went upstairs to put Blake down and look in on the shrinking. Everyone was the same size as before.

'Mm, this is delicious,' Stephanie enthused at the dining table. 'I love curry.'

'Me too,' Michael said. 'Melissa made it.'

'He made the rice.'

'It's interesting, isn't it,' Stephanie said, 'how stew, or curry, is one thing all over the world. It's the same thing, tomatoes and onions and some kind of stock all cooked together into a gravy. But at the same time they're all different – in Russia it's stroganoff, in Italy it's bolognese, in India it's curry, in Morocco it's tagine . . .'

She was sitting next to Damian, who was sitting opposite Melissa, who was sitting next to Michael. Damian was trying hard to block out Stephanie's voice and not look directly at Melissa because he was afraid he would stare at her and everyone would see him staring. Why was she so lovely now? Why did he have this bizarre feeling that he was supposed to be with her and the couples were the wrong way round? It was difficult to behave as if everything was the right way round. He lost track of the conversation in his absorption, and didn't understand what she meant when she asked him, 'What about you, Damian? Ever think of moving back?'

'Back where?'

'To London.'

The children were sitting on the rug on the other side of the ecclesiastical arch, having a dinner picnic. Amy Winehouse was singing in her way, as if she were not going to remember the next line, though she always did, she always returned.

'I think about it a lot,' he said. 'I'd love to move back.'

'Really? Why? It's so rough,' said Stephanie. 'How many teenage stabbings or shootings or whatever have there been so far this year? Forty or something? Jerry, don't wipe your hands on your top, use the napkin.'

'Twenty-eight,' said Michael.

'Twenty-eight. Well, that's enough, isn't it?'

'Those are the ones reported anyway.'

Damian took the last sip of his wine (he was driving home). 'You shouldn't hang on to every word of the news all the time,' he told Stephanie. 'It's not a realistic picture. Just makes you paranoid, creates panic. You watch too much news, man.'

'But there is a problem with gangs here. That's a fact, isn't it? I've seen them.' She told them the story about the man with the rock at the mini-roundabout in Forest Hill and how that had been the last straw. 'Some of these kids, they look as if they'd kill you. It seems like they've lost all scruples, all sense of boundaries. It's not their fault, I know, it's their environment. But what's being done about it? What are they going to do about crime?'

As if in answer to Stephanie's question, a siren whizzed by

on the high street at the bottom of the road. 'See. You don't hear many of those where we are.'

'There's sirens everywhere, for all kinds of things,' Michael said. 'It's not just about their environment. It's about who they are, knowing who they are and what they could become, and having control over it. These are exactly the kind of kids I used to work with at the youth clubs,' (when Michael was doing radio presenting he'd run workshops sometimes in youth centres around London). 'Some of them were just plain bad, through and through, no lie. But most of them weren't. They were just . . . inchoate.'

'And that's when they're most in danger,' Damian said.

'Right. You can't just round them all up and throw them in jail. What a waste. Let them find something they love, music, science, architecture. If they're enthusiastic about something the gang life isn't attractive any more.'

'I read somewhere once that boys in gangs have homoerotic tendencies,' Melissa said.

'I want to be in a gang!' cried Jerry.

'No you do not,' Stephanie said firmly, but laughing with everyone else, and going over to wipe his face. 'This is what I mean, though. I'd hate them growing up around all this trouble and strife. London may be the centre of the world to some people,' meaning Damian, 'but I'm sorry, I just don't think it's a very good place to raise children.'

There was a cry from above, loud and insistent. 'Blake's crying,' Ria said, still wearing her white glove on her left hand. 'Can we go back up now?'

'I thought you wanted to watch TV?' said Michael. Melissa was getting up, but Stephanie asked, 'Can I go? You relax, I'll get him.'

She went, eventually the crying stopped. She came downstairs holding Blake, his face thick with sleep, his hair flat against the back of his scalp over the golden patch where he'd been lying. She was cradling him against her, soothing him with a soft murmuring, 'you lovely, tired thing, you little blast of sunshine, look at you, such a prince, it's all right, it's all right,' and he was content, languid, limp in her embrace. When he saw his mother his arms made a sudden glad song, his body jerked and flinched, a small smile exploded. Melissa took him.

'I tried to put him back down but he wasn't having it,' Stephanie said. 'I think he was cold. It's quite cold in that room.'

'Really? I find it cold in there too sometimes.'

'Well if *you* find it cold, he'd *definitely* find it cold. Why don't you give him another blanket?'

'Isn't that dangerous, too many blankets?' Since the night of the bad omen, Melissa had been wary of too much heat. Now she was worried about too little heat. In motherland there was always something to worry about. She felt she was learning everything all over again. 'I read something in *The Baby Whisperer* about —'

'Oh, whisperer-shmisterer,' Stephanie balked. 'Don't listen to those stupid books. He's your baby, you know what to do. There's so much literature around these days about how to look after your child, it's just bossy, don't you think?'

'No. I find it quite useful.' Sometimes Melissa peered into these books in the middle of the night when Blake wouldn't stop crying. Sometimes she clung to them with both hands, desperately seeking a wonder sentence, a celestial bean of wisdom to get him back to sleep. Sometimes she reached for them *before* she went to sleep, instead of reaching for one of the novels she was trying to reclaim, or some good poems, and this seemed a dangerous thing. 'I don't read all of them,' she said defensively, 'just that one and the Gina Ford, to remind me . . .'

'Gina Ford!' Stephanie's voice was getting louder from the wine. 'That woman doesn't know the first thing about being a mother. She hasn't even got any kids! She's a nanny, for god's sake. What gives her the right to go around telling people how to look after their own babies, telling them they have to wake up at 7 a.m. and go back to sleep at 9 a.m. and have lunch no later than 11.30 and have their nappy changed at 2.24 p.m.? You can't put a baby on a schedule like that, it's cruel, it's unnecessary. You change the nappy when? When it needs changing! You put him to sleep when? When he —'

She was interrupted by a knock at the window.

'What was that?'

Michael went to look, pulling aside the venetian blind. 'It's Mrs Jackson. In this weather. Jeez.'

Mrs Jackson lived five doors down at number eight. She was in her seventies and lived alone, and she was in the process of forgetting herself, what her name was, where her coat was, what number she lived at. Every couple of days she would walk up and down Paradise Row, usually in her slippers, her hair wild and unkempt, trying to explain to people that she couldn't remember where she lived, but they didn't always understand what she was saying because her sentences got lost on the way and ended up in unrelated things.

'I better take her home,' Michael said, and went out into the darkness.

Mrs Jackson liked Michael because of his kind face and kind way. She was wearing only a green housedress, no coat, her thin brown calves poking out from the hem like sticks. The wind railed against them as they walked.

'It's too cold and late for you to be out like this,' he told her. 'It's number eight, see? Here's your house, this one, with the yellow door.'

'Thank you.' Mrs Jackson held his hand with both of hers and smiled up at him. 'Thank you, darling. You are so kind. You look just like me son Vincent, he is coming back from America on Saturday, he always bring clothes and saucepans and shoes, he's such a good boy . . .'

'Someone needs to look after her,' Melissa said when Michael returned. 'It's the third time this week.'

'The poor woman,' said Stephanie.

For dessert they had New York cheesecake with pistachio ice cream. Damian drove home in silence, the occasional fox appearing at the edge of the road, its flashing eyes making him think of the glinting tassels on her top, the curve of her neck where it met with her hair, the particular shape of her nose in profile. He did not write anything when he got home.

Later that night, Melissa lay awake in the master court. The children were asleep in the second room. As usual she had checked on them last thing, that Blake was breathing, the blanket was not over his face, and that Ria was unshrunk, which she was, her cardboard house closed for the night. Tomorrow she would play with it some more, and they would pass a long familial Sunday in the culture of the crooked house – a visit to her mother across the river, the roasting of a bird, anticipating Monday, when Michael would go back to work and she would stay here in Paradise with Blake.

Michael was also asleep. He liked the romance of recent rain, and he had reached for her amidst the red, his hands across her waist, asking, but she could not tune in to his eventual beauty, to the boomerang light next to his heart. Outside the fast wind was still blowing, shaking the raffia, most vigorously at the left-hand window where the draught was coming from. Melissa got out of bed and tried to open it again so that it would close properly, while doing so glimpsing the dark windows opposite, the front doors, the square front gardens. She missed the view of the sky from the old place. It had been on the seventh floor of a tower block. The stars had been so close there, the moon at the window. She had become used to an affinity with the Milky Way, and this view of the houses on the other side of the street felt like a theft.

No matter how much she pushed and tugged at the handle, the window would not budge. She began to have a strange sensation, as she was standing there, that there was someone standing behind her, very still — a night thing, her mother used to call them, beings who walk in the night hours, not quite human, who watch us. It had always frightened Melissa when Alice mentioned them. She turned around to look, but there was nothing there, only the shadows in the room, the door ajar, beyond it the landing, the skylight. The window shook and trembled in its frame. It was almost as if someone, or something, were trying to get in. Or possibly out.

4

I CAN MAKE YOUR ZOOM
ZOOM GO BOOM BOOM

Michael took the bus to work, preferring it to the tube as he could look out of the window and anyway he had read somewhere once that a seat on an average Central Line train is less hygienic than licking the bowl of a toilet. Even if he had wanted to go by tube, residing now in the London the tube forgot, he would have to get a bus to Brixton or Elephant & Castle first and then change, down into the crowded tunnels and stairways, and he didn't like being underground over long distances. To get his stride going he walked the long way through the back streets to the Cobb's Corner roundabout, his bag slung over his shoulder and in it a small bottle of sanitising hand gel, and waited there for the 176, which took him around the back of Forest Hill via Upper Sydenham, through Dulwich and Camberwell, into the fuchsia explosion of Elephant, onwards to Waterloo, and over the river to the other side. Because he got on near the first stop he usually got his favourite seat, the top deck, second from the front on the left-hand side, and all the way he stared out at the knuckled city trees, the pigeons grouped greyly on the grass, the early smokers at bus stops, the winter palms outside Dulwich Library, the building projects paused in recession, babies pointing from prams with concern in their faces, the suya hut in the shadows of the fuchsia, the Walworth Road nail salons, the trough-like tenement balconies, the evacuated Aylesbury Estate, the community police officers performing slopey walks, the church steeples amidst the rooftop satellite dishes, the shady high-street hotels, the men on their phones, the women in their clothes, the boys with their boxers showing and their new uncuddly brand of urban pet dog, the rail tracks, the hedgerows, and the peeping greens and streams. On the approach to the river the roads widened into boulevards and became in fleeting moments almost Parisian, the buildings slightly smoother and the stonework somewhat grander, shaking off a downbeat southern mood and a roughness of edge like a woman with messy hair neatening it up as she walked across the water which glittered, which churned and twisted and rolled with the wind as she went, the vista of the north rising up before her, the Houses of Parliament and Somerset House with its pillars and flags and the children in stucco on the roof trim. In the centre of the city it was a different kind of dirt, the dirt of money and extreme lack or excess of it, and it became a little like New York along the glitzy stretch of the Strand, then onwards towards the last stop at Tottenham Court Road there was the great wide opening of Trafalgar Square where Nelson soared up and the galleries flanked, where so many birds swooped, as if it were holy, on to the cold blue fountain pool.

On the bus it was easier to convince himself that he was not part of the rat race. He was wearing a suit, yes, he had three suits, the black, the navy and the grey, two of which he had acquired only recently when starting work at Freedland Morton. But he wore it with nonchalance, with a sense of disconnection between skin and fabric. His real self was untouched, unaffected, was actually wearing khakis, and over the suit he had on a large, quite trendy winter coat so he looked less square, less like a cardboard box with legs. On the bus there was a greater mix of people, and rather than facing each other and staring miserably into the murky darkness of below-ground-level windows, they faced the front. They were private and unscrutinised in their journeying, and not all of them were going to work. Here was a woman in a yellow hat with a little girl a year or two older than Ria, possibly on their way to the passport office in Victoria or Madame Tussauds or the Museum of Childhood in Bethnal Green (this was a game Michael liked to play in his head, to imagine other types of living, other types of Monday or Tuesday). Here in the front seat in the opposite aisle was a middle-aged man, drunk and pink and grey, slumped forward over the bar and being shifted from side to side with the hurlings of the deck (job centre on Walworth Road, or the pub, to wait at the entrance until it opened, or maybe he was red-bus-rovering without meaning to, he gets to the end of the route and doesn't know where the fuck he is so gets on another bus same thing again). And here were two teenage boys in school uniform ('If you beat him, yeah, I'll give you ten pound. *Ten* pound!') who were not on their way to school. Michael knew what youngsters looked like when they were not on their way to school. He himself had been not on his way to school many times as a kid, and there were only three places he would go, the park, the shopping centre or to his friend's house, with a silly cocksure swagger and a loudness overcompensating for his fear. Down Denmark Hill they came, these strangers, past the hospital where Blake was born, past the rundown Pentecostal church on the shopping parade, and Michael pretended that he too was going somewhere different, somewhere spontaneous, someplace where less was required of him. He didn't really want to be a corporate responsibility coordinator at Freedland Morton. Deep down he identified with that old pink drunk. He had always thought of himself as the type who could either die young or end up a crying park-bench bum. He had been sure that he wouldn't make it past thirty, and now that he was thirty-seven he was slightly bewildered, mindful of the projected alternative.

If he were ever released, or ejected, for whatever reason, from the grave and beautiful responsibilities of this life, he sensed that he would sink down easily to a truthful reunion with a shabbier self, like a hot-air balloon that had lost its flame.

En route he listened to his iPod. There were a handful of artists on his Most Played list, including Shuggie Otis, Nas, Dolly Parton and Jill Scott, but the Most Played album was John Legend's 2004 debut *Get Lifted*, which was a journey of a different kind. It began with a little waterfall of piano and an invitation from John to go with him and see something new, and in a surging sequence of warm, gospel-percolated melodies it followed, as Michael interpreted it, the odyssey of a man changing from a womanising, nightclubbing, phone-number-collecting, good-time cheat into a responsible, mature and committed life partner. It was a slow and difficult road, strewn with conflict and temptation. He loved his girlfriend but he loved his freedom also, and couldn't his girlfriend see, he sang in She Don't Have to Know, that just because he slept around it didn't mean he didn't love her? Just because he snuck off to Washington DC so that he could hold hands with the other woman in public wearing sunglasses to shield his identity, it didn't mean she wasn't still his Number One? No, she did not see, and the thing was that this girlfriend, this Number One, was not just any girl. She was special, she was bombastic, she was 'off the *hizzle*!'. Snoop Dogg scolded him about it in I Can Change. He said if you come across that kind of woman, you have to change, because they are rare, and you don't meet them often. It is a moment that warrants a grand and decisive destruction of the wayward phone-number-collecting guy, a passing over on the bridge of justice to all that you can be, your best self, someone who is deserving of her. And he didn't want to do it. Oh it was tough, he loved those women, all of them, all the warm and luscious women in the world. But he did it. And he spent one song in an agony of uncertainty called Ordinary People, where his love was undeniable but constantly running into hardship and there were arguments every day and no one knew which way to go. There were two choices, to Stay With You, or not to stay. He stayed. And at some point beyond that crossroad he, they, reached a sublime plateau. They came out into the wild and peaceful air of the ninth cloud and there was wonderful love-making and deep understanding and they walked onwards, together, So High, into a future that would repeat their parents' lives, that is, the ones who were still married. When it was cold outside they were a Refuge for each other, a sweet washing of the soul, a sunny path. He came to embrace the value of family and developed a nostalgia for the simple days when the family was central. Those were the important things, to spend time with the people you loved, to continue to love them. He had grown. He had arrived on the other side. He was lost but now he was found, and all the way through, piano, strings flying in the distance, fingers clicking, cymbols whirling, John's voice like rich autumn gravel. He ended on a high note with Live It Up, a definitive, undulating bassline, the violins euphoric, a final celebration of love, of life in all its struggle and complexity and fullness. It was one of the best soul records ever made.

Michael, in this his thirteenth year with Melissa, did not quite know where he was positioned along this narrative. He would like to say that he was at So High or the less exciting Refuge, but this would not be true, although there were sometimes fleeting moments of these, particularly the latter, for example when the children were asleep in the evenings and Melissa was doing something in the kitchen or surfing the Internet at the dining table and there was a feeling of calm and warmth and safety in the house. He had long ago passed the one-song agony and made the decision to Stay, but it seemed at times that he was slipping back, wondering whether he would be happier with someone else, or on his own, a bachelor again, living in a one-bedroomed flat in

Catford, near the children, taking them at weekends to soft play or the Broadway Theatre or to his mother's. Maybe he should be one of those men, who fathered from a distance. Perhaps he had never really deep down achieved that grand and decisive destruction of the phone-number-collector and he was still in the vicinity of She Don't Have To Know. Because frankly these days it felt like he and Melissa were nothing more than flatmates. In the not too distant past, when he would arrive back home from somewhere, she used to walk into his arms and embrace him, smile that dust-busting, magnificent smile of hers and they would talk, immediately, in tumults, about what had happened that afternoon or who they'd seen or something they'd read or something cute Ria had said or their next trip away. Their talking was like a river, always flowing, delirious with move-ment. It was oblivious to their physical separation and continued within, so that their coming back together was merely an increase in volume. It was not like this any more. Now when he got home from work, wearing his suit, Melissa would be standing at the kitchen sink and would hardly look up. There was no smile, no hug. She no longer put kisses on the ends of her texts or emails during the day. Now it was only, 'Can you pop to Lidl on way hm, chick thighs, pots, tissues, milk', or, 'Bog roll pls', or, 'Can you be home by 6.30 so I can go to zumba?' He would go upstairs to change into his tracksuit and there would be three plastic bags on the floor next to the washing basket containing his hair-cutting clothes, which she was waiting silently, with mounting irri-tation, for him to wash. Then once the children were in bed they mostly retreated into their separate realms, he on the sofa in front of the TV, and she in the bedroom reading. They lived in two different houses in one small house. *Relationships can get old*, John sang as the 176 approached the river, *have a tendency to grow cold*.

Michael's romantic odyssey had been similar, though less

brazen, to John's, this Mr Legend, walking in a better tailored suit than his down the aisle of a church in the CD artwork. Like him, or this man he had created in his music, he, Michael, had also enjoyed his share of women before settling down. He was shy in love, inquisitive, and they had liked him for it, the fellow Politics student at SOAS, the model from Honduras, the girl he'd met in Tesco. With all of them he had held a part of himself back, sleeping with them in percentages, only going to a hundred when he felt it was warranted and when he was sure he would not catch a sexually transmitted disease. He was preserving himself for something, someone, whom he had no concrete idea of, only that she would be softer, purer, higher. His passion was imperious. He was a man who was made for a great love. And in searching for this love, like John in Used To Love U, he also, at one point, had found himself in a relationship in which he was dissatisfied, in which he had fallen out of love, or further still, in which he had come to question whether he had actually been in love in the first place. Her name was Gillian and she had adored him with a molten desperation that had left him suffocated. She was studying to be a paediatrician and played the flute. She had soft, rich, flutey lips. She was gifted, she cared about the world and making it better, she made soaring silver birds with her mouth. But she had wanted him too much, more than everything else she was capable of having. On her twenty-second birthday, when Michael was twenty-three, she had asked him across their table in a Brick Lane curry house to marry her. She was a little drunk but she had meant it, and Michael said 'maybe', maybe one day, without really meaning it, because he hadn't wanted to hurt her, for she had experienced terrible pain in her life. There were men at every turn who had wanted to harm her. Her foster father had fondled her in secret nights. She was molested by an athletics coach when she was twelve. Then there was the man in the cupboard (she didn't like cupboards because of it, especially when they were closed, she had a habit of keeping them open) who had come initially to fix the boiler, but finding her there, little, in her green summer shorts, had ended up touching her inappropriately in the cupboard while no one was looking, and *then* fixing the boiler. It was amazing, she told Michael, how many men there were in the world who just wanted to take a girl for a minute to quench some passing horrific urge. It was incredible how many.

Gillian had a thick, downward way of walking as if she were forever going down into a cellar. The only time she seemed light was when she was playing the flute. She cried easily. When she and Michael were in public she wanted them to walk arm in arm or hand in hand, to appear as a woman on whom a claim could be made, a woman who was protected. She enjoyed cooking for him. She liked the spaces tradition had made for a woman and did not object to the alleged constraints, the great shadow of the patriarchal umbrella. While she was with Michael she eased herself into the warmth of his happy family, which was the only happy family she knew, this strange collection of people laughing, these loving smells emanating from his mother's kitchen, this quiet house in the suburbs. She stayed with him three nights a week, four nights, five, loved him in the early morning when his parents were sleeping in the opposite room, slipped her mouth around him asking for nothing, only that he would lie there breathing beneath her and cover the back of her head with his palm in that mode of protection. Michael thought of her now in the chorus of Used To Love U, although she was not the kind of girl John was singing about, a girl for whom nothing was good enough, who had a high opinion of herself. Gillian had thought nothing at all of herself, it was the central manifestation of her trouble. She considered herself lucky that someone like Michael, someone good and clean, had accepted her, and once she had him she had nestled in his life like a small and fearful animal. His father had adored her. She was just the kind of girl he'd hoped for, someone who would

73

love his younger son in stern abundance, someone with sensible career plans. He came to see her as a daughter (once, while out shopping in Wood Green, he had introduced her to someone as his daughter-in-law).

All of this had made things difficult for Michael. Two years into the relationship, he came to the conclusion that he didn't love Gillian and never would. They did not, the combination of them, amount to what it took to send two people off the cliff-edge in faith that they would float as one. He tried hard. He tried to position his mind permanently at the exact point during lovemaking when she set him out to sea and he was awed by her power, or at some point in their first few months when she was completely new to him, a gift still to be unwrapped and containing unknown possibilities. But it wouldn't hold. He slipped back into a sensation of wanting to be away from her, a feeling that she was trampling on his life and preventing him from seeing and thinking clearly, from *being*. He began to dislike certain expressions on her face, the blank serenity when they were sitting on a train together, the absorbed, oblivious way in which she ate, almost roughly, or the habit she had of playing with the ends of her braids. When he was out at clubs or bars he began to look at other girls. He didn't have the courage to end it with her, so like John in She Don't Have To Know he played around, in low percentages, and was eaten by guilt. He found every excuse not to be with her. Eventually she became suspicious, and it was only then, at the tail end of an argument, that he told her he wanted to end it. She responded exactly as he had feared, tears, begging. But then she had quietened. She sat down on the edge of his bed, looking downwards into her cellar. After a while she quickly stuffed some of her things into a bag and left, politely saying goodbye to his parents, not hugging them like she usually did. Eight months later he received a phone call from her during which she asked for him back, but by that point he had met Melissa.

If you come across one like that, Snoop said, it's time to change. Melissa the mermaid. Melissa with the distant eyes and glistening skin. Melissa walking lightly along a London street in khakis, trainers and bracelets and Michael walking behind her with his friend Perry ('Look how fit she is, she is *fit*'). She was the softer, purer, higher. She was way, way, way off the hizzle. She liked to swim. That was where the glistening came from. If she didn't swim she felt too dry, like something beached, her mood would descend. The day after he first met her in Jamaica, at the carnival in Montego Bay (they were both covering it, Melissa for a magazine, Michael for radio), they were on a beach, Michael and Perry and a few other reporters, talking, sunning, playing ball games, and she broke off and went into the water. She was wearing an old-fashioned black swimming costume with a diagonal white stripe across the middle that covered her to the tops of her thighs. He watched. He watched her walk into the waves with her body for days, the water reaching for her as she went, alone, fearless. She swam out. Her brown body twisted in the blue, her mermaid flow, she was a new world turning. She went further and further out and he watched the waves rising and falling, coming in and slipping back. He saw her strong brown arms wheeling in front crawl. He saw the edge of the sea where it turned with the circularity of the earth until he couldn't see it any more and he saw the rocks and the island across. He kept his eye on the brown arms turning but it became harder and harder, the sea took over in its expanse. Then he lost sight of her. She was gone. She had turned the ocean corner. Or maybe she had slipped under, maybe she was being pulled down. He began to panic. He felt his heart quicken, that she was here, this shining new thing that he wanted to know more of, and now she was not. He couldn't swim a stroke but something took hold of him then and he started walking. He rolled up his jeans and waded out, long-legged. He had no idea what he was intending to do, and when he got as far in as he could go without swimming he stopped, and waited, looked around the corner as far as he could. But he couldn't see her. After a while he went back, soaked, and stood stupidly on the shore in his wet jeans, wishing he could rescue her, wanting so much to be her hero, feeling already, as he often would in the future, that he was not enough for her. Then he began to feel angry with her, that she could just go like that and worry someone and act as if she didn't exist, as if he didn't exist. She came back twenty minutes later, laughing and out of breath. All the anger fell away as she walked towards him, her strength, her thighs, her face, her happiness, 'what a sea,' she said, 'what a swim,' and he was laughing too, 'I thought you'd drowned'. That was she. She was The One. He wanted her. He wanted to make her zoom zoom go boom boom. He liked her so much that it felt dangerous. He said to Perry, 'One day she's gonna break my heart. I know it.'

Her hands were small like her feet, she wore silver rings with jade and amber stones. She was doll-like, almost sexless. Her profile was dreamy. He stared at her a lot. She liked adventures. She wanted to go to Argentina. She had heard that there are a series of mountains at the top of Argentina that are red, especially during sunsets. She wanted to go to Seville and the south-eastern coast of Corfu. She wanted to go to Mexico and visit the house of Frida Kahlo and climb the Andes in Peru, to live somewhere other than England, to exist elsewhere from where she had begun; she wanted to eat the world. She was unlike Gillian in every way, self-heeding, self-possessed, defiant. She said that she would never be tied down and she would never occupy a space in which she felt trapped. Michael was full of questions, more so than with any woman before, and she liked him for it, the way he listened, so closely. He wanted to know every corner of her mind, every corridor. There was no end to her unwrapping. The more he found the more there was to explore. She had a mystical perception of the future, in that she seemed to believe that she was going to a different place from everybody else, that life would not happen to her in quite the same way, that in every moment she was preserving herself, enriching herself in secret like Michael Jackson in his glass coffin, remaining at a distance from people so that she would not be distracted. Those far-off eyes, always cryptic. What are you thinking about? he asked her on the beach in the evening, right now, right this minute? He tried to catch her in stills. She was slippery. I'm looking into my thoughts, she said, instead of 'I am thinking'. She expressed herself in the picturesque literal. Later she would write him poems, a line while she was away in Rome: *I miss my mouth in your pubic chin* (a reference to his goatee).

What followed, after that first meeting in Montego Bay, were three months of talking on the telephone, during which they discussed their pasts and their futures, the two houses of Edgar Allan Poe, the drama of Mary J. Blige, the depths of Cassandra Wilson, the National Front, the police, Margaret Thatcher and the things she did, volcanoes, their mothers' countries and the times they'd spent there, the decreasing distinction between R&B and pop. He made her laugh. That was the thing, she used to laugh a lot. She used to laugh so hard that he could hear sticky sounds at the back of her mouth, she embarrassed herself, she told him, because the office she was working in at the time was small and everybody could hear her. During these conversations there was nothing else but the talk, they were completely absorbed in each other's voices, seeped in chemistry, yet it took him three months to lie with her. She was living in a room in Kensal Rise with a sink in the corner and she would let him stay after a party or a date but he always slept on the floor. Their first kiss happened only after he asked her, he couldn't find another way, it made him timid, how much he liked her, and this feeling that she would break his heart. They were standing by the sink and they had eaten a meal of spaghetti with fake mince (she also ate pumpkin seeds, muesli and other things meant for birds). She was wearing a blue and pink dashiki with explicit armholes and all evening he had been peeping and trying not to peep into her brownness, her sweet shallow mounds, and now the evening was over and he was about to leave because her friend Hazel was coming over and he still hadn't kissed her. So he came out with it and asked her, like a boy, to which she said yes, like a girl. He bent. Their lips arrived together, and the *softness,* the *warmth* of it was a swirling, explosive surprise, it was a kiss that needed no input, it operated by itself, was fully formed, intrinsically euphoric yet nonchalant, had its own psychology and personality, could be called Franklin or Desdemona or Angelina, and he was so taken that he lifted her up on to the bed so that she was above him where she belonged and went with his hands inside her dress and touched, at last – and then they were interrupted by Hazel's knock at the door. It was the interruption, the cutting short of the thing, that made it even more momentous.

After that with long nights and hashish she let him in. She was bashful. She was loosely innocent. She hid herself, even after everything, behind the wardrobe door when she was changing, but she also went bra-less and oblivious in her flowing African dresses, allowing him the secrets of her little breasts, the gentle line of her upper back. By the time she moved into the flat on the seventh floor they were more or less itemised and he soon moved in with her, although she still courted him like he was some kind of accessory that she might one day leave on a train. He asked her once, when he was already too deeply in love with her to call it healthy, 'What is this? What are we doing?', because he felt like he was drowning, to which she replied, in her infectiously reasonable, noncommittal way, 'Do we have to define it?' She was always at a slight distance, withheld. It was not that she was unaffectionate, at least not then. Their lovemaking was constant. It was impulsive and ecstatic. It made them shout. It made the man who lived downstairs bang the communal central heating pipe in protest. They would leave the bed in the afternoon with the light swinging in from the balcony and go to the kitchen for toast, and in the kitchen just sitting there watching the seventh sky beyond the railing and talking, always talking, it would begin again by some long touch on a waist or the comparing of their different-sized hands or a linking of eyes or something else that made her laugh, and they would go back to the bedroom, or to the living room where the windows looked out on the city all the way to the river, and the night would fall in sepia upon their bodies. Every Sunday evening she would steam her face over a basin of essential oils. He remembered one time in particular when he had stood naked in the doorway, watching her like that, swaying under the towel to Tracy Chapman or Al Green or some other steam voice, in her blue satin slip, and she had eventually lifted her head and seen him standing there, smiled at him in that gorgeous way that made him feel so full and happy as if she were pouring sunshine into him. The tower block became the palace in the sky. It glittered like the lesser Eiffel at night. She said that she could 'just be' with him, that she didn't have to pretend or put on a front, and he felt the same way, for they were united in a large disquiet with the world, instilled partly by its everyday cruelty, partly by a common, second-generation distance, that no matter how much they tried to belong here they were never fully accepted, never fully seen. 'I've found you,' she said. 'My sweet brown, I'm so glad I've found you.' They warmed each other. They burned for each other. They just be'd, and more than once during these times when they were just being they spoke of marriage, he would ask her to become his empress one day, she would say of course I will, seeing as it's you, as if it were nothing at all, or as if she were speaking in a dream, it seemed a foregone conclusion, like a station they would arrive at on a train. In that seventh floor palace they went through Ordinary People, Stay With You, Let's Get Lifted Again, So High and Refuge. If they argued they always came back to a good place, they forged on, they continued, always returning, the flame still high only harder to find. John sang it on the replay, as the 176 took The Strand . . .

Even after eleven years together, on his birthday, Melissa had dedicated a Pussy Cat Dolls song to him, Stikwitu, about how no one else could love her better, no one could take her higher, that she must 'stikwitu' for ever. And gliding along now in the dancey haven of his iPod, Michael remembered one day in Finsbury Park after a job interview, back in those first halcyon years. He was wearing his big black puffa coat and it was freezing cold. Throughout the interview all he'd been able to think about was her, his empress, about going home to her, back to the palace, that she would be there, waiting for him, and that was all that mattered, all that he needed. He didn't care about the job. He didn't care about money. He just wanted to be with her, to be made complete by her. Next to Finsbury Park station there is a round-about. In the descending dusk, in the rush-hour traffic, he bounded across the road, bypassing the pedestrian crossing with giant, euphoric strides, and found himself stuck in the middle of the green grass circle. The cars were going round him. He took out his phone. She was on him, in him, all around him, she was the dusk, the greying light, the green, he was dizzy with her, spinning in her universe. He laughed at the sound of her voice when she answered the phone. 'How did it go?' she said. 'I don't know. I don't care.' 'When you coming home?' she said. 'I'm on my way.' Then, 'Melissa, I love you,' he cried. He shouted it, 'I *love* you!'

So how do you get from that, to this? How do you get from 'I miss my mouth in your pubic chin' to 'Bog roll pls' no kiss? What happened to Angelina, to Desdemona? How can all that love just disappear? Michael did not doubt that he still loved Melissa. His passion for her was unwaned. She could harden him at the removal of her rings, a catch of light in her collarbone, the taking off of a sock. She was in his heart through all the hours and all the strides of his day. But he doubted whether she still loved him. Would she listen to Stickwitu now and see her truth? Did she look at him and feel herself melting like she used to, like she'd told him she did? How could she, when she could look at him in that other way, this new way, with utter coldness, as if she wanted him to vanish? He disappointed her, he knew it, his uninteresting job, his inferior thirst for adventure. He embraced the land while she hungered for the sea. Adventures, for him, were inside, of the heart and spirit, whereas for her they were outside things like volcanoes. He was in the way of the volcanoes. He was her dam, her Gillian. There were days when Michael really questioned his sustainability in this relationship, when he wondered whether he had come full circle to Used To Love U, and Melissa was now a different kind of woman, the kind John was singing about, superior, demanding, judgemental. Maybe that other Melissa was gone for good and he should just let go. But he couldn't. He still believed that somewhere the fire was burning and she remained there as she had been, waiting for him. As the bus moved slowly along The Strand, past Charing Cross station, past St Martin-in-the-Fields where he'd taken Ria to do brass rubbing – the memory of this causing him to well up (the warmth of her small hand in his, her skippy walk) – the words of Used To Love U resounded in his head, about living a lie and being tired of it, no longer being willing to justify it. He felt, with a new, emergent spite, that yes, Melissa *was* this type of girl now, unkind, materialistic, a Puffy-wanter, a Jay-Z-chaser, that yes, they *had* come full circle, and all he had to do now was just try to stop loving her. Simple. Simple, yet so difficult. And arriving at Trafalgar Square in the final mist of the morning with the swirl of people and the swift walking and the birds in descent towards the icy pool, he was taken by that memory of the roundabout at Finsbury Park, the world turning around him and she a green universe, the perfection and the joy of it, and how sad it was that even such things disappear.

Coming off the bus, down the dirty narrow stairway, avoiding the poles even though he was wearing gloves, he had an urge to stand in Trafalgar Square and tell her again that he loved her, to make her remember. But he did not. He went down Whitcomb Street. A young woman came out of a building and walked past him, glancing (they often looked twice). He turned left towards his office and just as he approached it he turned off the music. It was very important that the two forces, the music and the office, remained separate, so that the music would retain its power, would remain untouched by the too bright panelled ceilings, the dead serenade of the photocopier. Now Legend was gone and Michael assumed his official façade. He went in through the shiny turning doors. He proceeded through the leafy, marble-speckled lobby, towards the circular island at its centre, another green circle, where three dynamic receptionists spoke coolly yet pleasantly into their headpieces, tapping buttons, crisp, clear and infallible in their rendition of the company's standard telephone greeting, 'Good morning, Freedland Morton. How may I help you?' He went by, taking a clandestine look at the one on the right with the long, thick black hair and the absolutely beautiful eyes, *god* those eyes, mysterious and somehow mournful, a type of caramel, almost golden, shaded by sharp and sweeping eyebrows. He did not know her name. They passed each other sometimes going to and from the office and they always tried not to look directly at each other for there was an obvious attraction, but it had come to a point where it seemed rude not to say hello, then once they had started saying hello the chemistry between them had become too pronounced and she sometimes flushed a little (she was a flushable colour, olive-toned), so that now they were at a kind of stalemate where sometimes they said hello and sometimes they did not.

Today, he did. He even waved, lightly, by accident. Uncertainly, she waved back. They smiled at one another, embarrassed.

5

MEANWHILE

'Good morning, babies! Good morning, mummies! I am *so* happy to see you all – I hope you're ready to have some fun! My name is Chun Song Li and I am your Baby Beat instructor!'

Chun Song Li, sitting cross-legged at the helm of the rectangle of women and babies on primary-coloured mats in the high-ceilinged hall of the Nunhead Christian Worship Centre, opened her arms wide, smiling with equal breadth and effervescence and leaning forwards in a gesture of determined outreach and inclusion. Melissa was to her left, the fourth woman along, wearing a Prada blouse she'd got free from an *Open* photoshoot and feeling overdressed, while Blake was in front of her, ignoring Chun Song and staring instead into the kaleidoscope of his early-life confusions. To Chun Song's immediate right was a thin black woman, Chun Song's protégée, whose face was steeped in boredom and the friction it was encountering in trying to appear enthusiastic. Melissa smiled at her, out of a vague, old-fashioned comradeship, but she did not reciprocate. It was 9.30 a.m. and nobody in the room was wearing shoes.

'Now,' Chun Song said, picking up a set of cards. 'For those of you who are here for the first time,' she smiled and leaned towards Melissa and another woman opposite whose baby was wearing a denim dungaree dress but was otherwise androgynous, 'we start every Baby Beat session with some fun and happy songs and baby signing! Don't worry if you don't know the signs yet, they are very easy to learn. Just sing along and give it a go, OK?! OK, babies? Everybody ready?'

Chun Song's protégée pressed a button on the CD player. A soft, twinkling music flowed into the room and Chun Song started to sway. With one hand she held up the cards, one at a time, on each a singular naturalistic object such as a sun, a cloud or a flower, and with the other hand she demonstrated the sign for the group to copy. The sun, for example, was a circle formed by the joining of the tips of the thumb and index finger, the other fingers splayed out to suggest rays. For the sake of their sign-literate babies, for whom this could mean the difference between a grammar school and a comprehensive, the regularly attending mothers swayed also and sang along, holding and assisting their babies' hands in front of them:

> The sun is warm and bright
> The clouds are soft and white
> Flowers and trees are green
> And rain makes them so clean

Reluctantly, Melissa joined in, swaying and singing at a minimum, making the signs with her hands in Blake's line of vision while also trying to look into his eyes encouragingly like the other mothers. She felt ridiculous, but she told herself that it was only an hour and she was doing it for him. After five months of relative seclusion from the parent-and-baby community, not a rhyme-time, not a breastfeeding café, she had come to the decision that it was time to take Blake to a place frequented by other small beings. This was her Baby Beat taster session, which, as Chun Song had explained over three telephone messages and a long email, would be free of charge if Melissa signed up for ten classes at the end of the class – that's *ten* sessions for the price of *nine* – and if they came on Monday, today, she and Blake would have the delight of experiencing the pirate-ship adventure!

The pirate ship was the large bright plastic object in the centre of the rectangle moored on top of a shiny blue aluminium sheet evocative of the sea. It was manned by four teddies wearing pirate hats and had a large orange sail, fixed to the deck with a red pole. Beyond the rectangle, in the further expanse of the hall, a second shiny sea of high-quality toys awaited the little people. There were multicoloured abacuses and scintillating rockets, building blocks, rattles and touch-and-listen play mats with woollen creatures dangling above them from arches made of felt. There was an inflatable ball pond, a psychedelic tent, a variety of light-up walkers and a scattering of noisy fabric books. White sunlight fell in from the tall windows, suggestive of a distant outside world, making the colours even brighter, more saccharine.

'Wasn't that *fun*!' said Chun Song. 'And now we are going to discover some very exciting noises and textures, before we go for a ride on our wonderful pirate ship!' The protégée handed round tissue paper, ribbons, maracas and pompoms from a decorated crate, and when everyone was adequately provided for, the babies already shaking the maracas and filling the air with the sound of fizz, Chun Song shouted, 'Now, mummies and babies, we're going to have some more great music and shake our instruments to the beat! Can you do that? Mummies, make sure you help them shake if they need it! OK?!'

The music resumed, an upbeat acoustic folk, and the babies, some of them dumbfounded, made jerky grasps at the ribbons and paper, which they scrunched up in their arms or put in their mouths or accidentally rolled over on top of it all in moments of maternal failure. Blake had a startled look on his face, his default expression, but it was tinged with a deep interest and abandonment as he toyed with a maraca in one instant and squashed tissue paper in the next. Melissa was in the process of deciding not to sign up for ten sessions for the price of nine, but it was Blake's enjoyment that kept bringing her back to the bittersweet idea of sacrifice. When the shaking was finished the babies were encouraged to climb on board the ship. It was big enough only for one or two at a time, but the child in the dungaree dress wanted to be resident captain. Her mother cajoled her to share, in a shy, extreme tone ('You've got to *share* the ship, Isabella'), but two babies were elbowed overboard and another hit in the face. For a while it was a mini riot, clambering limbs and bellies shuffling along the ocean in the development of motor skills. 'It's not designed for younger babies,' a woman next to Melissa complained under her breath, stealing a mutinous look at Chun Song.

Then it was bubble time. Out they came floating from the momentary mirrors of the soap mixture, blown by Chun Song and her assistant as they circled the rectangle, dipping and pausing like saints offering holy things. 'Aaaaah,' said babies, and 'Oooooo,' said mothers. Little arms reached up to catch. Warm cherubic faces lifted. They stared, spellbound, as round air danced before them, fleeting and translucent and suddenly bursting, all by themselves, like happy deaths. Chun Song began to blow the bubbles outwards towards the second sea, coaxing the children towards the waiting toys, they followed, jumping and reaching and clapping at the air. Once there they became engrossed in fascinating buttons and things that spun, in the luminous inner pink of the tent and the throwing around of feather-light balls. Their mothers sat near them on the floor, having disjointed, anxiety-fuelled conversations about such things as nappy brands, nurseries, infant rice cakes and the healing benefits of arnica.

'I did baby signing with my first child,' one woman said. 'It took her almost a year to pick it up, but eventually she had a vocabulary of about eighty words.'

'I pulverise absolutely everything,' another said. 'He eats the same thing as us, just mashed up. Minus the salt.'

Melissa was drawn into a conversation with a tired-looking woman by the ball pond. 'It's harder to keep them entertained in the winter,' the woman said. 'I got one of those stretchy things you attach to the door with elastic on it so he can practise his walking. He's almost fourteen months now and he's still crawling.'

'My daughter started walking at fourteen months,' Melissa said. That thing was happening again, where her mouth made sentences it wasn't interested in saying and her voice came out flat and monotonal. The talk bordered on the competitive. If one woman said she never used manufactured baby food, another would feel inferior and try to justify her use of manufactured baby food. If one said she used the Ferber method to get her baby down, another would explain the long-term attachment benefits of rocking an infant to sleep. Melissa was guilty of it herself. It was a highly contagious, psycho-verbal leprosy. She thought of Michael out there in the larger world and could not help but feel resentful towards him. In this room men were elsewhere. They were distant, virtual beings referred to in the Queen's English – '*we* don't use a pram', '*our* three-year-old gets jealous'. Here was the continuance of an old and indestructible tradition. History was here, fully intact, wearing modern clothes yet fundamentally unchanged, like a dirty secret.

During this chatty interval, Chun Song Li meandered around the play mats mingling with the mothers, showing interest in their babies and reminding them of the ten-for-nine deal (she had given up a high-flying career in investment banking to fit Baby Beat around caring for her own children and marketing was key). As she crouched down next to Melissa, Blake vomited on to the Super Scribbler. Melissa fished in her bag for baby wipes, while the woman she had been talking to gave off a faint air of distaste. 'Oh dear,' Chun Song said. 'Is pumpkin sick?'

The second half of the session was given to a name game, a dance stand-off and more signing, finishing with a goodbye song which involved waving to each other across the rectangle.

'So?' Chun Song said at the registration table afterwards. 'Would you like to sign up for ten sessions?'

'I don't think I can come next week.' Melissa was desperate to get out of there. She felt like she was suffocating in the ghost mist of the happy deaths of the bubbles. 'I'll just pay for today and maybe come back the week after.'

But Chun Song's face darkened at this reply. She said in a scolding tone, 'You don't get the free session if you do that. It has to be ten *consecutive* weeks.' She looked deeply into Blake's eyes, wiggling his hand. 'Did you have fun, Blake? Did you like the pirate ship?' Blake simply stared at her in his worried, startled way. 'I can give you until Friday to sign up for the ten sessions if you like,' she told Melissa. 'Just give me a call. After Friday, though, I don't know if there'll be a free place.'

With that she capitulated. She smiled and waved at the babies and the mummies as they dispersed from the hall, gathering their bags, their milk bottles, their coats, their slings, talking in twos and threes and fours about the excellent high-quality joy they had just delivered to their offspring. Outside a slow line of three- and four-wheeled buggies formed, rolling up the ramp back on to the street, where they waded away into the white day beneath the stark November branches of the plane trees, to lunch, to naps, to empty houses.

According to Gina Ford, the woman from Ireland who had no children, Blake should sleep for approximately two hours, between 12.15 p.m. and 2.15 p.m. It was now 10.45 a.m. Lunch was at 11.30 a.m. Due to the tremendous excitement of Baby Beat, he fell asleep in the car on the way home. He did not stir as Melissa prised him out of his car seat, nor as she removed his coat in the hallway, nor when she turned the kitchen radio up high to Choice FM, nor when she took off his socks, nor when she propped him up on the living-room rug and shook him a bit, nor when she left him there slumped against a cushion and turned on the TV in the hope that he would be lured awake by the effervescent blare of CBeebies, where a gang of talking vegetables were showing a group of children how to plant a turnip. In the end she had no other choice but to go against her mother's staunch Nigerian conviction of never disturbing a baby's sleep, and wake him up by blowing on his eyelashes and making spiders over his cheeks with her fingers. He was not pleased. He cried while she was pulverising, and when the food was ready he took his time eating it, sabotaging the 12 noon pre-nap nappy-change deadline. By the time she carried him upstairs it was 12.25 p.m and he was wide awake.

A different kind of Monday or Tuesday. Melissa did not board a bus. She did not put on suit or boot or ride the low black tunnels to an office far away from home and progeny. Her office was in the house, in the room at the top of the stairs off the halfway, skylit landing, lying dormant until the moment of that glorious and longed-for post-prandial nap. The nap was the holy land, the place of materialisation. When Blake finally fell asleep, with the blinds down to block out the light, and a lullaby playing in the background (*if that diamond ring turns brass, Mama's gonna buy you a looking glass*), Melissa would go immediately to her desk and work for those two sweet hours, feeling reawakenings in her brain, a recharging of the mechanisms of intelligence, a mature peace borne from human fulfilment and earnest endeavour. But first there was the prelude to the nap, which stretched all through the morning and was composed of such infant delights as pop-up books, animal books and transport books read to him one after another, a circus of toys laid out on the living-room rug in a similar though less extravagant way to Baby Beat – a farm puzzle where a sheep must be slotted into the shape of the sheep and a cow into the shape of a cow, etc. Or they would play nursery rhymes, or they would play some proper music like Whitney Houston or Kanda Bongo Man and dance together in a homely, insular disco. At some point between ten and eleven, Melissa would begin to experience that dubious emotion made dubious by its association with one's own precious child: boredom. A deadening, soul-destroying listlessness. An insistent yet involuntary closing of the eye. She would become acutely aware of the hollowness and the silence of the house, the insides of the walls, the crooked angles, so for a change of scenery they might go out to the library that didn't understand that words had relinquished their midweek sleep, or if it was a Wednesday and they therefore could not go to that library, they might stop in the polluted children's playground next to it, or go to some other park where other paused women walked among the trees with their prams in weekday workday hours, where they pushed their little ones back and forth on the swings, singing to them, tickling them, making faces, trying to do everything right, trying to appear as perfect, wonderful mothers.

It was so different from her days at *Open*, when the world had indeed been open. Every day she had been out, at a catwalk, at a launch, at the office, at a party. She had travelled the city, would go for drinks at All Bar One, go shopping on the King's Road and buy all those swish and colourful clothes that now were hanging in the wardrobe collecting mildew and dust. Occasionally Melissa regretted her decision to change her life and go freelance. Being freelance, she was realising, meant being off, not off the hizzle but off the scene, off the *A-Z,* out of the game, nowhere. During her pregnancy she had pictured a blissful new life of evenly balanced and creative working motherhood, of Blake lying happily in the papasan with the sun filtering in through a window while she sat happily at her desk working. She would pick her subjects. She would go beyond fashion, into features, the arts. She could finally dig out those old poems she'd been meaning to look at. She could at last get closer to connecting with that neglected part of herself, to finding herself again, understanding herself, therefore fully *being* herself, more meaningful, more profound, more truthful. For there was a niggling paradox inside Melissa that meant that she was still not sure exactly which kind of person she was – did she belong to the world or the world of the soul? Was she inward or outward? Was she a poet or a hack? She had hoped that she would be able to address this paradox in this new, different, quieter life, to dissect it, but what she was finding was that two hours a day was just not enough time in which to do this.

And Blake did not always sleep. Sometimes, like today, he wanted to stay awake and be the same as the daylight, and he would resist with all his might as she lulled him and rocked him and paced up and down the room (as she was doing now). Or he would sleep for only a little while, and it would be time to stop working when she had only just started. She would read him more books. They would do more puzzles, more sheep-shape finding, more xylophone hitting, and she would again think of Michael out there on the outside, absent, oblivious. By one o'clock she was a little bit annoyed. She got to thinking about patriarchy. She thought about all the women who had burnt their bras and died for the vote. She thought about how the Victorian age was not really over, about the prison of tradition and how so many women over the centuries had spent their lives rearing children when they could have been so much more. She thought about Simone de Beauvoir and Lucy Irigaray, about Gloria Steinem and Angela Davis. Oh she was a failure, a coward! She was allowing herself to be oppressed. All the feminist theories of her Women's Writing literature module came back to her. All the ferocity of Audre Lorde and Alice Walker came back, so that by two o'clock she would be floundering in a chasm of rage and depression so dark and venomous that she would be unable to smile at Blake. And even her depression would be a feminist depression. It was the depression of all women, all the oppressed women all over the world, and Michael was no longer Michael but a patriarch, *the* patriarch. He was no better than the patriarch of Charlotte Perkins Gilmore who had confined her to the yellow room and made her disappear. He was the patriarch of Jane Eyre who had banished Bertha to the attic and by three o'clock it would be time to pick up Ria from school, so she would push the pram up the mean, manmade street and back again, then wait desperately for Michael, who was no longer Michael but the patriarch, to get home. The real Michael was lost. That two-tone Michael was gone. That Michael who had asked her questions and walked into the sea to get her. Michael who had changed the configuration, who had changed her mind.

Melissa's journey in love was a different story from Michael's. If it had a song it would be Dido's Hunter or Gloria Gaynor's I Will Survive. She didn't need them. Before Melissa met Michael, her attitude towards men was one of indifference. They were strange and hungry beings. They had strange bodies. They wanted things. They wanted to stroke, pull, kiss, enter. She didn't like the squirt and salt of their semen. She didn't want to be a fantasy, a Coke bottle, as she had once been described. She preferred to walk alone. She was stronger on her own. Men were a distraction, a kind of erasure. It had often happened that she would be with someone mostly because of how much they liked her. There was the Irish man she had met in Paris when she was seventeen (the one who'd called her a Coke). There was the boy who had kicked her in the leg when she broke up with him. There were brown boys who wanted something pale, and pale boys who wanted something brown, and through them all she was unaffected, untouched, only physically touched (it was a thing from childhood, a father who was cruel, she had turned to stone). The only exception to this indifference was a boy called Simon whom she had met at university in Warwick. He had started off as her friend (this seemed a better way for her), he was tall, blond and soft-eyed, a London boy. They would talk for hours, lie down together platonically in his room in the middle of the night, until one day she realised that she felt something. She was not quite sure it was love, but it felt like what she thought love must feel like, it had felt very close, so she'd told him that she loved him. It was as if she were saying this from a distant compartment in her brain, though, and once they were lying down together unplatonically, she realised that they'd lost something. 'Do you think, sometimes,' she asked Simon, 'that people who like each other are not meant to touch each other?'

She was alone after that, for long enough to learn that she was capable of loneliness. Then came Michael. He was kindness, heat, persuasion, something unexpected and idiosyncratic. He wore glasses and bright silk tops and various adornments incorporating the Jamaican flag – wristbands, caps, tracksuit stripes. There was a strange combination in him of sloth and quickness, he flicked when he moved but there was a laziness to it, his hands were the fastest thing about him, they scissored the air when he talked, danced and dropped and sprang up again. He was no Tyrese. He lacked the musculature of D'Angelo. But what he did have was more valuable than these shallow things: he was kind, both in the face and in the soul, he was supremely sensual, and he had a way of looking at her that made her melt inside. She liked his questions, that first time in the Montego deckchairs, leaning into her with his very white teeth and looking square into her face, hungry, but for knowledge of her, of what was deepest within, beyond the flesh. It allowed her to still hold herself close, while also trickling out towards him, trickling in the blue Jamaica heat, towards his heat. She came to discover that there were two sides to him, two tones, the boy and the man; he was juvenile and stallion, clown and lover. He was her secret, her eventual beauty. Through Michael, Melissa finally came to understand what all the fuss was about, the thirst for the stroke, pull, kiss, enter. The way he touched her, his smooth and lengthy hands, the sparks they made within. That look in his eyes, the way he laid them on her. She would lie on her back and let him do everything. He was the master, his energy boundless, his long arms disarmed her, he was everywhere, all-encompassing. 'You're like an octopus,' she said, succumbing to him again and again and again.

Yet despite such rightness, not everything about them was right. Sometimes she felt that he wanted her to be more Nubian, that she was too English for him, had too much of white. He wanted her so badly to understand the anger that charged out of him at random moments, at the police, for instance, at passport control, at anyone or anything that seemed to pose a barrier because he was black and male. And she did understand, but not all of it, for their lives had been different, their early terrors different. It was hard, she found, blending with someone in this way, no longer walking alone, and taking these differences into your mind. It made her feel cluttered inside. She did not want to blend. She did not want to be two. Yet she wanted Michael, or the part of Michael that was the same as her. Even now, she thought as she rocked Blake and paced up and down with him, as one lullaby ended and another one began, even now, in some way, Michael still had that power to persuade her, to change her mind. But it was fainter, getting fainter by the day. Now she went with Blake out on to the landing and into the red room, the master court, to change him again. He was another body of awareness as she walked, she was thinking twice, beyond herself, his helplessness added to her, while she was being erased she was also being extended. She lay him down on the mocha bed. This is how it happens, she thought as she did her best to smile at him. This is how you get from 'I miss my mouth in your pubic chin' to 'bog roll pls' no kiss, and Blake was smiling at her nevertheless, waving his legs in the air, pulling her out of the shadows, a small face looking out of light. She turned away from him for a second to get the Vaseline –

When she turned back, Blake was no longer smiling. He was staring, pointedly, amazed, at something over her shoulder. His eyes had widened. He was struck still, frozen, like an animal stiffened by a sudden glare.

'What?' Melissa said.

She was standing again by the window, that window. Babies, Alice had always maintained, could see night things. They were in the same world. He continued to stare, and she looked behind her to see. She could feel it, the stillness, the cold, detached watching. Again, there was nothing.

'A night thing? Now?'

In the next moment he was back. Waving his legs in the air, shining from the inside out, released from the grip of whatever it was he had seen. Melissa kept looking behind her and around her as she carried him out of the room on to the landing. A flash passed through her mind of Lily standing beneath the skylight that day, the sunlight balancing on her white-blonde hair. In the second room she tried again to get Blake down. He still resisted, cried when she left him, stopped when she came back. Only when she paced with him and rocked him through the entirety of one more lullaby did he let his muscles go loose and his eyes go heavy. She lay him down in the cot for the last time, and he finally fell asleep, holding a Smurf.

That left fifty-five minutes in which to materialise, to reawaken in the holy land of work. Melissa went immediately to her office, where her desk was waiting like an abandoned ship, and sat down in the velvet chair. She stared at the screen, which contained the first two sentences of her *Open* column, this one about the resurgence of the colour yellow. *The sun shines on catwalks this season*, it began, which was lame. She tried to think of other things associated with yellow, buttercups, mustard, but it was hard to concentrate, the day seemed already defined by something else. Taking a deep breath, forcing herself into the zone, she brought her hands to the keyboard, was about to write a word, to begin a new, better sentence, when there was a knock at the front door. At first she thought it was a knock on the door of the sentence so she ignored it. Then she realised that it was an actual knock on the actual front door of the house, but she still ignored it because it was probably just a gas meter-reading person, a loft-insulation person, a replacement double-glazing pusher, a karate-club canvasser or a door-to-door organic-vegetable supplier. She held on to the hem of the yellow sentence. It wanted to get away. There came another knock, and she threw back her chair and went to answer it. Standing on the front path, holding a black canvas bag, was a large, pear-shaped man in a red and grey anorak and woolly hat. He had a square moustache and a small British smile.

'Rentokil?' he said, tipping up his badge.

Melissa looked surprised, then blank. He was waiting. She remembered. Monday, 2.15 p.m. Rentokil. Mouse. Under the bath.

'Oh. Yes.'

'Ah,' he said relieved, and filled the hallway with his bulk, setting down his bag. 'It's *very* chilly out there today, isn't it,' he remarked while taking off his gloves. 'Nice and warm in here, though. Very inviting to the mice also, unfortunately.' He smiled, without it taking up very much space in his face.

Housewives, Melissa remembered at this point, in the films, offer tea to visiting handy persons. It was her responsibility to offer this man some tea.

'Would you like a cup of tea?' she said.

'That would be marvellous. I'm white, two sugars.'

He bent down and started unpacking his equipment from the canvas bag. In the kitchen she found him a mug. She searched for the sugar, which was at the very back of the tea cupboard. No one in this house took sugar. Housewives, though, have a supply of ordinarily unneeded groceries in the kitchen in order to feed and provide refreshment for passing workers like this. There were no biscuits. She should but could not offer him a biscuit, just the tea, which she stirred for quite a long time, as if the spoon had its own will, and placed on the dining table. He did not say thank you.

Proceeding to business, his clipboard ready, he said, 'So when and where did you catch sight of our little visitors?'

She realised that he was talking about the mice. She had not had a bath since the sighting, only showers. She had been picturing a village of mice living their lives under the bath, playing violins, going to school, having dark picnics. 'It was just over a week ago,' she said, showing him to the bathroom. She described how the mouse had crawled up the side of the bath into the gap at the top.

'Just one?' he said.

'One what?'

'One mouse.'

'Well, I only *saw* one . . .'

'Hmm,' the Rentokil man tapped his clipboard with his pen. Their voices were echoing in the cold generator of the bathroom, the extractor fan was on. 'Hmm,' he said, 'they do tend to like bathrooms, especially in the winter when they're trying to get warm. The last place you'd want them, though, eh?' and he gave a little chuckle. 'Have there been any other sightings anywhere else?' Had they put down traps? Had she noticed any food eaten into? Melissa said no, lamenting the loss of her sentence, aware of the minutes passing. Then he started talking shit. Droppings, he told her, were the best indicator of a mouse presence. They were unmistakable in appearance, small brown pellets the size of a Tic-Tac but obviously less appetising. He spoke of mice as though he was a friend of their families, empathic yet grave, a kindly executioner.

'They're incontinent, you know,' he said. 'The average mouse releases about eighty droppings a day.'

'Really?' Melissa was horrified. She wondered how he knew that. Did he surf the Internet for information? Did

he have an office? A mouse hut? A rodent encyclopaedia?
Here I am on a Monday afternoon talking about animal shit,
she thought. What is the bright side? Well, it is better to be a
housewife than a mouse. I have my human dignity. I know
how to use the toilet and I can stay dry. Plus no one is trying
to kill me.

'. . . sometimes even more, with the larger ones,' he was
saying 'a hundred, a hundred and twenty. And don't forget
they're constantly urinating. Movement is pee, as it were.
Have you seen any droppings?'

'No,' she said. Or had she? Had she mistaken one for a
clove? A raisin? And eaten it? Or fed it to Blake? The matter
of the mouse extermination was taking on a heightened
urgency.

'Ah, here,' he said, pointing to the bottom of the fridge.
'There's some. Predictable. That's where people often forget
to clean. Half the job of getting rid of them is making sure
there are no crumbs anywhere. That's what they're after, you
see. They use the house as a feeding chamber.'

He knelt down to open the kickboards, revealing murky
regions unconsidered, and placed a bright-blue substance held
in transparent hexagonal containers in the dark space. Poison.
He also put some under the bath and behind the fridge. 'It's
the gradual kind. It doesn't kill them instantly. They'll eat it
and then go and find somewhere to die, hopefully outside.'

'What if they don't make it outside?'

'Oh, then you'll smell something, eventually.'

'And what *then*?'

The Rentokil man looked at her, apparently confused by
the obviousness of her question. 'Just sweep it up with a pan
and brush and pop it in the outside bin.'

'Urm, I don't think I could do that.'

Melissa had a frightened look on her face, which he notice-
ably registered. He smiled a little. The sight of a terrified
woman. Is this why he had gone into the field of mouse

attack, to see women scared on a regular basis? Might he otherwise have been a rapist? She was aware that this was a twisted thought.

Now he rose, drawing attention to his creaking knees, and sat down at the dining table with his miniature printer and walky-talky which connected him to the rest of the mouse-attack world. 'I'm almost finished here,' he said into it. 'I should be there in about thirty-five minutes. Over and out.' He concentrated on preparing her report. To make conversation – for she was overwhelmed by the smallness, the crucifying mundanity of this moment (such a large man, for such a small job) – she commented on the dinkiness of his printer. It turned out that this was not an original observation.

'If I had a pound for every customer who's either expressed an interest in this thing or said they were going to buy one of their own, I'd be a rich man,' he said. 'Yes, it's very nifty, isn't it? It fits in your pocket. I remember the days when I used to have to take all the notes back to the office with me and print the reports there. It was so much more drawn out. Now I just print and go. Don't know where I'd be without it.'

Melissa was nodding stupidly. As he handed her the report, she asked him if he knew how many mice there were. He said about four. 'They tend to go in pairs, like married people. The real problem comes if they start breeding. That's what really increases the activity.' And can they get upstairs? 'Oh yes, they can use the stairs.' Across the landscape of her inner eye, she began to see marriages of mice, not just under the bath but bounding upstairs and entering darkened bedrooms, nestling in the warm caves of quiet shoes and relieving themselves obliviously. The yellow sentence was dead. She was at full attention as he gave instructions to keep the house as clean as possible, to check the poison every three days for signs of consumption, to fill any outside holes with wire wool.

'Can you just check upstairs?' she asked as he was going out into the hall.

He agreed. The bedrooms were clear, but of the loft, he said, 'It's a bit strange up there. Wood chippings. I'm thinking something bigger than a mouse. Possibly squirrels.'

'Is that good? I think I'd rather have a squirrel than a mouse.'

But he was shaking his head. 'Now that's where you're wrong. Squirrels are like rats. They just have better publicity. They'll eat through your plaster. They'll shred your carpets. They can get through wood. They work very hard to get what they want, whereas a mouse will just eat whatever's available. Anyway, keep an eye on it.'

He opened the front door, revealing a slap of crystal daylight. He would be back in two weeks to check for bodies.

Blake's crescendoing cry surged into the air five minutes later. They went to pick up Ria from school, and the rest of the afternoon was spent in the craze-making realm of house-wifery, which involved trying to fry plantain while holding the baby while exemplifying patience in the overseeing of Ria's homework, sweeping rice grains and bits of damp salad off the floor, discovering that they were low on washing-up liquid and texting Michael (hugely devoid of Desdemona) to get some, and answering the telephone to a market research company who wanted to know if she was happy with her home broadband package at exactly the point when Blake bashed his head with the edge of a spoon and howled, causing her to go into the bathroom to scream. When Michael got home at 6.37 p.m. she was calling him bad names in her head, making her lips curl in on themselves with the inward mouthing of the words. Michael saw her like that, standing at the sink in her housey clothes, the Prada blouse was gone, her hair in disarray, not even a turn of the head in his direc-tion, and it saddened him. The digital radio was playing

Pietro Locatelli's violin sonata in D major on Classic FM, the type of music Melissa would have balked at in the days of the palace, deeming it tedious and morose, but now endorsed as pacifying, mature-making, educational, and more sophisticated than Busta Rhymes or Nelly and Kelly as a children's mealtime soundtrack, thereby further marking the disintegration of her character and a fading awareness of her identity, her likes and dislikes.

'Hey,' he said.

This came on the tail of Ria and Blake's daily celebration chorus of Daddy coming home. 'Dad-*dy*! Dad-*dy*! Dad-*dy*!' Ria sang, out of her chair dancing, Blake pumping his arms in the air and trying to sing along. They were overjoyed, every day, by this sight of him. Ria ran into his arms and he swung her around in the way of men returning from work, and Blake wanted to be swung too so he lifted him out of the highchair, making it more likely that he would puke, and swung him around as well. They were all so high on each other, the three of them, that the 'hey' directed at Melissa had a rotund, glorious air to it, full of a complete, resounding happiness and well-being. She managed a quiet, monotonal 'hi' in return.

Michael had prepared himself for this. Walking back from Cobb's Corner he had tried to anticipate her mood on the basis of the day's communications, the kissless washing-up liquid text, apart from that nothing. And the weather was grey, which was also a factor. It was not looking good. He had pumped himself three times on the chest turning the corner into Paradise Row. Don't get angry. Be positive. Be understanding.

'How was your day?' he asked.

'Oh, it was full of joy and bright, vivid colours.'

He did not know what to say to this so he took out his phone for reassurance. He was slightly terrified by the chilliness of the deep sarcasm in her voice, as if she were a mask of herself, an imposter.

'How was *your* day?' the imposter asked.

'Cool,' he said, which infuriated her. Cool did not mean anything. Cool was his answer to many questions and did not answer questions, a question, in this case, whose answer she had not been interested in anyway. She did not want to speak to him. She did not want to speak to anyone, but then he dared to ask her – in order to express caring, to be understanding – whether she'd managed to do any work today.

'Work? Work? Me? Hah!' she cried, like Bette Davis in *Nights of the Iguana*, throwing back her head, flashing a furious look at him in his thin suit. She hated seeing him in a suit. Suits did not suit him. They made him look angular.

'No I did not manage to do any work today,' she snapped. 'Blake wouldn't go down and then the Rentokil man came. He said the mice can go upstairs and get married. He said there might be squirrels and the squirrels are like rats but they have better publicity. Have you had to think about things like this at any point today, hm? Did you know,' she said, leaning with one hand on the side of the sink making her elbow jut out and her other hand holding a knife, 'that the average mouse shits eighty times a day?'

'What?' Michael said.

'Yeah. It's true. Sometimes even more than that. And they're weeing, all the time weeing, wherever they go.'

Michael sat down on the edge of the sofa and mouthed 'fuck', so the children wouldn't hear. Mouse piss, all around them. What an unbearable thought. He needed to look at his phone. He glanced at it, and Melissa clocked him glancing at it. Then he actually looked, steadily, at it, like someone on the edge of a pool, preparing to softly dive, he would go in, the water of technology would submerge him, he would sink into the neon serenity of his iPhone . . .

'He put poison down,' she was saying. 'They might die inside and then we – you – have to sweep them up and put them in the bin. There's something weird about this house, you know. Today when I was changing Blake – Are you listening to me?'

'Yes.' He looked back up at her, like a soldier in line before his colonel.

'You haven't even been home for five minutes and you're already staring at your phone. Can't you just be here now that you're finally here? Can't you just be *present?*'

'I *am* present.'

Melissa thought that when Michael was looking at his phone he was basically just sitting there doing nothing, but she was wrong. When he was 'staring at his phone', as she put it, he was not just staring at his phone. He was looking for more exciting jobs he might apply for. He was checking for important messages, checking the news, keeping up to date with Barack Obama and Lewis Hamilton developments, checking house prices in less crime-ridden areas they might move to, buying music, getting a recipe for chicken patties, and now, very usefully and imperatively, he thought, asking Google for any sure-fire tips on eliminating mice. Everything, *life*, was in his phone, a whole world of information and activity. She was so yesterday. She was so prehistoric.

But still hopeful of a peaceful evening, he put the phone back in his pocket and walked to the kitchen, to make her see that he was actually here, all of him. She was holding Blake on her hip and she kissed him with her tight lips which untightened for the moment of the kiss – Blake, the imme-diate transformer, a little wizard, the fact of him a wand. 'He said we have to put wire wool in the holes on the outside of the house,' she carried on, wiping the countertop with a frantic motion, 'because they come in from outside to use the house as a feeding chamber. So we need to buy some wire wool. It's wool, made of wire.'

'OK. Are you feeling all right?'

'I'm *fine.*'

'OK.'

Michael was hungry. His stomach was growling. He opened a cupboard, looking for food. There were some crackers, some apple rice cakes. There was a pot of rice cooking on the hob but nothing to go with it, apparently, not that he was expecting her to have cooked him dinner, hell no. He opened the fridge. A box of eggs (Michael did not like eggs), some pulverisations in little tupperwares, some condiments and a few other things like that, and a fromage frais the size of a thimble.

'God there's no food, man,' he said.

Melissa bristled inside. Her inner man-hating despiser of patriarchy was computing that he had just berated her for not maintaining their domestic plenty during her non-working day.

'What?' she said.

'What?' he said, because in fact he had been half speaking to himself, exclaiming, rather, at the lack of existent munchies, which he always liked to indulge in on arriving home from work ravenous. But she didn't see it that way.

'Are you *complaining*,' she said, bearing down on him, or bearing up because she was short, but it felt like bearing down, 'that I haven't made you some dinner?'

'No,' he said.

'It sounded like you were.'

'I wasn't. I was —'

'Do you actually expect me to have your dinner ready for you on the table when you get home?'

'No.'

'Do you think I spend the day preparing for your empty stomach?'

'No.'

'Do you think I have nothing better to do with my time than look after your children?'

'They're our children.'

'Yes,' she said, '*our* children,' and she roughly handed Blake to him. 'The children we both made together, remember?, and are supposed to be looking after together. Except that we're not. So now, *I* am going for a swim, and *you* can stay here and look after *our* children. Blake needs a bath. Don't forget to take Ria's bobbles out before she goes to bed. And can you listen to the rice, it should be done soon. I'm outta here.' She left the room but immediately came back again, realising she was still holding the dishcloth. 'If you don't want me to behave like a housewife,' she added, 'don't treat me like one.'

She slammed the dishcloth down by the sink and was gone. Michael was left in the kitchen with Blake trying to pull off his glasses, feeling deflated and misunderstood, wondering what she'd meant by listening to the rice. He was too afraid to ask her before she left, and while she was gone he forgot about the rice entirely, apart from once when he looked at it cooking in the pan for a while, even bent slightly to put his ear to it, acknowledging its wet, bubbling sound. It was only later when he smelt burning that he remembered. He ran to the cooker, dismayed, fearful for his future. Melissa returned refreshed by her backstrokes, her shoots from the edge, her wheeling arms and watching the night sky through the slats in the ceiling of the swimming pool, all of which was quickly superseded when she discovered this new failure. Listening to rice, Michael learned that evening, means listening out for when the wet bubbling sound becomes a dry popping sound, and when it does, you're supposed to turn off the heat and put the lid on the pan. This allows the hot air to do its final intrinsic softening in 'the house of the rice' (these were her words).

6

MULTICULTURALISM

In case the people of Bell Green had not noticed, or not duly appreciated, the variety of nationalities and cultures living in their vicinity (the Africans and Caribbeans, the Eastern Europeans, the Indians, the Iranians, the Turks, the Nigerians, the Jamaicans, the Chinese, the Greeks and so on), Ria's school held an annual cultural evening in December to celebrate the rich and expansive meeting of all these disparate lands. There were folk songs and dances performed by children wearing their national dress. There were poetry readings in high-pitched voices exploring the positivity and mellifluousness of diversity. There were comedy sketches and gospel singers, recorder recitals and carnival choreographies, a fashion show in which adults and children alike paraded up and down the makeshift wooden catwalk in the cramped assembly hall flaunting their far-flung fabrics, their wrappers, their saris, their headwraps and their dashikis. In the adjacent hall was an array of international food donated by the parents, an aromatic meeting of fufu with samosas, of moi moi and egusi stew with tabbouleh and baklava – and while you were there you could also get your hair braided or your palms hennaed or your face painted at one of the stalls, or take part in a spot of Tamil calligraphy, or Polish Wycinanki. This year there was going to be a guest appearance by a former pupil of the school called Justin, who had been strong in music and was going to sing for them.

Michael was taking Ria to the show. It would become one

of her favourite memories, she knew, walking with her tall father up the road, right at the top, left at the church and left again in the early-winter darkness. Blake would be in bed but she wouldn't, because she was oldest and mature, and they would go up the ramp into the busy, bustling hall where her school friends would also be up late, Shanita, Shaquira, Emily. They would watch the show, and afterwards they would go into the other hall to eat crisps, custard creams, Haribos, Chupa Chups and other things that were forbidden at that time of night, and they would peruse the stalls, and just skip and jump around. Michael would lose her in moments as she revelled in all this fun, and catch sight of her in a corner twittering with Shaquira or negotiating jellybean portions in the corridor with Emily. They roped him into their games and made him give them swing rides. He was the comedian father, one of those easy adults who understood the importance of playing, who could do it almost as well as them. Ria was not taking part in the show. She preferred to watch, craning her neck and peering to get the best view. At the end of the evening she and Michael would walk back home in the even deeper dark, the moon there, the lamplights, the quiet streets, and she would fall asleep without protest on a long, smooth slide made of joy.

The preparations for the event went on for many weeks, for that time robbing the children of PE. Instead they practised their songs, they rehearsed their dance moves, or if they weren't performing they made the backdrop, or painted the national flags to be hung on lines of string across the ceiling. At home the parents got costumes ready. They found wrappers, and if they did not have wrappers they hemmed pieces of cloth to make wrappers, and if they did not have pieces of cloth they went to Brixton or Peckham. The recent women of Africa considered what headwraps they would wear, how they would wear them, with what quiff and shape, with how much coverage of ear – half, whole or none, depending on the sensitivity of your gristle and whether or not you wore glasses. They talked to their less-recent children who had never been 'home' about how they were going to take them home one day, so that they could see the true country, where they were really from, and if they were naughty children or showing signs of possible future street-gang involvement, they would focus on the educational virtues of that country and how respect for your elders and authority was an unquestionable, unnegotiable part of life on the basis of important ancient customs, and the declaration about taking them home would bear a tone of threat. Meanwhile, the peoples of the Mediterranean dug out their historical skirts, and those of the Indian subcontinent assembled little tunics and saris so that they could watch their cubs twirl around on stage, celebrating all together the wonderful exuberance of the beige nation, which was something that just did not really occur to them on a day-to-day basis.

Ria had a wrapper and matching top that Melissa had made for her to wear to a Nigerian wedding last year. But she wasn't going to wear it because she wasn't in the fashion show and the audience didn't have to dress cultural, they could wear whatever they wanted. She was going to wear her new grey Primark jeans, the Moshi Monster top her grandmother on Michael's side had bought for her, her black and pink trainers, and her white puffa. And she wanted her hair all out and bushy with a hairband in it. Melissa and Michael also planned to take their children 'home' one day, to both Nigeria and Jamaica, but these were expensive, complicated trips (multiple vaccinations, high flight costs out of school term times, a visit to the Nigeria High Commission in Northumberland Avenue, where you would have to wait in a hot, overcrowded basement for possibly hours with a lot of annoyed Nigerians, only to be told when you got to the counter that you had to come back next week), so they were going to wait until Blake was at least old enough to know where he was and what it meant when they were there so that they could get their money's worth of heritage awareness. Melissa did sometimes attempt to make eba and stew – Ria always enjoyed eating it at her mother's, and Alice was eager for all of her grandchildren to eat Nigerian food – but it never tasted as good when she made it herself. She could never get the consistency of the eba right and the stew was not as tasty, and it was such a long drawn-out process, getting the yam and shaving off the bark and boiling it and mixing it with the gari and mashing them together in a pestle and mortar, and for what? For a sub-par, second-generation travesty. So the occasions when Melissa did make it had become just that, occasions. She preferred to take the children to her mother's so that they could have the real thing. To Ria, though, it was all irrelevant. People were not black or white. They were brown, beige or pink.

'Mummy,' she said one afternoon on the walk home from school. That day she had been painting the Jamaican flag. 'I've got three countries in my blood – Nigeria, Jamaica and England.'

'Yes, that's right,' Melissa said.

'I'm half English, a quarter Jamaican and a quarter Nigerian.'

'No, you're a quarter Nigerian, a quarter English and half Jamaican.'

'Why?'

'Because I'm half Nigerian and half English, and Daddy's completely Jamaican.'

'But I want to be completely Jamaican too,' Ria said. 'I want to be all of them.'

'You can't be all of them and only one of them at the same time. You can either be just one thing or a mixture of things. Anyway, you're British as well.'

'So I'm four things?'

'No. British is your nationality. This is where you're born and bred.'

'What?'

'Pardon, not what.'

'Pardon?'

'What?'

'What did you say about bread?'

'Not bread that you eat. Bred means growing up.'

'Oh. OK.' Then she skipped off ahead and waited at the corner opposite the church for Melissa to approach with the pram, at which point she jumped out spectacularly in front of Blake with her arms in a flourish and her mouth wide open and made him laugh. His laughter was a new toy and she did everything she could to make it go.

Every day they did this walk, other children skipping nearby with their mostly female guardians of the afternoon. They saw the same people, the short, very white girl from the estate with the large head and hard face, the slow man in the tracksuit who walked like a cat, the leopard-print woman with the leopard-print leggings and relaxed burgundy hair clasped at the back with a matching clip. As they walked they talked of many things, sometimes the hood of Ria's coat would be balanced on her head, the arms left unused. They talked about insects.

'Ants can get under any door they like,' Ria said.

'Yes, they can,' Melissa replied.

'Flies can't. They're too big. What if lots of flies wanted to crawl on me? I like it when flies crawl on me.'

'Do you? I don't.'

'I do. What if a line of flies was queuing up to crawl on me?' she laughed. 'Not all over me, though. I wouldn't like to have flies crawling *all* over me, especially on a hot day. Mummy, why do flies like bins?'

They talked about the Queen.

'My friend Aaliyah said she's been to Buckingham Palace and met the Queen and stayed there for a month. She had to wash her feet —'

'Whose feet?'

'The Queen's feet, and scratch her feet as well and wash up and cook her dinner. She had to do loads of stuff, I can't remember all of it. I think I should start learning to cook.'

They talked about ghosts.

'Mummy, do you want to die peacefully or not peacefully?'

'I definitely want to die peacefully.'

'I don't.'

'But why not?'

'Because then I won't get to come back as a ghost. It would be fun being a ghost. You get to stay up late all the time.'

And the perils of Coke.

'If you drink Coke it makes your teeth shrink. If you drink it every day then after about two or three days all your teeth shrink smaller and smaller and then they just fall out. My friend told me.'

From the corner opposite the church they could see the Crystal Palace tower in the distance beyond the rooftops and treetops and telephone wires. And they talked about that palace too.

'You know in Crystal Palace Park there used to be a massive big palace made of glass and it got set on fire and burnt down?'

'Yes,' Melissa said. 'In 1936.'

'How did you know?'

'I read it in that book we got from the library.' Ria had recently done a school project on it. 'Do you know about the train as well?

'What train?'

'The one that got stuck in the tunnel with the people inside it?'

'What? Did they all die?'

'Probably. If it's true, that is.'

'That means there must be ghosts there. Can we go to Crystal Palace Park and see one day?'

'OK.'

Ria had inherited Melissa's wanderlust. They were adventurers, explorers. It was not just talk. They would go and see.

'When?' she said.

'Soon. I think you can get to the tunnel entrance through the woods. It's sealed, though, so we won't be able to go in, just look.'

'OK.'

The houses either side of them, the red-stone witch-hat terraces. The gardens, the stony driveways, the silver birches, the estate. There they turned left and came down Paradise Row, along the bend, across the road to their line of Victorians with number thirteen halfway down and the high road at the bottom where the sirens ripped crazily through the air. They were a constant presence, their endless wail of trouble. Like Stephanie, Melissa did not want Ria and Blake to grow up with this sound, to develop the hardness that enabled you to become insensitive to it. She wanted them to live somewhere calmer, somewhere greener, somewhere the emergency services were less busy, so that they in turn could be calm, and keep the purity of themselves. She was aware that in the area in which she chose to live, in walking Ria to school, taking Blake to the park, to the local shops, in the things they came across on these journeys, she was assembling their childhoods, building their store of memory. Would Ria remember the sirens? Would she remember the day they walked home from school and the road opposite the church was blocked off by white ribbons?

That day Melissa went to pick her up as usual at 3.30 p.m. They went to the administration office to give in a reply slip, then exited through the school gates. They crossed the road, turned right, turned the bend, playing a game of I-spy, but when they reached the church they had to stop. There was a white cordon ribbon blocking the way. Another was fluttering in the wind further along, while inside the two ribbons was a police van and several policemen standing about. A group of onlookers had gathered by the church. It was not difficult to guess what had happened. There had been a shooting, right there at the top of Paradise Row, at 3.35 p.m., as children were walking home from school.

To address the problem of women's equality, Blake had started going to a childminder twice a week, Ria's friend Shanita's aunty. She was a loud, buxom Jamaican with a red weave. She said, 'Hi there, sweet bwoy!' snatching him out of Melissa's arms at the front door. He didn't like being left and he cried a lot. She could still hear him crying as she walked away, feeling lopsided, as if she had misplaced something very important. Blake was more attached to her than Ria had been. She felt that in leaving him there she was tampering with the natural order of things, depriving herself of an offering, a new direction. She looked back at the house and regretted that she would not know the tissues of his day – the tissues used to wipe his nose, and the tissues of his new mind experiencing moments.

Michael said, 'He'll be fine. He'll settle.'

'How do you know?'

'He will. He has to.'

In the second week he cried less, and set a brave face when the door was closed. But Melissa still rushed to him when the day was over, desperate to reclaim him.

'How do you manage it,' she said, 'spending so much time away from him? You see him for a minute in the morning and two minutes in the evening. Doesn't it bother you? Don't you feel bad? Is this just a woman thing?'

'It's different for you. You're his mum.'

'Well, you're his dad . . .'

'I know, but . . .'

During that walk to the Cobb's Corner roundabout in the

mornings and the ride on the 176, everything fell from Michael's consciousness, the house, the baby, the dust, the draining board and whether it was full or not. The world was distraction and extraction, from smaller worlds. It was getting more and more between them, this imbalance, the hours spent with and without. It was another presence, darkening and becoming solid.

'Your life hasn't changed,' she said.

'My life *has* changed. How can you say my life hasn't changed?'

'How? Tell me.'

And he told her, about the after-work drinks he didn't go to, the meet-ups he couldn't make, the rush to get home every evening so that he could be ordered in an unfriendly tone to listen to rice. He did not like this Melissa with the hard mouth and loveless eyes. He wanted the other Melissa, that old, original Melissa, with the soft and skyward face, the gentle dreaming eyes. Where had she gone?

'OK,' he said angrily, 'how about you get the 176 at 7.35 every morning instead? You're never satisfied! You go out to work then, and I'll stay here.'

'I do work,' she said. 'I don't need your money. I can make my own money.'

This exchange took place at the intersection between the living room and dining room, beneath the ecclesiastical arch, Melissa standing at the bottom of the stairs, Michael sitting on the sofa in front of the TV. Afterwards Melissa went upstairs without saying goodnight and Michael poured himself another glass of red wine. When he lay down next to her later in the red room he thought to encircle her in the way of the old palace days, but she was all closed to him, breathing deeply on their ship, as if their bodies had never belonged to one another. In the morning he got up before her. Blake called for his mother and he lay him next to her in the place that he had just vacated. He put on the grey suit. Before leaving he went to say goodbye to Ria. She was awake, lying on her back. He sat down next to her.

'Hi, Daddy,' she said.

'Hey.'

'It's Thursday today.'

'I know.'

'And you know what that means.'

'I know what that means.'

'Can you stay with me for a minute?'

'OK. A minute.'

'A long minute.'

'I've got to go to work now.'

'But it's too early.'

'I'm going to a breakfast meeting.'

'A breakfast meeting? What's a breakfast meeting? Do you eat your breakfast together with lots of other people or something, with different cereals?'

'Yeah, kind of, and talk about work.'

'Oh.' Ria pondered this. 'I don't like breakfast meetings. I think you should have your breakfast first at home and *then* go to work and talk about it there. You're always at work, Daddy.'

Michael laughed. 'I know, but them's the breaks.'

It was a holiness, the sight of this child. She had a power over him that no one else had. She washed him clean of any darkness, any disappointment or yearning. With this holiness in the palm of his hand, he stroked the side of her head and her rich hair. 'I'll see you tonight,' he said.

Ria beamed. Multiculturalism was nigh. 'Tonight! I can't wait!'

Egusi was stewing. Chapattis were frying. Rice was steaming and plantain was undressing. Later that day the tables in the second hall were pulled into place, making loud scrapes across the parquet floor. The flags of the world were hoisted on their strings across the ceiling of the first hall and rows of child-sized blue plastic chairs were laid out for the audience, with the piano set just so at an angle to the stage. Across Bell Green traditional outfits were ironed and final-checked, and the light was falling early in its new frame of mind. It was not yet winter, but the season was already well underway on this island of eager coolness. The green chandeliers of the birch trees were gone, their arms naked above their stoic white trunks. Snow was coming. You could feel it, in the knife of the air, in the rip of the breeze. It was almost dark when Ria came home from school. It was thick and deep by the time she'd eaten dinner and changed into her uncultural clothes. She unleashed her hair. She chose her Hello Kitty hairband. She put on her socks. She put her things into her fuchsia felt bag, and waited eagerly for Michael to get home.

After the breakfast meeting, Michael went to the office and passed the girl at reception with the beautiful eyes and said hey. Now they always said hey, he hey, she hi. He even knew her name, Rachel, because they had found themselves in the lift together one day and he had said, 'Michael,' offering his hand, and she had said, 'Rachel,' accepting it, and the discomfort of avoiding each other was thereby resolved. He worked through lunch so that he could leave early to get back for the show. On his desk he had a picture of Ria and Blake which he looked at periodically and got a warm and purposeful feeling from. At 4.45 p.m. he cleared away his things and headed for the door, and he would have got back in time if it had not been for a number of things, as he tried to explain to Melissa later that evening. First of all (this is the bit he didn't try to explain) he ran into Rachel in the lift again and they got chatting about cricket (her father, it turned out, was once a national player in New Zealand, where she interestingly had lived until she was ten before moving to England, and Michael of course had played lots of cricket when he was a teenager, so there was much to enthuse about, the white running, the flight of a ball, full of chance, the seeking in the arm). They carried on talking as they left the lift and walked through the lobby together, during which he noticed how pleasingly tall she was and how her hair smelt nice, flowery, and it turned out that she also was leaving for the day so he waited just very briefly for her to get her bag from the island and they carried on out the door shoulder to shoulder, even walked a little way through the streets together until they parted on Charing Cross Road, next to one of London's last red telephone boxes. For a moment there he had felt like John Legend in sunglasses in Washington DC walking out with his forbidden woman, and it had given him a thrill, another pinch of yearning doubt about where he was in the *Get Lifted* narrative. Who was she, inside, this Rachel, this fellow aficionado of cricket? He looked back at her as she walked away, her leather handbag tapping against her hip, her thick legs and that slightly heavy walk. What might she feel like, touch like, be like in her newness? How might it be? Those eyes, the luxuriance of them, such depth, such gold . . .

And then he had the most horrendous journey home. He waited ages for the 176, he told Melissa, ages and ages, twenty minutes at least, in the deepening city-lit darkness, but it didn't come, which is very unusual for the 176, and indicative of the unusual, somehow otherworldly nature of this particular journey home. So he had no choice but to get the tube (who gets a bus, anyway, from central London to the deep south, during rush hour? Melissa interjected as he was telling her this). He ran – for now it was 5.40, the show started at 6.30 – to the crowded tube entrance at Charing Cross, bracing himself as he began to descend from the safety of the upper air into the claustrophobia of the lower air, the tunnels, the dreaded tunnels, stretching and shooting through miles of dirt, populous with all kinds of incontinent vermin, susceptible, he could not help but imagine, to disastrous collapse and random bombings, as demonstrated by 7/7 which had marked the beginning of his serious tube boycott. The stairs were crowded. The ticket hall was teeming, there were wide walkers everywhere, the name he gave to people who wade rather than walk, or have bags on either side of them, or have some other kind of inconsiderately expansive gait. He finally got through the barriers and down the escalator on to the southbound Northern Line platform, only to find that also was crowded, two trains went by before he could even get on. Same thing at Waterloo, where he changed to the Jubilee, though thankfully the one he did get on was less crowded and he at least had some room to breathe. He stood there, bound for London Bridge, listening to Jill Scott on his iPod, reading the ads above the windows, studying the tube map, looking at the people around him but too anxious to play the 'where are they going?' game – the man with the guitar in the suede shoes, another man with bright-green eyebrows who kept opening and closing a piece of paper and mouthing words from it. He found that if he focused on these small things, the suede shoes, the green eyebrows, he could cope better with the problem of being under the pavements, though what he was predominantly thinking about was Ria waiting at home for him, the minutes going by, 5.54, 5.56, 5.58. At 5.59, as if purpose-fully to madden him, somewhere in the blackness past Southwark, the tube came to a gradual, infuriating halt.

Darkness enfolded. The silence was total. No word from the driver. Sighs, tuts, shufflings, teeth kissings. Michael started to sweat. People were rubbing their necks, scratching, folding their arms. From somewhere further along the tunnel there was a tremor. From somewhere closer there came a jolt. People glanced at each other. Another jolt, closer still, a door at one end of the carriage opened, and a man stepped in, wearing a dirty coat and emitting a bad smell. Holding on to the two poles where the seats began, he cleared his throat and gave the following speech: 'Now listen for a minute,' he said. 'I'm not a drunk or a junkie or anything. I'm unemployed, got a sick wife to support, lost my job last year then became homeless cos I couldn't keep up the bills . . . Now as I said, I don't drink or take drugs, I'm just going through a rough patch, you know, we all have rough patches . . . If I'm gonna eat and feed my family this evening, I have to raise six pounds. I ain't got no money, but there's enough of you here to help me eat even by giving me just a few pennies each . . . I don't do this all the time, honest, only when there's nowhere else to go. Thank you for listening, and if you can't hear me you don't want to hear me.'

He shuffled through the carriage holding out a bag for people to drop their pennies into, which a few of them did, more so towards the other end of the carriage, Michael gave him two pounds. The train moved off again, the beggar went into the next car, and at last they arrived at London Bridge where Michael shot out through the open doors, weaved through the wide walkers – oh so many wide walkers! – up the escalator, through what seemed like a series of more and more tunnels and walkways so that it began to feel as if he were going nowhere and would never get anywhere ever again. He passed a busker who was playing Aaron Neville's *Hercules* on the guitar, and another busker playing a flute, the silver trail of sound suddenly making him think of Gillian. He was running now, up the final escalator, and *then*, after all that, he told Melissa, he had to wait *ten minutes* for an overground train – that is, an actual train, as opposed to a tube – to take him to the London the tube forgot. It was not until seven o'clock that he was running down the high street gripping his Oyster card past the chicken shops and the pound shops towards Paradise Row, full of a violent, stomach-churning guilt that Ria had missed the beginning of multiculturalism and it was all his fault. To his surprise, the house was empty. This is because forty minutes earlier, sacrificing the evening order of the Gina Ford bedtime and thoroughly piqued, Melissa had gathered up Blake, put his bodysuit over his pyjamas, put him into the pram, and the three of them, she, Ria and Blake, had gone up Paradise Row in the dark and the cold, right at the top, left at the church, up the slope, and into the brimming first hall, where they found a seat in the fifth row and waited for the show to start.

The pianist was in position. The stereo was playing highlife. The children who were performing were sitting on the floor in front of the stage, while their mothers, fathers, aunties, uncles or grandparents were sitting in the rows of chairs behind them, their buttocks, some denimed, some legginged, splurging over the edges. The room was hot and getting hotter, as the chairs filled up and more people gathered, standing at the back, leaning against the climbing frames along the walls, or watching from out in the corridor when there was no space left in the hall, as Michael did when he arrived halfway through the show. All the windows were open and misty with steam. There was a feeling of bright, accepting chaos, of gushy expectation, the smells of many stews drifting in from the second hall.

Presently, the headmistress, Mrs Beverley, stepped up on to the stage, with her grey cornrowed crown, her cultural effort of Kente dashiki top and fishtail wrapper with fluorescent orange sling-back heels. She had squinty, bespeckled eyes and always lurched forward when she spoke in a mode of grand compassion. The audience quietened. She pressed her hands together and thanked everyone for coming. 'I am always so *impressed* with our children and all you dedicated parents who make the effort to come to our show every year,' she said, her earnest eyes blinking, 'It really makes it all worth it, doesn't it, children?' and she swept an affectionate gaze at the ones waiting and assenting below her. 'Now, the children, as you know, have been working very hard to prepare for tonight, learning their songs and helping to decorate this hall – doesn't it look wonderful?' The audience agreed that indeed it did. Blake did not agree because he was starting to cry. Melissa bounced him up and down on her knee while Mrs Beverley asked everyone to switch off their mobile phones and to extract 'overwhelmed' infants from the hall if they really weren't happy. She finished her speech with a request for some encouraging applause for the opening act, and the performance began.

First up were two young Tamil dancers in red and turquoise saris, biting their lips and looking at each other. As the music played they span and bent, letting their viscose fabric flow, then rose up again and checked what the other was doing to see if they were doing it right. Too frightening it was to smile out at the audience or attempt eye contact, their mothers and fathers and possibly especially their mothers being the most frightening people of all to be studied by in public, so there was a complete absence of audience–performer connection, which made them more endearing. '*Ahh*, bless 'em,' said a woman next to Melissa, who was sitting next to the one from the estate with the large head. The Tamil dancers were followed by a gospel song from the school choir, then a middle-aged Greek solo dancer, somebody's mother, in a traditional dress with frills at the front, embroidered hems of aubergine velvet and short puffy sleeves, accessorised by green sequinned gloves to the elbow and a pair of tight gold pumps on her chubby feet. She was a stark contrast to her dancing predecessors, with her absolute lack of shyness and her bull-like, charging movements. Every time she did a skirt-lifting spin or something flourishing and climatic with her sequinned arms the audience clapped. She had a white flower in her hair and a black clip. Her musical accompaniment was throaty and substantial, thick with guttural strings and a heavy continental bass. During her performance she began to sweat. It glistened in the emerging wrinkles of her forehead and darkened her armpits, but she continued unabashed until the music reached the peak of its crescendo and she finished, victorious, one knee on the floor and arms extended. There was a blast of applause from the crowd, honouring the bravado and lustre of her performance, her commitment to celebrating life whatever your age and setting a shining example to the children. It's never too late. Live. Live completely. Dance like no one's watching.

After this came the Trinidadian carnival troupe, then a recital of a poem by Benjamin Zephaniah. The final act was Justin, the ex-pupil who had come to sing, though, it turned out, not as well as people were expecting, considering the build-up. He was given a magnanimous introduction by Mrs Beverley and a round of applause as he climbed the steps to the stage, wearing an ordinary white polo-shirt and Adidas trainers. He walked with his head tipped back, as if he were about to ask the world a question. There was no overture to his song. He did not smile or speak, merely took hold of the mic with both hands, looked blankly ahead, and delivered a crucifying rendition of Robbie Williams's Angels. He put that song on a hard black nail and mounted it to a deathly cross on a dark and desolate hill, where it died slowly over many long and painful bars. 'Oh my god, who told that boy he could sing?' the woman next to Melissa said. He was no Legend, not even a Robbie, and when he had finished the relief was palpable, the people who had been trying to close their ears invisibly by using the muscles inside them could relax again, they sat back and watched the fashion show, frills and fabrics swishing up and down, the earless ladies in headwraps.

Michael took Ria to Wycinanki, hair-threading, fufu-sampling, henna-palming and Haribo-munching afterwards while Melissa went home in a huff with Blake. Later he would explain the horrendous journey home complete with the Hercules busker and tunnel pause but she was icy with him. Definitely no Desdemona. Was Desdemona dead, and all of her offshoots?

It went on like this. They fell to distances. Her body forgot his hands. They were partners, in the very tedious sense of the word, and the difficult thing was that they couldn't talk to their best friends about it, because they had been each other's best friends. One night Melissa called her friend Hazel instead.

'I need to go shopping,' she said.

'Me too!'

'You always need to go shopping.'

Hazel was always beautifully dressed. Probably even now on this gloomy Sunday evening she was sitting in her swinging designer wicker chair in a dress and lady slippers.

'Life is cloth,' she said.

'I believe you. Retail therapy. Works every time.'

'Why, what's wrong?'

'Nothing.'

'Oh really.'

'So when are you free?'

'Next Saturday?'

'OK.'

'OK.' And they arranged to meet at Topshop.

7

DESDEMONA

'I don't understand women sometimes,' Michael said to Damian.

'Me neither,' said Damian.

'Like the other night, I went to give her a hug and you know what she said?'

'What?'

'She said you just want me to service you.'

'Service?'

'As in petrol. She's Esso, I'm the tank. I'm not a tank, I told her.'

'And what did she say?'

'She said you are. All men are tanks. You use women like fuel. You come home and expect me to be lying there waiting for you wearing Ann Summers underwear.'

'And what did you say?'

'I said that's not true. I was just showing a little love and affection, remember that? And she goes yes, you want to be loved passionately your whole life, don't you? And I said well yes, I do, what's wrong with that?'

'And what did she say?'

'She said I need to get real and life ain't like that any more and it can't run like that now. I don't know what's happened to her, man. It's like she's turning into a different person.'

'Maybe it's postnatal depression. Stephanie had that after

Summer was born, it makes them crazy. You have to just go with it and be meek.'

'Meek.'

'Yeah.'

'I don't wanna be meek.'

'I know, but it's the only way.'

'God.'

'So how did you leave it?'

'She went to bed. Then I went to bed.'

'The same bed?'

'No. I slept on the sofa.'

There was a grave silence at the seriousness of this disclosure.

They were in the Satay Bar in Brixton on a Friday night having an after-work drink. They had initially met at the station and walked down to the Arcade to find a bar, but they were alarmed at the lack of black people in there, they were nowhere to be seen, it was as if they had been shooed away into small, dark mouse holes where the buildings met the streets, so Michael had said cha man, let's go to the Satay. And here they were, a fuchsia glow at the glitzy end of Coldharbour Lane, opposite Kentucky, around the corner from the Ritzy cinema, meeting point for dancing at Plan B. It was one of the few places in Brixton that had triumphed against the bleaching conquest of gentrification. It was full of weaved women, dressed to the maximum in shimmer tops and cute jackets and silky dresses, their hair flowing smoothly from their fibbing scalps, their fingernails dynamic. This was a place you made an effort for, guys too, well-snipped, best denim, musculature optimised if applicable. Damian felt conspicuously lame and provincial in his bad suit. Michael was wearing a suit as well, but his was a better cut, a slick faint navy, more fitted, and there was only half of it, he was wearing jeans and a trendy belt, and his stomach didn't bulge out against the belt the way Damian's did. They had discussed before the wearing of the suit and how they felt about it. Damian could never seem to pull it off, the shoulders were always a bit too wide for him and the trousers too tight, and no matter where he'd bought the suit it always looked like it came from Blue Inc on Oxford Street. Although he claimed also to struggle, Michael did not share these failings. He power-dressed powerfully. He had swagger. For him it seemed effortless, like many other things.

In order to attend to the issue of his ailing mental health, as Stephanie thought of it, Damian was trying to spend more time in London, to reconnect with himself, and it was his idea to meet up tonight. What a relief it was to walk along Brixton Road in the evening hubbub and to be sitting here now in these cosy leather armchairs next to the bar with a good friend and a bowl of wasabi nuts and Roy Ayers playing from the speakers. It made him yearn again for his former life, and the dangerous thing was that the feasibility of returning to that life seemed less impossible, sitting here with Michael, than it ever did in Dorking. He could get a studio flat somewhere, he was thinking, it wouldn't have to be anything fancy just a roof over his head, he could visit Stephanie and the children at weekends, finish his novel, surely in London he would finish it, maybe even get a publishing deal. The idea of it was making him sweat, as was the bad pleasure he was feeling at Michael pouring out his heart to him like this. All was not well in M&M paradise. He was enjoying every word.

'It's oppressing me now, this relationship,' Michael was saying. He was on his second whiskey. 'Sometimes I feel like walking out, like not going home after work, just going somewhere else instead.'

'Like where?'

'I don't know, to a hotel, a club, just *somewhere*.'

'But that's the thing,' Damian said. 'There isn't anywhere. It's a fantasy.' At least this was the theory he tried to live by.

'Is it?'

'Isn't it?'

'You know the one thing that stops me from leaving?' Michael said. 'The kids. I wanna be with my kids, man. I wanna be there when they wake up. I wanna smell their morning breath.'

'Yeah, I know. It's all about the kids.'

'But it shouldn't be all about the kids. I don't want to live like that either.'

Melissa did have a point, Damian thought, about Michael needing to get real. Marriage, it *was* all about the kids. He himself had accepted this a long time ago, that children claim the love, they change it, they drink it, they offer it back to you in a sticky cup and it never quite tastes the same. The romantic love from which they sprang becomes an old dishevelled garden visited on rare occasions fuelled by wine and spurts of spontaneity, and the bigger, family love is where the bloom and freshness lie. But Michael and Melissa were not married. That was the difference. They had not crossed that line, and Michael could keep on walking without paper, and he could look around at all these fit, shimmering women – as he was now, intermittently, particularly at the one on the table over there in the ivory dress who was looking back at him – and wonder at other futures, more experience, more pleasure. Damian did not dare look at them. If he looked at them, really looked at them, he would be faced with the ugly and excruciating abstinence of his own life.

Michael turned from the honeys and stared into his drink with deepening bleakness. He wanted Melissa, not them. But he didn't know how to get to Melissa any more. He was stuck. It was hard to stay and hard to go.

'What do you do,' he said, 'when you reach a point where you know it's just not going to work out with someone? It's never going to be good again. What do you do, huh? You have to make a decision, right? You accept unhappiness, or you do something different. I've been thinking about this a lot.' He moved his drink to the side of the table and drew a square with his finger. 'There's a window. This is the window. Everyone, at some point in their lives, is faced with this window, and in the window you can choose not to become what you seem to be becoming. You can take a leap, do something off the wall, something reckless. It's your last chance, and most people miss it. They just walk past it. Then one day it closes, and once it's closed it's closed for ever. This moment right here with Melissa, this is my window. I can either risk it and jump, or stay where I am.'

'But *could* you jump?' Damian said. 'Do you have the courage to jump?'

Michael pondered, sighed. 'I'm such a coward.'

They drank from their glasses, both looking through this metaphorical window, which for Damian was closed (or was it?) and for Michael was still open.

'When are you two gonna get married? This long engagement is one long engagement.'

It had been announced in the closing embers of the last century. There had been the meeting of respective families, the gathering of friends, champagne, cashew nuts, then nothing. The century turned. Babies, a house. What were they waiting for? They should just damn well get married and put the nail in the coffin like everybody else.

'I think we've missed that boat,' Michael said.

'It's never too late.'

'Ain't gonna happen.'

'Have you ever thought that might be half your problem?' Damian said, energised, calling on a line of reasoning he employed often with some doubt. 'That you haven't taken that step together? That final step? You haven't fully *committed*. The grass on the other side is still available to you. You think it's greener but it's not. You're torturing yourselves, man. Just close the door, seal it shut, and get on with your lives. Deal with what you've got, innit.'

'That sounds like a really dry reason to get married,' Michael said, at which point Damian felt belittled and stripped of the protection of his reasoning and a bit irritated, and wanted to do something mildly violent like poke him in the eye.

'Do you and Stephanie ever fight?'

'Yep.'

'I can't imagine you fighting.'

'We do it by not talking.'

Which ranks high on the list of dangerous domestics, close to the exit door. When you are only tolerating each other, avoiding each other, becoming to one another mist, vapour, ether. Damian went to work. Stephanie took the kids to school and went to work. In the evenings they put the children to bed and did their own thing. All was not well in D&S land either, though Damian was less open about it, there seemed more at stake. He was not exactly contemplating divorce, but last week while Stephanie was putting the colander in the kitchen cupboard and he saw her bending down like that with her shoulders all thrown into it and the side of her face flushed from the kitchen heat, then standing up and leaning on the edge of the counter, just at that moment he had felt like being perfectly and devastatingly honest and saying, 'I can no longer live this life and I am going to go and save myself.' But of course he didn't. He couldn't. The evening passed, the next day came, and things went on as normal. If you entertain and act on every impulse that passes through your mind, went his line of reasoning, you will find yourself in chaos. Hold on to the things that bind you. The self is a doomed and wayward creature. It can be neglected and this will not kill you, at least not in every way.

Stephanie had said to Damian the night before last, 'Get a therapist. That's what people do when they're depressed. It's not something to be ashamed of.'

And Damian had said, 'I'm not depressed.'

'Oh really,' Stephanie drawled with her now frequent sarcasm. 'Well, I beg to differ.'

Her well of comfort and support was running out. Exhausted were the don't-shut-me-outs and I'm-here-if-you-want-to-talks and blah blah blahs. Wrung out and stiff were the soothing cloths of cool water to mop his brow through this momentous time of bereavement and adult orphanness. It was time for psychology, for she herself was not adequately trained, and there was only so much a wife could do to help when her husband had turned into a ghost, when he spent entire evenings sitting at the computer looking at random websites or whatever he was doing. Sometimes with horses that won't drink you have to just drag them to the water and dunk their face in it. Forget about their feelings.

'I have three children, Damian,' she had said, 'not four. Please, for all our sakes, get some help.'

With that she had removed herself from the dining room, leaving behind on the table some leaflets for local counselling services that she'd picked up. Since then she had practically ignored him, and he had ignored the leaflets, putting them on the shelf where the maps and telephone directories were kept. He couldn't imagine sitting in front of some nodding stranger in a little room with a plant and a box of tissues and unveiling his heart. It was not in his make-up. His father would never have done such a thing. He would see it as self-pitying and white. Did the slaves have access to therapy? Were they treated for post-traumatic stress disorder? No, Laurence would opine. They got on with it and mustered strength and sang songs and drew on their *spirits*, and they had a whole lot more to complain about than one measly little family bereavement. They were being bereaved every day, every hour, every minute, en masse, their throats cut, their sweethearts raped, their brothers whipped, their fathers lynched. Who are you to complain?

Two weeks ago, Damian had gone to his father's flat in

Stockwell to clear out the last of his belongings. The books, the African carvings, the crocodile skin shoes were now in boxes in the garage at home waiting to be sorted through. He wasn't sure what to do with it all, and its presence there was having the effect of magnifying the feeling that he was being haunted. He'd been having absurd dreams. He'd dreamt that he was in an airport and he had to catch a plane and he was running but his suitcase was too heavy and when he opened it he found his father inside but he was a boy instead of a man. There was an unnerving instant last week when Summer, who bore a striking resemblance to Laurence, had looked at him in a particular way, and it had seemed exactly as if Laurence had come to say hello to him in her face. And then just now, on the walk from the Arcade to the Satay Bar, crossing Railton Road with Michael, a chilling moment of déjà vu. On that same street, about a year ago, he had been walking towards Brixton station after a meeting, when he had seen coming towards him a shabby old man in dirty jeans and a threadbare denim jacket, his hair wild and matted, his face long and haggard, a hopeless, wayward gait, almost like a drunk. It was Laurence. He hadn't recognised him at first, his own father. When he did recognise him he was shocked and embarrassed, for them both. They shook hands. They stood there for a while trying to have a conversation but it was stilted, and after a few minutes Laurence had walked on. Watching him go, Damian's strongest thought was that he would never, ever end up like that. He would never become a penniless, staggering drifter of a man whose own son did not recognise him. It occurred to him now that Laurence must have already been ill on that day. It was only in the last six months of his life that they had seen each other more often.

'My bad,' Michael said, as if reading his thoughts. 'Been meaning to ask you, how you getting on without your old man?'

Damian nodded, fake lighthearted. 'I'm getting through.'

The spectre of Stephanie rose before him, with her therapy leaflets.

'You miss him?'

'Not much. I guess. A little. Not really, though.'

'Look, you don't have to talk about it if you don't want to, bro. I get it.'

Damian did think about telling him about the déjà vu moment back there, but he was ashamed. Michael wouldn't understand. He came from a happy family where the mother and father were eternally in love and the children were adored and did not call their parents by their first names. Instead he went to get more drinks, after which they talked of other things, eventually returning to the problems with Melissa. It was the pressing issue, and Damian had always been more the listener in their friendship. It also made him feel better about the recent 'feelings' he'd been having, which sitting here drinking with Michael he could see were off-key.

'What you need is a date,' he said. 'When was the last time you went out alone together?'

'Last month some time,' Michael said, and just then, as though conjured by the memory of it, Bruce Wiley stopped by their table, a largeness of belly and scruffy jeans, beer in hand. He was with one of his models.

'What's up, Mike,' he said, clamping his shoulder in greeting before giving dap.

'Hey, big man, you just crossed my mind. That was a bashment to remember,' Michael said.

Damian and Bruce shook hands as well, having not seen each other in years. 'And where's the mighty Melissa tonight?' asked Bruce. 'Friday night is date night in Obama custom, you know. I hope she's not at home all by herself.'

'He brings the message,' Damian said. 'You see? Date night.'

'We're not the Obamas,' Michael said when Bruce had

moved on, running into someone else he knew, which was practically the whole bar.

'Doesn't matter. It's the same principle.'

'I don't like booty schedules, they don't work. It kills the spontaneity. I prefer things ital.'

'Who's calling it a booty schedule? It's just a date,' said Damian. 'Look, babies throw a spanner in the works. Take her out, that's all. Go out dancing or to dinner or something. Make her happy.'

'Oh, that's not easy, to make a woman happy,' Michael laughed. 'Men shouldn't be held responsible for that.'

'True,' Damian was laughing too. 'But you've got to try at least. Look what's at stake.'

Michael thought about it, downing his drink. 'Maybe you're right,' he said, and looked around again at all the honeys. None of them compared.

'We've got to do something, I guess. She's the love of my life.'

★

'OK. I need tops, skirts, trousers and shoes,' Hazel said.

'I need a red dress. I don't have a red dress. I'm trying to be more feminine.'

'You always say that.'

'I know, and I always end up buying more jeans. Don't let me.'

'OK. Where do you usually get your jeans from, by the way? I like your jeans.'

'Topshop.'

'Oh theirs never fit me, I'm too fat. They don't make them for women with hips.'

'You're not fat,' Melissa said. 'You're Amazonian.'

Having met at Topshop as planned, they were walking now through the central avenue on the ground floor of Selfridges that led from perfumery to the clothing concessions. Why wade and trawl through the Oxford Street hoi polloi, tramping from shop to shop, when you can come here, where everything resides? This was Hazel's view, lover of the department store, frequenter also of John Lewis and House of Fraser. Melissa liked the tramping, albeit less on a Saturday when you could walk only in slow motion – concessions were only highlights, you missed stuff. Ultimately she preferred a more bohemian kind of shopping experience like Portobello or Camden, where from the cubic shade of a market stall a face might look out, lined and wanting, as you touch earrings, pendants, fabrics, and a little hut nearby might sell falafel or mulled wine and you could drift along drinking it in the cold air, in the strange colourings of light, the charisma of the cobblestones, the dirty sheen of the canal. Department stores had no personality and they lacked fresh air. And Selfridges was a beast of a department store, a glittering homage to materialism, the shop assistants were like overseers, standing around with their open pots of cream and eau de toilettes, their faces extreme with paint, all around them a dizzying profusion of objects and escalators and wild electricity. High and multiple-ceilinged as it was, it was more of a subterranean experience.

It had been some time since Melissa had been shopping for clothes, not since buying maternity wear. Everything looked over-bright or over-tight, too frilly, clothes for clowns and nubile nymphs, tacky colours, strange concoctions of garments. It was making her feel weary, not excited like it always had. 'Look at all this stuff,' she said.

But Hazel was already delving. 'I love this place.' She picked up something bright green made of lace with holes in it.

'I don't even know what that is.'

'It's a dress.'

'Wow.' Melissa noticed a grey skirt and held it against her. 'Hm. Not sure how I feel about pleats.'

'Pleats are for schoolgirls and the over-fifties. You told me that,' Hazel said.

'Did I?'

They trailed the cotton. They perused the chiffons, silks and satins, meanwhile chatting.

'I must come over and see him soon.' Hazel was talking about Blake. 'I'm such a bad godmother. I did warn you, didn't I? Why do you have to live so far?'

'It's not that far. Just go to London Bridge and get a train.'

'But a *train*! An actual train!'

Hazel was one of those Londoners who perceived the south as another state. West was best. The river was the end. Beyond it was no-man's land, the streets were alien, the skies were darker, the people were base. She did not understand Melissa's relocation to a random road in such a southernmost enclave, far away from friends, family and civilisation. She herself lived in Hammersmith. Oxford Street was a short bus ride away, or she could take the tube. She only ever took trains to places like Margate, to the provinces.

'You westerners, you get a nosebleed if you cross the river, it's pathetic,' Melissa said.

'I seem to remember you were the same once.'

'Yeah, well, I've evolved. Actually, I'm getting used to the train thing. It's good reading time.'

'If you say so,' Hazel snorted. 'What are you reading? I need some recommendations.'

'I'm trying to read *Middlemarch* but I'm thinking about giving up. Hemingway as always, some of his stories. And I just read *The Road* by Cormac McCarthy. It's good but very depressing, end of the world kind of thing.'

'I hate those kinds of books.'

They were long since agreed that Jeffrey Eugenides's *Middlesex* was one of the best books ever. Melissa liked *The Corrections* but Hazel didn't so much, she had found it wayward and self-indulgent. She was a fan of *The Kite Runner*, which Melissa hadn't read yet. As for the Chekhovs, Delmore

Schwartzes, Grace Paleys and the more obscure books Melissa liked to read, Hazel didn't have time for it.

She was Melissa's oldest, boldest friend. They had gone to the same primary school. Hazel worked in advertising. She had a wide and glamorous smile behind which was an oft-foul tongue, and long, bouncing, half-French, half-Ghanaian curls falling down her back, the most beautiful, the most envied of their schoolgirl pack, the one the boys always went for first and then made do with a lesser girl if she was already taken. She was gutsy, self-actualised and tactile. Today she was wearing a clinging blue wool dress, caramel eye shadow and high-heeled sock boots. And a red coat. She was that type. She twinkled.

At the shoe section she sat down to try on a pair of pink wedges but didn't like the way they looked in the mirror. She put them back and they walked on, passing boiler suits, jeggings, a blind man tapping his stick with a young Asian woman holding his arm, two people with buggies, wide walking. The music coming from the speakers was a Mariah Carey remix. Melissa recommended another book, which Hazel asked her to put aside for her. 'I'll get it when I come and see Blake.'

'You don't have to come and see him, you know. I'm always reminding him that you love him. Your main duty as a godparent is that you take him in if something tragic happens to me and Michael – that's if I don't kill him first.'

'Don't be silly,' Hazel said.

'I'm not being silly.'

'You love him. He's your beau.'

Melissa had already talked about the current hostilities at Paradise, the tiffs, the time Michael neglected to pack a night bag for Blake when they were visiting his parents, the time he forgot to change his nappy before going to the park, because he didn't *think* of things like that, men just don't *think* of things like that, meanwhile Hazel's eyes had started to glaze

137

over and Melissa, noticing, quickly fell silent, ashamed. Hazel put the arguing down to common post-baby disruption. It would settle down. They just had to keep the peace and enjoy Blake.

'Come on, it can't be that bad. You and Michael are solid.'

'Right now there *is* no me and Michael. It doesn't flow any more. It's too much like hard work.'

'Wait,' Hazel paused in her perusing, 'you're not thinking of splitting up with him, are you?'

'Um, no . . . kind of . . . I'm not sure. In a way it feels like it's happening all by itself, like we could break up any minute.'

'But, you're M&M. I mean, you're chocolate. You *can't* split up.' Hazel had stopped shopping completely now and there was a look of dismay and urgency on her face. 'If you and Michael broke up I'd be devastated. You're my favourite couple. You still love him, don't you? Tell me you still love him.'

Melissa didn't answer the question. 'Chocolate *can* break, actually,' she said instead. 'It crumbles, when you break it into pieces.'

'Not M&Ms. It's really hard to break an M&M in half.'

They both laughed. 'Even if I do love him,' Melissa said, 'I don't think it's enough.'

'Of course it is. Now you're just basically being cynical.'

Hazel was disturbed, though, by the look of hopelessness on Melissa's face, an absolute lack of faith. Grasping the severity of the situation, she pictured Ria and Blake without their father, which to her was a terrible thing, a sad and tragic thing. 'The children!' she said. 'What about the children?'

Melissa had started looking through a rack of tops in French Connection, not really seeing anything, not concentrating. When she thought about the children she entered the realm of the caves. There were no answers. There was only darkness and fuzz, a sense of groping and things happening as they happened. 'They'll be fine,' she said distantly. 'As long as they still see both of us, they'll be OK. There are other ways of bringing up kids than the nuclear family, you know. Why are we even talking about this anyway? I haven't said we're definitely splitting up.'

'You're *not* splitting up.' Hazel put her arm through Melissa's quite firmly and they walked on. 'You and Michael are perfect for each other. You're just not seeing straight. Do you really want to be a single mother?'

'What's so wrong with being single? I'd love to be single.'

'No you wouldn't.'

'I would.'

'You think you would but you wouldn't. It gets lonely being single. Believe me, I know. You're lucky to have what you've got, a good man who adores you. Michael's good for you. He's a catch. He's something to be celebrated. You know what? Your life really started coming together when you met him. Remember you were living in that horrible room in Kensal Rise?'

'Yeah, and?'

'And you had to share a bathroom with that horrible girl? And there was that nasty fuckhead upstairs who was threatening you? What was his name again?'

'Victor?'

'Yeah, him.'

'What about him?'

'Don't you remember the way Michael looked out for you? That day he was banging on your ceiling and shouting at you and Michael went up and dealt with him? He protected you. He defended you.'

'I defended myself. I went up there too, remember. Michael didn't need to be there. Anyway, the place wasn't that bad. My room was nice.'

'If it wasn't for Michael you'd probably still be there.'

'No I wouldn't.'

'You could be.'

'I wouldn't.'

'Where would you be, then?'

'That's what I'm always asking myself, where *would* I be? Maybe I'd be somewhere different. Maybe I'd be living in Brazil or Peru or the Caribbean, who knows? Maybe he's holding me back. There might be another way, another course I'm being kept from. If things hadn't happened the way they did they would've happened a different way, and that way might have been —' Melissa's phone started ringing. She found it in her bag and answered it, 'Hello?'

'Hi!' said a sprightly voice. 'Am I speaking to Melissa Pitt?'

'Yes.'

'Hi! It's Chun Song Li from Baby Beat. How are you today?!'

'Fine.' Melissa rolled her eyes at Hazel, who in turn was rolling her eyes at what hippie-shit confused rubbish she had just been spouting and now returned to perusing the merchandise.

'I was calling to see if you're ready to sign up for ten weeks, that's ten for the price of nine! Remember the special offer? And I can also —'

'I'm shopping, can I call you back?' Melissa said.

'OK! That's fine! There's only three days left to take advantage of the revised special offer, though! I'll wait to hear from you!'

'OK, thanks, bye.'

'Bye!'

'God, that woman is so pushy! I hate it when people are pushy, it has the opposite effect. Is there no escape from capitalism, from everyone trying to make a buck?'

'Who was it?' Hazel was assessing a two-tone blue coat against herself.

'Oh, just baby stuff. What was I saying?'

'You were saying that if it wasn't for your gorgeous man you'd be living in Peru and there's not only one way of living life and things might have happened a different way if they hadn't happened the way they happened, or something like that. Do you know you seem to have this ridiculous fixation with being *strong* and *alone* and unconventional and – what's the word? – *resistant*. Like, you can't just live your life the way other people do. What is that? You're dog-headed, that's what you are. It's gonna mess you up. Lots of women would love to be in your position. What do you think of this coat?'

'Hm, don't know, I think it would hang cheaply . . .'

'Hm.' Hazel put it back. 'Do you know what you and Michael need?'

'What?'

'You need to spice things up a bit. I bet you haven't fucked in ages, have you? Look, here's one for you.' She picked up a red dress, tight, bulge-clutchy, low at the bust. 'How about this?'

'It's slutty.'

'It's sexy!'

'It costs sixty-five pounds.'

'Yes, that's cheap, for a whole dress? God, the fashion industry is so wasted on you. Try it on, go on. Sometimes the best garms are the ones you'd never pick out yourself.'

'Well, I'd definitely never have picked *that* one out. OK, I'll try it on. Are we going to MAC? I need powder.'

They went to the changing room, Melissa with the red dress and a couple of tops, Hazel with a mound of skirts, trousers and blouses, several of which she bought. Melissa bought the dress, commanded by Hazel ('Michael will love you in it, he'll eat you up'), and afterwards they went to MAC, which was situated by the main entrance in the make-up hall. It was guarded by a gang of beautified creatures in black clothes listening to dance music, the MAC ladies. They wore their make-up pouches slung on belts around their hips, from which they flipped out eye pencils, mascaras and colours to paint the faces of the weak. They were deliverers of blue, scientists of pink. They knew the secrets to lifting a dull skin and mattifying a stubborn shine. They had understanding browns, many shades of it, placing them above those brands who allowed only a few dark tones to be flawless. At the entrance to the enclosure was a podium above which a muralled face with cascading hair waited with pen and paper, making appointments for makeovers. Her eyes were meticulously designed, broad streaks of shadow, temple-bound, a layer of silver studs along a light-blue background, and beneath this, cool green eyes staring nonchalantly out, acknowledging their hipness, their futurism. Around her women lingered by the cabinets, trying out the glosses and putting lipstick on their hands, looking for better versions of themselves, or they sat on high stools with their eyes closed and their faces lifted to the power of the lady, hoping for transformation.

Among the staff were two gay men in tight jeans and leather waistcoats, likewise heavily made up. 'You OK there, babe?' one said to Melissa, who was studying the pressed powders.

'Do you have NC45?'

'We're out of that one, sorry babe. Do you want to try something similar? We've got a new range come out. Gives more coverage.' He slipped a compact out of one of the revolving display cabinets and opened it. Melissa said she'd try it and her name was added to the list. A few minutes later she was sitting on a high stool while he puffed at her face with a thick brush.

'Oh that goes nice on you.' He dabbed and flicked with his brush some more. 'Have a look,' and handed her a mirror. She was lightly almond, perky.

'Looks nice,' Hazel said.

'Isn't it too dark?'

'No! Gives you a glow. You're just not used to it. That's the mistake a lot of people make with make-up. They see it and think too light too dark too red too yellow or whatever, cos they're so used to what they see in the mirror. But what you see in the mirror is only like a blank sheet of paper, right? It's *meant* for colouring in.'

'Exactly. That's what I was basically just saying,' Hazel said. 'I think you should get it.'

'OK, I will.'

MAC ran a special offer of a free lipstick if you returned six empty compact cases, which Melissa loaded out of her bag.

'Babe, I don't mean to be rude but your eyebrows need doing, love.'

'Yeah, I'm always going on at her about her eyebrows.'

'Changes your face. It does.'

'I know, I haven't had time to get them threaded lately . . .'

'Got to keep yourself beautiful. You've got a lovely face, darling. Don't waste it.'

'See,' Hazel said as they walked away, linking Melissa's arm, though she was taller so Melissa changed it round and linked hers instead. 'Don't you feel like a new woman? You've got a red dress, a new face, new lipstick – time to get it on. I promise you, all you and Michael need is some time alone together and you'll be sweet. Get a babysitter for a night. I'll come over and babysit if you like.'

'What? You? Will cross the river? To babysit?'

'Of course I will, what do you take me for? I can see when two people need some emergency loving. You and Michael are *not* going to break up. I won't let it happen. I mean, if you two broke up I'd stop believing in love! I'd stop believing there was hope for any of us!'

'OK, OK, calm down,' Melissa laughed, out through the revolving doors with their bags, out from the subterranean whirl and back into the weather, cool air on their faces, into the pigeon-stepping crowd. 'You don't need to worry, though. You've always got men on your heels. Tell me about *your* love life. What's happening, anything interesting?'

Hazel, going on thirty-seven, had for some time been on the lookout for 'the man'. She did believe that there was one man, a right man, of the fairy tales, and she wanted to find him and marry him and buy a house and have babies who would run around the garden wearing nappies that she couldn't be bothered to change. She wanted to go the traditional route, but she was beginning to worry that it might never happen.

'There has been a development, actually,' she said.

'Really? Oooh.'

His name was Pete. He was Greek–Moroccan via Harrow. They met at the milk-and-sugar stand in Starbucks, she putting chocolate on her cappuccino, he putting cinnamon on his latte, his shoulder half a foot higher than her shoulder, pleasingly, as she liked it, possible prince material, they lingered, a lot of chocolate and a lot of cinnamon, drew it out with more sugar, by the time they looked at each other side-on these were two very sweet beverages, he smiled, she smiled, and they had a little conversation about how they liked their beverages, and then they were sitting at a table by the window talking and getting to know each other. He was a travel consultant and liked clubbing and going to the gym. He ticked all the boxes, muscles in the forearms, apparently intelligent, sense of humour, does not live with his mum, has no children – but Hazel was not going to get ahead of herself.

'You don't meet the man of your dreams in Starbucks,' Melissa said.

'Well that's what I'm thinking, innit, it's like meeting someone in a club or something. But you never know. I'm leaving it to the stars. Right now we're just hanging out. It's only been two months. He's gorgeous, though. He is gor-geous. He looks like Al Pacino.'

'Let's see.' Hazel handed over her phone. He did look a bit like Al Pacino. 'So have you slept with him yet?'

'What do you think, it's been two months, of course I have. Can't you see the bags under my eyes? We're at it like rabbits. He is *wild*, you know, even by my standards, but he's sensitive with it. Best cunnilingus this side of Kentucky. That boy knows exactly where to flick me.'

'Do you mind, I'm trying to eat my edamame beans!' Melissa spluttered.

They were now sitting across from each other in Wagamama waiting for their mains.

'You asked.'

'He sounds almost too good to be true. Maybe you *do* meet the man of your dreams in Starbucks.'

'We should have a foursome some time – you, me, Michael and Pete.'

'What kind of foursome?'

'Not *that* kind of foursome,' they were both laughing, 'God, some people just have sex on the brain! You know I wouldn't be able to share you with anyone else.'

Despite their joking, Melissa was remembering with nostalgia those exact same times of helpless, compulsive honeymoon love with Michael and feeling jealous. A foursome was a terrible idea. When new couples get together with old couples there is only unhappiness for the latter, watching the lovebirds glow at each other and gaze at each other and lock hands uncontrollably under the table. She mumbled something vague, avoiding the suggestion.

Hazel noted her noncommittal tone. 'But you and Michael have your twosome first. Seeing as we're on the subject, when exactly *was* the last time you fucked?'

'Do you *have* to be so crass?'

'I'm serious, man, this is important. If you stop having sex it just dies. It's the life force. It's crucial, you've just got to do it. Tell me, when?'

'I don't know, months. We're basically flatmates.'

'Oh no. Me and Oli were like that in the end, it's horrible.'

'There's no time, though. I can't be all the things my life is asking me to be. It's too much.' Melissa was hiding it but she was close to tears.

'But he's a man, Lis. He needs it. You've got to make time for him, otherwise you'll lose him.'

'I don't *want* to make time. The little time there is left I want for me, not him. I don't want to be answerable to someone's sex drive.'

Hazel was appalled. 'Jesus, listen to yourself. You're disturbing me now. Answerable? Is that how you see it?'

'Yes, frankly. We're not lovebirds any more like you and Starbucks. It's been thirteen years. How many times can you keep having sex with the same person without it becoming vapid?'

'What does vapid mean?'

'Kind of dull and flat.'

'Why don't you try something different, then?'

'Like what?'

'I don't know, use your imagination!' Their food arrived. Melissa was having ramen and Hazel was having vermicelli. 'All I know is that you've got to make love. Men need to feel wanted. So much can go wrong when they don't feel desired. Instead of thinking of it as something you have to *do*, for *him*, make it for *you*, know what I mean? It's a two-way thing.'

'Hm,' Melissa said, unconvinced.

'Wear that red dress. Go on, get penetrated. Give him blowjobs. Everything will be fine.'

'You're so disgusting.'

'You know you want to,' said Hazel, and they tucked into their noodles.

★

Thus cajoled, thus alerted to the imperatives of their partnership, their perfection, their chocolateness, Melissa and Michael went out on a date. Not to a party, no fraternising with other people and forgetting about each other. Just the two of them, a nice quiet dinner in a good restaurant, some wine, some music, easy adult conversation, perhaps followed by a walk hand in hand in the romantic winter's night, an evening of remembering each other and feeling like a couple again, of laughing together, flirting, a tipsy, canoodly ride back home in a cab afterwards, then rounding off with some steamy, redemptive copulation.

That was the plan. In preparation, for they had to look their best, dress up for each other, Melissa went to the mall in Bromley to get her eyebrows threaded. There was a pod there where three Nepalese women worked all day holding the string between their teeth. They hewed at her brazen follicles, snipped at stray hairs, eventually achieving a sharp, thinned-down brow which always made her look alarmed for a couple of days until it softened. While she was there she also bought some red high heels to go with the dress, the kind of shoes Hazel might wear, in fact it was as if she had spotted them with Hazel's eyes. Meanwhile Michael attended to his own follicles, setting his clippers to a close grade 1 and shaving three weeks of growth off his scalp. It always gave him a cleaner, chiselled look, and there was that promising moment when Melissa was finishing it off for him, as was their custom, gliding up with the blade from his neck to his crown, neatening the edges, rubbing at the stubborn patches, she had to stand very close to him in order to do this, between his knees, her arms raised over him, and already they were reminded of how perfectly her smallness slotted into his largeness, his length, his octopus arms. He couldn't help but stroke lightly down the backs of her legs as she stood there, a blush of Saturday afternoon sun coming in from the window twins. It was a warm, natural moment. So there was hope. They could return. Perhaps it really was this easy.

Hazel arrived in a blaze of southward trauma. 'God, my satnav wouldn't work. It just died on me, I had to read a map! I ended up taking Vauxhall Bridge instead of Battersea. Didn't know where I was. You need to come back to civilisation, man. Wow, you two look be-*auu-tiful*.'

They were pictures of themselves. Oiled, snipped and

perfumed, Melissa in the new lipstick and powder, the dress and shoes, darker and taller than she knew herself to be, and Michael also wearing red, a new V-neck sweater beneath the chestnut leather jacket. They were matching.

'I don't know *why* Mummy and Daddy have to go out tonight,' Ria said. 'Why can't you just stay in and have a nice time?' She hated it when the two of them were leaving her for some private adventure. It made her feel bereft, like the world was dissolving.

'Sometimes,' Hazel said, 'adults need time on their own, and anyway you've got me to hang out with now. What shall we do?'

Make cakes, watch TV, have a disco, eat cakes, make a house, have some hot chocolate, shrink, not have a bath. These were just some of the things. Ria stood in the doorway watching them go, wearing her one white glove and her strange nightwear of cotton strap dress on top of fleece pyjama suit. She watched them right up until they turned the corner into the high street and all that was left to see was the plane tree leaning out into the road and the moon behind it. Then she went back inside.

Open air! Childlessness! Pramlessness! And carlessness. They walked. It was a windy night. That was the first thing. It was the kind of wind that blew at you from all directions so that whichever way you went your hair still got trashed. Melissa got frizzy up the high street while Michael was trying to hold her hand, down the slope they went to the station to take the train to Crystal Palace, where they were going to have dinner. Michael had booked a table. They were going to a secret gig afterwards as well, which Melissa did not know about. He was trying to re-enact another long-ago night when he had taken her out for her birthday to the Soho Theatre, afterwards they had walked through the London streets in the dark as she loved to do, bound for a restaurant in Covent Garden, holding hands, he a little way ahead, leading her, she enraptured by the mystery of it, the excitement of not knowing. Tonight was going to be just the same. He would lead her and she would follow, enraptured. As they stood on the platform he put his arms around her and she sheltered in his leather coat. It was stilted, though, that was the second thing, not like before during the haircut. They felt that they were putting on a show for themselves and watching it uncomfortably. The train came slowly in, its low lights shining over the tracks. They got on and sat next to each other, facing the dark windows.

When the Crystal Palace was still standing, when people had come from miles and miles to see the colossi of Abu Simbel and the tomb of Beni Hassan, there had been two ways to get there, via the High Level line or the Low Level line. The High Level line was no longer in use; it was the Low Level platform on to which Melissa and Michael disembarked, climbing the many steps up to the street after a rustling, verdant journey (the foliage thickens and closes in around the tracks along the way, as if you are going into a different world). Dutifully hand in hand they emerged on to the street, into this rolling, hilly town on the far south edge of London, where from the pinnacles of the steeps the city centre is a shimmering, distant valley view of many coloured lights. You can hear seagulls, possibly bound for Brighton, it is so far out, it has a seaside sensation, and they and other birds soar amidst the peaks of the two Eiffels, the taller standing in the park on the flat plane of Crystal Palace Parade, the shorter at the top of Beulah Hill towards Thornton Heath. Up they walked in the frizzing wind towards Westow Hill where all the restaurants were. There were lots of people about, spruced up for Saturday night, people who had moved out here for affordable places to live, thus joining in with the endless expansion of the city, bringing Kent and Bromley into the party, making Brixton central and Dulwich hip. With these people had come the trendy furniture boutiques and wholefood juice bars, the vintage clothes shops and Paperchase, and the indigenous folk, those who had watched all this happen, carried on in their own sweet way, the boys who came down from the tower blocks with their dogs, the old folk who couldn't believe the price of a flannel in Sainsbury's these days. There were other couples too, walking hand in hand more naturally, peering at the menus in the windows beneath the awnings.

The place Michael had booked was one of those chic and stately modern places with elegant chairs and no music, where the food is considered the only music necessary and actual music an unnecessary distraction. There was gold panelling around the doors and windows, light-grey tablecloths. A stern, unsmiling host placed them next to a pillar in the centre of the room, neither discreet nor intimate, and they struggled in this classy sterility to vibe. Melissa ate wood pigeon for the first time in her life and didn't feel right about it. They tried hard not to talk about the children, but it was difficult, and they ended up talking about the mice. Between intermittent silences they sipped from their different wines, his red, hers white. At the next table sat an old couple who also had nothing to talk about and had given up trying to make it look as if they did, both of them with tight looks on their faces and deadened eyes.

'You look beautiful,' Michael tried at some point between the mains and the desserts. At exactly the same instant, the candle in the middle of their table went out.

'Thanks,' Melissa said. A deep melancholy was rising within her. She wanted to be miles away from him. But they were here. And here was her chocolate cake. It had a bitter orange-peel edge, a dark chocolate cream running out of it. She ate it with a grave and absolute absorption. When the desserts were finished, Michael checked his watch.

'You ready?' he said.

'What for?'

'Come on.'

He got up and pulled out her chair for her. He held open her coat as she slipped in, and it was something, these small attentions, it might still turn out well. Around the corner, off Westow Hill, there was a black car parked at the kerb. A man got out as Michael approached it, they conferred for a while, then Michael opened the door for Melissa to get in. 'Where are we going?' she asked him, but she was beginning to enjoy the mystery, to remember, the evening was changing. Michael just smiled. He got in next to her and they took off at some speed down the hill.

The driver was playing loud R&B. He was a bald, plump Ghanaian in a black polo-shirt, the Ghanaian flag dancing from his rear-view mirror. He drove like a maniac, down and up over crystal hills, through the southern quarters, ripped through them as if he were evil, as if he were Knievel, as if there were no paying customers in his car. Melissa leaned into the enclave of Michael's arm. Grey tinge of night leaves in the curves of Honor Oak, flares of lime flowers and holly leaves in the secret crescents, they flew by, the driver knew all these back streets, silver birches were here then gone, mere suggestions in the night and the speed, other trees, fast lights, sweeps of green. He beeped at slower cars, driving right up to their bumpers. He jerked at turns. Every brake was an emergency. When he almost jumped a red light, Melissa was thrown forward in her seat.

'Will you slow down!' she shouted over the music.

'Sorry, sorry.' The driver slowed, momentarily, bopping to Jodeci, but soon charged off again. The next time he slowed down was to swing into a petrol station, where he pulled up next to one of the tanks and got out. 'Wait now, back in a minute,' he said.

'Hey, you can't stop for petrol when you've got customers!' Melissa baulked.

He filled the tank anyway and went off to the kiosk.

Michael refused to pay him the whole fare, which Melissa said was only right. 'We're your customers not your homies.'

Looking at her in his rear-view mirror, the driver said, 'You are from Nigeria, I know.'

'I'm half Nigerian.'

'Your mother or your father is Nigerian?'

'My mother.'

'Eh, I know.' He chuckled. 'You are just like my wife. She is always making trouble.'

He chuckled some more, and drove on with continuing recklessness towards the river, along the vast urban tarmac of the A2, turned off at the exit to the O2, and there ahead of them was that once-failed Millennium Dome with its twelve yellow cranes sticking out of it like monstrous and very painful acupuncture, pointing to specific points in the solar system, a suggestion of alien transmission. So much grand expectation had been placed on this building at the turn of the century, to be mighty, to be showy, to be somehow sci-fi, and they had gone too far futuristic with it and forgotten all about beauty. People were disappointed with the thing after all that hype, and once the new century had begun no one knew what to do with it for a while. What do you do with an empty, 80,000-square-metre, disc-shaped spaceship grounded in an ugly concrete desert off the A2? What else? You give it to music, let music make it sing. Here in this enormous space, in these stretching auditoriums, popstars and crooners, the angels of the modern age, delivered their voices. Prince had sung Kiss here, wearing a pair of high-heeled white boots. The Spice Girls had made a comeback over seventeen consecutive nights. Beyoncé would come and swing on a flowery trapeze with her weave flowing. The O2 was the Wembley of the south side, and it had better acoustics, most of all in the IndigO2, the smaller auditorium where the lesser divinities sang, the ones not quite arena-famous, the niche, the lovers rock line-ups and R&B revivals, a jazz hip hop soulstress from Philadelphia known as Jill Scott, who stood there, swaying in green smoke and a misty light, as Melissa and Michael entered.

'It's Jill,' Melissa said.

'Yeah, it's Jill.'

She was their early music. The music of the palace, the seventh sky. She had seeped through the rooms with her honey molasses and her love moans, her hip hop beats which sometimes pumped and churned and then slowed again, or disappeared entirely. Jill Scott shimmering before them in pale-green smoke. It lifted from the stage, whispering to her afro puffs, wafting around the band. The backing singers wore black and did the finger-clicking gospel two-step. The pianist was lost in jazz, and Jill was gently dancing, her wealthy waist, her wide American smile, her voice deep and saccharine at the same time. From a distance away her eyes glittered. The lights went pink, went yellow. She was singing Do You Remember. In between songs she made chains of words. Whether she was speaking or singing, her voice was constant melody.

In the audience were soulheads and hip hop fans, observers of the culture, headwrapped Afrocentrics and followers of the new jazz. Couples swayed against each other intoxicated by her sound. There were single people sipping at her wisdom, men in good shirts looking for women, knowing that this was a place to find them, that Jill would make them open and heat them up inside. Jill had the power to make a world, with her sweetness, her girlishness, which was soft and malleable and wholly woman. Sometimes she sang hard, *wanna be loved*, sometimes the guitars stilled and she brought her voice down to a whisper, and everyone in the room if they closed their eyes felt almost that she was whispering only to them. They listened, spinning on her axis. The trombone went submarine. Trumpets cascaded in flashes of gold.

In the middle of a song, Melissa felt Michael's hand on her

waist. He wanted to dance with her. In a gentle closing around her with his arms he sent them moving, he behind her, she with her back to him. But here, even here, in this musical mirage, there was something else that was not right. They didn't dance right. They never had danced quite right together, because of how they were different inside when it came to rhythm. Melissa was obedient to it, directed by it, she danced on top of the beat. But Michael instead went inside it and did his own thing, slower than the beat, loose and nonchalant, as though he believed that his inner rhythm was superior to that provided by the music. The effect was that as they swayed they did not sway as one. There was friction, a slight forcing. Halfway through the song, the music slowed down again. The trumpets hushed, the drums subsided, the piano watered down until it was gone. A single blue spotlight centred on Jill. She was going to talk to them again.

'Ladies,' she said, 'Fellas, I wanna tell you something. Can I tell you something? Come here . . . come closer . . .'

The audience stilled. They were held in her palm, in this big disc by the river, huddled in her light.

'Tonight,' Jill said, 'I stand before you a divorced woman.'

The music returned for a brief twirl and subsided again.

'Yeah . . . I was married, and I gave him *all* of my heart . . . I gave him *everything*, we were *happy* in our love, in the morning, in the evening in those cold – night – hours . . . I loved him *all* the way *through*. I was married for *life*, for *always* . . . But you know what he did? Ladies, do you know what that man did?'

'What?' the women called.

'Well, he went to somebody *else's* house. Hmph, yeah. You'd think he woulda known there was nobody else like me, nobody's love so fine like mine . . .' now she was fully singing again *'one is the magic number . . .'*

It was a message for the world but it seemed to come directly for them. It was the loudest moment of all, louder than the trumpets, the brass, even than the finale when Jill came back on for an encore. The music that had married them was now telling them to divorce. There was no more dancing after that. Michael went to the bar, and while he was gone Melissa looked around her at all the other people, other couples, other men, and wondered. Those words were sitting on a swing in a back garden in her mind, going back and forth, *I stand before you . . . a divorced woman . . .*

The drive home was quiet, very quiet. There was no canoodling in the back seat and the tipsiness was private and going dry. As they approached Bell Green the disappointment of the evening thickened. It manifested in the bleakness of the high street, the stony mannequins in their bridal gowns, the sinking into Kent. In the distance the towers were half cut by a thick fog that had descended, smothering their peaks, so that they were half of themselves. And this man and woman sitting in the back of the cab were just like those two towers, in their distance from one another, their separateness, he was Beulah and she was Crystal, and there seemed no way, in this fog, in this pretence, that they might come together as one. The cab turned into Paradise Row and slowed at number thirteen. The house glared out at them with its narrow face, the window twins murky, foreboding, tightly shut against the cold.

Hazel was mid-doze on the sofa in front of 4 Music, where a host of bikinied girls were languishing around Nelly's musculature. She came to at their footsteps.

'Oh hi, you're back. I conked out. How was it?'

'Good,' they both said, their faces tight like the old couple in the restaurant. 'We went to see Jill Scott,' Melissa added.

'*Did* you? Oh yeah, I heard she was playing – was she good?'

And while they filled her in on the amazingness of

Jill – that voice, that sass, what poetry – a hard, nudging pressure built up in their midst, reminding them of what they all knew must now be done, that thing up in the red room, that overdue sail, the drowning ship. Hazel started getting her stuff together, her nail varnish, her Russian hat and her red coat. 'By the way,' she said before she left, 'does Ria sleepwalk? I found her standing at the top of the stairs and she didn't hear me when I called her. I took her back to bed and everything, she's fine, it was just a bit weird, that's all.' Soon afterwards she was bound for the west with her satnav (which was working again) and craving Pete, hoping that she had contributed in some way tonight to the preservation of long-term romantic love in London, while her chocolate pair were left stranded in their hallway, burdened by the task ahead.

'I'm going to check on them,' Melissa said.

She had that flash again of Lily under the skylight as she was going up the stairs, except that now it was Ria under the skylight, asleep, unhearing as Hazel called to her. She was glad of this distraction. She had been hoping for Blake's bleating cry, a pressing need, a detour, but both of them were supine in their swathes of cotton, breathing deeply, Blake lying on his front with his mouth open and one tiny arm stretched upwards. She rearranged his blanket, for it was cold in there, colder than usual, most of all next to Ria's bed closest to the window. Looking down at her – the crescents of her lashes were completely still, a sliver of moon lay across her cheek – she wished that she could sink into the newness of their years, that she could fall into their innocence. It was such a strong wish that for a moment she had the sensation that she was falling down into Ria's body, and she was not sure any more whose mind she was in. When she left the room there was a sadness, faint but definite, enough to make her look back, that this childhood room was no longer her world. He was waiting for her.

Passion, at its truest and most fierce, does not liaise with toothpaste. It does not wait around for toning and exfoliation. It wants spontaneity. It wants recklessness. Passion is dirty, and they were too clean, once their faces were washed, their mouths freshened, the doors, windows, cooker and taps checked so that the house would not burn, flood or explode. Michael had wanted to undress her, to prise her out of the red dress in the red room, but he was again too late. By the time he got there she was hanging the dress up in the wardrobe. She was wearing the rich cappuccino gown, the same colour as the raffia. He took in the sight of her, the shape of her gentle brown waist and the soft, shadowy dunes of her thighs beneath the satin. Oh how she threw him, electrified him, by doing almost nothing, just standing there with her back to him, her gold arms raised. He wanted to drink from her sweetness and break her until she was set to flowing. He wanted to take her higher, like a Legend, past the sublime plateau, into the wild and peaceful air of the ninth cloud. Tonight he was going to lift them up from under this old love and make it new again.

But the wardrobe is so dusty, Melissa was thinking, so much dust on my red dress, on my clothes. The air in here is so old. The floor is creaking. The window is shivering. It needs fixing, he hasn't fixed it. She tried her best to relax as he kissed her neck, but the light was still on, it was freezing, she wanted to get under the covers. Once these things were done she tried once more to relax, to think of the sensation, how nice it was. This is a nice thing that people do together, *a nice . . . gentle . . . stroll . . . along the calm . . . water's . . . edge.* And it is available to you, this warm, relaxing thing. Think about nothing else. She held his head with her palm. It felt like the fur on a newly skinned animal. She wandered across the plane of his back and his whip marks with trailing fingers as he smelt her for chicken but found none. He was breathing deeply, quickly. He was racing towards her, in fact almost past her, she could hardly keep up.

The kiss. Kissing her on the mouth. This is the centre, the core. This is how you know. He kissed her, a long, moist, demanding kiss. But it was so far away from that first, fully formed kiss, the one with its own psychology and personality. Desdemona was not around. Neither was Angelina. It was dry despite its moistness, neither swirling nor euphoric, and he had the feeling, as he was kissing her, that while she was kissing him she was also pulling away from him. This kiss was mean and finite, whereas Desdemona had been infinite and boundless, was in some form possibly existing even now, in some other young new kiss. A little saddened, he drew up, unbuckled his belt. There was a scramble between them to pull away the denim, she out of an eagerness to be proactive and helpful, and he out of her failure to be the latter. He became self-conscious at the falling fabric, too aware of his feet, one of which got caught in the hem as he was trying to struggle out so that he lost his balance and almost fell down on top of her. With the socks it was no more graceful. He stood up to take them off to avoid further stumbling, the floorboards groaning beneath his weight, an ugly serenade to their clumsy foreplay. But you can't make love in socks, unless passion allows it.

Meanwhile Melissa shrugged off her gown, her skin was free, his skin was free, the light next to his heart the shape of a boomerang which made the skin a touch yellower there, was free, he came back to her. There was another, meeker kiss, warmer and tender this time though still not wholly satisfying, so he moved southward to seek a better kiss in her breastplate. The left, the right. This old order, this weather-beaten script. She yearned for something new, something else. He wished that she would tell him what she liked, where she wanted to be touched, with what pressure. He didn't know any more. He couldn't read her. Michael had always tried to propose a path of adventure, to keep things interesting. Adventures, he believed, were in the cavities of what already exists, in the folds and possibilities of your own life. You do not need to travel to the south-eastern coast of Corfu or climb the Andes or go to Chile. You can travel right here, in spasms and leaps, to heavens close by. He had tried new things, new shapes, different kisses, bolder gestures, but such flamboyance was wasted on her. She was no match for his level of aspiration, and eventually, reluctantly, he had accepted this slow moderation of the burning inside of him and succumbed to routine. They had become missionaries, she below, he above. After all, it worked. It was highly adequate.

And all was quiet, so very quiet, hardly a moan, hardly a tremor. Melissa let it continue this grazing around breast-plate along torso, concentrating on the *feeling*, the actual biology of it, but her mind was wandering (Blake's blanket, school-dinner money, mice who might be coming upstairs, the night thing, Ria under the skylight . . .). But then he kissed her hip bone. And when Michael kissed her hip bone that meant only one thing, the next thing, that lush and rhythmic licking, the thing she always came back for, if she was sailing over the south-eastern coast of Corfu or climbing a mountain in Peru or considering celibacy. He stayed there a long time, calling her, swirling her, drowning richly. Her sex to him was a celebration, its soft and falling walls, its avalanching liquid, she was a waterfall. She stretched out the blankets over them to keep them both warm, and she lay there with her arms by her sides swimming out to him, in a kind of soft self-erasure, for part of her still remained else-where, was in a cave, where the truest part of her lived, waiting for the glorious summit to pass, that frightening yet delicious surging, that oh my *god* what's going to happen? sensation, which often felt to her like rising to a peak with great expectation and the peak being less than what was promised, an explosion that disappeared as it happened, or a train arriving at a station that was no longer there.

Afterwards she felt that she should return the gesture, and

she held him in her hand but her hand was dishonest. This dishonesty had an effect on her heart, was a kind of poison, though she continued with it, with a sense of terrible duty. She took him in her mouth, made flowers on the head with her tongue, making everything seem all right for a while, almost natural, and he surged and came up full again. Yet there was something cold and clinical about it all. He still, even now, did not feel fundamentally desired. He was racing, reaching, breathless; she was cool, reticent, retreating. They were not flying. There was no ninth cloud in sight. They had not even left Bell Green. Irritated with her, yet ready, needing, he went inside and she received him. It took her breath away, how he filled her, but so disappointed did he feel at the prospect that it should end like this, in this awful monotony, that in a ferocious reach for that Legendary cloud he encouraged her to turn over, though she didn't quite want to so she clung to him, resisting. With these conflicting longings they rolled on to their sides in complete disharmony until she gave in, feeling herself fading, becoming just biology, just the science. For the sake of love, for the sake of chocolate, for the sake of their children, she did what he wanted.

This, however, was not Melissa's favourite shape. The length of him was such that he reached right to the end of her and, unable to go any further, shoved and bulged against her, causing an unpleasant ache. 'Ow,' she said. 'Does it hurt? Lift up.' 'No, it's OK,' she said, not wanting to prolong it. He put a pillow underneath them to help, then further taken with his desire for more, *more* adventure, *more* transcendence, more *love*, he coaxed her up on to all fours, which did not suit their difference in height, she was forced to assume a downward dog shape. There were several of these shiftings to make them match better (we used to match, we used to match so *well*, thought Michael, what *happened*?), and at the pinnacle of this disaster, he straightened to full height, straightening her with him. Her hands were flat against the wallpaper, his legs awkwardly bent. He pumped at her, over and over, he couldn't quite reach the place, kept on angling himself in different ways, going harder and harder, until he finally arrived at his own lonely summit, then crashed forth, defeated and upset, his knees buckling. When it was finished he deflated like the hot-air balloon that had lost its flame, pulling her down with him, and they collapsed in a heap on the mattress.

They were sweating, embarrassed, crestfallen. It was not what they had planned, not redemptive, not romantic. In the leak of the late raffia moon Jill's words echoed through the air like a ghost, *I stand before you . . . a divorced woman.* They lay there, in the cooling red darkness, in the failure of their feast, unable to look each other in the eye. For they both knew, with a sharp, cold definition, that an end point had been reached.

8

CHRISTMAS

Well, thought Michael, if she doesn't find me attractive, someone else will.

Mayfair, a week before Christmas, the city dressed up for Jesus, windows aglitter, balconies flashing. Michael was on his way to a fancy black-tie, end-of-year trustees' event at a fancy restaurant in this the fanciest part of town, wearing a new suit, shoes polished, coat open to the cold (he never buttoned his coat), and generally experiencing the world differently. It is remarkable how the defining edges of passing women become sharper when love is slipping from your grip. Everywhere he went now he was aware, like extra-vision, like surround-sound, of all their shapes, contours, sizes and colours, the olives and browns, the talls and shorts, all the warm and luscious women in the world. He was backtracking up along the John Legend tracklist. He was regressing to a post-teenage, pre-Melissa state. Just now, for example, on the bus, standing next to him, the soft, voluptuous, gothic brunette with the slightly cruel lips and heavy mauve eyeshadow. He had not been able to help but notice her trembling porcelain cleavage, the jewels in the soft line. And he could not help but think about how she reminded him of Rachel, of what Rachel would look like if she wore more make-up, though he was glad that she didn't. Rachel, he hoped, would be there tonight at the trustees' dinner. Rachel found him attractive.

The restaurant was almost equal to The Ritz in status

terms. Freedland Morton really went to town, literally, for their trustees, among them aristocrats, lords, a lady and a baroness, with peremptory, stuffed-up voices and static hairdos. Michael never knew what to say to these people. They were virtually another species even as they shared his citizenship, and he always felt overly conspicuous yet circumferential in their multitudinous presence. Usually he skirted around the edges of these events, feeling too tall and dark in the middle, he would find a friend or a comfy group and chat in a corner in his cocktail party stance of palms together a bit like a priest, head down, feet level, assuming the air of someone who was commanding and entirely calm within, someone dashing and wise. As he approached the venue he checked himself – were his lapels straight? was his shirt tucked in? were his hands smooth and adequately moisturised? – wondering as usual whether he would be the only black person in the room. It was hard to believe, the ice caps melting, the crater expanding, Obama, the recession, the fact of the twenty-first century in general, that he was still asking himself this question. The last thing he did before entering was turn off his iPod, and he strode on in, ready for whatever.

The tables were to one side covered in white. On the other side people were standing around, drinks in hand, talking. There was a central chandelier and canapés, colourful paintings along the walls, and that mass murmur that rises from parties where people don't dance and becomes louder the more they drink. Rachel was there, wearing a dress of a soft purple fabric with a belt at the waist, her long hair falling over her shoulders. When she saw him there was, he was sure of it, a moment of molten eye contact between them that made it seem perfectly natural, expected, in fact, for him to go over to her and say hey.

'Hi,' she said.

And like the eye contact, this particular hey and hi bore a substance of something that must be attended to, a waiting.

He knew, for instance, that sometimes, in the dead of a night, she thought of him.

'Do you know Michael?' Rachel said to the two men she was talking to, sallow creatures in dark suits.

'No,' they said, all shaking hands.

'Michael is one of the CSR team.' She turned to him, her eyes wide open, beaming a colluding let's-get-out-of-here beam, or at least that was how he interpreted it.

They sat next to each other for dinner. They drank Merlot. On the other side of her was Brendan from HR and on the other side of Michael was Janet from Accounts.

'This is good wine,' Rachel said.

Before that they'd had champagne.

'Your hands, they're so smooth,' she said suddenly, as if about to touch them.

Brendan looked at Janet and Janet looked at Brendan.

'You should play the piano,' Janet said.

'That's what people always say,' Michael said.

'Honestly, with hands like that. Who says a man's hands should be rough and calloused?'

Brendan looked at his own hands. They had panna cotta for dessert, and liqueurs, followed by more wine. It began to feel like they all knew each other better than they did, like Rachel was his sweetheart. At one point he even pressed her leg under the table with his leg, the way people do in films.

'You two, you know what?' Brendan said, pink-cheeked, referring to Rachel and Michael. 'You two would make a very good-looking couple. Do you know that?'

Oh alcohol this most joyous of drugs.

'I feel like dancing!' said Rachel.

'I do too!' said Michael.

'Let's get out of here!' cried Brendan.

It's funny when you're drinking how the place you started begins to feel like another day and you're someone else. Someone not quite Michael, nor quite Rachel, or Janet or

Brendan, all of them heightened, connected, turned up yet somehow muffled, walking, teetering out the door through which they had entered as themselves. Into the night riot of festive lights they went, the late Mayfair traffic, leaving the trustees behind. They ended up at the Dover Street wine bar, a place for the mature raver, lots of people in their forties and fifties in sparkly dresses dancing to assorted disco and some live jazz.

'We are fully booked,' the thickly rouged woman at the door said in a Romanian accent.

'We don't want to eat. We just want to dance,' Janet said.

'We are fully booked,' she said again.

'But look at them,' Brendan said of Rachel and Michael, 'they just got married. They've come all the way from Leicester.'

A crowd of people left so she let them in. They went down shiny, discoey stairs, the fake newly-weds holding hands for a minute, and Michael didn't even think of Melissa all the time they were there, apart from once when he was waiting to be served at the bar and he began to feel tired and had a sudden yearning for her. He imagined arriving home to the quiet house in the quiet night, and she would be waiting for him in her cappuccino slip, reading Hemingway, smiling at the sentences, he would walk into the red, she would lay her book aside, lift her arms, and he would accentuate the smallness of her breastplate by laying his head against it. He could not help but compare them, Rachel and Melissa, as he returned to the dance floor with another round of cocktails, Melissa's small breastplate, Rachel's larger breastplate, Melissa's smaller feet, Rachel's bigger feet, which danced differently from the way Melissa danced. He liked dancing with Rachel, Legend was echoing in his ears, singing to him of the weakness of his nature, how the conflicting sides of him were yet to be reconciled. Her eyes, their uncommon clarity. True, naked eyes. Eyes that did not slide away like

Melissa's eyes, did not hide from him or hold anything back. Attractions like these, John said, are ordained by the angels. They are droplets of bliss to make us remember our aliveness. And should they not be followed? When the switch is turned on, should the light not be made use of, the room walked into, the carpet walked, the sheets troubled? Yes they should, Michael agreed emphatically from his tequila high. She swirled in her Cinzano high, and he watched her, her shining teeth, her cream-coloured neck. She was virtually off the hizzle. She was possibly worthy of a hundred per cent. I want to make your zoom zoom go boom boom.

'How old are you?' he shouted.

'Twenty-five. How old are you?'

'Thirty-seven.'

This aroused secret checks for compatibility, positive speculations. Next thing they were in the Christmasy street and Janet and Brendan were nowhere to be seen.

'I'm so pissed,' she said.

'Me too.'

Next thing they were in a cab, going her way, east, to Whitechapel.

'I didn't know people even lived in Whitechapel,' Michael said.

'I love Whitechapel!'

'You must be loaded.'

'I'm not. I work on phones, remember.'

But it turns out that you don't have to be loaded to live in Whitechapel, for there are many kinds of digs all across London to suit every budget, this a tiny flat with two bedrooms and a kitchen, living room and dining room all in one. Rachel's flatmate was asleep.

'Ssssshhhh,' she said as she went ahead of him up the stairs, he studying her ankles, inferior to Melissa's ankles, yet pleasing, stirring. So the cooker was in the same room as the sofa, and there was a smell of recent dinner, and in Rachel's room there was a sink in the corner, like there had been a sink in the corner of Melissa's old room in Kensal Rise, where they had first met Desdemona and Angelina. It bothered Michael, the sink. It made him sad, and he wanted to run away back to his own woman and her Hemingway. Around the sink there was some dirt where the grout had fallen away, which also bothered him, deeply. He tore his eyes away from the sink, away from anything to do with Melissa or his actual grown-up life. Here they were. Rachel. Rachel's room. Rachel finds me attractive.

'I'll put on some music,' she said. Boyz II Men lifted out from the CD player on the dressing table. They had another drink. It began predictably with 'I don't normally do this kind of thing . . .'

Their kiss was no Desdemona, no distant relation whatsoever. It was too drunken, too wet. They did not know each other, had not laughed enough together to make it comparable. On her bed was a purply-blue bedspread with ridges in it which was quite coarse and uncomfortable. They did not make it under this bedspread but stayed on top. The whole thing was fast, all the way through there was an awareness that Michael would probably leave soon afterwards. She unbuckled him, he pulled up her dress, and in the speed of it they became glorious, she straddled him, her hair brushing his shoulder. He managed, almost completely through it, to erase Melissa from the shadows of this experience. She was only a small ghost floating in the vicinity of the sink, and it was not until the end, when Rachel piled on top of him in a shuddering mass of moistness, that Melissa, and with her Ria, Blake, his mum, dad, brother and Aunty Cynthia (his father's sister in America), gathered in an appalled congregation around the hard, purply-blue sea.

'Oh I like you,' Rachel said.

'That was, wow,' he said, into the collapsed curtain of her hair, which got caught in his throat so that he started to cough. The coughing was such that she felt obliged to roll off him, and once that was done any tenderness that might have concluded things seemed inappropriate. She got him some water, from the tap at the sink, *that* sink, from which he could only take a miniscule, polite sip, first because of the traumatic emotional connotations of the sink, and also because it was essentially Thames bathwater, not technically drinkable, which made him think badly of her. She covered herself in her dressing-gown and sat back down on the edge of the bed.

'Rachel —'

'Sssssshhh, I know. I know I know I know.'

'Yeah.'

'It's late.'

'I better go.'

He quickly washed, kissed her on the cheek, found his other sock, checked his lapels, and went to find a night bus. All the way across the water into the south he felt like a shit. How would he face them? What had happened to his careful percentages system? Had he become so desperate as to engage in such seedy one-night-stand behaviour? What if she found out? What if he talked about it in his sleep? He felt sullied, frightened. The Christmas lights laughed and pulsed in his face as he walked back from Cobb's Corner. He tried to remember what he was before, how pure he was, how righteous, to place it, but he couldn't. When he opened the door, he was startled to find Melissa walking up the stairs in her cotton nightdress. It was 4 a.m.

'Oh, hi,' he said, so happy to see her nevertheless.

'Hi,' she said.

There was that immediate warmth between them, that first, indestructible warmth that stays even when love itself is going. She had come down for medicine. Blake had been coughing.

Michael felt the need to explain his lateness. 'I had to get three night buses. I couldn't get a cab. I only had ten pounds on me.'

It was the first lie of this kind, and it made him feel even shitter.

★

The Christmas tree was ruled by an angel. She had a fine kingdom. It seemed to float, above its glossy mound of presents, a mist came off of it, the magical mingling of tinsel with fairy lights, of dust and pale daylight from the bay window, of faded olive-green foliage with many colours and forms of decorative bauble. The tree was bought from Woolworths in 1978. The baubles were stored throughout the year in their original partitioned boxes in the attic until it was time to radiate and scintillate. They were planets with curly waves of gold glitter circling around. They were purple discs with pink combs at their edges. They were icicles and snowmen, foil-wrapped Santas made of chocolate, which over the course of the day were unwrapped and eaten by the various children and adults liming in the armchairs, corners and nooks and crannies of the old house. The angel sat on top of it all in a long white dress and halo, watching over with inanimate blindness.

The blindness of Cornelius, Melissa's father, however, was animate. Pertaining to one eye, his left, a recent result of accelerated glaucoma. With his other eye he went about the usual events of his eight-and-a-half-decade life, which were pegged in a neat, supportive order along a mental washing line leading towards the final eclipse: wake up, watch television, smoke, shave and dress, smoke, watch television with lunch, smoke, watch television with dinner, smoke, go to bed, smoke in the middle of the night if happen to be awake. In macro terms there was Easter, birthdays, and of course Christmas. Christmas was the largest of these events, and although he lived alone now, it was done in the same way he had always done it, with copious papery and tinselly adornment. With just one eye, an albeit sharpening eye in the demise of its friend, and with the help of Adel, the oldest daughter, who lived on his side of the river, in the third week of December Cornelius gathered the boxes of decorations on the dining table and checked their contents. From ladders lengths of motley patterns went up. They criss-crossed the ceiling and frilled the cornices, obedient to their drawing pins, for Cornelius would not be able to handle the event of a failed drawing pin, a collapsed frill, living alone as he did, and no one there to fix it for him. So they used hammers. Up went the festive Chinese chandeliers in the hallway. Over the mantelpiece went the string of Christmas cards from what was left of his family in the north, and there they all stayed until no later than midnight on the fifth day of January, that is, of course, the twelfth day of Christmas, when Adel returned to help him take them back down.

Adel had two children, Warren and Lauren, nineteen and seventeen. They always came to visit Cornelius on Boxing Day, Carol came with her five-year-old son Clay, Melissa and Michael with Ria and Blake, and finally Alice, their home-land connection and matriarch, who also lived alone now, in a little flat in Kilburn. She and Cornelius maintained a cordial communication with one another for the sake of festive family occasions like these. Long gone were the days of Cornelius's fearsome dictatorship, when he had ruled over the house with a strict disciplinarian regime and large amounts of alcohol. Now he was just a withered, white-haired old man with high anxiety levels, and everyone did their best to pretend it had all never happened. It was a lot to handle for Cornelius, this sudden crowd of people in his space, their strange urbanesque speech, the unbearable mass displacement of kitchen items and other household wares that he desper-ately needed to be in their rightful places. He spent much of the time shuffling around with his walking stick picking things up and questioning people angrily about whether they belonged to them. Meanwhile he drank lots of wine, which gradually made his lips go purple, and smoked cigarettes to their starkest conclusions. The air smelt of tobacco and damp plaster. Carpets were curling from their corners, emitting tiny screams from the seventies.

Currently he was sitting in his green chair, TV-centred, a wrinkled leather pouffe by his feet, next to a knee-high table upon which he dealt with business: lunch and dinner, the cleaning of one-sided bifocals, the unwrapping of presents, for which he used scissors. Ria was sitting on the floor next to him, as she often did when they came here. She felt a wild pity for him, and a fascination and a distance. He was so *old*. He couldn't jump. He couldn't run. He was like an old street that had been rained on and walked on and wheeled on and hailed on for a long time. There were potholes and dents all over his face. His hands were grey-veined like the remains of a mercury volcano and somehow blind also. At intervals she watched him, by way of exploration, which Cornelius did not much seem to mind or notice.

Warren and Lauren were sitting on one arm each of the sofa, with Melissa and Carol between them talking about yoga, specifically, how long to hold the warrior poses of the primary series. Michael was over at the dining table beyond the partition, drinking Dragon Stout and playing with Blake, while Alice and Adel were in the kitchen with Clay. The TV was on. Conversations rose and fell. Lauren was talking about her forthcoming eighteenth birthday plans. 'I'm gonna hire a limo,' she said, 'a pink one.' Ria asked what a limo was.

'It's one of those stupid long cars with twats inside it,' Warren said. He was wearing a red sweatshirt with GOLDDIGGER printed across the front.

'What's a twat?'

'Language, Warren, please,' Melissa said. She hated being in this house. Every time she came here she tried not to stay for too long, and she found it difficult to converse directly with her father, she could still see thunder in his eyes. When she was a child that thunder had felt as if it could break the house, as if the house were made of glass. It was always easier when Carol was here too.

'You can hire one for seventy pounds,' Lauren was saying, holding a hot comb which she was pulling down through her weave. 'They've got TVs inside. You just drive around, drive to the club, whatever. They take you home afterwards as well.'

'Yeah and who's paying for it?' Warren said.

'I *have* a job. I can pay for it myself, innit.'

'It's my birthday too,' Ria said. 'I'm going to be eight. Can I get a limo?' This made everyone laugh. Cornelius said, 'Sssshhhhh!' turning up the TV. He was trying to watch *Dad's Army*.

From the kitchen Adel came in looking flustered. 'Isn't anyone going to help with the food?' She was hard done by and taken for granted, but at the same time she did not want to relinquish control of the food, and when Michael went in to help she eventually told him he wasn't needed, muttering that Carol should help because she hadn't done anything yet and never did.

'What are you doing to your hair, Lauren, are you relaxing it?' Carol said. She sported dreadlocks and believed in the Nubian approach to the contested afro follicle.

'I'm straight-combing it.'

'You should just be natural. Just be you, be free.'

Lauren had smoke lifting off her head. She was trying her best to supersede herself. Her hair had once belonged to someone else, someone Indian, she revealed, which was why it had been expensive. Her eyebrows were drawn on, sharply defined and dark. She wore tight blue jeans and a yellow blouse a similar colour to her skin, upon which, once a week, she applied bronzing cream, to darken her too-light beige-nation complexion. She was a fantasy of herself, permanently materialising.

'You're hot-combing someone else's hair,' Melissa said.

'It's *my* hair.'

'It's on her head,' Warren confirmed, 'so it's her hair.'

Meanwhile, Ria and Clay had gone out into the hall and were sitting halfway up the stairs. They were eating the chocolate Santas and playing with Clay's stickers.

'I've got lots of bones in my body,' Ria said to Clay.

'I haven't,' said Clay.

'Yes you have. You've got one here, here, here,' she pointed at them.

'No,' Clay said. 'I haven't got any bones. I've only got one bone, in my belly button,' and he pulled up his jumper to show it to her.

Back in the living room the adverts were on, Warren was watching music videos on his tablet. Cornelius was intrigued by this new kind of screen, smaller, maybe better for one eye. He watched it. People, things passed across it, music of the new world, rappers with bulky arms and tattoos and very white teeth.

'I saw you on Facebook last week,' Melissa said to Lauren.

'Is it? What did you think of my Facebook page?'

'It was . . . nice?' Melissa was not much of a user.

'Fanks,' Lauren said.

'Let's see it.' Warren looked at Lauren's phone. Both their phones were ever out. There was group Facebook perusal, meanwhile watching the music. A tune was on, 50 Cent's In Da Club.

'Is that P Fiddy?' Cornelius said suddenly, his voice breaking in to the midst of them with a familiar foreign tone soaked in the building fog of senility.

'I think you mean Puff Daddy,' Warren said.

'But I thought he'd changed his name.'

Warren and Lauren were astounded by their grandfather's unexpected pop-culture awareness. It was particularly surprising because these days he said a lot of things twice and forgot names, and the names within the names, words like 'table' and 'wire'.

'He did change his name,' Warren said. 'He changed it to P Diddy, though.'

'Well, that's what I said.'

'No. *Diddy*,' said Lauren, 'not Fiddy.'

'But isn't there someone called Fiddy?' Cornelius said, confused.

'Oh, *Fiddy*,' Warren laughed. 'You mean 50 *Cent*. He's called Fiddy for short.'

Into the room now came Alice, wading, gliding, her head up, her glasses shining in the light of the ancient chandelier, her wrapper and slippers swishing, holding a glass of sherry. She took a seat by the window, the Christmas tree floating next to her, adding to her mysterious light. She was looking forward to going back to her empty pink flat. On the subject of yoga, she felt that both Melissa and Carol were foolish to try and keep it up while raising children and she regularly told them so. And on the subject of night things, which Melissa had talked to her about upstairs earlier, Alice had various recommendations: you hang up some garlic by the front door, cut an onion in half and leave it on the windowsill, put Vicks on the place where the night thing is coming and some cayenne pepper on top of it, and you pray.

'Another thing,' she said, after taking a sip of her sherry, the voices continuing on in the background, 'use salt water in the bath, and make it very, very hot.'

'OK, Mum,' Melissa said dubiously.

'And sometimes you put one plantain under your pillow at night.'

'What, a whole plantain?'

'Yes. It stop it going inside your mind.'

Of this last observation Melissa took no notice whatsoever. She had also dismissed her mother's theory that if there was a night thing in her house it was because it had a downstairs bathroom.

'One day you get a better house than that,' Alice said.

★

Two days after Christmas was Ria's birthday, and around that time two things happened that convinced Melissa once and for all that there was something jinxed about 13 Paradise Row. The first was to do with fire.

For Ria's fourth birthday, she had been given a fairy dress with wings. She had immediately put it on and climbed on to the sofa. She had stood there, preparing herself, anticipating the first hover and the higher air. When this did not happen, when she had simply landed on the floor like any other jump, she had shouted, 'Mummy, these wings don't work! You have to buy me some more!' So every year now they went to the theatre, Melissa with Ria, to offer her flight of another kind, to reward that she had so deeply believed. This year they were going to see *The Nutcracker*, a first ballet. Ria wore a new black dress with sequins across the bodice and a full skirt that became a semi-circle when she lifted it at both sides, which she did, standing beneath the skylight, then soaring down the stairs with the black satin billowing after her. Before they left, Melissa told her to put some cream on her hands because her skin was dry.

They took the train into town, Ria's feet just touching the floor, swinging. Melissa felt an enormous pride in her and a great protection. They saw the blue-lit trees along the riverbank, the misty dome of St Paul's in the distance. The whole city was blazing, the lights all around, the way they fell and danced on the water. 'I like having my birthday for Christmas,' Ria said as they walked along The Strand. She ran ahead as usual, her red tights sparkling, a dirty city wind was blowing, and it occurred to Melissa that Ria was who she was in part because of this city, that she, they both, belonged to it.

The lobby of the theatre was crowded. They went up a circular staircase and found their seats near the back of the auditorium. They were high up, the stage waited, closed and secret, to give the afternoon a dream. Soon the curtain rose, and here was Christmas most of all, a giant tree in the corner surrounded by presents, a pretty, ornate room in a made-up house. The orchestra was gold and silver, lit up in the pit with the conductor's dancing arms. A little girl, Clara, tiptoed into the room, and then the bigger dancing began. The ballerinas were synchrony, together on their toes, weaving across the space. Ria stared at them, straight-backed, she whispered, 'I can't believe my eyes.'

The simultaneous arms, the turns and glides, the certainty of direction.

'How do they know what to *do*?'

Melissa told her they'd been practising.

'But how can they point their toes like that?' Then, 'Why is Clara dancing in her pyjamas?' And, 'Why is the Christmas tree made of paper?' Meanwhile sucking on a lemon Chupa Chup.

'Is that blue man the handsome prince?' she asked.

'Is that the king mouse?'

'Is that real snow?'

All this before the interval. After the interval, 'Why is that gold thing on the curtain going up?' 'Why didn't those people on the stage have any food?' 'I don't believe that Clara's still wearing her pyjamas.' 'Is it finished?' 'Is it finished now?'

Back out in the lobby, from the bottom of the circular staircase, Melissa took a picture of Ria standing at the top holding up her skirt in a semi-circle. One foot was in front of the other. Her legs were crossed, as if infected by the ballet. There was a smiling look on her face containing the kindness and the selfishness of children. This would be the last picture of her taken on two good feet.

But first the fire, which happened that evening over the birthday cake. Ria was sitting at the dining table, still wearing her dress, and Michael was standing opposite her holding Blake. Eight candles. The lights went down. Melissa emerged from the paprika glow of the kitchen with the cake as they were singing. There was a feeling of deep togetherness in this singing, that in the singing was the ribbon that linked them all together, and Michael lost his sense of nagging unease for a moment and laid his hand lightly on Melissa's back. Melissa put the cake down on the table. When Ria bent to blow out the candles, her loose hair got caught in a flame, and the flame then lifted. A high orange sweep went up, quickly monstrous. To Ria it felt like just some warm air by her neck; what upset her was the sudden look of horror on her father's face, even on Blake's face. Frantically, Melissa batted her hand against the flame. It went out, and Ria was not hurt, but the image stayed there in Melissa's mind, a burning child's head, a terror at the dining table. It was another bad omen.

A week later Melissa and Ria went to the woods to find the tunnel as they had said they would, the tunnel where the train got stuck on the way to the Crystal Palace. They entered the woods from the street, and walked down the dark, uneven path to the clearing where the light opened out and there were stretches of thin, tall oaks and hornbeams. The sound of the traffic slipped away. There were only birds and the rustling of the trees above. They had stood for centuries, these trees. They had witnessed the walking of yesterday's beasts, the egrots, the beavers. There were bats and owls here, and three kinds of woodpecker. Dogs flashed through the trunks, their tails in the air, upward with freedom.

'Can we go inside the tunnel?' Ria said as they walked. A bit of her hair on one side of her head was shorter than the rest and singed a lighter brown.

'I think it's sealed,' Melissa said. 'But let's see.'

They reached the footbridge from which Camille Pissarro had painted the view of his time – a pale open sky, a train taking a bend away from him, empty fields on either side. They went past the algae pond that didn't move and threw a stick on it and watched it not sink, past the golf course and the rope swing, and eventually, at the bottom of a slope, they came to the tunnel entrance. It was black, sealed shut. A tiny blue bird flew out from a slit at the top. Ria was disappointed. She had wanted to walk all the way through it to the glass world on the other side. She had wanted to see Leona Dare hanging from her hot-air balloon, doing gymnastics in the sky.

'I saw pictures of her,' she said. 'She used to hang from her mouth. It cost one shilling to watch. How much is one shilling?'

'About ten pence.'

Ria imagined crowds of people in long dresses and high hats at the other end of the tunnel, looking up at Leona. Melissa imagined it too, walking through the tunnel, past the ghostly abandoned train, and it was very quiet, and she was walking into history. Michael was not there. He did not exist. They did not exist. It was a beautiful kind of solitude. The way was wide enough for two people to walk side by side. When she got there she wandered through the courts, saw the frescos and tombs and the lions in a circle in Alhambra, and had a glass of rhubarb champagne.

'We should go back,' she said. The light was changing. 'It's going to get dark soon.'

'OK,' Ria said. They began making their way back up the slope.

That was when the second thing happened. Just as they reached the top, Ria stumbled in the mud and twisted her ankle. She carried on walking, but near the algae pond she stumbled again and started to cry. She held on to Melissa, hopping and limping, or being half carried, for the rest of the way out of the woods. By the time they got back to the car it was dark, and her ankle had swollen to the size of a tennis ball.

Instead of going home they went to the hospital. The anklebone was fractured at the outer edge. She would wear a cast for two weeks. She lay on her front on the stretcher as the nurse arranged plaster of Paris around her thin brown calf. She fell asleep like that and dreamt of the palace. It was after midnight, in the London borough of Lewisham.

9

CONFESSION

The man on the radio was saying, 'We're always reminding them, myself and my wife, that we're a gang, we're a team, we work together, and anything we've got, we've got because we all make it happen. So say they ask for the latest DS game or whatever, we'll say to them, well, there are some children who don't have a DS at all, let alone the latest game, and we'll encourage them to do something else with their time if they're bored like play cards, we play cards with them a lot, play games, you know, remind them of the concept of the team, encourage them to make the most of what they already have. That's not to say that they never get what they ask for, because they do, only in moderation. And we never do that thing, that terrible thing of going on about how much things cost and how hard we had to work to buy them, but we try and make sure they appreciate things. And really, as a result, birthdays and Christmases and Easter and all that are no big deal to them. It's not this crazy extravaganza of presents and *things*. It's a time when they get to see their grandparents a bit more, some quality time with the family, you know? So it's about what we teach them, the messages we're sending them as they grow up . . .'

Despite the irritating, sanctimonious, somewhat nasal voice of this anonymous parent, Melissa was making a mental note, while driving the children to soft play, of the worthier elements of his sermon – the importance of the team, the thing about not going on about how much things cost, which of course *was* terrible, and she was wracked with guilt and self-loathing at the thought of yesterday when she had told Ria off for putting her Hello Kitty Cool Cardz in the bath as part of an impromptu science project, stating that they had cost twenty-seven pounds. What, indeed, was twenty-seven pounds to an eight-year-old? An eight-year-old on crutches, with a hard white left leg, who was isolated from her school friends and needed to find in-house entertainment to keep her occupied. That Cool Cardz experiment had been conducted on one leg, bending over the bath, with the bad leg supported by its big toe and the crutches leaning against the wall. She had limped there, as she limped everywhere, clattering around the rooms, hopping, leaning, holding, sometimes swinging a crutch around and throwing things off the bookshelves, but how determined, how exploratory, how imaginative, how much more physical and disability-refuting than sitting on the sofa watching CBeebies. And all Melissa could do was berate her for it.

On and off for the last nine days, after an initial appearance at school where Ria received leave of absence and immediate celebrity status ('Lord have mercy, what happened to your foot?' and 'Wow, let's have a go on your crutches!'), she and Melissa had been united in their daytime occupation of 13 Paradise Row. Melissa spent as much time as she could in her office working, and the rest of the time with Ria, making lunch, making snacks, encouraging homework, ensuring adequate fresh air through occasional walks and clattering expeditions into the garden. There is only so much you can do with a leg in Paris. No running, no swimming, no scooting. All is hoppy and slowed and sedentary, and Ria spent many hours sitting at the dining table engrossed in imaginary worlds made of Lego, Peppa Pig furniture and chess pieces, muttering to herself, enjoying her freedom from fractions and this new, homely independence while Melissa longed inwardly for her to go back to school. When Blake was home with them, like today, Friday, a freezing, dreary morning in the second week of January, it was worse, and she had decided on the expedition to soft play to make things easier. It was not the obvious place to take a cripple. She couldn't climb, she couldn't slide, but perhaps she could sit on the edge of the ball pond and she and Blake could throw balls at each other, or she could roll around on the cushioning or fiddle with the netting, while Melissa, she hoped, could finish her column (she was late with her deadline). It had been cumbersome getting them both into the car, Blake and his straps and Ria with her crutches. There had been hardly any time for Melissa to make herself look nice, she was wearing her grey anorak with the roughly sewed-up rip in the hem, a beige jumper accentuating the thus far unflattened calamity of her postnatal stomach, and her trainers which were still muddy from the fateful walk in the woods. She had applied some lipgloss at the last minute, but this, apparently, was the only allusion left to the high-flying, world-eating woman who had once edited the fashion and lifestyle pages of *Open*. She had put the radio on to provide an alternative to her bad mood and the chattering in the back ('Mummy, when my cast comes off can I go swimming with Shanita, Shaquira and Emily?', 'Mummy, where did you put that Brat doll that came with my shoe?', 'Mummy, did you know that little lies lead to big lies and big lies lead to terrible lies?'). They were passing Tesco Express. A drizzle was falling on to the windscreen. She turned the radio over to Radio 4, *Woman's Hour*, Jenni Murray's soothing, determined voice, a moment of reinforcement, a reminder. She turned up the volume.

'Mummy, can you turn it down, please?' Ria said.

'I'm listening to it.'

'But it's too *loud*, and I can't *read*.'

'You're not reading, you're talking.'

'Now I'm reading.'

'Oh, *now* you're reading. What about me? What about what *I* want? *I* am a person too, you know. I have desires and pastimes and hobbies, thoughts, emotions and feelings too. What am I supposed to do while you're so desperately reading? Just sit here looking at this grey street, this grey rain, huh?'

'Oh just forget it'.

Urged again by guilt, Melissa turned it down a tiny bit. Then Blake started to cry. She tried to calm him down by reaching back and holding his foot, which did nothing for him.

'He's tired,' said Ria, smugly familiar with his not-quite-working Gina Ford routine. 'Now, Blake, remember what we told you,' she said. 'You wake up in the morning and then in the daytime you can have two little sleeps and one big nap then an *enormous* sleep all night long, and then you wake up again in the morning and you do the same thing over and over and over and over again, OK?'

To this he cried harder, obliterating the radio. He cried all the rest of the way to Little Scamps apart from just as they got there when he unhelpfully fell asleep. There was further clattering getting Ria out of the car, the unfolding of the heavy Maclaren which Blake didn't want to inhabit just now, so Melissa carried him with one arm, pushed the pram with the other, and the three of them proceeded awkwardly through the icy wet air into the house of hell.

The path to Little Scamps is a three-turn slope downwards into an underground dungeon composed of primary-coloured apparatus, shoe pouches, and a small café. On the first slope you brace yourself, on the second slope you sense that you are drowning, on the third you are fully submerged. You hear the shrieks, cries and wails of scamps of all sizes and ages and that is the only music. You are surrounded by netting and padding. Everything is padded, the walls of the ball pond, the runways of the fun, netted tunnels, the stairs going up to the fantastic curvy slide and the landing strip at the bottom. The scamps bounce and cling against the netting, their shoes stored in the red, yellow and blue pouches, running, leaping, climbing, whooshing. Their mothers and generally not their fathers sit nearby on hard wooden chairs with lines lengthening on their faces, cowering over their beverages or even reading material if they are very ambitious about this being a chance for me-time amid the frequent requests for crisps, juice, toilet, inter-scamp conflict resolution and alternative entertainment if they are bored. And then there is the other kind of mother, who takes a more hands-on approach, or rather feet, who has taken off her shoes, who steps, flushed and clammy of forehead, into the ball pond to help her baby enjoy the blowing machine which makes the balls hover in the air with a clever magnetic mechanism, she dangles little Jimmy or whoever it is above it and he laughs and laughs, she hopes, or else just dangles there feeling windswept and bewildered, at which she presently deposits him back on the padded floor and lets him sit, and she will also sit, with her legs tucked underneath her in minimal comfort, maybe chatting to another of these mothers who is also sitting in the ball pond, both accepting that although they are two large bodies obstructing some of the children's passage between net tunnels, they have just as much right and purpose to be there, more in fact, because they are needed. Melissa belonged to the former of these categories.

'How many children are you signing in?' said the green-shirted Little Scamps warden at the desk.

'Two.'

The girl looked Ria up and down, taking in the crutches in her armpits, and tentatively handed Melissa two wristbands. 'Sign them in, please,' she said, pressing the gate-release button. It swung open, bright-yellow and also netted, and submersion was complete.

The ball blower wasn't working today. Some of the

children were using it instead for something to stand on and jump off but the babies weren't interested. It being a school day, Ria was the only one here of school age. There was no one for her to strike up a spontaneous, soon-to-be-forgotten friendship with. She would not be able to climb the nets or run through the tunnels, only play alone amidst the padding or be a medium-sized duck. Permeating the thick subterranean air was a warm smell of food additives and coffee, of cheese toasties lately consumed, evidenced by some stray crusts on the floor by one of the chair legs. Melissa made her way to a relatively deserted corner, steering the pram along a crooked path between the chairs and tables with Blake still hoisted by her free arm. Ria followed and took a seat at their table while Melissa removed Blake's shoes. Nearby two women sat talking, another sat alone over a newspaper.

'Mummy, can I have some crisps?' Ria said.

'We just got here. Go and play.'

'But I can't.'

'Yes you can. Go on, take off the shoe. Wait, put some cream on first. I told you, you need to keep creaming your hands. Why are they so dry all the time?'

'I don't know.'

She creamed her hands and took off the one proper shoe. The other was a huge felt flip-flop designed for legs in plaster. Melissa put the three shoes in the pouches and Blake in the ball pond, asking Ria to keep him entertained. She watched her for a while, she was lovely in her limping, in her flared blue skirt, her one actual thin leg sticking out of it. She and Blake threw balls at each other, laughing, while Melissa ventured tentatively back to her corner and took out her laptop. It was difficult to concentrate, trying to keep one watchful eye at the same time, but she managed to write a sentence. Soon, though, there was an approach of UGG boots, a powder-blue coat, a large four-wheeler. 'Hi, Melissa!' a voice said. It was Donna, a motherland acquaintance, also frequently run into at the local playgrounds and in the aisles of Japan. She motioned to take a seat, but Melissa was not quite smiling, her fingers shadowing the keyboard.

'Oh, sorry!' Donna paused with her vehicle. 'Am I disturbing you?'

'No, no . . . it's OK, sit down . . .'

Donna wore blue glasses the same colour as her coat. The eyes behind them seemed always staring and blank, through her light, foody chatter, about mousse preferences, good cakes, the difference in quality, for example, between a low-fat Marks & Spencer's blueberry muffin and a Sainsbury's low-fat blueberry muffin. There was no one who could beat Marks & Spencer's for their low-fat muffins.

'I'm more of a savoury person,' Melissa said. 'Give me a packet of crisps over a doughnut any day.' The more they talked the more the world receded, they were sinking, the dungeon was going down deeper, and deeper. Around them the voices of the scamps whipped through the air, beneath the ugly neon lights, beneath the ground itself, and among these shouts came a sharp, distinctive cry belonging only to Blake. He was lying on his front on the padding, crying. Ria was limping back over to the table with only one crutch.

'Mummy, Blake's stuck in the balls.'

'Where's your other crutch?'

'I don't know.'

'What do you mean you don't know?'

'I don't know.'

'Well, where did you leave it?'

'I don't know.'

Melissa collected Blake and went to look for the other crutch, which she found lying under a table. Blake didn't want to play in the pond any more He wanted to go inside the tunnels, to rise into the upper echelons of the netting like the bigger kids, but the only way he could do this would be for his mother to aid and accompany him, and thus take off her shoes. Intent on his wish, he lunged towards one of the padded mounts leading to the first level.

'Blake, come here. Blake, you can't go up there,' Melissa said.

He arrived at the mount and pulled himself up to standing, attempted to mount it, cried when he couldn't, and looked around for his mum. She was now on all fours. Donna was watching with her staring eyes. Melissa entered the tunnel, keeping her shoed feet outside, trying to coax him away. 'Sweetheart, you're too small. Come here, come out.'

Then he was wailing, mouth wide open, full volume, throat visible. At some point in the parenting war between what you know you should do and what you do not want to do, there is capitulation. You must let go of yourself, perhaps only for a little while, though these many little whiles may gradually build into larger and larger whiles, joining together like cells and building another person, until you are no longer quite yourself. There was her son, her crying little crawling son, who only wanted to rise, and how could she deny him this, when she had already denied her crippled daughter the full enjoyment of a wet Hello Kitty science experiment? When you try to be selfish in a situation that requires selflessness, there is unhappiness. There was only one thing to do.

'OK, Blake,' she said. 'OK.'

She sat down on the bright-red padded ground. They would climb together. They would rise. She untied her muddy laces, took off her trainers, and placed them in the pouch next to the others.

After lunch the mouse man came back to Paradise, which looked more and more now like a live, menacing structure with its white and stony face and those two window eyes looking out, holding in. Dust was swirling in the air. The crooked floors were getting crookeder. The narrow hall was getting narrower. During lunch Ria refused to eat her fish fingers. 'Don't cut them,' she ordered, so Melissa cut them, out of spite. 'Mummy, if you do that again you'll make me angry, OK?' and she left them on her plate, also out of spite. Melissa considered what to do about this affront – should she force them down her throat, punish her, over a fish finger? 'Motherhood is an obliteration of the self,' she said. 'What?' Ria said. 'Pardon, not what.' 'Pardon. What?' 'Motherhood is —' Then came that tight, British knock at the door. She recognised it. Rentokil. The same anorak and hat, the same Hitler moustache.

'So,' he said, striding into the kitchen with his clipboard. This was his third and final visit. Ria stared at him from the table with her scaly hands. 'Any other sightings? Any bait bites? Droppings?'

'Bait bites?' Ria said. 'What's bait bites?'

Blake was careening out of his high chair in such a way that it looked like it was about to tip over so Melissa got him out of it. He shoved some mashed potato into her ear, found this hilarious, and tried to do it again. Meanwhile she provided a mouse update, no more sightings, no droppings.

'I didn't check the bait, though.'

'Ah,' he said loudly, bending down by the kickboards. 'This one's been eaten into, look.'

There were sinister bites in the blue poison, which meant that something was dying, here in these walls, or was already dead. The corpse could be anywhere. 'Do you know when? When it was eaten, I mean. How long it takes for them to die?'

'Oh, who knows, who knows?' the Rentokil man said, apparently satisfied at the opportunity presented by the question. 'It depends on the size and the constitution of the little fella. Whether it managed to make it outside *before* the poison began to take effect. Inside deaths definitely take longer. The cold speeds things up a bit, you see . . . But I would say,' he rubbed his chin, 'judging on the size of the bites here, that it's a smallish mouse. The smaller they are the quicker they go and the less likely they are to get outside. They don't *want* to go outside, that's the thing, especially when they're expiring. They want to stay here in the warm chamber.'

Melissa laughed. The warm chamber! So much information, so much specificity. The Rentokil man didn't think it was funny. He looked at her, mystified, his eyes glinting with empathy for the soul of the lost one who had bitten. And suddenly Melissa thought of Brigitte. Brigitte had wanted to leave this house. That was why she'd lied about the mice, why she'd tried to keep Lily hidden away in her room. The house was poisoned. There *was* something wrong with it. Brigitte had wanted to get out of here and she hadn't wanted to let anything stand in her way.

'Actually, is there anything else?' she asked the Rentokil man. 'I'm kind of busy, so . . .'

Onions. Garlic by the front door. What else had her mother said?

'I just need to print off your invoice,' he said, sitting down opposite Ria and getting out his nifty machine again.

'Don't worry about the invoice. Post it to me.'

She practically threw him out. He started to say something more about the mice, something conclusive, a rounding off, handing over to her the baton of kindly extermination, but she had no ears left for it. He scuttled away, letting the gate slam after him. It was January in Lewisham, and she was still in Lewisham, in the London borough of.

★

Lidl was cheaper. How ingenious that Dieter Schwarz who had made it possible to buy granola for a quarter of the price you could get it for in Japan. How much cheaper their chicken, their kitchen towel, their fruit juice and their vegetables, all of adequate quality if you stayed away from the lowliest brands. It was half factory, half shop. Why go to the trouble of taking hundreds of items out of their distribution packaging and putting them on a shelf, when you can keep them in the packaging and put that on the shelf one time, and people can just take it out themselves? And is there really such a great inconvenience in buying four tins of Heinz baked beans instead of one or two, or a pack of four kitchen towels rather than a pack of two? There is a quiet delight in the hearts of people who shop in Lidl, and with it a mild camaraderie. They have been changed. They buy in bulk and have discovered new names, new tastes, such as honey-flavoured walnuts from Denmark. Those freezers full of meat and pizzas and ice cream and seasoned rice they feel almost affectionate towards, as if they were their own freezers, so little do things cost. There is no unnecessary music, no 'Lidl Radio'. It is just bare, barren, basic silence. And what does it matter that there is hardly any room at the tills next to the cashier's elbow to pack your goods, or that you have to queue for longer than you would in Japan because there are only two cashiers, who, incidentally, are underpaid and the women penalised for becoming pregnant and denied the right to join unions, when you can walk away with a receipt for only eighteen pounds and forty-seven pence for a week's sustenance for a family of four? You could even buy a tent at the same time if you wanted to. Lidl was a miracle.

Michael had received a grocery text (without kiss, as now standard) from Melissa in the afternoon and was walking through the aisles looking for things, the things that she had asked for and other things he might come across – at the moment he was studying a large packet of tikka-flavoured crisps. He found Lidl comforting. It was a poor man's shop, an arcade for the working class. There was no pretence, everyone was on the same level, all united in their recession-inspired economising. Also browsing was a dark-skinned man in long white Islamic dress and hat pushing a trolley full to the brim, with an engrossed, good-natured look on his face. They came across each other again by the soya milk, where Michael was trying to decide whether or not he should get the unsweetened one. The man pointed at it saying, 'It's good, that one's very, very good', and although Michael was in his way for a second, there was no impatience, no trolley rage, which is rare in Lidl. They both just carried on about their shopping with a faint and fleeting brotherly connection. It was pleasant. It was soothing.

On this particular cold and drizzly Friday night, Lidl was also a place to hide. He did not want to go home. Friday nights, traditionally assigned to partying and relief and enjoyment, were becoming increasingly depressing. He did not want to go home at the end of yet another week to the woman standing at the sink with the different mouth, to feel the wide emptiness that gripped the house after the children were in bed, he so wanting, of something, some loving heat, and Melissa wanting something too, but not him, something else, somewhere else. He did not want to live this way, and in addition to this, he was burdened with guilt about the thing with Rachel. They had seen each other a couple more times since that first time, once in her flat, again in the vicinity of the sink, the other time at a hotel, because of the sink, when he had gone as far as to book a room for the evening and lie to Melissa about where he was. Both times she had given him that heat, that fast enclosure that he needed, her soft and open body, and he felt that her heart was truly kind, but for him the quenching was purely physical. Afterwards he was left with a profound sense of spiritual shrinking, a self-loathing that walked with him everywhere he went, and when he looked into the children's faces the love in their eyes was hurtful, the power of it, it could not wash him clean any more. It was easier, in fact, to look at Melissa, even though it was she he felt he had most wronged, because in Melissa's eyes there was no love to receive and he could meet her in her blankness, her withholding of what she, and he, might feel.

He had never been with a white woman before, not to a

hundred per cent. It was minimal, physically, the difference between them, his brown against her cream. The real difference was in her life, in her history. She could never know him completely because she had not lived as he had lived. She did not belong to the brown world in which he had learned his fear, his fury and his distrust. He found himself explaining things to her and not liking that he had to explain, whereas with Melissa, or with Gillian, all the others before, they already knew those things and he didn't have to tell them anything. Even if they had not felt it themselves, they knew it, because they were of the same texture, or a variation of that texture. The difference between him and Rachel was inside, in the lenses behind their eyes, in the prisms of their minds, as defined by the outer side. And when he walked with her, the tension he felt, besides the obvious worry of being a cheat, was not what people might think, of him, of them, as a possible couple, but that she did not know what he saw when he walked, the necessity and the laughter and the sadness of the blackness around him – the beauty of three black boys singing in the street yesterday, or the menace in a St George's flag hanging from a deep-southern balcony, and in that same deep south the never-ending sorrow for Stephen, for all the Stephens and the murdered ancestors of Stephen. Or the sweetness of that moment at the soya milk just now, that passing brotherliness. She would not smile. She would not know, as Melissa knew. Her life was a different language.

Michael admitted to himself now, in the safety and the glaring lights of Lidl, that Rachel could not give him anything, no matter what she gave. Nothing lasting, nothing enough. Rachel was just a way of missing Melissa. Rachel was a way of needing Melissa. Melissa was the hizzle, she still was the real hizzle, while Rachel, anybody else, was lesser, and in realising this he understood that he had betrayed her, his empress, his mermaid, pointlessly, because he had known it all along. All that he was left with now was this need for her, physical, and in his soul, in his mind, he wanted all of her, he still did, and he wanted her to need him too, the way she had in the beginning. But the only way to make this even remotely possible, to return to a place where it was good, was to tell her about Rachel. The knowledge of this was like a strike coming out at him from the granola shelf, because it was only Melissa who ate the granola and he was thinking very hard about which granola to buy, the orange and cranberry or the coconut and tropical fruit. You have to tell her, the granola said, and you have to do it now, tonight, so that you can begin again with the truth firmly intact, with a perfect honesty. Truth is the only foundation for broken things, as earth is the only foundation for the rebuilding of a house. Go home. Go home to your house and tell your woman what you have done, and whatever happens, however she responds, take it as it is, be prepared for anything. Let avalanching stones fall down on your shoulders. Let lava flow. It's the least you can do. And it was the coconut and tropical fruit granola specifically, he felt, that was telling him this, so he put it in his basket and went immediately to the unspacious till.

Down the high street into the belly of Bell Green he went, light rain falling on his forehead, the smell of the long winter in the air, the sound of the early weekend sirens. The tower blocks surrounding the green next to the library were lit up in their windows, along with the estate at the top of Paradise and the thin houses along the sloping bend. Mrs Jackson was out again. He took her home again and she stared up into his face the way she always did. 'You look just like me son Vincent.' He waited a while to make sure she stayed inside, though really he was stalling. Outside number thirteen he paused at the door, frightened.

The first thing he noticed going in was that there was some garlic hanging up by the front door, on one of the coat hooks. He heard the sound of bathwater. Melissa came walking through with Blake wrapped in a towel, she gave him a sharp

snap of a smile and said, 'I'm going to put him down, he's tired.'
'I'll do it,' Michael said. He hadn't seen him since dawn. How
had he grown through the hours? What new expressions on his
face? You could miss so much. You could miss so many small
moments of a whole boy turning into a whole man. He took
him upstairs and dressed him for bed. He read him *The Little
Red Hen* and laid him down in the second room. He watched
him as he fell asleep, the diminishing of blinks, the extraor-
dinary youth of him, his innocent face, untravelled by circles,
lines and time, and he had the reassuring sensation that this was
the only thing that mattered, the preservation of this small but
crucial kingdom. Before going back downstairs he got out of
his work clothes and put the world away so that he could
concentrate fully on the task at hand. While he was doing this
he noticed half an onion lying on the windowsill next to his
wardrobe. He picked it up, confused. The granola was still
whispering to him, *Now, you have to tell her now.*

'There's something wrong with this house, Michael,'
Melissa said when he came into the dining area. She was
picking up place mats, wiping them and putting them in a
pile. Each time she added one to the pile she pressed it down
hard, as if it could walk away. 'I know it. Don't ask me why,
I just know.'

'Why is there half an onion in the bedroom? I found it on
the windowsill. It smells.'

'Did you move it? Put it back where it was, I put it there
on purpose!'

'Why? And what's with the garlic, what's going on?'

'My mum said it would help.'

'With what?'

She looked at him doubtfully. He wasn't going to understand. When she'd mentioned the night thing to him he'd
been dismissive, saying ghosts didn't exist, even though she'd
tried to explain to him that it wasn't a ghost as such, it was
an energy, a pressure, a dark touch in the air.

'Have you noticed Ria's hands lately?' she said. 'They're really dry, like sandpaper. I keep reminding her to put shea butter on them but it doesn't seem to be making any difference. They're – dusty. Like this house. Can't you see the dust? It's everywhere. And there's this white gunk on my flip-flops? I think we should move.'

She waited for him to speak, some encouraging response, which must not include the word cool.

'I think you're overthinking it,' he said, slowly putting the onion away from him on the table.

'I knew you'd say something like that.'

The avenue of communication was clamping down. How would he find the channel for his crummy revelation? He must tread carefully and not let her think he thought that she was mad. He must obey the granola. It might not speak to him again with the same force and then they would be lost for ever.

'It's an old house,' he shrugged. 'Old houses have excess dust, I guess.'

'Which gets into a child's hands, and dries them out?'

'What's the dust got to do with Ria's hands? It's probably just eczema or something, man, just take her to the doctor.'

'*I* take her to the doctor?' Melissa said waving a place mat for emphasis. 'Not *you* take her to the doctor? Why am *I* always the one to take them to the doctor, the dungeons, the Baby Beat, the fields in the middle of the day, the hospital, to Little Scamps?'

'Oh, Jesus, not this again. I'm at *work*. It's not like I'm —'

'Yes all right, all right, I know. It's the Unsolvable Problem, isn't it? But anyway, I'm digressing. Did I ever tell you about Lily?'

Michael held back his anger, obstructed as it was by this question. He didn't know what she was talking about. She wasn't fully present to be angry with. He sighed. 'Lily who?'

'The girl who was here when I came to see this place that second time. Brigitte's daughter. She had a limp. Well, she had strange hands. I remember them. They were very white, dry-looking, almost powdery. Maybe . . .'

'What?'

'Maybe there's something here that . . . She was off-key, that girl. There was something wicked about her. It was like she wasn't, I don't know, like she wasn't a real person, in a way? Or she was possessed or something? I can't explain it . . .' Here she trailed off, because Michael was looking at her in an erasing way so that the strength of every word faded once it had entered the area of his auditory range.

'I'm listening,' he said.

'No you're not.'

'Yes I am. You think that girl Lily's got something to do with the dust and Ria's rash, and that —'

'It's not a *rash*. It's *different* from a rash. And anyway it's not just that, it's her leg, her hair caught fire – remember that? – right here at this table. Ever since we moved here there's just been – oh for goodness sake, Michael, will you please stop picking your dick when I'm trying to *talk* to you!'

Like many men, Michael had a habit of adjusting his scrotum for comfort of positioning when he was at home, a private thing that he felt he had a right to do in his own house, which was fair enough, but no matter how much she tried Melissa couldn't stand it.

'Look,' he said exasperated, 'I have a penis, OK?'

'I know, and I feel sorry for you. Why can't you just keep it to yourself, huh? Why do you always have to make me aware of it in such a crude way?'

This seemed like the perfect time, as they were in the subject area, to make his confession, which under the circumstances did not come out in quite the way he had intended, as there was a touch of nastiness in it. He wanted to make her feel bad, to remind her, indeed, of the importance of this very scrotum, its neglect at her hand, which had thus necessitated the excursion into another aperture. He said, 'Well, *someone's* got to be aware of it. In fact someone *has* been aware of it, someone . . . else —'

Then he stopped, losing scrotum, therefore adjusting it again in his anxiety which made Melissa hate him, more, actually, for this second adjustment in such a short space of time, than for the content of his confession, which in this moment seemed quite by-the-by.

She laughed at him. 'Oh, really? So what, you're seeing someone now?'

He became meek, like a little boy anticipating punishment, but there was a smugness in it, he wanted the punishment. 'I wouldn't say I was *seeing* someone. I'm not *seeing* her. There were just a couple of times, when, stuff happened. It's not still going on . . .'

But she didn't seem to be listening any more. She was neatening the place mat pile with a crazy exactitude, not even looking at him. Her face had faded from awareness and turned its dark corner. 'Those mats are straight,' he said. 'Do you hear what I'm saying to you? It was just a stupid glitch when I was feeling like I needed some attention.' He was thinking of the John Legend song in his head, Number One, the gist of which was going to be the finale of this explanation. 'And I wanted you to know about it, so that we could —'

Again she laughed, giggled this time and shook her head. Melissa had a tendency to giggle when extremities of feeling were all cluttered together in her brain – frustration, anger, hurt, disgust, hunger. 'Men think they are better than grass,' she said.

'What?'

'It's from a poem, by W.S. Merwin. Men really do think they're better than grass. I understand exactly what that line could mean now. I didn't quite get it when I first read it but I liked it so I made a note of it. I mean, what makes you think I give a shit? Grass grows. Trees stay standing. Wind carries. You men think the whole world is your dick. Well, I can tell you that it's not. You can spare me all the details and the emotional backstory, honestly, it's fine, Michael, you are free to wave it where you please. Frankly it's one less thing for me to think about.'

Michael was taken aback. Where was her *lava*, the avalanche? Where was her feeling, her goddamn *heart*? 'Hold on a minute. Do you love me?' he said.

'What?' She turned back to him from her departure into the kitchen, pausing in the doorway, against the fiery glow of the paprika floor.

'Do you love me?'

'Why are you asking me that now?'

'Because I seriously want to know. I'm interested. Go on.'

His face was twisted, older than it had been just a few minutes ago. He looked shabby and weak. Melissa felt sorry for him, and she was suddenly full of an old image of their big love and it made her sad. She missed him. She missed them. Somewhere she was hurt, because he had belonged to her through that love, but she couldn't quite feel the hurt as her own, couldn't work out whether it was there only because it was supposed to be there. Who was she, really, inside? It was as if there were two of her, one at the back, drowning, and one at the front.

'It's not exactly the absolute greatest time to ask me a question like that now, is it?' she said.

'Of *course* she loves you, Daddy,' came a smaller voice from beyond, through the double doors, from the bathroom. The door kicked open, there was a clattering of crutches, and there was Ria, naked, leaning with one arm on a crutch and the other hand holding the door handle. Her damp black curls were loose and sleek and falling down her face like a slow black prehistoric waterfall. Her eyes were huge, bulbous and shining, the lashes like sooty sunrises. She was a vision of early brownness, the most beautiful broken thing they had ever seen.

'Hey,' Michael said softly, crouching, reaching out his hand to her, as though to a saviour.

She hopped towards him. He wanted to cry. There is something monstrous about seeing your child limping.

'Can you buy me a present?' she said when she reached him, when he was holding her hands and looking up into her face. 'For when my cast comes off?'

Ria knew, at this moment, that she could ask anything and would receive. She smiled for them, enjoying the attention. She knew her power.

'Just one,' she said, 'a small one.'

Michael grabbed her, folding her into his lap, glancing down at her hands.

IO

SOMETIMES IT SNOWS IN FEBRUARY

In February it snowed. It was a wild, white surprise. The snow fell for days, in a confusion of climate. Long past Christmas in the wings of spring, the world was white. Ice on the corners. Snow on the hills. Traffic formed on the A roads and the back roads. The white stuff piled on rail tracks, halting trains and increasing signal failures. London does not know what to do with snow. It lives in hope that if it falls it will do so lightly, and leave smoothly, pulling away into ice, the ice disappearing into light, the streets returning to themselves. But this February, no. The fall began on the first day and came down heavy. Before it could disperse there was more, another layer of difficulty which smothered the rooftops and the tiny surface areas of the thinnest of naked branches, making pretty winter trees. Cars would not start and schools were closed. All the buses were cancelled and Heathrow was closed. Even in the centre of town, in Piccadilly and Covent Garden and Trafalgar, those places whose endless activity had the power to nullify movements of weather, where the city itself was the defining factor of experience, making songs of rain, laughing and tooting in the face of sleet, even they could not shrug this off. It was covered, everywhere, the city, the suburbs, white. The Thames formed rafts of ice, and closest to the water was coldest of all.

Damian was at work in Croydon, whose high metallic skyscrapers were also icing capped, as were the tips of the telephone masts, the railings of the ugly flyover, and the ledge of the fifth floor window that looked in on the blue-carpeted area of his desk. There were three other desks in this corner, belonging to Angela, Mercy and Tom, who watched *EastEnders* religiously and owned a tie with prints of tiny pineapples on it. Angela and Mercy were talking.

'You know what happen?' Angela said, her red earrings matching her red fingernails, her black braids swirled into a bun. 'When you climb on people's heads to get to the top? Well, guess what? When they all leave, you fall right back down to the ground.'

'That's it,' Mercy said, munching her mid-morning marshmallow, which matched her baby-pink shirt. 'And you think someone's gonna come and put out their hand to help you up when you're down? No. They'll just be watching you and laughing innit.'

'You know. And not *with* you, but *at* you. What goes around comes around. God is just,' said Angela. 'Treat your neighbour as you would want to be treated yourself.'

'Reap what you sow.'

'Yes.'

Their fingers clattered for a while over their keyboards and Mercy offered Angela another marshmallow which she accepted, even though, as everyone was aware, she didn't like marshmallows because they were an unsatisfying, disappearing kind of food, but the snow was such that it caused aberrations of character and habit. The person they were talking about, Heather, had recently been promoted, using, they felt, underhand and treacherous tactics. They now decided that they were going to just go the whole hog and bitch about her.

'She's one of those people,' Mercy lowered her voice, 'who thinks she's better than everyone else, better than you or me. I hate people like that.'

'Going around with an inflated sense of themselves, yeah.'

'But you can't hide who you really are.'

'Maybe that's why she wears so much make-up . . .'

'It's the wrong colour as well. Next time look at her neck, you'll see it . . .'

From there they went on to talk about comfort duvets, the special, very old duvet that is kept by the television and that you wrap around yourself at times of extreme pampering and hibernation, the perfect thing for this kind of weather and the very item they would both be making good use of when they got home that evening. Damian listened to them, rather he heard them, hoping that they would not try to include him in their conversation as they sometimes did. He was having particular trouble being at work today. There had been another in-lawed Sunday roast with Patrick and Verena two days ago that he was still recovering from, plus he had a headache, and he resented more than usual the irritating nature of nine-to-five existence, that you chat endlessly with the same people simply because they are stationed in your patch, that you come to know their daytime physical intimacies, Mercy's need for regular face powder and lip balm, Angela's chilblains and resulting office slipper-wearing, what Tom and his keen-hiker wife and their two boys were going to be doing this weekend. The snow was making everything more intense, louder, closer. He felt shut in. The heating was on too strong. The cold whiteness outside the window was both inviting and incongruous.

At 11.30 a.m. the sandwich trolley arrived, a tall silver vehicle which lately had developed a squeaky wheel. It came at the same time every day, too early, at the lunchtime of children. The arrival of the sandwich trolley was Damian's proof that school was preparation for this kind of future, that from a very young age our training for captivity is in motion – the uniform, the fifteen-minute breaks, the ridiculous premature lunch. The sandwich trolley was the moment in his working day when he felt most strongly that his life required a dramatic change, a splintering, some kind of scandal or shock or tremor, when he most wanted to flee, to rip off his suit and run screaming from the building, and go – where? Not home, not to Dorking, but to some loose, untethered place, any kind of ocean or other country, to a transcendental sphere where breath itself was marvellous and the breeze was open and palpable and there was nothing in the way of it to make it seem irrelevant. Instead though, usually, he got up from his navy-blue swivel chair like everyone else, stretched, and walked over. The hungry huddle bantered amidst the crinkling of plastic sandwich wrappers and packets of crisps and the jangling of change, returning to their desks afterwards temporarily enlivened by the approaching meal, through which their computer screens would remain switched on, so that they could peer at them, or enjoy a moment of unbridled and legitimate net-surfing. Today Damian could not join that brief, low-ceilinged voyage to the sandwich mecca. The sound of the crisp packets and the squeaking of the faulty wheel made his head ache even more. When Tom nudged him and asked him if he was coming to the trolley he just wanted to beat him down. He looked out of the window, saw the clouds moving slowly across the firmament, and from somewhere very close, yet also seeming to come from the sky, he heard his father talking to him again, in that now frequent harsh whisper, those same seventeen words, *How long will you go on living your life, as if you were balancing on a ribbon?* That was when he fled.

He did not scream as he left the building. The screaming was internal. The cold, after the claustrophobic heat inside, made him shiver. And not just that, but the sharpness of everything, the enormous difficulty of each moment. He had not been to the grave yet. He had not laid flowers or knelt in the necropolis, or taken care of the boxes in the garage. He was afraid, afraid of the emptiness, of finding reflections of himself, and now they were hounding him, these small failures, so that he couldn't think straight, and yet it was so much more than that, everything, *everything*, was wrong – specificities were fading, foundations were crumbling. Indeed he *was* walking on a ribbon, tripping, falling, with Laurence on his heels, pulling him down, along this white-cushioned southern pavement, on this alternative journey to another kind of sandwich, to Pret A Manger, which he now entered, realising, beneath his turmoil, that he was nevertheless hungry.

Damian was a Pret frequenter. He came here on such days when he couldn't handle the trolley. Inside all was retro and metallic, silver floor, silver cabinets, silver ceiling. He stared at the sandwiches. There were other people also staring at the sandwiches, in their neat office clothes, their dark winter coats, considering what they wanted to eat in this single, special hour, this small portion of freedom. Should it be meat or fish, cheese or egg? Should he pick the sandwich that foolishly claimed not to be a sandwich by forsaking its bread, and therefore was actually a salad? Or should he just have a plain and honest salad, a Niçoise, a bean feast? He stood there in this pressured Pret cluster, which was not really very dissimilar to the one in the office, it was just less friendly. Everyone was trying to appear as though they didn't care which sandwich they had, when actually they did care, a great deal. There was an acceptable amount of time that you could stand here for, between thirty seconds and a minute, and Damian was aware, as time passed, that his perusal was bordering on the excessive. The problem was that he was no longer staring at the sandwiches, but beyond them, into the silver of the cabinet, into the distractions and reflections there. He saw a picture of Stephanie, early this morning, putting on her dressing-gown to leave the bedroom, a reluctance in her movements suggesting defeat, dejection. He saw Laurence's eroding dead skull beneath the earth with soil clustered around it, yet still, in the midst of all this, he was supposed to choose between chicken-avocado and ham and Pret pickle. The more he stared, the more incapable he became of choosing. He glanced around and upwards, the ceiling swayed, a sweat was forming on his neck. Next to him a black thing reached out and took a sandwich, a woman's gloved hand. It seemed a sinister hand, he realised that he was trembling. In an attempt to pull himself together, he closed his eyes and opened them again. Then he reached out, following the movements of the sinister gloved hand, and grabbed the first thing he touched. Egg mayonnaise. He went quickly to the till and paid for it. Just as quickly, he went back out into the biting air and threw up on the pavement.

The rest of the day was spent in a smog of ongoing qualm-ishness, until at 5.45 p.m. he went to the station to get his train, only to find that it had been cancelled. The tracks were snow-clogged. There were red crosses all over the departure boards. He called Stephanie. He called Michael (Bell Green was only a couple of stops away and some of the local lines were running). When there was no answer on Michael's mobile, he called Michael's house. Melissa picked up.

★

She opened the door wearing a flared grey tracksuit with DANCEFIT printed across the chest and white cord string, and her slippers. She looked very young, yet older, closer into her face, some recent darkness around the eyes, an argument with her smile, an uncertainty. Or maybe people just look different when they're at home on a weeknight not expecting anyone special and it's snowing outside in February.

'Come in,' she said. He started apologising – the trains, I'll be out of your way first thing, rocking up on you like this . . . 'It's fine, Damian, honestly, it's really not a problem. Pass your coat,' which she hung to thaw over the back of one of the dining chairs. He left his briefcase leaning against the wall by the door.

'Where's Michael, is he trapped as well?'

He had expected to find him sitting on the sofa or coming out of the kitchen, but there was no one, just Venus and Serena Williams playing on a news clip, mythical, like shooting stars, distant yet familiar, and the radio on in the background.

'I don't know where he is,' Melissa said. 'I mean, he's away with work so, I don't know.'

This was not strictly true. Michael was staying at the Queen's Hotel in Crystal Palace, on a temporary sojourn away from unmarried life, at her request, after another argument that had started with his objection to the returning of the onion to the bedroom windowsill, but which was really about deeper things. The frost between them had thickened further after his confession. Michael had moved to the sofa full-time because the master court wasn't big enough any more to hold their distance. For a while they had lived purely by the light of the children, but during that last quarrel Melissa had said, 'I can't take this any more. I can't live like this, it's making me sick. I want you to go.' 'What about the kids?' Michael had said. 'I'll manage,' she'd said. And so he was gone, return date as yet unspecified. Which meant it *was* true, in answer to Damian's question, that she didn't know whether he was trapped in the snow or not. He could be, there were lots of hills in Crystal Palace, a train could have come off the tracks or he might have stumbled in a ditch. Strangely these possibilities were out of her jurisdiction. For now he was not her man. He was a snowman, out there, and she was in here, in the crooked warmth, with her sleeping cubs, and now this other man, who was drifting around as if embarrassed by himself.

'Why don't you sit down? Sit down, chill.' Damian took this as an order, descending into the sofa at the last pop of Venus. He couldn't chill, though. It was weird being here without Stephanie and Michael. It was releasing all kinds of unacceptable feelings in him. 'Are you hungry? I just ate but there's some couscous left over if you want some.'

Couscous. Stephanie did that sometimes, cooked couscous. Couscous, Damian believed, was not meant to be eaten
in the home. It belonged in North African restaurants where
they knew what to do with it, so there was not much hope
for this meal that she strode across the room into the kitchen
to prepare for him. She put feta cheese on top of it. There
were chunks of grey aubergine and carrots. She laid it out on
a place mat with a glass of red wine and a spoon. 'Thanks,' he
said, sitting down to it. He wanted to ask for a fork but he was
paranoid that he might say fuck instead.

'When I was growing up,' Melissa said relatedly, 'we
always ate rice with a spoon and fork.' She was sitting on the
edge of the chair diagonally across from him with her leg
tucked underneath her, watching him eat, making him more
self-conscious. 'But Michael and *his* family ate it with a knife
and fork, so that's how *he* always eats it. So now, whenever
I'm having rice or couscous or something like that, there's
this confusion in me that wasn't there before, about whether
to get a knife or a spoon to eat it with. Don't you think it's
problematic how when you're in a couple you lose your grip
on who you really are, on how you do things, on your own
private culture? Do you know what I mean? Do you ever
have this issue? I mean, what kind of a person eats rice with
a knife? I don't want my children to grow up to be the kind
of people who eat rice with a knife.'

She was looking at him with genuine interest. She wanted
a response. She wanted him to engage with her on this.

'Well,' he said, 'you definitely can't eat couscous with a
knife.'

'Thank you.'

'But you do need a f-fork. You always need a fork, unless
it's cereal.'

She gasped. 'You haven't got a fork! I'll get you a fork.
Of course you need a fork, to get the dregs on to the spoon!
You see? You see what's happening to me? I'm confused. My

inner make-up has been rearranged and now I'm spoiled. It's so sad.'

She went away and got the fork and gave it to him. He was chewing on some tough aubergine. It all tasted quite nice but the textures weren't necessarily the best. 'Actually, you know what?' she said. 'I think I'll have some wine too, even if it is red. It's Michael's wine. He's the one who drinks red. I prefer white, as you know, but I'll have some red with you. It's no fun drinking alone.'

It was a two-thirds-full bottle of Rioja. Soon they were chilling at the table postprandial listening to Jaguar Wright. She had a sharp, hot voice rafting over choppy beats. Melissa nodded to it intermittently as she was drinking. Damian had discreetly left a few bits of aubergine on the side of his plate.

'Space is good,' she was saying, in an upbeat rumination about coping with stress. 'I like it when Michael's away. I feel different, brighter. Even this house feels different. I'm returning to myself, experiencing myself clearly again, you know? It's like, I'm not opaque any more, I'm stronger in fact, more positive. Positivity is the way to go – that's what my sister's always saying. It's our mental landscape that holds us back.' (Since Michael had left, Melissa and Carol had been chatting more on the phone in the evenings.)

'Um-hm,' Damian said nodding, because he could see that she really wanted him to get her, and he really wanted her to get that he was getting her. 'Yep, space is the thing. Whenever you can get it, take it. I could use more of it myself. When's he coming back?'

'Er, Thursday,' she lied, 'maybe Friday. How're Stephanie and the kids?'

'They're fine, they're good . . .' But he didn't want to talk about Stephanie. He did not want to bring her, or anyone, into this perfect, warm and temporary cave where every-thing was just so, Melissa, all to himself, even if she was going on and on about Michael, but it was OK, it was just the two of them. They were alone together in a world of snow. Everything was still and soft. There were occasional sounds from the London outside and he liked that too.

'OK, look,' she said suddenly, 'I hate lying. Michael isn't away with work. We're having space' (she made quote marks with her fingers) 'from each other. You know, space space. That kind of space. There, I've said it. Everything got too much so I kicked him out.'

'You kicked him out? Seriously?'

'Well,' the Jaguar Wright LP ended and Melissa got up to change it, 'I didn't *actually* kick him out per se, as in, literally, with my foot. I just asked him to get out of my face for a while and he agreed. It was kind of a mutual decision in the end. I thought you would've known. Didn't he tell you?'

'No, I haven't seen him.'

'But I thought you were buddies.' She found Susana Baca on the shelf and slipped her out of the CD case. The congas came in, the taps of the xylophone. In the kitchen she washed up Damian's plate straight away so that dust wouldn't build on it. She still had the image in her mind of Michael packing his tiny blue suitcase, the way he'd looked at her as she'd walked into the bedroom. She had wanted to lie down with him on the bed, a last holding, but he'd given her such a hard, hollow look.

From the way she was talking about it, so flippantly, Damian sensed that Melissa was fronting about Michael, that she was more upset about it than she seemed. There was a picture of them both with the children on the shelf above the television that he was trying not to look at. 'I guess he must be lying low,' he said, assuming the same levity in his voice, though really he wanted to know everything, all the details. He felt spurred, guiltily so. 'Anyway, I don't think Michael considers me a bonafide spar on that level that he'd go out of his way to call me up about something like that.' Not that he wanted, in any way here, by thus speculating, to imply that

Michael was not a close enough friend for it to be such a big deal if something were to happen here tonight, something unrighteous, something secret. No. Absolutely not. Because that would be dark of him. But if only, in this sweet snow . . .

'What happened?' he asked as she came back into the room.

'Oh, nothing and everything. He slept with someone but that's not what happened. It was everything else that wasn't happening that happened.'

'Wow. He cheated,' Damian said.

Melissa looked at him, bemused, a little condescending. 'He doesn't belong to me. Fidelity is so overrated. I think it's childish, the way people think of it.'

'So it doesn't bother you?'

There was a suggestion in his tone, a hint of expectation, that made Melissa see him for the first time in a different way. She noticed the roundness of his shoulders and the thickness of his waist. There was a rich warmth to him that she had always thought of as brotherly, but now it was alluring, rugged. His fingers were very thick, not smooth and elegant like Michael's. She studied them, for long enough for him to notice. The Rioja was going to her head.

'If it bothers me it's my problem, not his,' she said.

Damian could feel a wide, foolish smile trying to take over his face and he suppressed it. It was just that he was content, being here in her company, so different from how he'd felt earlier today, and the way she'd looked at him just then had given him something, it had lifted him. 'I think I had a panic attack today,' he blurted.

'Did you? How come?'

'I don't know. I was trying to buy a sandwich and I just . . . I don't know. I freaked out.'

'Do you know what caused it? Was it something to do with the sandwich? Michael hates egg mayo, it turns his stomach.'

She was like a record on repeat. Michael Michael Michael. 'Sorry,' she said, realising, as Damian got up from the table. There seemed to be a collusion emerging between them, unspoken, a secret twoness. 'It was egg mayo, funnily enough,' he said, turning away from her towards the bookshelves. Melissa shuddered. It was getting colder. She went to adjust the heating and wrapped the blanket off the sofa around her, by which time Damian was sitting on the floor looking through the records on the bottom shelf. His shirt had come untucked at the back. His back was like a warm mountain, thick and rotund.

'You've got some classics here, man. Millie Jackson. My dad used to listen to her.'

My dad. Had he actually said that? It sounded absurd coming out of his mouth, yet he'd said it so naturally. He was shocked.

'Why don't you play it?' Melissa said.

She showed him how to change the speed on the record player. Millie sloped in slinky, white with the snow in her white jumpsuit and long cape. The voice took Damian right back to a time when Joyce, he and Laurence were sitting at the table playing blackjack. It was all crisp edges and clusters of colours in his head, Joyce's purple cardigan, the gold buttons, the flowers on the table, the orange curtain. The vividness, the immediacy of the image, brought tears to his eyes.

'Are you OK?'

He was hunched on the floor, staring at the turntable. He breathed deeply, a long, violent exhale. 'God, it's amazing how music can make up your life, your whole life, and bring it back to you in bits, things you thought you'd forgotten.'

She agreed with him, and he felt that she was gently listening to him. 'Are you thinking about your dad?'

The song played on, both of them inside it. 'It just struck me that he was alive once. I mean, really alive, before he died in his life. Do you understand what I mean? That's what happened to him. He was already dead.'

'The greatest challenge in life is not to die before we die,' Melissa said. 'I read that somewhere. It happens to a lot of people.' She was going to add, 'I think it's happening to me,' but didn't.

They were both a little drunk by now. They were next to each other on the rug with their backs against the sofa in the zigzag lamplight. Damian wanted to put his arm around her, to hold her, just for a minute. He'd never talked like this about his father to anyone and he felt lighter, as though a touch could carry no guilt, no reproach.

'I think my dad's going to die soon,' she said. 'He's getting frailer and frailer, every time I see him. I should go and visit him more.'

'Why don't you?'

She paused. 'It's a long story. It's in the past and I don't like to go there . . . Lots of people have difficult childhoods. The important thing is how you rise above it to meet yourself.'

'Where did you read that one?'

'Nowhere.'

There was an extended silence, for the dead and the undead. The vinyl too fell silent, in the space between songs. Melissa finished her wine. 'Have you tried writing about it,' she asked, 'about what it feels like, in a diary or something? It must rock your foundations when a parent dies, no matter how you felt about them or how close you were. You should just splurge it all out. That's what I used to do. It helps.'

Damian had never kept a diary. 'It seems depressing, staring your problems in the face like that, writing them out . . . I have written about him, though, in a way, a long time ago. I wrote a novel that was sort of based on him.'

'Did you?' She sounded impressed. 'Did you finish it?'

'Kind of. Not properly. It fizzled out in the end.'

'What's it called?'

He was shy. 'It doesn't really have one title. There were two or three of them. "Canon and the Storm" was the main one.'

'Canon and the Storm. Hm.' She rolled it around on her tongue. 'Canon. That's an interesting name. Is Canon the father? . . . I like it. It's a good title. It's intriguing.'

'So it gets your approval?' Damian was overjoyed. It was beginning to come to him again, the finger-tingling writing feeling, the cocooning thrill of it. She even said, 'I'd like to read it some time,' glancing over at the empty bottle on the table and draining her glass again, even though it was definitely finished.

'Are you serious?' he said.

'Yeah, seriously. Email it to me.'

'OK, I might.' (He would.) 'Once I've got it all together . . .'

'God, I don't know how anyone could write a novel. It must take ages. All those words. All those sentences.' She was getting up, clinging to the edge of the sofa. 'I couldn't do it. Two thousand words is about my max.'

The music had ended again, throwing the room into emptiness. 'You know what I'd really love right now?' she said.

'What?'

'A cigarette.'

'I didn't know you smoked.'

'I don't. I used to.'

'I've got some Marlboro Lights if you want one.'

'I didn't know *you* smoked.'

'I didn't. I gave up.' On giving up, that is. On New Year's Day, to spite the resolution culture. Don't stop, start. Stop denying yourself and live. Life is long, not short. Smoking kills? Life kills. This was Damian's current philosophy, and it had been enabling abundant Marlboro Light puffing in the driveway at home and subsequent gum chewing to hide the smell, which wasn't working.

Melissa tried to fight the craving but gave in. 'Let's have

one, I don't care any more,' she said. 'We have to go outside, though. You know it's minus out there.'

She went to check on the children. Blake was sleeping through now, returning to her the night. It was Ria who had been restless recently. She had tried to sleepwalk downstairs at 2 a.m. with one crutch, before the cast was removed, and Melissa had found her under the skylight. But now she was sleeping deeply. They had gone out in the snow today, in the morning, and on discovering that the school was closed, they had gone on towards the park, along the silver birches, in through the gates. It was deserted, the snow a white floor untroubled. Amazed, Ria had run across the field, a decreasing figure advancing towards the tenements, her small dark foot-prints a trail of recent Rias. There was a slight limp in her left leg, which the doctor had said would disappear in time.

And they had made snowmen, a family of three, in the garden, who stared with their hard sultana eyes as Melissa and Damian lit up. Their noses were carrots. One of them, the tallest, was wearing Michael's scarf. Other inanimate beings in the garden were the yellow teddy bear sitting stiff-haired on the red bench, and the toy figures in the white-topped playhouse. The sky was cold and lilac. The snow was turning to ice, making the snow family lose their definition. The wind chime sang as the ice wind blew.

'Are you sure about this?' Damian said when he offered the pack.

'I'm sure.' She took one. It felt big between her fingers. The first inhale was air-spinning, gorgeous against the wine. They had found more to drink at the bottom of the fridge, a half bottle of leftover Liebfraumilch which was pleasantly sweet. 'Sometimes when you want something you just have to let yourself have it,' she said.

For Damian too, it was one of the best cigarettes he had ever smoked.

'Just don't blame me if you start again.'

'I won't. I don't wanna get cancer.'

'If you smoke it to only halfway down it's not as bad. Most of the cancer's in the butt.'

The arms of their coats were touching, which didn't seem a thing. They blew up at the sky, the skeletal aerials and the silhouettes of the chimneys. Long clouds lay out, some moving and pink and slipping away, and at one end, to the south, the moon slid full, round and golden into a case of silver wisps, until it was swallowed, whole, and all that was moving was a fading glow like a sun reduced to a common star. A bay tree, blackened in the darkness, stood up above the fences, watching over them with its still, black leaves.

'I like it out here,' Melissa said. 'Sometimes I come out here at night to think, to be by myself. It's not that private – I feel like people are watching me from the windows over there – but I can hide behind that tree.' She looked up at it. 'That tree is my friend. It understands me. It knows.'

'What does it know about you?' Damian said.

'Everything.' He was looking at her profile. She could feel him looking at her in a certain way. It reminded her of how Michael had looked at her in Montego Bay, waiting for her to answer his questions. 'Everything I was and what I am now,' she said, 'whatever that is. I'm not sure I know any more. I seem to be losing a sense of it. It's quite frightening. Do you ever feel like that, like you're losing track of who you are?'

'Most of the time I feel like that.'

She turned to him, stealing her profile away, emboldened. 'And you're looking for yourself, but can't find it? You don't even know where to look any more? Like you're groping around in the darkness?'

Dominant in her face was that look of extreme youth he'd seen when she'd opened the door to him. The face of a child, the façade all gone.

'It's because we're in the wrong place,' he said. 'It's because we're not living how we were supposed to live.'

'Why, though? Why don't people live the way they're supposed to live? It should be the easiest thing in the world.'

He shrugged and lit another cigarette. 'It's scary. That's why.'

So quickly does smoke enfold. Melissa wanted another and motioned for one. She took it in deep, right to the bottom of her throat before blowing back out, adding smoke clouds to cold clouds. The wine and the snow and the smoke were a red and white dance inside her and she felt carried with it, afloat.

'Can I tell you a secret, Damian?' she said.

'Yeah, course.'

'I've never told this to anyone before. I'm almost afraid to tell it to you.'

'I won't tell anyone, I promise.'

'It's not that. It's not that kind of secret. I'm just worried something bad will happen if I do.'

But she wanted to tell it, to say it out loud, in this quiet pure white, so she moved her fear out of the way.

'When I was younger, before I had children, before I met Michael, when I was around twenty-four, I used to have this feeling. I'd had it all through my life, right up until about that age, twenty-four – that's the age when I can still remember it being completely intact, as much as a feeling, a sense of something, can be intact.' Her hands were shivering, partly from the cold. She took another sip from the Liebfraumilch, followed immediately by another inhale. 'You might find this strange, or arrogant maybe, it was a feeling that I was protected by something, a kind of guide. A guardian angel, if you want to think of it like that. I had my own angel watching over me. It walked with me. She, I think it was most like a she, was there, everywhere I went, through everything that happened. I felt like I was untouchable, invincible. I used to walk across roads without looking, convinced she would stop the traffic. I used to take all kinds of risks with myself . . .'

'What kind of risks?'

'Oh, things I wouldn't do now. Staying in strange men's flats, getting into meat vans with them, jumping off —'

'Meat vans?'

'Another long story.'

'OK.'

'Anyway, the point is that I'm scared now, and I didn't used to be scared. I used to live off my instincts. The instinct was guided by the angel and the angel by the instinct.'

Before Michael had left, Melissa had taken to going out alone in the evenings. She hadn't felt like seeing friends. She'd go to the V&A, to galleries, to look at pictures, to see if maybe she could find it, what it might look like, this angel that she had always taken for granted. At the Tate Modern she had found something, a painting by Gaugin of a woman standing facing the sea. It was called *In the Waves*. The woman had long, bright hair and she was naked, the sea rising around her. She was open and unhindered, alone and whole in her nature. Melissa had stood there for a long time, gazing at this picture. There it was. That was what it looked like. How could she get back there?

'So that's my secret,' she told Damian. 'I can't feel it any more. That thing that belonged only to me, that no one could ever take away. It's not there any more. I think it's gone.'

'It hasn't gone,' he said.

'It has, it has. Where is it, then? I've looked for it. I've been thinking maybe Blake's taken it. Maybe that's what happens with sons, they take their mothers' souls away. Do you think he'll give it back? He's quite good at giving things back, like if I ask him usually he gives it back, whatever it is, my hair clip, my wallet, he'll just give it back to me. Did you give your mother's soul back to her? When does it happen?'

'My mother never gave me her soul, so I never had to give it back.'

'Oh sweetheart, I'm sorry. It's so cold, I'm so drunk now I

don't even know what I'm saying any more. I must remember to think positively. Put your arms around me, let's keep each other warm. I don't want to go inside yet.' He did what she asked, rubbing her shoulders to warm her, feeling that this was enough, they had transcended something.

'It sounds like you're talking about God,' he said. 'Your angel, your guide. Isn't it God?'

'It's my own god. What do you do when you lose your god?'

'You haven't lost it,' he repeated. 'I can see it. It's right there.'

'Where?'

'There. In your face. Your face is beautiful.'

She looked past him, into the lilac, the mist. 'But I can't feel it,' she said, with tears in her eyes. 'I don't know who I am.'

He slept on the sofa, aware of her above him, every movement, the noise of the floorboards under her feet. He was the sea churning and drifting beneath her bow, and he fell asleep in the liquid motions of this longing and dreamt of the fishes he'd seen in the aquarium last week with Avril, the snake pipefish making question marks with its tail. In the morning, in the very early light, she came downstairs. He was already up and was standing pulling on his trousers. She paused, for just a breath of time, in which they reached for each other from inside themselves, only with their eyes, in that first purity of morning. She saw him, the whole possibility of him. Her vision swept up and down him and he felt it. He would have gone to her, right then. But he couldn't move, only look at her, asking silently for her to remember. Then the moment was gone.

'Morning,' she said, and went to warm Blake's milk.

II

THE INITIATION

White ribbons blowing in the breeze around the chicken shop. The police in the road. The song of the sirens. Apart from that there was a hush. The air was slow. The sun was incongruous. Last night the streets had felt the lifting of a boy. His blood ran down and his soul ran up. No one knew who he was in the first hours except for those who had lost and those, less so, who had killed. By morning everyone knew. His name was Justin. The boy who couldn't sing, the boy who had crucified Angels.

A woman on the corner said, 'I never go to that park. Now you see why I never go to that park.'

Another said, 'They chased him, like a pack of dogs. Animals. They're animals.'

It was possible to get the story by walking up the street. Further on by the church, 'It was Pauline's boy, the younger one.'

On the next bend, 'He ran to the chicken place for help . . .'

'. . . the ambulance was too late . . .'

'. . . thirteen years old . . .'

'I am so angry. I am so angry,' a mother said, leaning against a garden wall, one hand on her pram, a flush of early white roses behind her. 'When I heard the news I just had to pray.'

'Yes. Yes,' another one said.

'You know the kind of prayer – I prayed and cursed at the

same time. God is so cruel. Why does he let this happen? My faith is shaking.'

'It has to stop.'

'Too many of our children are dying.'

What happened was this. Justin had an older brother, Ethan, and Ethan was Justin's beacon in the world. It had always been so. When Ethan ran, Justin ran. When Ethan rode his bike at high speed down the park road to the round-about, Justin wanted to do the same, though his wheels were smaller, and his legs were shorter. He wanted to be as tall as Ethan, as fast as Ethan, as cool as Ethan, with his cap sideways on his head like Ethan, and his jeans slung low on his hips like Ethan, to walk like him, a broad, soft, cat-like tread, his trainers smooth and neat and guarded on the pavement, knowing of it, every turn and crack of his manor, owning it. And watching them, Pauline had always worried. She knew that there were limits to her power, that Justin would always go with Ethan, he would always follow him. Ethan had not finished school as she had hoped, so all the hope she had left for her sons was in Justin, who had always been good, capable, hardworking, a good student, she pictured him as a lawyer one day or a professor, tall and proud, in a smart suit. Ethan liked to hang out with the boys around the way, the boys who also did not finish school, who smoked on the corners in the moonlight, in the courtyards outside the flats, in the deserted children's playground, who had nothing special to do. The things they did, they were shady things. They slung weed, hustled skunk. They aimed for Ferraris that way, not the other way, the right way, which was too hard, too long, too compro-mising. In this kind of life there were distant hierarchies and contentious postcodes. You could step into Dulwich and be doomed. You were barred from Peckham, from Camberwell. There were showdowns, between these young postcode armies, with silver-blade weaponry and sometimes gunfire. And last night, there was one such showdown in the park next to the library opposite the TM Chicken joint between the tattoo parlour and the barber shop not far along from the bottom of Paradise Row, because Ethan and his crew had had a fight with some people from Catford about a gun he'd asked Justin to hide for him and that Pauline had found and taken to the police, who had then traced it back to the owner, and now that crew from Catford wanted blood, specifically, at the hands of their newest and youngest member, a fourteen-year-old girl, who happened to have not yet earned full initiation into the crew with a bad enough act.

Aside from asking him to hide the gun (which originally hailed from Berkshire, where there is a gun factory), Ethan had also let Justin hang out with him a few times in the courtyard, after school when their mother was still at work. But mostly he told him no, you have to do what Mum said and do your homework. Last night as well he told him no, standing before the mirror in his room putting on his cap and his studded belt and assessing himself overall to see whether he looked like a hard enough man. In the mirror he could see Justin sitting on the bed behind him, still wearing his white school polo-shirt and black trousers, saying, I wanna come with you. Justin liked the feeling of being Ethan's young partner in the pack. He liked the way they all called him Little Man but treated him like a big man. They also called him The Singing Professor, because of how much he studied and how much he liked to sing and listen to music, all kinds of music, especially his mum's old soul records. Come on, let me come, Justin said to Ethan. No, Ethan said again. Well I'm coming anyway. You can't stop me. I can walk where I wanna walk. You best stay here, man, I ain't joking with you now, Ethan said. Just stay here. I'll soon come, all right? All right? All right, all right, Justin said, and he went into his room to change his clothes, jeans and a yellow T-shirt, his favourite T-shirt, a T-shirt he felt was down, because he was surely going out to the park tonight no matter what Ethan said. Justin was getting to an age where he felt he could almost equal Ethan, where Ethan's word was almost level with his own word. Plus he was worried by something, the tone in Ethan's voice just now, the sudden frightened flash in his eyes. In the mirror Ethan took one last, long look at himself, and put a blade into the pocket of his jeans in case he would need it. It was a small, sharp Swiss brand, small enough for discretion, large enough for defence. He took one more last look, knocked his brother's shoulder with his fist in the living room, left him there watching TV, and went cat-like in the twilight down Paradise. The day had walked into night without a look back. The clouds were thick. They had joined themselves and made darkness.

When Pauline got home the flat was empty. It was well past nine. She felt something. Something was wrong. She'd felt it on the bus, a flip in her stomach, an inexplicable dread, and now again as she turned the key. She had the sensation that she was turning it into an emptiness that would never stop turning, and once inside the silence was ominous. Where was the sound of the television? Where was Justin? The sky seemed a strange colour tonight, an end-of-world kind of colour, black and red mixed together. And there was no moon. It was hidden by the clouds. She called Ethan's phone and he did not answer. Justin had lost his phone and she hadn't replaced it yet. She went out again and walked by the courtyard and up and down Paradise but did not see them. Instead she saw Mrs Jackson who again could not find her house, and was wandering up and down in her thin green dress and slippers. Pauline did not have the patience for Mrs Jackson tonight. Her heart was bulging. Her ribs were snapping. Mrs Jackson, it's number eight! she shouted. Have you seen my boys? Have you seen my boy? But Mrs Jackson did not know what she meant. Mrs Jackson allowed Pauline to lead her back into her house, then Pauline went back home and waited.

And how Justin loved his mother. Pauline had no idea

how much Justin really loved her, how he wanted to look after her when she was old and walk with her for the longest he could until there was no further to walk and he would have to say goodbye. He never wanted to say goodbye. She was in his thoughts now as he walked around the park looking for Ethan, along the tunnel of trees leading up to the tower blocks whose windows were lit up with the many evenings of disparate people and always made a beautiful sight. The traffic was swishing by on the high road. The tattoo parlour and the barbershop were closed but the bright red lights of TM Chicken were on. He went into the courtyard where he'd hung out with Ethan recently. He walked around to the green at the front. No one, none of the pack, no one who called him The Singing Professor. Ethan, actually, by now, was miles away. He had been dragged into a car and taken away, and they were going to fix him, really fix him. That's what happens when you cross this one, this baddest one from Catford, when you get too close to the devil. You get fixed indirectly, in ways you might never have imagined could happen to you in your life, in your family. They hurt you by hurting what you love, by taking it away, by destroying it.

So Justin walked out of the courtyard back on to the dark green, singing to himself because he felt nervous. There were people gathering amidst the trees, their thick jackets and loose strides. They were prey-conscious, metallic. There were blades in the pockets of their denim. They were alert, existing at the very edge of themselves. Justin thought he recognised someone from the pack and he went towards them, but as he got closer he sensed danger, he turned in the other direction, soon he was running, and when the time was high they leapt for him, jumping, their silver toys flashing, get him, they said, while across the road the chefs at the chicken shop were putting more oil in the vat and they were restocking the chicken and the place smelt burnt because they'd had a little fire in the back just now, a spark of a flame that started suddenly, from nowhere.

They had doused it in time and now they were making more chicken. They were both wearing TM Chicken caps and red polo-shirts. It's quiet tonight, one said to the other, Yeah, it's always quiet on Tuesdays, the other said. Aadesh said he was glad he wasn't working tomorrow, Wednesday was his day off. What you doing? said Hakim, poking at the chicken with the long fork. Taking Lakshmi out, innit. Is it, I heard it's gonna rain tomorrow. Shit, said Aadesh. Then they heard someone shouting. They looked towards the door. A figure was coming across the road, a falling, running, crazy kind of walking like he wouldn't make it to the other side. A car swerved by him and beeped. The figure came closer. He was clutching his side and feeling the air with his free hand. His heart was beating faster than it had ever beat. He was living in just this one single moment, and in this moment there were memories, pictures, his mother was in this place, in this one single moment. She was waiting for him in the flat and he wanted to go back to her, to his first country, to his mother who was his first country, and walk with her to the end of her life for the longest he could. At no other time had he wanted this more strongly than now. He tripped. He stumbled. He saw the red light of the TM Chicken banner. He saw the strange bright haze over the street, the final gold, everything had a shine on it. He didn't want to die. He didn't want to die. He was crying because it hurt so much and he didn't want to die.

That was the other big thought, aside from his mother. Pain. They had found him, they had clocked him, the brother of Ethan. They found him in their midst among the trees and the chosen one went for him with her small girl hand. The blade crunched through the spine. Pain unfolded. It spread through him like a storm, like flames. It flung out, hot searing rips right through him. It hurt so much that he could see it, the wide gold shine, the red, the distant stars, he looked up as he reached the curb and at that moment Pauline stood up in her living room and looked out at the night, an unbearable thought, a heartbeat missed, she held her stomach, she walked out of the room into the hall, towards the door, opened it.

There was hope right up until death. Hope is the last thing that dies. Justin staggered across the pavement to the red door of the chicken shop. He grabbed the doorframe and with a last strength hauled himself forward. Help me, he whispered (he felt so quiet, like he was dreaming). Oh shit, Aadesh said. Shit, Hakim said, Oh my god. They went to him, just as he fell, half in the shop, half outside the shop. He was bleeding so much it was just pouring out of him like an ocean all across the pavement. The yellow T-shirt was soaked through, his jacket over it. His final thought, the one after his mother, the very last sensation, was that he was freezing cold, even though the place he felt himself entering was full of heat. A door was open. He went inside and the door closed behind him. It was too late now for anything. Even for Pauline, who was running down Paradise Row to cradle him on the wet, red floor.

The blood continued to run into the mortar around the paving slabs outside the chicken shop. It would never quite rub off, through all kinds of weather. It was there if you knew it was there.

★

'Hello?'

'Hey, it's me.'

'Me who?'

'Michael.'

'Michael . . . Oh, Michael, what . . . ?' There was a sleepy pause. 'Do you know what time it is?'

It was 2.15 a.m., and Michael had been staying at the Queen's Hotel in Crystal Palace for three and a half weeks. It was a vast, cream-coloured building in the colonial style set away from the parade along the road to Croydon, the Beulah tower to its right, the Crystal tower to its left. There were flags of the world adrift on the roof, a red path leading up towards the entrance, but inside it was not so grand. The reception desk had the feel of a motel or an airport stop-off. There was a murky fish tank in the seating area where people watched music videos on an overhead screen. The carpets, the same throughout, a pattern of navy blue and beige, were curling away from the skirting boards, and there were passing smells of body odour and detergent. It was not the kind of place he wanted to come home to, but it was close enough to the children and it meant he could avoid his parents' questions.

His room, where he was now, lying flat on his back on the carpet, was at the front of the building on the fourth floor. To get there he had to take a tiny lift up, containing that same dichotomous smell, then walk along a series of corridors, through a door into a stairwell, and up a short flight of stairs on to a secluded landing. He always felt like he was entering a labyrinth, until he went inside and the room opened out to him. It was big and bright by day but sad and sepulchral by night. He had two huge windows looking out over the crystal hills towards the park, where the palace had been (the edge of the gravelled platform where the main transept had stood was just in view). There was a sunken armchair in the corner where he threw his coat and bag on entering, and there were two beds, a queen and a single. He slept on the queen and used the single as a sofa, but at night he imagined it as Ria's bed – a wisp, a thought of her slept there next to him in the dark, when he missed her so much that he could almost hear her breathing. He did not like this absence of himself in his children's nights. It made him feel absent in himself. He wanted to carry Blake downstairs in the morning, to descend into breakfast with him. He wanted to feel Melissa's incidental presence nearby, doing her hair, reading her Hemingway. All of this pathos and loneliness he needed to express to someone. He had tried both beds tonight but neither of them were working, he couldn't sleep, so he had decided to try the floor.

This also was not working, and he had been fighting the urge to call Rachel for over an hour. Would she mind? Was it too late? Might she be lying there likewise unable to sleep, hoping that he might, maybe?

'Sorry. Did I wake you?'

'Yes.'

'Sorry. It's all right, you go back to sleep.'

'What is it? What do you want?'

The hard edge in her voice made him feel bad. He hadn't expected annoyance, only sympathy. He wanted to hang up but it was too late now.

'I can't sleep,' he explained. 'I thought I'd call you, to chat . . .'

'To chat . . .'

'Yeah.'

She sighed. 'I've got work tomorrow.'

It had occurred to him to call Rachel when he'd first checked in, once he'd cleaned his room with bleach and unpacked. He could spend whole nights with her here. He could be with her fully, spread out on the queen. They could be magnificent together before these windows, this wide open sky, but he had decided not to out of loyalty to Melissa. It seemed important, not least for his conscience. So instead he had gone down to the hotel bar and had a whiskey and Coke. It slipped, ice cool and copper, down into the region of his heart, down into his boomerang light. He had followed it by another and then gone out for a walk, away from the high road into the steep streets leading off it, turning corners, coming out into silent crescents and clusters of greenery. It had become a habit, this whiskey and walking in the evenings, right into Fox Hill, left on to Tudor Road, left again on to Cintra Park, along the curve of the pavements, through the pools of the street lights. This evening he had gone into the little park near the hotel and sat down on a bench, faintly inebriated and craving another whiskey. On the next bench there were two pink drunks drinking from cans of Asda beer. They looked at him. Their coats were dirty. There was a thin space. A very thin space.

'You can't just call me in the middle of the night like this,' Rachel said. 'It's not OK, OK?'

And she was right. It wasn't. There are very few people you can call. He had one more drink and fell asleep around four.

*

'Tell me how to make the stew,' Melissa said. She was on the phone to her mother. It was late afternoon in Bell Green.

'I've already told you.'

'I know but tell me again, I forgot.'

She had her pen and paper ready.

'Take the Oxo,' Alice said. 'Pour it in and mix. Then, bitter leaf. At last the chicken.'

'The chicken at the end? When do I put the Maggie in?'

'Any time. Doesn't matter. Make sure you mash the eba properly. Put water.'

'OK.'

It was probably going to be another failure, but she'd had the urge to make eba, yesterday on the high street passing the plantain shop. You could buy three plantains there for a pound. The fat man at the meat counter put them in a blue plastic bag, and then she had added the yam, on a whim, some chicken and some okra, there was gari at home already. It seemed like a comforting thing to do, a way of being somewhere else. She wanted to escape from these dark British streets, their haggard, downtrodden faces, their meanness and menace and the stifling air.

'Is Michael come home yet?' Alice said with concern and determination in her voice.

'No.'

Now the lecture on the imperative of the male presence in the parenting household delivered with traditional Nigerian outrage.

'You cannot manage on your own. You must let 'im come back. What about the children? You know men must live at home with their family. Don't leave him away. If you do that he will start to drink and and and smoke and go to nightclub. That's what they do!'

'Mum —'

'Women cannot do without husband. All that time I stay with your daddy because of you children, I cannot manage alone. I take, take, take. Parent must be together, until the children grown up. Tell Michael to come home this week on Friday. I don't like him to live somewhere else. It worry me.'

'All right, Mum,' Melissa said. 'I'm going now to make the eba.'

'Listen to me!'

'I *am* listening.'

'Put water slowly and mash it properly.'

'OK.'

'Tell Michael to come home,' she repeated.

Every few days he did come, to see the children and put them to bed. Then he went back to the hotel. Sometimes he had dinner with them. He was coming again tonight, and Melissa decided, as she was stirring in the Oxo cube, that he must also have some eba and stew. He had been looking quite thin.

Since yesterday the flowers for Justin had amassed at the entrance to the park, as they would continue to amass in the coming days and weeks. There were balloons and bouquets. There were pictures and candles on the pavement while the traffic went on back and forth past the chicken shop. In the evenings his school friends gathered and sat around weeping. It became a pretty site of early death, and a common site. There were other flowers, for other children who had gone too soon, which were wrapped around the lamp posts, around the railings by the sides of the roads. The flowers would be replenished, most of all by mothers, again and again, becoming less bright, less shiny, until one day even the mothers would let them die, withdrawing and sealing the love, all the memories, finally within themselves.

'Did you hear what happened?' Melissa asked when Michael arrived.

'What?'

'Dad-*dy*, Dad-*dy*, Dad-*dy*!' went the song.

'Hold on, darling. What?'

'Another stabbing.' She said it quietly so that Ria couldn't hear. 'Down next to the library.'

She had seen it, a dimension of it, a component in the project of the death, though she did not know that she had seen it. When Ethan had walked down Paradise in the twilight towards the park with his blade in his pocket and his cap sideways on his head, he had never made it there. Before he had reached the bottom of the road, Melissa had heard a car screech to a stop outside, and she had looked out of the window of the master court where she happened to be changing Blake. Two men got out of the car carrying clubs. They dragged the boy wearing the cap into the car. Then they got back into the car and it sped off again with the devil inside it, and now they were going to really fix him. It had made her shiver. It had made her stomach twist, because it was clear to see right there in the street with her baby on this side of the window and the devil on that side that a boy somehow was going to die tonight and nothing was going to stop it. She had walked away from the window, into the inner recesses of the house.

Michael said, 'No,' his shoulders dropping. 'Another one?'

'Another one.'

He seemed deflated, exhausted. His black coat was loose around his shoulders and he was stooped slightly, a faint bow, a salute to age. A melancholy was creeping into his face and changing its atmosphere, which was frightening, from the outside as well as from the inside.

'You look mashed,' she said as he dragged off his coat.

'Thanks.'

'I didn't mean that horribly.'

'I didn't sleep well last night.'

'Why?'

'Are you staying here tonight, Daddy?' Ria said. She missed him so, especially at night, and in the early morning.

Both these questions he answered without really answering. He stared into the children's faces with a warm and frowning intensity, studying their noses, their chins. Melissa watched them from the kitchen as she was pounding the eba. There was an extreme rightness in his presence, in the four of them together like this under one roof. She had felt it every time he'd come, and a wrongness every time he'd left. All of them were being deprived of something that belonged to them, an aspect of home.

'Do you remember the boy who sang at Ria's school?' she said. He had come into the kitchen. Nina Simone was there in her baritone with her friend Mr Bojangles. 'Justin, his name was. He couldn't sing to save his life, remember? – well, literally.'

'It's him dead?' Michael said.

'Yeah.'

'Jesus. That's fucked up. He was only little bit.'

'I know.'

The eba was lumpy. Melissa carried on mashing it like her mother had said, and added a little water. The stew was simmering on the cooker, along with some okra in a smaller pan next to it to add for gooiness. Michael poured himself a drink, still knowing this kitchen, inhabiting it. Every so often he moved past her and touched her gently, almost subconsciously, in the small of her back. She realised that she missed him doing that, the possibility of him doing it.

'I heard it was a gang initiation, a dare. That's what someone said.'

'Where'd you hear that?'

'Just round the way. Apparently it was a girl who did it.'

'A girl?'

'Fourteen years old.'

Michael tried to digest this information. He had to sit down to do it, on the paprika step, shaking his head. A long, beaten sigh came out of him. 'What is happening in this country, man?'

He often walked past these kids on the high street, standing outside the chicken shops, smoking by the park, looking out at the world and refusing it. He always wanted to say things to them, to tell them how enormous one person's capacity was to achieve, how intrinsic we all are to the mechanisms of this world, and the reason why it didn't work properly was that we lacked the crucial combination of power and hope. He wanted to slap their faces and tell them that the world did not owe them anything, it had only led them to believe that it did by taking away their power, and by expecting some compensation, some consolation for this theft, they were continually forsaking their power. It was unjust, but it was so.

'I love you,' he said.

Melissa paused, her hands raised to her waist. She was separating the eba into chunks, arranging the bowls for the stew. It was a comfort to watch her, to witness her smallest gestures and movements, which in some way seemed to take place inside him, to be connected to him. Despite the frustration and dismay he was feeling, there was a supreme sense of balance in his body as he watched her.

'Love you too,' she said softly, without looking at him.

They carried on talking. She told him about the car and the men with the clubs outside and the boy being dragged away. 'I mean it now. We need to move away from here. It's not just about this house, it's this whole area. It's not safe. I want the kids to live somewhere safe.'

'Yeah, I know,' he said, and he liked that she was saying 'we', as if this 'we' were not contested. 'Move where, though?'

'I'm not sure – Sussex, maybe? Kent? Somewhere near the coast?'

'What, you mean leave London?'

Michael was having images in his head of the children playing on an empty beach in foul weather, with lots of white people in the distance.

'We could . . .'

'I'm not leaving Londinium,' he said adamantly. 'I need to be around brown people.'

At this Melissa felt a familiar tightening sensation in her face, the cold hand squeezing around her mouth. Michael's reliance on brownness was a prison, hers as well as his. It cut him off from other possibilities, from certain unknown skies and distant blue grasses. He did not want to go to France because his race-detector read high levels of fascism. He did not want to go to China, to Australia – too backward, too white. But what about the sunsets there, or the mountains, the canyons, the particular lights, and other beauties? Colour was in his way of all the other colours. It had given him a script for his life, or forced it upon him, and he was compelled to follow it. If the script were taken away, who would he be?

'London is not the only place,' she said, spooning the stew into the four bowls. To each she then added the okra. 'Ria and Blake are more important than what we need. It's about what *they* need. I don't want them to get killed by a stray bullet one day just walking to the shops to buy toothpaste.'

'They won't be, stop exaggerating. You sound like Stephanie. They need brownness too, you know. I'm not only thinking of myself. If everyone started packing their bags every time something like this happened, there'd be none of us left.'

'But they *are* their brownness. It's inside them. It's part of them. God, why are we even talking about this? It's so basic.'

She shoved past him with two of the plates. Blake was crawling across the room away from the TV towards Michael to try and stand up by holding on to his back. It was that same old predicament. He did not understand who she was. He would never understand, because they were different creatures. When Melissa tried to see the world through Michael's eyes she could not see all of it. It was half closed. Yet as she brushed past him again on the step, his wide shoulders taking up most of the doorway, Blake grasping them with his thick infant fingers, she still saw a home for herself, a place that she could inhabit, somewhere to sink into. She was being pulled away from him and towards him at the same time.

He went on, persisting with his point. 'I want my kids to see black folk around them, not just feel their blackness inside.' Those words, blackness, black people, whiteness, they were crude, contagious. The children would be infected by them, dragged also into this prison, this malady, this towering preoccupation, robbed also of a love for canyons, for particular lights. 'The less they see it around them,' he said, 'the less they'll feel it inside.'

'No, the more they'll feel it.'

'Yes, but in a bad way.'

There was a brief silence. Melissa said, 'It wasn't like that for me, though, Michael, the way it was for you. I had other things to worry about when I was a kid.'

They ate, the four of them, at the dining table under the white light. The eba calmed them, it soothed them. Like Alice, they ate it with spoons, dipping it into the stew, adding some chicken with a fork or curtailing the goo of the okra. Blake used his fingers, Melissa helping him. It was good chicken. The taste went right down to the bone. The chicken essence that had once lived in Melissa's neck seemed to Michael now to live more widely, to have caught her hands that made the chicken, that stabbed it, seasoned it and cooked it. Whenever he ate her chicken he still thought of her neck, and the hollows of her collarbones . . .

'The eba's still not right,' she said. 'It's too grainy.'

'I like it,' said Ria, who did not yet understand the nuances of eba consistency. She ate two more helpings, saving a wing for the end, pulling it apart with her hands.

'Do they sell gari in Sussex? Plantain?' Michael joked as they were clearing away. Then Ria called him into the living room and they danced there together the two of them in that way she liked where he held her and they twirled slowly and at the end he bent her backwards over his arm and looked down at her with his eyes full of adoration. Melissa watched them from the kitchen doorway. That very slight limp in her left leg, it was still there.

Afterwards he went upstairs with Blake, beneath the skylight, past the birds of Tanzania, past the indigo dancers on the wall of the master court. He was glad there was no onion or garlic hanging around any more – it was true, it wasn't about the house, it was more than that and he was glad she could see that now. Standing by the window, he was aware of the street below and the darkness of it, thick with vengeance and violence. There was unrest in Bell Green. The skies were rich with sirens. He had a yearning to be back on the other side of the river, the other side of the divide, where he knew the people better, where he understood them more. People in the south were too rash. They would take something further than it should go. There was a sharper edge, a lawlessness in the air.

'Maybe we should cross back over the river,' he said.

She had heard him coming down the stairs, the sound of his weight on the timber, the tumbling as he took speed. She missed, too, that tumbling sound of him.

'It happens across the river as well,' she said. 'It's every-where. This whole city is infected.'

There was a song playing on the system by I Wayne, Living In Love, lamenting the fighting among his people, the bloodshed. It made them think of Justin and the blood on the pavement, and the children north and south who were dying in this war. It seemed an endless war. The weapons were becoming more deadly. The children were getting younger and younger.

'You know what the worst thing is?' Michael said. 'I don't understand my people any more. The things they do, how their minds work to make them do those things. I don't know my community.'

She couldn't help it any more. She could no longer suppress the desire to be in the place inside his arms, that warm country. She remembered something Carol had said on the phone the other night, that if there is someone in this world whom you love, whom you think you can share a life with, it is important to hold on to them, to work to do what it takes to keep it strong and good. She stepped into him, where he was sitting on the bench, stood between his knees and brought his head to rest easily against her, and his arms came up all the way around her. Octopus.

'You know me,' she said.

'Yeah.' He looked up at her. 'I know you. You're my woman.'

She liked the sound of that, the ownership in his voice. It was sensual, the same supreme sensuality that had drawn her to him in the beginning. Maybe love was ownership, she thought as she was kissing him. All the things she had avoided for as long as she could remember: safety, settlement, home, surrender, a step away from the spiky demands of the self into sweetness; a reduction, yes, but an opening. Was there so much shame in belonging to someone? Could it imply not weakness, but sheer strength, the risk of it?

This kiss was like another first kiss. In fact it was an advance on that kiss because of everything that had come since, all the absence and distance of the past few weeks and months.

Desdemona was present, in full effect. So was Angelina. And like before, those thirteen years ago by the sink, he slipped inside the armholes of her dress so that his hands could roam her skin.

'We're Londoners,' he said, as another siren rang out and the night sky flashed blue.

He was aware that he was supposed to go, back out into that blue, back to the hotel. He didn't want to go, but he needed to be forgiven.

'I'm sorry, for everything,' he said.

'Don't say sorry. Stay with me.'

'Are you sure?'

'Yes, I'm sure. I don't want to be by myself. This is no time to be alone.'

So he lifted her and went with her to the rug, her small-ness in his tallness, and they lay down there before the window twins. All he knew was that he needed some part of her in his mouth, in his hands, against him, in every moment. She pulled his work shirt away, pulled him out of the world that detained him. He lost himself in the kingdom of her body and they moved into the safety of one another, until she was swirling in her river and dancing low, and this time when she approached the top of the mountain she did not fall back down just before the summit but went right high over it and fell down the other side, the right side. This time it was not erasure. It was addition, fullness, completion. Now they were travelling, high over Bell Green, high above the towers, away from the city, further and further out towards the ninth cloud of Legend.

'I didn't know we could still be like this,' she said when it was over.

He was still lying on top of her, their arms wrapped around each other. She basked in the weight of him.

'Let's go away somewhere at least. I need to get out of here. I need to get off this island.'

'OK,' he said. 'Where d'you wanna go?'

She was thinking of Jamaica, how much she'd loved it there. She had felt so at home, the warm air, the bright colours, the black country, the lack of inner questioning.

'Somewhere pretty,' she said. 'Completely different from here. Somewhere where there's no English people.'

'I'm with that.'

'And soon.'

Outside at the top of Paradise Row, the light in the living room of Pauline's flat remained switched off. She was inside, listening for the newly historical sound of one person's breath.

NEAR TORREMOLINOS

Not Chile, not Peru. Not Jamaica or Brazil or Madagascar, or even the unspoilt, rugged country along the south-eastern coast of Corfu. Not Sicily, not Tuscany. No orchards or olive groves, or some remote village pleasantly untouched by a tourist footprint. Not even to Morocco, or Tunisia, or some other shore along a different, browner continent that would feel like they had really travelled. They went to the Costa del Sol. Mass-market Spain. A two-hour flight on easyJet. Crawling with Brits. A little place near Torremolinos amidst the bays, dunes, cliffs and estuaries of the wide, flat valley between the two mountain ranges of the Baetic Depression. The shopping centre by the beach featured an Indian restaurant and an Irish pub. There was bingo above the discotheque. Almost everybody spoke English, and the paellas were less than Spanish.

Not a cottage in a long-grassed wild or woodland vicinity. Not a barn with original features and rustic charm, or a cabin by a river, or a lighthouse, or a tower, or some other circular gesture of architecture. This villa was square. The rooms were sharply angular, the roof a flat, square asphalt plane, conducive, albeit, to group yoga, which Melissa initiated in the mornings. The floors were cool speckled tiles devoid of rugs, apart from one, beneath the Moorish coffee table in the lounge, which was stained with circles from the drinks of previous Thomson Holidays package-deal customers. A hard staircase led from the hall into the upper rooms, four bedrooms and two bathrooms; a fifth bedroom with its own en-suite was situated downstairs off the lounge. There were two faux-Roman terracotta pillars flanking the main sofa at a distance, and an arch into the kitchen. Everything else was either square or rectangular and the overriding colour was magnolia, except for passing wisps of colour in the occasional painting, amateur renditions of Baetic landscapes, one signed by a Q. Bertonell, and the ugly brown and yellow curtains behind which a dragonfly was discovered on arrival by Stephanie, who did not express her alarm in order to set a good example to the children. Another major insect was found by Michael, a cockroach, floating dead on its back in the middle of the swimming pool. He fished it out with a net and cast it into the crisp, dry bushes surrounding the garden, hoping that Melissa would think him heroic.

They were here with Damian and Stephanie, their respective children, and also Hazel and Pete, who were still rapt in the first throes of new love and finding it impossible to keep their hands off each other. All the time they were kissing and touching and caressing and sitting on each other and massaging each other's feet and rubbing suncream into each other's backs. Pete was a strapping, six-foot, six-packed, bronze-toned hunk of a man with dark designer stubble across a wide and chiselled jaw, a diamond in one ear, seductive eyes and a slow smile. In his presence most other men paled into aesthetic inadequacy, and he knew this, Hazel knew this, Michael and Damian knew this, but everybody tried their best to ignore it and not be jealous. It had all come about when Hazel, intent on her foursome idea, had suggested to Melissa a week in Spain with their men – she had a friend who worked for Thomson and could get a cheap deal. Melissa was so desperate to get away by then that she'd said OK, but they'd have to bring the kids, which was fine with Hazel, her being permanently broody, but then Michael had invited Damian, partly for moral support, and somehow it had become a sixsome, plus the five children, in one big villa for seven nights in May. They would all get to know each other. They would have rolling, raucous fun, stay up late, get drunk, jump waves, play games. In the middle of the night everyone met at Stansted airport and offered their lives to easyJet. They touched the Depression at dawn and came out into the valley of heat with the sun already high. The parents found taxis and checked the children's seat belts, feeling middle-aged and boring as Hazel and Pete, seasoned from a recent backpacking tour around Central America, decided to take a bus. 'A bus?' Stephanie queried, 'Yes, a bus,' Hazel replied, 'you know, one of those vehicles that takes people to places for a small fee?' And they watched, pretending not to notice, pretending not to be irked by it, as the fresh new lovers wandered away along the line of airport palms with their arms around each other, both in their G-Unit flip-flops, Hazel's hair falling down her back, in the deeper distance she hooked her thumb into the khaki shorts pocket upon Pete's right buttock and just left it there, and they were gone.

Now everyone was in the garden, after yoga, which all the adults had participated in except for Stephanie. Damian in particular had struggled with the balancing postures of the primary series, almost falling over twice in trying to keep his palms pressed together above his head while standing on one leg. Michael, though, was surprisingly supple, Melissa had discovered; he had a hidden Buddha. He was sitting in a white plastic chair next to the white plastic table on the patio, upon which were the remains of a late breakfast, Nutella, the spread of holidays, a chocolated knife lying across the upturned lid, brioche, croissant crumbs and a carton of orange juice, all gently congealing beneath the shade of a dirty Heineken parasol. Melissa was nearby, sunbathing and reading *Tar Baby* on a deckchair while Blake played on the grass beside her, apparently nodding his head to the sound of Justin Timberlake coming from the speakers. On a neighbouring sunbed were

Hazel and Pete in an affectionate straddle. Hazel was wearing an orange bikini and kept laughing as Pete made little taps on her abdomen in a private game, which was getting on people's nerves. Meanwhile everyone else was in the pool, the children splashing through the water doing handstands, jumps, dives, flips and float rides. Balancing cross-legged on a foam island, sun-kissed and sailing across, was Ria, her back perfectly straight, her arms the shape of champion. Since arriving here her limp had disappeared and her hands were no longer dry. Avril was watching her from the edge of the pool, afraid to jump in. Stephanie tried to coax her.

'Come on, sweetie,' she said, her arms raised, thick and untoned by the primary series, which Damian could not help but notice. 'I'll *catch* you, come on!'

'I don't *want* to,' Avril insisted.

'Just *jump*!'

It was important to Stephanie that her children did not entertain fear. Avril had a lot of it, and she didn't quite know what to do about it. She went closer and got hold of her hands.

'Come *on*.'

'*No.*'

Damian said, 'She doesn't have to jump if she doesn't want to.' He was sitting on the edge of the pool with his legs in the water, looking on. 'Let her be, man.'

'Can you stop saying "man" all the time around the kids? I'm always telling you that and you don't seem to take it on board.'

This was said with no attempt at discretion and Damian was embarrassed. He said quietly, 'I shouldn't have to change the way I speak.'

'But you *do*. You *do* have to change.' Stephanie also lowered her voice. 'You're selfish.'

These tiffs were frequent now in the Hope household, and here in the Depression they continued. At Stansted they had fought about how many bags to put in the hold. In the taxi they argued about Jerry's forgotten inhaler ('you said *you* were going to pack it, so I assumed you'd packed it!'). In the kitchen, before the first evening meal, they had argued about the cooking. It was not even about Damian and his father any more. It had gone beyond that, and now they just couldn't seem to get along. The situation was exacerbated by the presence of the others, the canoodling of Hazel and Pete especially, and the apparent harmony of Melissa and Michael, who were less demonstrative in their passion but still linked hands sometimes, still were friendly with each other. Damian had thought it might go the other way, that out in the sun, extracted from their normal routine, he and Stephanie might reconnect. There had, admittedly, at Michael's invitation, been a flicker of excitement within him at the thought of spending more time with Melissa, but that absolutely had nothing to do with his agreeing to come.

Avril did not jump. She went instead to play with Blake, whom she liked. Damian walked over to the patio, sharing a fleeting moment of eye contact with Melissa on the way, and picked at some brioche.

'It's hot, man,' Michael said, one eye open, squinting.

'Yep.'

'You cool?'

'Yeah, I'm cool.'

'Cool.'

'Hi! Hi!' A woman appeared in the garden, entering from the side, raising a skinny, tanned arm and heading for the patio. Under the other arm she was carrying a folder. The Thomson holiday rep, due at noon to offer general tourist advice and check whether everything was OK with the villa.

'Oh, hi,' Hazel jumped up. 'Are you the rep? I was wondering, do you have any other mattresses? My bed is so hard.' (Hazel and Pete were sleeping in the ground-floor bedroom.) 'And do you have a salad-dryer as well?'

'A salad-dryer? Um, I don't think we have a salad-dryer,'

the rep said. Her name was Debbie. She was vaguely wish-
fully blonde, her elbows saggy, her neck wrinkled from the
Andalusian sun. Her accent was possibly Billericay, possibly
Bermondsey, and she belonged to the category of British ex-
patriot who believes that work should be kept to a minimum,
should not cause any undue stress whatsoever. 'Anything you
want you can buy from the supermercado on the main street,
no?' she said, with the Spanish twang at the end. 'But they
don't sell mattresses there. We can't change the mattress.
Those are just, the mattresses.'

Avril thought Debbie was a witch and it made her feel
homesick.

'Have you been down to the beach yet? You've seen the
information pack in the kitchen been left there for you? It tells
you where everything is, no? The supermercado and where you
can change your money an' that.' She mentioned a castle they
could visit and some sightseeing tours on offer in her folder.

'We asked for a cot,' Melissa said, 'but there isn't one. We
had to keep the baby in the bed with us last night.'

'Oh,' Debbie glanced again at her folder, 'It should be
there if you booked it, no? Did you look in the wardrobe?
Sometimes they put it in the wardrobe.' Michael went to
check. 'I'll get one sent over then,' she said when he returned,
and before anyone could ask anything else (the black people
were always so demanding, she found), she went on her way.

'Helpful lady,' said Hazel.

'I can't stand holiday reps,' Melissa said, yearning again for
somewhere more like Jamaica.

'Shame about the mattress. At least the sheets are clean,
though, and a little hardness isn't necessarily a bad thing.'
Hazel gave Pete a sweet, sly look and went and sat back down
on their sunbed.

'I'm just looking forward to firing up that barbecue,' Pete
said, his diamond blinking in his ear, his chin coming to rest
on her shoulder. The barbecue was a rusted, burnt-out cave

submerged in foliage at the edge of the garden. Hazel smiled about him and rubbed his leg.

'You can get my fire going any time, sweet thang.'

After lunch Melissa and Stephanie opted to go to the super-mercado to do a big grocery shop. Stephanie wanted to make sure there would be enough wholesome food for the children to eat amidst all the beer, wine and Haribos that had been requested, and Melissa wanted an open-road drive. They had hired a car for a few days, a green Fiat. They took off out along the sizzling highway while the men stayed at home with the children and Hazel and Pete had an early afternoon 'nap' in their room.

'Oh wow, this is just what I needed,' Stephanie said, her hair flying back in the wind, the sun doing salsa on her eyelids. 'Sometimes you have to just get away, no matter where you are.'

'I know,' Melissa said.

An expanse of ease and spaciousness opened out between them with the unfolding of the landscape. Stephanie was a different atmosphere away from her children. Usually her propriety, her conventionalism, made Melissa feel uneasy, but she was looser on her own, less parental, less alert. She spread out the map on her lap and perused it without commitment.

'Do you ever feel that men and women were not meant to live together or raise children together?' she said. 'That they were meant to live in separate villages, maybe visit each other sometimes?'

'Are we talking about Damian here, by any chance?'

'Oh god. Sometimes I want to kill him. Sometimes I want to cut off his head and throw it in the sea. He just *riles* me these days. I don't know how much longer I can stand it. I'm seriously considering asking him to leave.'

'Is it really that bad?' Melissa was surprised by Stephanie offloading like this. They were not generally so open with each other about their relationships. She wondered if she knew about Michael's recent defection from Paradise. Had Damian told her?

'It's about as bad as it's ever been,' she said. 'We don't see eye-to-eye on anything any more. He doesn't help me. You saw what happened with Avril earlier when I was trying to get her into the pool. Whatever I'm trying to do he comes in and makes it harder, and in front of the kids too. He refuses to form a united front with me. I'm just trying to help her get over this *fear* she has. I don't understand where it's come from. She didn't used to be like this. She used to love the water and now suddenly she's terrified of it.'

'Did something happen to make her scared of water?'

'No. Not that I know of.'

'Ria's scared of toilets. There's something about water that's frightening to them maybe, the way it swells up and overflows . . .'

'Hm, maybe.' Stephanie leaned her head back against the headrest and looked out of the window at the boundless hot blue sky, the hills of ivory sand and the ocean appearing and disappearing as they went. Her mind was full of all the things she wanted to say to Damian but would not be able to remember when she set eyes on him again and resumed the struggle of being in his company. She forgot all about the map-reading.

'Wait, are we supposed to turn off soon?'

'Oh shit! Sorry!'

They ended up in a different supermercado to the one that they'd intended, in the next town. It was full of salmon-coloured Brits in shorts. They cruised the aisles of Mediterranean fruit, the heat-softened apples and the Italian salami. They found a friendly system. Stephanie pushed the trolley and Melissa fetched, sausages, burgers, cereal, Red Stripe, vodka. There was a barbecue planned for the final night. The idea was to save some of the alcohol until then but the likelihood was that they would have to restock – Hazel and Pete drank like fishes.

'I think I agree with you about the village,' Melissa said

when they were driving back. Stephanie had been talking again about Damian, this time in a calmer way, more resigned. She had been interested to hear that Melissa had been going through a similar thing, and impressed that it had led to an actual split, if only temporary.

'Aren't things better now, though, after some time apart? You seem happy. You always do.'

'Please don't say we're chocolate.'

'What?'

'That's what Hazel always calls us.'

'Oh. No, I wasn't going to say that.'

'Things are better, I guess,' Melissa said. 'But they're the same as well. It's the same problems. Life consumes us. We get caught up in it and forget about each other. Sometimes I think we're just fundamentally not enough – he's too much for me and I'm not enough for him, or the other way round, I don't know. It must be that, what you were saying. Relationships and children simply don't belong in the same place.'

'It's because we want to do things our way, how we see fit,' Stephanie said. 'Instead of some big hairy man coming along and messing everything up.' They both laughed, and Damian was so extremely hairy, she added. 'You have to live with these things. You put up with them. What for?'

'But say there *were* these two separate villages,' Melissa said, slowing towards a roundabout, 'isn't it a bit unfair, the kids staying with the women? Why wouldn't they stay with the men? Why should we get dumped with all the work?'

'Because they belong with us. They came from us.'

'You sound like my mum. That's just what you've been taught —'

'No, it's *true.*'

'. . . women *and* men, we've all been given this old script and don't know how to let go of it. It seems indestructible, almost. We're stuck. We're all stuck. We haven't moved forwards at all in some ways. Society makes patriarchs of decent men.'

'Oh, listen to you, Susan Sontag or Germaine Greer or whatever your name is. Are you sure *you're* not the one with the script? See, I've always steered clear of feminism because they're always so het up about everything instead of just getting on with their lives and just *living*, you know? It might have done a lot for women in the long run, but I think an essential thing it's taken away from us, or at least contested in us, is an innocence of instinct. They talk about choice, yet they seem to look down on a woman's choice to prioritise her children, as if she's been forced into it. I'm not oppressed. My children don't oppress me. They free me. It's the man that's the problem.'

Melissa did not see it that way, but she liked the boldness of Stephanie's thinking, this great freedom inside of her. She admired her ability to exist loose from external expectation. She didn't care what anyone thought. She had a pure singularity of purpose and there was contentment and safety in that. She was a solid, straight house. It was not crooked and it would not fall down.

'All I'm saying,' she concluded, 'is that things don't necessarily have to be the way they've been put.'

'OK, Gloria Steinem. And by the way, men have been given their oppressive pre-assigned roles as well, you know. It's not just us.'

'Yes, but it's easier to settle into the dominant position than the inferior one.'

They drove the rest of the way in silence, listening to Spanish radio. It was a warm silence, with waves of understanding and connection going through it.

When they got back to the villa the activity in the garden had shifted from lounging in the sun to doing press-ups and sit-ups on the grass in some kind of testosterone-fuelled strength competition, in which Pete was in the lead and Damian and Michael were clambering somewhere behind. Damian was sweating profusely, the hair on his short legs clinging to his shin bones, for he was not and never really had been a man of exercise. He was only joining in because he felt compelled to compete with Pete, no matter how futile and ludicrous an idea this was. When he saw Stephanie and Melissa entering the garden with the shopping, he exerted himself even harder with his nineteenth press-up, though Michael was less eager to impress, and at the extremity of the press-up collapsed and flopped over on to his back, panting. Spurred by this demonstration of his friend's apparent physical inferiority, Damian soldiered on, right to the fortieth punishing push, by which time the women had disappeared into the kitchen.

Damian had not seen or spoken to Melissa, until that dawn meeting at Stansted, since the night of the snow. He had taken back with him to Dorking otherworldly memories of their white cocoon, their secret hours with Millie Jackson and Susana Baca, their intimate smoking in the garden by the black tree, and that lasting image of her at the bottom of the stairs in the early morning looking so wild and sweet, just out of sleep. For weeks and weeks he had been falling asleep next to Stephanie and thinking of Melissa, not in an obvious way, purer than that, more profound, he wanted to help her find her lost angel. Every day he thought about leaving, to go and live on his own, to find his own lost angel, and once he almost had left, in the middle of a Wednesday night, he had taken a suitcase out of the cupboard under the stairs and started to pack. He had even got as far as writing part of a note to leave on the bedside table for Stephanie, but Avril had woken up and come out of her room and asked him what he was doing, and the sight of her, her creased pyjamas, her sullen face, as if waiting to be hurt, had stopped him. The needfulness of his children, the shattering of their perfect normalcy and his fixture within it. He had put everything back where it belonged and thrown the note away. After that he had continued on as usual, work and back, work and back, the long, imprisoning weekends, falling asleep to thoughts of

Melissa, who now was almost a phantom in his mind, swollen and blindingly bright, with special powers, such as the ability to float and twirl in mid-air.

It was difficult, then, this sudden domestic proximity to her, in the morning, in the evening, in the afternoon, especially in the night, when she lay just across the hall in her stripy vest-and-shorts pyjama set, which he had seen when she was coming out of the bathroom yesterday. It was difficult, also, in the presence of both Michael and Stephanie, neither of whom should sniff or have the faintest inclination of his discomfort. He must assume an amiable, natural ease. She must not appear singled out for him in any way. Whenever he spoke to her he tried his best to achieve the exact right pitch of eye contact, not so little that he seemed evasive (he wanted to hold, after all, to that snowy closeness they had found), yet not so much that it became over-meaningful, which of course it was, to him, which was why eye contact was the trickiest thing. He tried hard to engage with the general jovial banter flying around, the constant gags and one-liners (Pete and Michael had hit it off straight away), and the two, implicit shores of maleness and femaleness that had established themselves almost immediately. The men watching football on TV at siesta, the shopping having been packed away by the women, the afternoon all quiet and still, and the three of them, he, Pete and Michael, staring at the screen as if it were the most important ball in the world, while drinking beer. How he wished to be a breaker of moulds, a different man. Hazel, admittedly, was watching it too, and at one point Melissa came in from her sunbed and stood behind the sofa, her hands leaning on the cushions, his cushion, almost touching his head.

'Ah,' she said after a while, watching the little long-socked men running around in the grass. 'Now I understand why men like football. It's a sexual analogy. It's about trying to score and the obstacles they face along the way. It's actually all about penises.'

Michael was appalled. 'No it's not!' he said. Damian laughed, or rather giggled.

'It is,' she said. 'You're trying to get the ball into the net. The net is the vagina. The ball is, well, the balls. What could be closer to a metaphor for sex than that? I can't believe I haven't realised it before. No wonder men are so into it.'

'And women,' Pete said.

'That's right,' said Hazel.

'I'm not saying it's *only* men who like it, just that they're prone to liking it.'

They all carried on watching, in a slightly different way, except for Michael who was used to this two-dimensional, uninformed downgrading of the game. Hazel said, 'She does have a point, though, when you think about it. In fact most games are about scoring, getting it over the net, getting it into the net, getting it into the hole. Golf, cricket.'

'Now you're being disgusting.'

'Chat 'bout, you started it!'

'Yeah but you always have to take it there, don't you.'

Hazel threw her flip-flop at Melissa's head.

'It's about technique, man,' Michael said. 'There's a strategy. It's mental as much as physical.'

'Innit,' said Pete, leaning forward over his wealthy, gladi-ator knees. 'Tactics, the route they're taking, who they're passing to, how they're passing, wait —' A roar went up in the stands, then sank. There was almost a goal. The pundits chastised the culprit. 'Come on, he's not penetrating enough!' Pete shouted.

'And there you have it,' Melissa said. 'Exactly my point.'

Over at the dining table on the other side of the left pillar, Stephanie was sitting with Summer who was doing home-work. Summer was writing, Stephanie was watching, her hands in her lap, waiting for any need for help, while also encouraging of the determination not to ask for help unless it was necessary. Damian wished she wasn't there. It made him more self-conscious and it became harder for him to join in with the other men. She had hardly spoken to him since their disagreement this morning in the pool.

He preferred it when he and Melissa came across each other in passing, for example when he slipped off on his own to read for a while, as he found himself having to do quite often, the perpetual communalness being too much for him. Just before dinner that evening he was reading Tolstoy on the landing, sitting on the top step – he was at the bit when Pierre and Prince Andrei are having their long talk after Andrei has returned from war – when Melissa came bouncing up the stairs after a swim, humming along to Always On Time by Ja Rule.

'Oh, hi Damian,' she said. 'Reading again, I see.'

'Yeah,' he said shyly. She smelt of the swimming pool, she was wearing her wrapper and a thin white cotton smock that was damp from her costume underneath. There was a pause, a nice, wanting-to-stay-here-chatting kind of pause.

'What is it?' She peered as he displayed the cover. '*War and Peace*. God, I had to read that for my degree. I couldn't finish it. It's just so *long*. Why is it so long? I gave up at around page seven hundred, I think. I just couldn't justify the amount of time I was spending on reading just this one book, d'you know what I mean?'

'Hm, it is long,' he said, 'it's true. But I'm enjoying it. I like Pierre.'

'Is he the fat one?'

'Is he fat? I don't know . . .'

'I think he is. That's one thing about that book I do remember. It gives a very physical sense of people. You really *know* what they look like.'

'And what they feel like too,' Damian said. 'That's why I like it. It gets right inside their hearts, so you know what they're thinking, how they're responding to things, why they do the things they do. Like that scene when Natasha almost elopes with Anatole and she gets sick afterwards because she's so humiliated. I think he does go on too much sometimes, though, in those sermons, well, they're essays really, on war and morality and philosophy and all that. I don't think they had proper editors in those days, that's probably why. If they had, a lot of that stuff would've been edited out. But still, I like the fact that he was bending the rules, playing with form. Who says a novel can't be an essay as well, or a sermon, or a philosophical text, or whatever?'

Melissa was looking down at him patiently. 'Yeah, I agree,' she said, but he sensed that she was losing interest, and he had gone on for too long. 'Speaking of which,' she gave him a light, scolding shove on the shoulder, 'how's yours coming along? You still haven't sent it to me.'

'Um, I've looked at it . . .' He had, and had realised, as he had feared, that it was terrible, that there was no other more rambling, self-pitying, stilted even in its ramblingness, leaden and torturous offloading of male twenty-something angst than this piece of literary shit, and this realisation had led to a newly rekindled depression lasting about five weeks, which had ended roughly six days ago, that is, as much as depressions can actually end.

'And?' she said.

'And . . . well, it needs . . . work.'

'OK. OK, that's *good*. Positive. Remember what we said, Damian, positivity is the way to go. It's our mental landscape that holds us back.'

'Yes, yes.'

'I've been reading Thich Nat Han,' she announced.

'Thich Nat who?'

'He's a Buddhist monk. My sister told me about him. He writes a lot about the importance of meditation and experiencing the present. You should try it, it's really been helping me with my stress and general state of mind. I've started meditating every day, or trying to, trying to stay aware of each moment, and it does make me feel calmer. It really does.'

'Actually,' Damian said, going back to the issue of the bad novel (now that he had opened this can of failure the stench of it was demanding more of her attention), 'I've been thinking of working on something completely new,' (but somehow trying to relate it to Thich Nat Han so that she wouldn't think he was being dismissive or self-obsessed), 'you know, living in the present, letting old things go. I've been thinking I should maybe just bury that novel and write something different, in a different form. Maybe a script or something.'

'Sounds good,' she said, ever bright, reassuring. 'Follow your feeling. Have faith in yourself.' Then Michael came along with Blake. He had fallen asleep in his arms. 'Oh he's not sleeping is he? What about our *evening*? How long's he been asleep?'

'Not long,' Michael said, meaning since just before her swim. He had been having a Red Stripe with Pete under the parasol and they'd been talking about boxing – and how comfy it had been, Blake getting heavier and heavier in his lap, and how cruel it would have been to wake him up then, when the sun was setting so peachly, and the air was so warm and silky, and the beverage was going down so cool and wet.

'Well, you're gonna have to wake him up, aren't you,' Melissa said, in a different tone of voice, and went to take a shower.

The next day they went to the beach, everyone, on foot, an exodus of flip-flops and beach towels and swimming apparatus and suncream, and buckets and spades bought en route from the shopping strip. The cool blue sea at the helm of the bay. The sandy shingle shore smothered largely with frying Brits. The heat was high and mighty. Ladies lay splayed in their deepening colours, sweat seeping saltish into the crevices of their thighs, and men with vast stomachs basked on their backs with their toes pointing upwards, floored by the meeting of beer and sun and breezelessness – for today there was none, only out there on the sea beneath the moving current, where the swimmers sought refuge. Brown heads bobbed among the buoys. The waves had attitude, a secret pulse and a throbbing surge that sent their white frills gently crashing. Stephanie headed straight for them, once her blanket was laid down, once her children were creamed and set to making sandcastles. 'I'm going for a swim,' she said, and charged out there in her flowered tankini, past the bodies, sunbeds and parasols, strode straight on into it. Melissa joined her, and they became two brown heads bobbing with the buoys, very far out, so far that Blake cried, and Michael was reminded of that time in Montego Bay when she had disappeared around the ocean corner and come back laughing, as she did again, this time with Stephanie, that particular look of oceanic elation on their faces, flopping down on to their towels. Weaving among the bodies was a man selling doughnuts, calling, '*Ah rosquillas!*' with his basket of sugared wares. They were warm and jamless, a hole in the middle, and sold well; the children, and Pete with his sweet tooth, slowly followed by the others, all together in the atrium of the heat eating from these soft rings of sweetness, the afternoon burning on, the light making glitter on the ocean.

As usual Hazel and Pete spent much of the time sprawled next to each other with their limbs entangled, their bodies well-oiled from mutual suncreaming, their ears almost touching and their lips continually moist from young and superior Desdemonas. Pete had a serene and blissful look on his face, he gave a long sigh of pleasure, 'Aaah, this is what I'm talking about,' and Michael could not help but feel envious of him. Somewhere in the skies past Stansted and the Baetic, it seemed that Melissa had left her love suspended. Up there in the softness of an inaccessible cloud they were perhaps embracing still, mythologies of themselves, dream figures, still languishing on Legend's number nine, but down here on earth the link had gradually loosened. She had cooled to him, like day to an evening, slipped back, stepped out. She had withdrawn her passion, changed her mind, did not come to him as Hazel went to Pete and lay her cheek in the less sinewy cushion of his shoulder. There was no original Desdemona here in the Depression, only forced, scrawny likenesses, a passing peck this morning on the patio, or a caress in the forgiving wings of dawn. He wanted her to stroke his head the way Hazel did Pete's, to cream his back with that same tenderness, to treat him the way she had when he'd moved back in, clinging to him in the nights, holding his face to her ribcage as if she were going to crush it. Since their reunion he had been trying his best to make things up to her, to be a good, faithful, attentive, non-phone-number-collecting life partner, father and potential husband, and for a while everything had been fine. But reality had slowly crept back in, the children, the hours spent with and without, the strangulating domesticity, and his efforts began to feel more and more draining, even futile. He lay next to her on the towel and felt the mist of the cool droplets of water on her skin from the sea, wanting so much to reach her again, to return to their special place. 'Hey,' he said, touching the damp small of her back, wanting her to remember, to think of it, 'how was the water, mermaid?' She looked down at him, holding back a piece of her smile. 'Amazing,' she said, then turned away and looked out towards the ocean.

She was looking at a woman lying on a blanket further down by the water, wearing a black swimming costume. She was middle-aged, somewhere in her forties, and sitting with her was a man of a similar age and two teenage girls. They all looked alike, the four of them. They all had straight brown hair and rosy lips, and the similarity of gesture that only happens in families. After a while the man and the two girls got up and walked into the sea to swim. The woman lay there and watched them go, the sturdy stride of her man, his thickened, hairy navel, and the two narrow-hipped girls, thin, with jutting teeth. Melissa watched her watching them, and she sensed a feeling of sorrow, a despondency, in the woman's beached body, slumped in the sand, seeing her family from a distance, this enclosure in which she lived. It was a way of watching herself from the outside, in different manifestations, and she would never escape it, this source of her love and this source of her constriction. In this woman Melissa glimpsed a slice of her own future, one of exhaustion and deflation and imprisonment, and it repelled her. She wanted to be at the beginning of something again, rather than in the eventuality of something. Out here in the midst of this jumbled sixsome, it felt as though Michael, she and Michael, were an old, safe place, and however high they went, to whichever number of cloud, they would always arrive back in this same safe and dusty place, where there was nothing left to discover, where the future was dressed in the past.

'Don't you just love it?' Hazel said from the next towel along, to everyone and no one in particular. 'I love this, that we can just do this, you know, come out here like this. We should definitely do it again. Maybe next time we'll have a sproglet of our own, hey sweetness?'

Pete murmured something in reply, opened one eye and closed it again, which Hazel took as adequately positive. She had whispered to Melissa in the bathroom last night, 'Isn't he perfect? I really think he might be the one. I really think he might be.'

And the children were architects. Castles were built. Moats were burrowed and the sea fell in at the visitations of the waves. As the tide came in the castles crumbled, and were taken out. They built more, further in, huddled together with their tools, patting rooftops, making grainy draw-bridges, their skin getting browner in the heat. Dusk fell blue and quiet on the mountains and there were evening birds. Only then did they make their way back, the children finally acquiescing, allowing themselves to be led away from the shore to the square white cool-floored house, to a late meal around the long dining table, the dark Spanish night so close and strange at the windows as they slept.

The following evening the children were put to bed early, as Stephanie wanted to maintain some semblance of order and normality amidst the debauchery of late-night drinking and music, which the girls, sparkled by doughnut sugar and Pete's endless offerings of Haribos, were often privy to at the top of the stairs, eavesdropping. They had heard the conversations about the resurgence of fascism in the West. They had heard the argument about the superiority of Foxy Brown over Lil' Kim. They had heard it when Hazel had announced that she liked having her big toe sucked during lovemaking, and everyone had since been instructed to keep their voices down, there being no door separating the staircase from the lounge. Now it was after eleven, there was a bottle of vodka being worked through on the coffee table, Damian was outside smoking, while the others were splayed across the sofa and armchairs, Michael on his phone, Melissa and Hazel playing a game of blackjack. Stephanie was watching a bad Spanish drama on TV during an interlude from the wine and cards, when there came a sudden rush of activity down the stairs, a flurry of pyjamas and gowns, Summer, then Ria, holding Avril's hand. Avril had a desperate look on her face.

'Mum, there's something wrong with Avril,' Summer said. 'She keeps saying she wants to go home.'

Stephanie stood and looked her over. Avril immediately clutched on to her, squeezing the fabric of her dress. 'What's wrong, darling?' she said.

'*Please* let me go home! Please, Mummy!'

The tone in her voice was shrill and unnerving, like someone being hounded. Stephanie hugged her and stroked her back. 'But we can't go home now, honey, it's too late. We're going back on Saturday. Why do you want to go home all of a sudden?'

'I just *do*.' She burst into tears, just as Damian came in from the garden and asked what was wrong.

'Gosh, you're shivering,' Stephanie said. 'Look, come here, it's all right, it's all right.' She carried on rubbing Avril's back and up and down her arms, crouching in front of her, but this didn't seem to help. Her eyes maintained that wild, petrified look and her breathing quickened.

'What's *wrong* with her?' Stephanie asked Damian, raising her voice.

He went and got hold of Avril's hands. She gazed right through him, breathing frantically. The expression on her face reminded him of the night she'd found him trying to leave. He carried her to the armchair, sat her down and told her, 'Avril, listen now. The plane to take us home is ready on Saturday. Then we can go home. The plane's not ready right now, OK? So we're going to stay here until then and have some more fun, OK?'

'But Mummy, Mummy I can't – I can't *breathe*!'

This sent Stephanie into a frenzy. She grabbed hold of her child and pulled her close. 'Get some water, someone!' she cried, 'Oh my god, what's happening? What's wrong with her? What's wrong with my baby?'

'I think it's a panic attack,' Hazel said, 'I used to get like that sometimes when I was younger.'

Panic attacks, coming from a family where outward expressions of mental extremity were uncommon, were nonexistent in Stephanie's pool of parenting knowledge. She knew what the best hayfever tablets were and how to bazooka a verruca and what to do about chicken pox, but she did not know how to simmer anxious shivering or restore the ability to breathe, and her futility in this scenario she found terrifying. She lashed out at Damian, 'It's because of you. She wasn't like this before. You've made her, we both have, we've —'

'Steph —'

'No, it's *true*, I know about this. They can feel it when

there's tension, it makes them frightened . . . doesn't it? Oh darling, it's all right, it's all right, you're fine, everything will be fine, sssshhhhh come here . . .'

It was clear that Stephanie was not the best person to comfort Avril, but she wouldn't let go of her. Damian went to get a glass of water. He stood uselessly watching as Stephanie stroked her head, rocked her, trying to calm herself down at the same time. Hazel gathered some cushions on the sofa. 'Let her just sit down quietly. She'll be fine. She just has to feel safe. If we all be calm, she'll be calm too. Show her the yoga breathing, Lis.'

And it was easier, Avril found, concentrating on sitting still like this, concentrating on breathing in and out, from the pit of her belly. Eventually she settled down. It was like a crashing wave changing its mind inside her and slowly turning back. Maybe it would not take her all the way out after all. Maybe she would be safe and the castle would not be washed away. She lay her head on the arm of the sofa and felt her mother smoothing her hair, making her sleepy, saying, her voice high and thin, 'Ssssh, sssh, ssshh.'

When she was calm again, her eyes beginning to close, Damian carried her back upstairs. Watching him go, Melissa felt sorry for him, the defeat and sadness in his shoulders, yet that warm paternal strength that endured regardless.

She was still thinking of this when she was lying awake next to Michael in the small hours of that night. She had been falling in and out of sleep. She had had a strange, brief dream, almost just one image, of Damian leaning over her in the darkness, his thick torso, his large hands carrying her in some way, and there was water all around them. There was a sense that the water was very cold but they themselves were warm within it, and that this heat was coming from his body. It was such a rich, immediate image that turning to find Michael's exposed back next to her, expanding and sinking with his breathing, made her disorientated. She heard a noise coming from downstairs, like a chair being moved, and wondered if it was Damian.

When she went down, she found Stephanie sitting at the kitchen table in her dressing-gown, drinking black coffee. She was disappointed. She had imagined talking to him again in this quiet night darkness, just the two of them. She wanted to tell him something, something that no one else would understand.

'Coffee? At this time?'

'It helps me sleep. I'm backwards. Literally.'

'What do you mean?'

Stephanie shook her head, dropping her chin into her hands. She was still upset about Avril. 'I was a mess before. I was ridiculous. I couldn't have handled it more badly, could I?'

'Don't be silly, you were overwhelmed.'

'But I should've known what to do. I didn't know what to do.'

'Stephanie.' Melissa dropped a chamomile teabag into her cup and came and sat down. 'You can't expect to always be the perfect mother, in every situation, in everything that happens. It's not feasible. Take me, for instance, I remember once I didn't even know the right thing to do when Ria had a high temperature. I kept putting more clothes on her, thinking she was cold.'

'Really?' She laughed, with a hint of scorn. There was a passing coolness between them. Stephanie began explaining, in a distant, more vulnerable tone:

'It's all I ever wanted, you know, the children. To look after them, raise them well, to bring them into this terrible world and make them shine in it and make it brighter. When they were babies, I remember there was this feeling of impermanence. It's all new. You're so afraid. You're thinking only of keeping them alive and seeing that they're healthy and growing. Later it's different, though. It gets more complicated, when they're leaning towards their own independent selves and there's less you can do to save them. That frightens me more. I can't always be what they need any more. I can't help them . . . I know, you think I'm a dinosaur, don't you?'

Melissa shrugged. 'That's just who you are.'

'Yes, but it's so frightening.'

'Hm, and there's that question, as well, of what happens afterwards, when they're fully grown, taking up space in the world, when they really don't need you, hardly ever.'

There was something about Stephanie's singular commitment to the work of motherhood that nevertheless troubled Melissa, even as she admired its focus, its confidence. It seemed to point to an inadequacy within herself, a possibility that she was suppressing in herself. A part of her wanted to kill this thing in Stephanie. She wanted to smash her house to pieces, to break it open and force her out of it so that everything entrenched would be thrown into the air and land differently, making new ways of living, new ways of growing. 'What will you be then,' she asked her, 'when all your work of raising is finally done? Will you remember yourself, how to get back to yourself? How much of yourself do you get to keep?'

Stephanie now studied Melissa, the way a grandmother might look at a child, wishing her a greater wisdom, further away in time, an ability to let go of something inside held far too tightly. Yet wondering also at her own self that she had let go, and how far back that was, trying to trace it, knowing it was impossible, unnecessary. 'Who knows about all that?' she said. 'I'll just find something else to be.' She laughed again. 'You do think I'm a dinosaur.'

'Actually, in a way I envy you.'

'Why?'

'Because you're patient with your life. You're not trying to be everything at once.'

'I've got to be someone's wife as well, though.'

Melissa lifted her cup, waited before drinking. This is what she had wanted to tell Damian but the words came out by themselves. As soon as she'd said them she regretted it.

'Michael wants to get married.'

'Oh?' Stephanie smiled. 'Did he ask you?'

'We've been talking about it. He says it's time. He said last night that we've reached the point where we either get married or split.'

'Hm. I understand.'

'So?'

'You're asking me?'

'I'm not sure.'

And Stephanie, in turn, wanted to kill this thing in Melissa, the thing that clung to the opaque, the intangible, to mere possibility. Be a solid person, a whole woman halved. Be firm and tethered and tied to something solid.

'Well, do it,' she said. 'Make the commitment. Accept this for all that it is, warts and all. Then you can just be happy, instead of fighting and questioning all the time. Go on, put him out of his misery.'

For the next two days it rained. It rained almost continually, between bouts of weak sunshine not strong enough to conjure rainbows, a gliding gentle drizzle that made a shushing sound in the air, a susurrus rising up from the ground. The beach was damp and deserted and the buoys were lonely. The pool seemed wetter, colder, though its surface was broken occasionally by the boldest of the children, Ria and Jerry, who could not see how rain could be a determent, it falling all around you as you were submerged, making water complete. On the third day a rainbow did emerge, spectacularly, on the wings of a new blast of sun, and not just one but two, a double arch of multicolour road against the background blue, the sun itself a neat apricot glow, like a great lost earring, risen from the gloom. The children ran outside to receive it. Slowly the heat sucked the water from the grass, the yellowed cotton of the Heineken parasol dried, and the barbecue was dragged out from its sheltering bush, ready for the final Friday-night fiesta.

For this highlight of the holiday they bought stacks of meat, kebab sticks, corn cobs. Potatoes and leaves for other salads. Burger buns and hotdog buns, and drinks, of course more drinks. The supplies had been drained in the rainy nights over long games of blackjack and another game called 'pile of shit'. Michael and Pete had stayed up all night yesterday and slept in until lunch, emerging loose-faced and delicate. More beer, more rum, more whiskey, more chasers. 'How much drink do we *need*?' Stephanie exclaimed. 'Don't worry, it will all find an orifice,' Hazel said, unpacking in the kitchen, finding fridge space and temporary freezer space to get it cold faster. They started drinking early, as drumsticks flamed on the grill, the coals working hard, as streaks of belly pork seeped their salty juices, as fish congealed and warmed in its foil. Towards evening the sun walked away across the grass in a dark-green cloak, leaving it crunchy again. Michael and Pete nursed their hangovers with Red Stripe, Pete at the barbecue, head chef, Michael his sidekick, both of them collusive, boyish, constantly joking. Damian felt left out, forgotten. Was his aptitude for humour inadequate? Was he less of a pal to Michael than he had thought? All the more reason why the sight of Melissa coming down the stairs as he was again slipping away for a slice of Tolstoy seemed an easier and lovely thing. She was wearing a yellow polka-dot dress with a white collar. Her hair was loose, no earrings.

'You look nice,' he said.

'Thanks.'

'That dress suits you.'

'Thanks!'

He couldn't seem to stop the flow of his thoughts to his mouth. Perhaps it was Pete's punch, which he had been sipping since three. It was such a punch that it tasted like strong raspberry squash with a splash of petrol thrown in. Now in its rich, fruity haze, Damian no longer considered his feelings for Melissa as a crush. No, it was more than that.

All the times at the beach he had been trying not to compare her to Stephanie, the springy physicality of her, the pretty feet, the yoga tone, the way she ate a doughnut, as if she were not eating a doughnut, whereas when Stephanie ate a doughnut she looked as if she was eating a doughnut. All week lying across the hall from her had made a new dimension of her in his mind. The sound of the shower water had a Melissa sound. There were Melissa footsteps on the stairs, her shapes were in the shadows, her voice was in the atmosphere, like a softly singing breeze.

'I feel a bit strange,' she said. 'I hardly ever wear dresses. I thought I'd make an effort for our last night.' She touched her naked earlobe, a sea of silver bracelets around the raised wrist. 'Blake's down, thank god, so I can party in peace. The plan is to get them all down as soon as possible so we're free for debauchery. You ready?'

'I'm just going to change my shirt.'

'OK, but if you're planning on reading I don't think Hazel's going to put up with any of that tonight. Tolstoy et al. are not invited.'

She tapped him fondly on the head and swept past him with a hint of body mist, into the clamour of Nirvana, which was playing from Michael's iPod. There was already a small disco taking place by a pillar. Summer was teaching Hazel and Avril (who was happier now, she had come round to the Baetic) a hip hop dance routine, interspersed with them taking it in turns to do moves that the others copied. Chicken bones were scattered on random plates. The grill was still going, the embers mellow. 'I want to stay up all night!' Ria said. 'Can we?' 'You cannot,' Stephanie confirmed. But only close to eleven did the children finally retreat from the upper stair, at last bored with the meandering talk of drunken adults rising up through the villa, their pontifications on ways of disciplining children, their gossiping on uninteresting media personalities and house prices, their earnest critical appraisals and recollections of movies they hadn't seen. Exhausted, they fell into their beds, dreaming of air flight, England-bound, their own beds empty, silent, waiting for them when the plane emerged downwards from the clouds, heading for home.

'Know what I feel like doing?' Hazel said. 'I feel like going for a swim.'

'You? You can't swim,' said Melissa.

'I can just dip. Come with me, go on.'

'No,' she shrugged her off, 'I don't feel like swimming at this moment. I feel like sitting right here in this warm, dry chair and being comfortable.'

'Don't let her swim, she's drunk. She might drown.' Stephanie was also beyond her usual limit. She felt like dancing. Michael Jackson came on and she did, bopping behind the sofa, holding her wine. The two big black and white table lamps on the sideboard were switched on, giving a copper hue. The door to the garden was open beyond the arch. In the bounce of P.Y.T. the conversation moved on to Michael Jackson himself, the fifty-date tour he had coming up.

'He's not gonna do all those shows,' Hazel said, 'no way. He can't even sing any more, I heard. How's he gonna do fifty dates?'

'He might,' said Pete. 'He must need the money.'

Michael said, 'It's a publicity ploy to get him back into the spotlight. It doesn't even matter if he can't sing. People just want to see *him*, because he's *him*.'

Hazel said, topping up her drink, 'Well, I heard he's loco anyway. My friend works for his management. She said she went to his house once and he answered the door with lipstick smeared all over his face.'

'What, Neverland?' said Damian.

'Yeah.'

'Your friend *went* to Neverland?'

'Apparently, yeah.'

'Wow. What was that like?'

'I don't know, I'll ask her if you like.' Hazel said this with an element of sarcasm. She didn't like Damian much. He was too intense and a bit weird.

Meanwhile Michael Jackson shrieked in the speakers. He said 'shamone' and 'woo-hoo'. It was Wanna Be Startin' Somethin', the opening song of *Thriller*. Heads were nodding, shoulders moving. 'Is anyone going? How much are tickets?'

'A one-a, a two-a maybe. Pete's taking me.'

'A friend of mine sorted me out.'

'Lucky cow!'

Stephanie sat down on the sofa arm, at the opposite end to Damian, throwing back her wine. Since the episode with Avril they had been civil with one another, avoiding any more embarrassing confrontations that might upset her again. They were like two acquaintances at a party. 'The poor man,' she said. 'I feel sorry for him. Do you think he did it, molested those children?'

'There's no smoke without fire,' Hazel said, as Jackson sighed and cooed and gasped, as he screeched and whooped and heeheed and audibly skipped. 'Ow!' he went. Melissa said, 'Listen to him, man. There's just no one like him. No one shrieks like that.' She got up to dance. 'I love this song.' She was clapping, making slidey steps with her feet. 'What exactly is he saying here? Is he saying "you're a vegetable"? I've always wondered about that . . .'

Damian watched her secretly, the copper lit pool of her throat and her whirling polka-dot waist. He had put on a good shirt, short sleeves, patterned, hopefully highlighting the work he had been doing this week on his musculature. He got to his feet as well and bent his legs in time with the music, bringing his hips into it. The music was a drug, Jackson dancing with them in his shiny white suit. Shamone! Ow! He was in the room, the lightening of his legs, the moon in his feet and the one white bright hand. It was a unique, cinematic music, a seething energy and electricity, a voice they all knew, from a time they all knew.

'One thing about Michael Jackson, though,' Michael said, 'he always seemed happy with his teeth. It's the one thing he didn't seem to want to change about himself.'

'How do you know he didn't change them?' Hazel shouted over the noise. 'He must have changed them. He's American. All Americans get their teeth done. Especially if they're famous.'

'Why are you talking about him in the past tense?' Damian said, followed by Melissa, drunkenness consuming her, oh this most joyous of drugs, 'It's kind of fitting, in a way. He *is* past tense, of himself, I mean. He's a different person to the one he was born as.'

Stephanie, who was practical about matters of the soul, said, 'We all are, aren't we? We're all different from who we started as. I would hope so anyway.' She believed in maturity, in the concept of the grown-up, not the inner child. But Melissa disagreed.

'Or are we just the same? I always think of myself as fifteen. When I was fifteen I decided I didn't want to get any older than that so I didn't. I think we're static inside. It's deviation from this static state that causes pain and friction . . .'

'Everyone has to grow up some time,' Michael said, which grated on her, as if he were talking specifically about her, which he was.

'Yeah,' said Pete, 'in your teens you get chirpsed, in your twenties you get laid, in your thirties you get married, in your forties you get —'

'Me, I'm never getting married,' Melissa said, 'I don't want to be anyone's wife. What a horrible word that is anyway. Don't you think husband is a so much nicer word than wife?'

'What happens in your forties?' Hazel said. 'Lis, you talk such rubbish sometimes. Ignore her, Michael.' He had shot Melissa a quick, dark look, a wince in the eyes, then it was gone. He swigged on his drink. He'd meant it, about this being the time to do it or split. She could make light of it, but he'd meant it.

'In your forties you get old, innit. Then the whole thing starts all over again —'

'. . . after you get divorced,' Michael finished for Pete.

Thriller, the song itself, came on. Everyone was up this time except for Michael, who didn't feel like dancing now, and Melissa danced with Damian, not quite opposite him. There was a drift of heat as they thrillered around each other. He actually danced well. He danced, in fact, better than Michael did, with her, the good, medium height of him, closer, his chunk of stomach, the hunger in his eyes, those thick hands caught in the beat. She remembered the dream of him above her, so vivid, carrying her like he'd carried Avril up the stairs, and she had a powerful longing to be engulfed by him, to be centred in his unfamiliar warmth. What would it feel like? What would those hands feel like? Hazel and Pete were also dancing together. Stephanie was swaying by the pillar like before, half holding on to it, the ceiling swinging back and forth. They all staggered, two-stepped and stamped. Hazel was laughing her head off trying to do the moves from the Thriller video.

'How d'you know all the moves?' she asked Pete.

'Come on, everyone knows the moves to Thriller.'

Forwards they stamped like the zombies. They became a mess of feet going left and arms going right, like in the video when Michael and the zombies gather into one dance routine. Hazel couldn't take it any more and she flung herself down on to the sofa. Melissa, Damian and Pete kept going, Pete dragging Michael up, he bopped for a while, noncommittal. He had not registered the sparks of terrible yearning charging out at Melissa from Damian's eyes just then, the loss in him, at that moment when the break came in and the pitch increased, of all scruples, all worry of propriety and consequence. The dancing got more and more wild, Pete was goggling his eyes, Melissa was shaking her head in fast motion, Damian was bouncing around her. When the song was over they fell about in their chairs, sweating, apart from Stephanie, who announced that she was going to bed.

'No!' Hazel said. 'No one's allowed to go to bed early!'

'It's not early, it's almost two!'

'Yes, early!'

'To you, maybe, Miss Drink-everyone-under-the-table, but I'm beat. Beat it – get it?'

'Ha ha ha!'

'Anyway, I feel sick. I think I'm going to —' She put her hand on her mouth, and rushed upstairs to the bathroom.

'Some people have no stomach,' Hazel said.

'Oh my god, I'm so drunk,' Melissa moaned.

'*I* know, let's play a game!' Hazel said.

'Doesn't she ever reach that point where you've just, like, had enough?' Michael asked Pete.

'What kind of game?' Pete said.

Hazel had poured herself more vodka. She was sitting with her legs slung over Pete's lap. By now they had a nickname, HP Sauce. She gulped the drink straight, no chaser. 'Let's play that game where everyone tells a bit of a story. Remember, Lis? We used to play it when we bunked off school.'

'Na, I'm rubbish at those kinds of games,' Michael said, his hand resting on Melissa's thigh in a determined gesture of ownership.

'It doesn't matter, let's just try it. I'll start.'

Everyone waited half-heartedly for Hazel to begin. The music was still playing but lower, the night thickset and mild around the villa. There were Cool Original Doritos on the coffee table, unanimously agreed as being a quality crisp.

'OK, here goes,' she said. 'One day, in the forests of Papua New Guinea, a little boy tripped over a rock and hurt his foot. . . . Your turn, Pete.'

'OK,' Pete said, assuming a confident narrative tone. ' "Ouch, that hurt", he exclaimed with aplomb.' (There was sniggering at the use of this word.) 'The boy's name was . . . Johannes, and he didn't have any plasters on him.'

Hazel was laughing and clutching Pete's bicep. 'You next, Damian.'

'Erm, so, to stop the flow of blood, he ripped off a bit of his T-shirt, which pained him because it was his favourite – Ben Ten – and wrapped it around the wound.'

'But alas,' Michael said dramatically, 'the cut was bleeding so much that the but-flimsy piece of fabric was soaked through in seconds, and Johannes realised, just before it fell off – his foot, that is – that it was more damaged than he had at first thought.'

Everyone laughed. 'That wasn't bad, dude,' said Pete. 'That was one of those situations where you smash it because you thought you were gonna be shit so you tried harder, innit.' Now Melissa. She continued, 'Poor, poor Johannes was so upset having only one foot, that he threw himself down on the ground and wept . . . Then he heard a voice.'

' "Hark", the voice said from the foresty air,' this was Hazel, on the tail of a huge yawn. ' "Do not weep, for I am your insect godmother, and I have come to save you." Go on, sweet thang.'

' "You have?" Johannes said. "Wow, that's ace! I thought I was really done for then. After that time in Mendoza, Argentina, when my nose fell off, I didn't think I was going to get any more chances. I thought I was going to have to hop to the nearest hospital holding my foot. Wouldn't *that* have been a drag! So, what do you want me to do?" ' said Pete.

Damian had his turn, then Michael flashed the godmother's wand sending Johannes back to Leytonstone, and Damian giggled as Melissa told of how glad he was to be back in the hood, but the price he'd paid for his freedom was that he had two left feet and limped. Michael's arm was slung lazily over the back of the sofa behind Melissa, she was leaning against him, but she kept gazing out at Damian in such a way, or so he thought, that he felt incapable of going upstairs and leaving the two couples to their own private games of love. She seemed to be speaking to him with her eyes, asking him for something.

'So you know what he did?' Hazel said, yawning again, for she wanted to go into her room now and eat Pete.

'What?' they said.

'Oh, I can't *think* any more . . . OK OK, he went to the nearest barber, with his funny limp, and said he was looking for work. The manager gave him a job cleaning the floors and the customer toilet. Meanwhile, Johannes' parents were really worried.'

'Indeed!' Michael said, 'For they hadn't seen their son in six months, and they didn't believe the police's institutionally racist theory that he must have run away from home, seeing as he'd had an important football match the day after his disappearance.'

'And so —' Melissa began.

'Oh sweetness, come to bed, it's time for gravity.'

'Oh, I see. *Now* you've had enough. You're not allowed to go to bed until the party's over. Your rule.'

'Who said the party's over?' Hazel was standing now holding Pete's hand, her drink in the other. 'Come on, hon, let's chip,' and Pete let himself be dragged up. He followed her, hazy, shiny looks on their faces, staggering as they went. He put his arm around her to steady them both as they bid their goodnights. They looked so rich and young together, as if gravity could not hold them even if it tried, like rustic angels, untouchable by mortal concerns, and Michael remembered that this was what love could do to you. He asked Melissa if she was coming up.

'I might have some chamomile first,' she said. Actually she

wanted a cigarette. She felt like smoking a cigarette with Damian, in the snow cocoon.

'OK, peace.' Michael touched Damian on the fist. He didn't look at Melissa again. Soon she could hear his footsteps in the room above, a silence, a familiar waiting. She didn't want to go.

Outside Damian lit up a Marlboro Light. He would have just this one smoke, he told himself, and then he would go to bed. It wasn't right, what he'd been thinking before when they were dancing. It couldn't happen, not here, not now, not ever.

'Have you got a spare?' she said, coming out to meet him. He felt her before he saw her. The stars were very bright. Pure silver, cyclical. Night clouds moved across them in a soft wind and then they shone out alone, brighter than anything. 'Thanks,' she said, blowing out. She slipped her arm through his and leaned her head on his shoulder. They watched the sky.

'I like you, Damian. You're on my tip.'

He didn't move, didn't speak, just concentrated on getting to the end of his cigarette and remembering what he was supposed to do next. There were two Melissas, he was coming to realise. There was the one who lived in the world, outwardly, who was bold and mocking and a little ruthless, and there was this other one, who was quiet and uncertain, much softer. He liked this one more, though it could not exist without the other. It was the price for the other.

'Can I tell you another secret?' she said.

'What?'

'I don't want to go home.'

'Neither do I.'

'There's something bad at home.'

'I know.' He put his arm around her. It was close, innocent, like last time.

'You always understand,' she said. 'You never try and solve

anything. I can't always explain how I feel or why I feel like that, or what's wrong, just that something's wrong. You're the only one who seems to —' She was looking at the swimming pool, the water, the lines on the surface moving with the breeze. It made her think of the dream: he was holding her body, they were surrounded by coldness but she was warm. How loose and oblivious the water looked. 'I want to be free,' she said in a strange murmur. 'I wish we could just be free. Why do we live this way?'

She was out of herself, and too deep inside herself, but he did understand. He understood completely. He said, 'How long will we go on living our lives as if we were —'

'— balancing on a ribbon,' she finished.

'What? Hey, what did you just say?'

But she was walking towards the pool. It was calling to her, the dark, silent water. She didn't stop, even when he asked her where she was going, what did she mean, how did she know? It felt as if she were inside him, even as she reached the edge, as she slid in in her pretty polka-dot dress, which billowed around her, that they were connected by this ribbon, which was white and silk and strong. She gasped at the cold water against her skin, laughing, and even then she was inside him, her mouth wide open, even as her face went under and came back up.

'Hey, be careful. Don't drown on me.' He was standing at the edge. His voice sounded like it was coming from somewhere else.

'It's *lovely*. It's f-freezing. Come in.'

She beckoned, with both arms, like a child, and held in her spell he sat down on the rim. It took him longer to go in, every inch of the ice was shocking, excruciating, but soon he was submerged. He was swimming, sliding through, trying to get warm, laughing with her, and there was nothing between them any more, nothing to say that it was wrong. They were free. The ribbon was broken.

He came close to her. He tried one last time to hold it back, but the next thing he was kissing her, and she lay back in his arms, afloat, curious. She opened herself to his mouth. Why not go and look for a cousin of Desdemona, some strange and waiting kiss, some sister of her friend or some friend of her sister? She went with him and he engulfed her as she had wanted him to, his thick hands slipped under and followed her skin quickly and with fear. It was a kind of gorgeous dreaming, a fantasy unfolding. They entered the dark possibility, and for a little while it still glittered, the warmth and the revelation of it, but what they ultimately found was that there was less there than they had thought there would be. There in the ice, hungry, fast, he was no kind of freedom, and she was no kind of saviour. His tongue was rough, unknowing, his stubble scratched against her face, and when he was inside her under the water she wanted it to stop but couldn't find a way to tell him, she was embarrassed, it seemed already too late, so she let him carry on, she turned to stone. While it was happening she thought of Simon, that boy from all those years ago when she was young, that there are people who touch, who should not touch, and once they touch, all their talking is ruined. That is how it was.

13

THIS IS IT

Sometimes in the lives of ordinary people, there is a great halt, a revelation, a moment of change. It occurs under low mental skies, never when one is happy. You are walking along on a crumbling road. The tarmac is falling away beneath your feet and you have started to limp, you are wearing rags, a cruel wind is blowing against your face. It feels as though you have been walking for a very long time. You are losing hope. You are losing meaning, and the only thing keeping you going is that stubborn human instinct to proceed. Then, immediately up ahead, you see something, something bright and completely external to your own life. It is so bright that it makes you squint. You see it. You squint. And you stop.

For Damian, this happened on the morning of Thursday 25 June. It happened in the television. A thin man stepped on to the road and centred himself in the middle of it. He had black shoulder-length hair and a pale unnatural face. He was wearing a pair of glittering electric-blue trousers that ended just above the ankle, white socks and black dancing shoes. From his thin, bone-coloured torso hung a jacket of the same glittering blue. He stood there in Damian's path, blindingly bright, blue fabric shimmering, ankle-swingers swinging, one white hand raised almost in beckoning, and Damian stopped walking. He saw him. He squinted. And he stopped.

★

On this morning of 25 June, he woke up late for the third time that week. The house was empty. The children had gone to school, Stephanie had taken them there, and then, he assumed, she had gone somewhere else, somewhere wherever he was not, which was now her way. When Damian was in the living room, Stephanie was in the kitchen. When Damian was in the bedroom, Stephanie was in the garden, sweeping the patio at strange hours, pruning the petunias to unbearable perfection. The garden was looking so good now that Damian felt he hardly had a right to be in it, let alone smoke in it, so he still smoked in the driveway, like a fugitive, late at night, and Stephanie didn't seem to care. She never looked straight at him at the dinner table any more, though since Avril's panic attack she was also extra careful to not let it be obvious to the children that there was a wall between them, resulting in occasional pseudo eye contact, she would look at his eyebrow instead of his iris, or sometimes perhaps his eyelid. She would say something like, Summer, tell Daddy about that experiment you did today. And Summer would tell him, there would be a strained, dull listening in which Damian was trying to appear genuinely fascinated, and when he had finished expressing this fascination with something like, That sounds really interesting, I wish I could have been there too, the conversation would turn back into the livelier, happier avenues they all preferred. Or so it seemed to him. He was an outsider, a ghost at the side of the house in the dark, risking cancer of the lung.

Did she know? he wondered, the first thought that entered his head every morning. There were no longer those initial moments of pure, thought-free consciousness that precede full wakefulness, which surely everyone deserves. No, it came straight away, every day – did she know? Was she waiting for him to confess, and the longer he didn't confess the angrier and more prone to divorce considerations she would become? Or did she not know, and she was angry about something else? Was she just tired of him and considering divorcing him anyway? Divorce. It seemed such a hefty, catastrophic thing for a person to go through. It didn't seem so revolutionary and dynamic any more, only scary, and not for him. And if she didn't know, to continue with this anxiety-fuelling line of questioning, should he tell her? Should he? Or should he let it slide? Would she even care if he did tell her? Was it such a big deal anyway? He didn't know what to do. He was stuck. The road was hard. The tarmac was crumbling. He was limping. He was wearing rags.

Specifically, a pair of old Nike shorts and a dirty white vest. Underneath the covers he was sweating. It was unusually hot outside and had been for days, a feverish, scorching kind of heat that made normal life seem ludicrous, where the only thing to do was to lie down and bathe in it, to drift, to dream hot blue oceanic dreams (of which, incidentally, he was having nothing of the kind. He was having frantic, terrible dreams, last night, for instance, of his head being cut off and then the head turning into Melissa's head). Plus he was having headaches. And he knew, with a quiet shame, that he smelt bad. He needed to shower (yesterday he had not been able to). He needed to get dressed and go to work. But all of this seemed impossible today. He couldn't go to work, because of all the things he had to do beforehand. Every easy thing seemed difficult and every difficult thing indistinct. The only possible thing was to have a cigarette, and it was this, this first matutinal craving, that finally gave him the motivation to fling off the covers and sit upright. For a little while he stared at the wall in front of him, the violet colour that Stephanie had chosen, within it a photograph of a short pier going out into the sea, which was grey, misty and mysterious; someone had just jumped, or someone was about to jump.

The cigarettes were downstairs in the vase cupboard. He wanted to smoke here, upstairs, with the curtains drawn, but he was afraid of Stephanie finding out. She might come back at any moment, or she would smell it, and that would make things even worse – she had always despised the smell of cigarette smoke. Damian was realising now, in this cold ostracism from her love and tenderness, that Stephanie's love and tenderness, and that ability of hers to transmit contentment, were a warmth in his life that he wanted. He had forgotten this. He had shunned her comfort. She had been there for him, when Laurence died, open and giving to him, and he had turned away, and now she was closed and hard-edged and he was a lone thing with nothing to hold on to. In the thick smog of his self-pity, barefoot, greasy and over-stubbled, he dragged himself up and went out on to the landing. The fact of daytime accosted him as he went downstairs, the light streaming in through the stained-glass window, the post lying on the doormat, an accusing symbol of industriousness and full functionality. In the kitchen there was a note from Stephanie: *Gone to work. So should you.* The time on the radio said 10:13. He would have to call in sick again, and he would, just as soon as he'd had his cigarette. When he lit it, standing outside by the back door, he inhaled deep and long the sweet small oblivion. Things were better for a minute. The garden was beautiful. He would find his way back into it. He would play with the children in the grass later. He would mow the lawn, be deserving of them again.

It was over too quickly so he had another, then another. Cancer would come, he knew. It would come on a Tuesday, because Tuesday was a cancerous kind of day. With the tar thick in his throat he came in from the sun, realising that he was hungry, he wanted toast, some coffee. He filled the kettle, put two slices of bread in the toaster and wandered into the living room, where he sat down on the blue calico sofa and switched on the TV. That was when it happened. There it was. The road. The thin man shimmering. A white hand, a turn in the leg. Music.

Michael Jackson was on every Freeview channel. He was the news, the music, the drama and the ads. He was turning on an axis in his fast and shiny shoes. He was dancing along a street at dusk after a girl in a tight dress, slinking down the Smooth Criminal stairs in a white tuxedo. A thousand pelvic thrusts. Flying sparks of skittering white socks. Idiosyncratic wavings of famous sad white glove. And then, not so mobile. Now the flashlights, the blue incandescence of sirens. A stretcher in a courtyard with a thinness on top of it too slim to be a grown man but which was Michael. The head was covered. The stretcher was going into the back of the ambulance. There were pills, bad pills, and a bad doctor, and he was dead.

Damian watched, stunned and shaken, as the songs played one after another, video after video, already history. The rolling skies of What About Us. The opening of the creaky door into Thriller, all the darkness of that song – his favourite bit, the heavy breathing to the beat of the music when Michael has just turned into the footloose zombie and the choreography begins. Michael Jackson understood the nature of evil, its presence all around. He understood that in being required to live side by side with it, we must learn to wear its cloak, to recognise it within ourselves. He knew that he had a demon inside of him and he knew that it was the stirring, delicious energy gathering within him when he sang and when he danced. The music was what named him. It was bigger than him. And now the music was finally stepping out from behind the terrible ridiculing shade of its creator. It was pure, loud, enrapturing, forlornly celebrating. Neverland was crowded with criers. The air was without Michael. He was ascending upwards, moonbound for his last act, the hypnotising feet, a jazzful ballerina. And it was only now, finally, with all of this exploding before him, that Damian fully understood and recognised what it meant that his father was dead. It struck him with a new nakedness, a jolt in the gut. He was dead. He was memories and dust. He would never see him again. He felt the true clarity of this absence, the permanence of it, and tears came rolling down his face.

For two hours he sat there, watching, the need for toast obliterated, all thoughts of work forgotten. He watched, snivelling, the talking about Michael, the dancing feet of Michael, his memories flooding back, these songs that had played through the dark rooms and tenement hallways of his childhood. Aside from the books, music was the second education his father had put to him. They had listened together, and danced for a time in the days of Joyce. They had watched together the gradual disturbing change, how he had moved further and further away from himself, trying to draw for himself a new face, if he could only finish getting rid of the old one. The more Damian watched, the more it seemed that it was Laurence's face staring out at him from the screen. He thought of him walking along Railton Road in his rumpled clothes, lying in the hospice on that final night, with that bruised, disappointed expression in his eyes. While remembering these things, an idea came to him. It was such a strong, clear, complete idea that when it struck him he felt a flash of joy. It was an idea that must be dealt with immediately, before it ran away. He knew exactly what he had to do, exactly where to begin. He stood up. Rather, he rose.

First of all, he went to the cupboard where his old manuscript was kept, found it and threw it in the outside bin. He did not read it, not a word of it. He must not look at anything else, not a single word or piece of paper that might distract him. He must do only one thing – actually, a series of things. He went back upstairs, took off his shorts and dug out the old peddle-pushers he used to wear when he was writing in his bedsit in Kennington. They were too tight, especially around the belly, but they were still the right length, just below the knee. Next, he threw the vest he was wearing into the washing basket – things to tend to later, along with brushing his teeth and having that shower – and replaced it with a red T-shirt. On his feet he put nothing. No socks. He remained barefoot as he went to collect from the bathroom the basin that Stephanie used for her home pedicures on Fridays. This he filled with cold water, the colder the better.

Carrying the basin carefully in both hands, he went downstairs and placed it on the floor underneath the desk in the dining room. He switched on the laptop and opened a Word document, then he sat down and put his feet into the water. It was just how he liked it, his calves were bare, his feet were cold. Finally settled, ready, he stared at the screen for a moment before bringing his hands to the keyboard. Just as he began to type, he remembered about calling in sick.

Mercy answered the phone. There were wet patches on the floor around his feet.

'What happened to you?' she said, eating a marshmallow.

'There's been a death.'

★

In the lost city to the north, Michael was surround sound. He was the hot high-street air and the common song blasting from car windows. Beat It whipped by and then Thriller. Liberian Girl sailed down Westwood Hill with The Way You Make Me Feel on its tail. The music was the crying bright June, slipping through the leaves of the birches, soaring up to join the white smoke trails of passing aeroplanes. It was gloriously free now, this music, no longer shrouded by its maker. Now that he was over, the songs were as pure as their first days, every beat was fine, the melodies pristine, the people were hearing them for a new first time and oh, such wide, sweet lamentation! There was a sense of moonwalking. There was a desire to walk backwards. In Paradise, out of respect and admiration for him, Ria put on her one white glove and watched the songs on TV, transfixed.

Almost as soon as they had returned home from the Baetic, on stepping over the thirteenth threshold, Ria's limp had returned. The same left leg. The same crooked gait. There was an ache in the left ankle which turned into a pain, and when the pain subsided it did so only as far as the ache, and so she limped, up the stairs, along the landing, down the stairs. 'Why are you walking like that?' Melissa asked her. 'It hurts,' she said. And not only that, but her hands became dry again, and pale. There was a white, powdered look to their surface. She had to use shea butter four or five times a day.

As for the house itself, something had happened in Paradise during their time away. It had deteriorated. Either it had happened quickly, over those seven days, or it had been happening already, and now, on returning, it was more visible. It was no longer white, the slim stone façade, but a slight and murky grey. The front gate was rusty and loose on its hinges and the sills of the window twins were cracked, big star-fish weeds pullulating in the seams of the concrete underneath. Inside, the hallway was narrower than before, the floors and doorframes more crooked than before, and the dust was like a snow all across the surfaces, building in its occupation. Giant dustballs had gathered in corners. The white film had thick-ened on Melissa's shoes between the two wardrobes of the master court, where the accumulation was greatest, along the headboard, for example, the picture rails, the bedside tables. Downstairs in the kitchen a gash had appeared in the wall above the dustbin, releasing a sawdust when pressed, another kind of dust, which came spilling out on to the paprika. And strangest of all, there was a black wavy line going up the stairway, just above the dado rail, which Melissa was sure had not been there before.

'Did you do this?' she asked Ria.

'No. Maybe it was Blake.'

'He wouldn't be able to reach.'

Ria shrugged and went into her room.

Another thing that had happened during their absence was that Mrs Jackson had gone. She had been taken away, to a home, a neighbour said. Michael no longer had to rescue her in the street on his return from the office, after the journey back on the 176, as usual wearing a suit, now one of four. The suit was becoming a part of his shape. Even in this heat he wore them, the jacket flapping open and his slim hands hanging out from the cuffs. The khakis were no longer underneath. They were being worn away by the rat race and the panelled ceilings and the dead serenade of the photocopier, which was partly why he looked thinner. And partly it was that he was thinner, and the bounce in his walk was lesser, as he took the road to Cobb's Corner in the mornings with his sanitising hand gel, which he was using more and more often. He had not mentioned the idea of marriage again to Melissa. He was trying to find a way to leave, but like Damian he couldn't do it. He kept waiting for things to change his mind, which the children did, every day, but not Melissa, though the children were almost enough. This is what happens to a man who was made for a great love and not a suit when he does not feel the love. He closes in. He becomes weary. On the bus he looked out of the top-deck windows and saw less of life and felt less sturdy, less sexy, less rich. He was beginning to forget his magnificence. A darkness was coming down over his face like the pulling of a shade.

Since Spain, Melissa had been attempting to banish from her mind all thoughts of Damian. She was ashamed. She was paranoid that someone had heard or seen them in the pool, one of the children perhaps. After the event, she had slept on the sofa in the villa, the room buzzing and spinning from the alcohol, and the next day she had found it hard to look anyone in the eye, especially Michael. She felt that she should tell him what had happened, yet she knew he wouldn't understand, he would take it at face value, so now it was another thing between them, which made being back in Paradise difficult, the narrowness, the sleeping side by side, the daily routine. As much as she tried to force herself to carry on as normal, the chaos and disarray in her head was overwhelming. It was everywhere, in the walls, the furniture, the light switches, the sloping floors. You have made the ground beneath me uneven, she said to Damian in her mind. You have made poltergeist of everything that was still.

The week after Michael Jackson died, she had a meeting in Waterloo with the *Open* editor, Jean Fletcher. They had dim sum, sitting on glossy black benches using black chopsticks. Jean was a dark, heavy woman with surprisingly bad dress sense for someone who ran a fashion magazine. She always wore primary colours, different combinations of them, and for this reason had been nicknamed by her colleagues 'the primary coloured woman'. Today she was wearing a red pleated skirt, a nursery-blue sleeveless blouse, enormous yellow earrings and yellow sandals. Her weave was damp from the heat, wisps of it clinging to her temples.

'So how is everything with you? Your new life, your beautiful baby, your wonderful man.' She perused the menu. She ordered a heap of dumplings, the chicken ones, the beef ones. 'I'm terrible,' she said when the rude waiter had gone away, 'I start off the day with such good intentions but by lunchtime I can't remember what they were.'

It had taken a long time for Melissa to decide what to wear that morning. She couldn't get out of the bedroom. She kept checking in the mirror, changing her shoes, which now were hurting, and misjudged, she felt, along with the flowered top-dress (too hippy) and the neck scarf. She wasn't out in the fashion world enough any more, in the world itself, for that matter, which was why she was here.

'I've been thinking about coming back,' she said, 'being on staff again. I miss the office.'

'Really?' Jean was amazed. '*You* miss the office? Are you sure, Melissa? You don't miss the office. All that politics and bitchiness. You've just forgotten it. You couldn't wait to get away from us, remember? You said you felt like you were dissolving in vacuity. Those were your exact words.' She stuffed a whole dim sum in her mouth and munched on it. Jean ate in public places with a sheer lack of inhibition – she drank from ramen bowls, breakfast meeting bowls, all kinds of bowls.

'It wasn't that bad,' Melissa said, although it was coming back to her now. She *had* been desperate to get out of there. It *had* become unbearable, soul destroying and demoralising, compiling lists of party dresses, the cocky photographers, the undernourished models, that basement office full of other women, only one man, the art director. She used to run into Bruce Wiley sometimes at shoots and once she had even cried on his shoulder about how unhappy she was (after which he had tried to sleep with her, but she didn't hold it against him).

Jean said, 'Anyway, my lovely, we're stripped down to the bare basics now with this recession. It's terrible. We've had to make redundancies. Malcolm's doing all the accounts himself. We've merged the fashion, lifestyle and culture together to reduce overheads, and a lot of our freelancers,' she reached over and put her hand on Melissa's, 'I'm sorry, we're having to let some people go, I'm afraid. We've got to do it all in-house . . .'

There was a dawning, eating pause, during which Melissa was determined to appear unflapped. She looked down at the platter, the pale dumplings like warm dead brains, their stuffed inner selves bulging against the skin. They looked revolting.

'I fought for you, I really did,' Jean was saying. 'You're one of the best columnists we've got . . . but Malcolm's doing the sums. We just can't afford you any more. We can't afford anyone except for ourselves.' She squeezed her hand again, leaving a shred of ginger on Melissa's knuckle.

'I remember that feeling, though,' she said after paying the bill (her treat, a leaving present), 'of wanting to get out. I felt like that when mine were very young. It's like going underground . . .'

There was only a month's notice and of course no severance pay. On the tube home people were sitting there in their suits and skirts and outfits, and she remembered being one of them, a swish hem, a ruffle here, some nice boots, a purposeful leather bag on her shoulder. She felt ridiculous and small in her hippy flowers, badly assembled. She leaned against the glass that separated the seats from the standing area, looking down at the carriage floor, and missed her stop, ending up in Crystal Palace. While she was there she wandered into the park, around the ruins and among the incorrect dinosaurs, climbed the steps up to the stretch of gravel where the palace had stood before it had burnt down. Not far from the base of the transmitting tower, she found a headless woman in the grasses, a broken statue from the days of glory. Melissa felt connected to the statue. She empathised with it. She and the statue sat together in the sun for half an hour, and then she went to get the children and take them back to Paradise. As she went inside, she became the woman who lived inside, and left the woman who had lived outside outside, because the doorway was too narrow for her to get in, and the hallway too narrow for her to walk along.

★

After the days of glory, when the people had come from miles and miles and across oceans to see the colossi of Abu Simbel and the tomb of Beni Hassan, the Egyptian mummies, the hemp, the Welsh gold and the rhubarb champagne, the Crystal Palace embarked on its long and steady decline. Joseph Paxton, the father of the palace, was dead. His gardens and fountains no longer sprang with the bright silvers of flora and water. The shine no longer dazzled from the so many acres of glass in the ferro-vitreous roof, for it was dirty. And Leona Dare no longer made shapes in the air above that roof with her famous elastic limbs. A year after Paxton's death, there had been a fire in the north transept, leaving interminable ash. The sculptures in the Grecian Court were crumbling. The frescos in the Italian Court were fading. At the top of the staircase leading to the entrance at the central transept, a Sphinx had lost its nose.

In order to get rid of the dust, Melissa cleaned and hoovered every day, because she still believed that the dust had something to do with Ria's hands. She attacked the swirling microscopic freedom around the TV. She clattered up the stairs with Mr Miele, which she thought of now as a cantankerous old man a little bit like her father. She went to visit her father, and she hoovered his house too, the armies of crumbs beneath the kitchen lino, the ash around the armchair. Cornelius smoked as she did so, insisting that he could do his own hoovering even though he couldn't and had trouble recalling the actual word 'Hoover'. The old house was like a shroud around her, full of bad memories and smothered resentments. 'You didn't prepare me,' she said quietly to her father in the living room, but he didn't understand what she meant. He offered the children Eccles cakes and Ribena. Then they went to Alice's flat in Kilburn and had eba. Ria didn't want any eba. She had gone off it.

'What's wrong with her leg?' Alice said.

'I don't know,' Melissa said. 'I think it's the house.'

'Did you put the onion and garlic, the pepper?'

'Yes, I tried it.'

'Take her to the doctor. And make her lie down in very hot water, with salt.'

Sometimes night things could get inside people, Alice said, and if this happened you absolutely had to use the plantain under the pillow. It was the only thing that worked. That was what Alice herself had done when Melissa used to sleepwalk as a child. She had made Cornelius drive to Harlesden to get the plantain.

'One day you get a better house than that,' she said. 'Bathroom supposed to be upstairs.'

In the car on the way home, Ria told Melissa about a dream she'd had about the palace: she'd gone to the woods, and while she was walking another girl joined her and they went through the tunnel and into the maze, had a boat ride on the lake. 'It was so funny,' she said. 'In the maze we couldn't find each other, then we bumped into each other and she disappeared.'

'That's a weird dream,' Melissa said.

The doctor told them the limp would go with time – if indeed there was a limp. In the surgery Ria was walking fine. When they got home the limp came back again.

'Are you doing this on purpose?' Melissa said to her in the hallway.

'What?' Ria said, and just as she did so, Melissa noticed another black wavy line on the wall going up the stairs, on the other side this time. She stared at it. 'I didn't do it,' Ria said, beginning to cry. 'Stop it, Mummy, you're making my heart seep.'

Garlic was reinstated by the front door, some onion on the bedroom windowsills. Vicks was introduced as well, a film of it on the same windowsills and on the banister post under the skylight, with the cayenne pepper sprinkled on top. At the end of July a card came through the letterbox addressed to Lily (there was no surname). A card of the same square shape had come this time last year, also for Lily, when Blake was just born. Melissa opened it. It was a birthday card, from a grand-mother who still did not know that Lily no longer lived here.

She didn't mention the card to Michael, she put it away in a book, but she pointed out the wavy lines, insisting he take them seriously. 'I told you. Somebody is drawing on the wall.' Michael looked at it, still wearing his suit, sweating, dying for a slow red wine. The hall smelt of garlic and he wanted to throw it in her face. Every time he removed onion halves from the windowsills she put them back while he was at work. Now he tried to muster some convincing receptivity towards the far-fetched and, yes, crazy belief in the mounting supernatural happenings occurring in their yard. 'I'm tired,' he said.

'So?' she said, not hearing him. 'Ria keeps saying it's not her.'

'So it must be Blake.'

'But he can't *reach*. He's one!'

'Well, who is it then? You? Are you sure you're not doodling the place up when you should be working?'

This was meant as a joke, but it didn't land well because work was a very sore issue with Melissa at present, with the final *Open* column filed and a job rejection from *Vogue*, a job she hadn't really wanted anyway but rejection was rejection. Plus school was out. The country had entered the mass endless meandering of millions of small people over six maddening weeks, where the weeks got longer as they went by, and the days went slower inside the weeks, and September seemed a far mirage of mercy on the cruel and distant horizon. School was a box in which a child could be contained with worthy educating and in-house entertainment. The summer holidays were a swamp in which the dreams, lives, personalities and everyday equilibrium of their carers were submerged and often swallowed.

'Yes, I'm sure,' she replied, without a hint of a laugh or smile, while inside she was thinking, *I know who it is*, but she didn't say this out loud because he would look at her again in that erasing way and then she would disappear even more.

'Maybe it's time to call Ghostbusters,' he said.

The Melissa who lived inside the house and not outside was further unimpressed. 'Why do you have to make a joke of everything all the time? Can't you take anything seriously? You're like a kid. You know what I think? I think it's us that's the problem. We're the ghost. We haunt each other. We don't work any more. I had a dream last night that we were in a boat and I was standing at the helm, rowing across the Thames. I was mad. I was wearing this old grey sack-dress thing and cackling like a witch, and you were lying down in the bottom of the boat, dead, completely dead. It was horrible. Is that what we're doing to each other? You're dying and I'm going mad?'

'Look, I've had enough of this,' Michael said. 'I've tried

and tried to make you happy and nothing ever seems to work. I give up. You're impenetrable. Pete was right. He said to me in Spain that no woman is for ever, it doesn't last, and I really think he's right.'

'Has he told Hazel that?'

'How would I know?'

'Well, he should,' Melissa said. 'She wants to marry him. He should do her the courtesy of letting her know he's not marriage material.'

'Oh what, like you let me know? That thing you said about not wanting to be someone's wife? Or don't you remember?'

'I was drunk,' she said, looking away. 'I don't know half the things I said that night.'

'You said that wife was a horrible word and you were never getting married. How do you think that makes me feel when you say something like that? Don't you think it might affect me even just a tiny bit? Sometimes I think you don't have any feelings, period. Not just for me, but for anyone. Maybe it's true, that dream you had. Maybe that is what's happening to us.'

Melissa had turned from him and was looking again at the black line on the wall. Last week in Japan she had been in the detergent aisle with Blake and he was crying because he wanted to get out of the pram and she wouldn't let him and she'd wanted to scream. Something had smashed on to the floor at the other end of the aisle, some lightbulbs, all by themselves, as if enacting the scream.

'Nothing is inanimate,' she said absently. 'Everything is alive.'

'Really? That's good to know,' said Michael, 'because I sure don't feel alive.'

Desperate for his wine, he sloped to the kitchen and unscrewed the lid of the bottle. All through this dark and feverish summer he drank like this, before he had even taken off his jacket, a full stop at the end of the working day, an aperitif to sometimish dinner. How deliriously and utterly he wanted to make love to her, to rise above all this friction and get back to what was important. But night after night they slept like soldiers in the red room, estranged. Morning was a cold white hand that lifted them by their clothes and dragged them up, both of them covered in dust. The mildew in the wardrobes was thickening. The dancers on the wall were dwindling. The joists beneath the floorboards were rusting.

One morning Michael tried to bridge the hostilities. He got hold of her when she was coming out of the shower. She was all wet and brown and shiny, and her thigh was so thick, he couldn't help it. His love for her was still deep and wide, it shattered him, it was destroying him, and while he knew that this was so he wanted it to carry on until the last drop was poured out of him, even though he knew that there was no last drop, no end, no way out. He slipped his arms around her and became the darker brown against her caramel. But only limply she held him back. She patted the backs of his shoulders, friendly, distant, and did not appear to experience any particular excitement or even registration of the weight of his forlorn warm sex against her leg. After an awful, empty moment, she extracted herself from him and dried herself with her towel. She was not there, the girl of the ocean. She did not put on her bracelets any more, her rings. She was nowhere in sight. The mummies in the Egyptian Court were vanishing. The statues in the Roman Court were withering. The flowers at the entrance to the Assyrian Court were dying. The arches of the Medieval Court were splintering.

And Thich Nat Han could not help with any of this. He said be present in each moment, notice the flowers and the little animals. Feel the calming surety of your breath, going in, and out, going in, and out. It was too basic. In fact it was infuriating, and during a lunchtime meditation session she threw the book across the room, hitting the picture of the twilight dancers which then fell down, violently, with more force than seemed warranted. When she put the picture back on the wall it was crooked. Every time she tried to straighten it, it gradually slipped down on one side again. The dancers looked so closed in in their indigo, as if they also were trapped, in their movement. Their arms were stiff and oddly shaped. Their feet were too small. After a while Melissa no longer tried to straighten their world. She accepted that the thing that lived in the house wanted everything to be crooked. Most of all Ria.

She limped. One white glove on the Michael Jackson hand and the other hand dry-white. Sometimes she whispered to herself. She got clumsy. At Little Scamps one day she fell over and hurt her wrist. In the park, in the playing fields, the swimming pool, all the places they went that summer to survive the swamp, she had that same crooked walk, and it always got worse the minute they stepped into Paradise, where the woman who lived in the house was waiting in the hallway mirror to take Melissa when she looked into it. She had harder eyes and a thinner mouth. She felt much tighter inside, joy was another country, her smile was a jetsetter. Frantically, Melissa searched for ways to get back into her body. She went swimming and looked at the weather through the slats in the intermittent ceiling, floating on her back, and came out still floating but the ground came back too soon. She went walking by herself in the evenings without telling Michael where she was going. He would picture her, a flash of denim, glinting through the city, her tasselled boots, the way she walked, with a shy power. She went to the Tate and looked at *In the Waves* again to see if she could get back that way. Another day she went to a yoga class at the lido in Brixton, where evening fell as they were breathing, and the teacher with his crossed legs spoke softly, almost inaudibly, about the way to peace. There it was, in the darkness of her, ever still, not destroyed, only disturbed by passing tremors. When the class was over she walked with this peace out into the park. She saw the grass spread across the hills and the few shy stars in the smoke of the vista. Tenements glittered. Brixton was night-blue. She skipped down the steps to the street, happy to be with herself again, but when she entered the house it was like entering a cave. It seemed that everywhere she went there was a cave, the same one, with different entrances.

On a Sunday evening after a visit from his parents (he looked tired, they'd said), Michael was sitting on a chair before the window twins shaving his hair. Out of habit, he waited for Melissa to finish it for him, according to the custom, to glide up with the blade from his neck to his crown, neatening the edges, rubbing at the stubborn patches. She stood very close to him to do it, her arms up over him, but this time he did not stroke lightly down the backs of her legs as she stood there. She was tense, silent. He was still, slouched. She rode with the clippers over his scalp and made tracks. Brown paths through black fields. The shape of his skull. He closed his eyes. She went harder over the stubborn hairs that clung to him, and as she did so she felt more and more taken, that she was another creature. He could feel it too. 'Careful,' he said.

'Sorry,' she said. *Do it harder,* said a voice inside. It was low-pitched and cruel. It was the other side of sadness, the voice of the dark. So she did it harder, and the voice went on to claim her body, and then the hand twisted and she cut him, behind the ear, drawing blood.

'Fuck! Be careful!' He slapped his hand over his ear.

'Sorry. These clippers are blunt,' she said. The floorboards upstairs creaked. Some sawdust slipped silently from the gash in the kitchen wall.

In August Blake got sick too. Red patches on his cheeks. Temperature ascending. The doctor said keep him in. But in the house the sicknesses were contagious. Melissa, the other Melissa, also tripped over, became clumsy like Ria, bumped into things, or things fell on top of her, the lid of the Dutch pot on her foot, the photograph of her, Michael and the children on her head when she was dusting. All by themselves these things seemed to fall, like the dust, a raining of certainties, of fixtures. One morning she woke up and there was a small dent in her forehead, which darkened and became a scar. She did not know how it got there. It had no mother. The only explanation was that it was the real Melissa trying to get back into her body during the night when the doorways were more flexible, and there had been a struggle.

The night after that she couldn't sleep. She was worried about being dented again. Michael's slumped form was turned towards the raffia. She had heard the twist of his bottle top earlier, the groan of the floorboards as he came to bed smelling of Listerine and the ghost of his drink. The floorboards were so loud now that they were like a demon presence, they were senile. She got out of bed and tried not to make a noise as she went out of the room. There was another wavy black line above the dado rail, this time stretching from the top of the stairs to Ria's room. When she touched it with her finger it smudged. And when she pushed open the door to the second room and looked inside, she saw Blake there, lying as usual on his front, his face to the wall, but Ria's bed by the window was empty, and the window was open.

She went down the stairs, past the wavy black lines. The window twins were silent and still in their frames, not moving, not open. The ecclesiastical arch was still attached to the ceiling and the paprika floor was low and being obedient to its gravity. She had expected a chaos of structure, a hump of a hurt child in the back of the courtyard, underneath the open window, but she was not there. She found her in the bathroom, whispering. She was washing her hands. She was wearing her dressing-gown – yellow, the same colour as Lily's.

'What are you doing?' the other Melissa said.

'Oh, hi Mummy. I went to the toilet.'

It did not sound quite like Ria's voice. It was deeper. 'I

know you did this,' she said when they reached the top of the stairs, Ria limping, one step, one slower step, one step, one slower step. She was afraid to hold her powdery hand to help her. 'It's fresh, look. You did it just now.'

'I didn't, I didn't, Mummy!' the little girl said.

She let her go to sleep in Ria's bed but she didn't kiss her goodnight. Before she left the room she found the box of crayons and felt tips and took it away with her and put it under her own bed. In the morning she was going to make her lie down in hot salt water, like Alice had said, and she was going to go to the high road and buy plantain to put under her pillow. But in the morning Ria did not get up. She slept through Michael's kiss on leaving for work. She slept through Blake's coughing, through the early sirens, through breakfast. At ten o'clock Melissa went upstairs and put her ear to the door. They were whispering again. The whispering stopped as she went inside. The walls of the Renaissance Court were quivering. The floors of the Byzantine Court were trembling.

She was lying in bed, wide awake. Her prehistoric hair was spread out around her face on the pillow. Melissa was afraid to go very close to her, but when Ria smiled and said, 'Hi, Mummy', in her own voice, she went and checked her temperature, as a mother is supposed to do. 'Are you sick?' she said. Ria nodded. 'My throat hurts.' Her forehead was unusually hot. 'I think I've got Blake's thing.'

She gazed up at her, those bulbous eyes, their sooty sunrises, the innocent, reddened cheeks.

'Can you stay with me for a minute?' she said.

'OK.'

'A long minute.'

'Who were you whispering to just now?' Melissa sat down next to her on the bed, feeling relieved. It was a warm and beautiful day. The sun was coming in through the window. It was tonsillitis, only tonsillitis, and Ria was just herself, her uncommon child with her coming and going teeth and her imaginary friend. 'Is it Coco? I thought you'd lost touch with her. Is she back now?'

Ria gave a coy smile and put the covers up over her mouth. 'No,' she said, starting to laugh. She wanted to play the game where Melissa had to guess which of her invisible friends was in the room, there had been so many.

'OK,' Melissa said. 'Is it George?'

Ria shook her head, giggling.

'Is it Taffy Bogul?'

'No.'

'Charlie R?'

'No.'

'Charlie K?'

'No.'

'Shanarna.'

'No,' Ria laughed.

'Oh, I give up.' Melissa threw up her hands. 'Who is it then?'

'You *know* who it is.' When she said this, she poked her arm out of the blanket for emphasis, the one with the hurt wrist, and the hand looked bigger. Also her voice had changed again, that lower pitch, with a wickedness in it.

'Who?' Melissa said, beginning to feel afraid.

'It's *Lily.*'

Now Melissa stood, took a step away from the bed. Ria was smiling up at her as if she couldn't believe how stupid she was for not guessing. Her eyes were still very large but they looked a different colour. There was grey in them, the colour of the dust.

'Who is Lily?' she said slowly.

But Ria typically did not give information about her friends, only their names.

'Is she the one who's drawing the lines?'

She shook her head and folded her arms, adamant.

'Is she – here now?' Melissa said.

A flicker of something passed across Ria's face then, a worry. She glanced over towards the door, to her right. Melissa glanced also.

'Is she? You can tell me. I won't tell anyone.'

'Promise,' Ria whispered.

'Promise.' They did the wishbone vow with their little fingers.

Carefully, Ria turned her head again to the right. 'There,' she said, still whispering, 'by the door. She always stands by the door.'

Melissa looked, but saw nothing. She had never actually met any of Ria's friends, but somehow she was expecting to meet this one. This one was different.

'She's wearing a brooch,' Ria said.

'A brooch? . . . Do you mean a broach?'

'Yeh, a broach.'

And the more she looked, the more she did begin to see a faint round shining by the door, the height of a little girl's collarbone or just below. There was nothing else attached to it, just the small round shine afloat there.

'Can you tell her I don't want to go to the palace today?' Ria was saying. 'It's not nice there any more and I'm scared I'm going to get trapped in the train if we go.'

'The train? What do you mean? I don't understand.'

The voice sounded all wrong and she seemed groggy. Melissa went to touch her forehead again but stopped just short of it, almost out of repulsion. There was a fire coming off the skin. She needed medicine. She needed a salt bath. But to get the medicine and the bath she would have to go past the door. She didn't want Ria to go past the door because then Lily might walk into her and take her completely, the way Brigitte had taken Melissa. The only thing to do was to leave her here while she went to get the medicine – and anyway, she also remembered, she had left Blake alone downstairs in his high chair. She ran down, pulling the door open wide to get out of the room without touching the broach (when she got close to it she couldn't see it any more, which made this difficult).

Blake was crying. She didn't know how long he had been crying for. His face was soaked with tears. When he saw her he cried harder, shouting at her for neglecting him, she wrenched him out of the chair and went to the medicine cupboard for the Calpol. Going back up the stairs, Blake trailed his hand along the wavy line and she batted it away, and going back into the room she shielded him from the shine, which became visible again once she reached the vicinity of the bed. That lullaby was playing from the chest, *Hush little baby don't say a word, Mama's gonna buy you a mockingbird*. She could not remember having put the music on.

'You have to stop this now,' she said to the girl in the bed. 'You're frightening me. You're not welcome here, do you understand? Get out. Get out now. Let me give her the medicine.'

Ria coughed and lifted her head. She drank two spoonfuls of the Calpol and lay back down. She didn't want to eat. She didn't want to get up, so Melissa let her sleep some more, into the afternoon, relieved that she did not have to look into those dusty eyes or hear that too-deep pitch in her voice. At three o'clock she came downstairs. She ate half a slice of toast, a little cheese and an apple quarter while Melissa was running the bath. She ventured outside into the baking courtyard but the sun was too bright, soon she wanted to go back to her room, she refused to get into the bath. Melissa backed down and gave her some more medicine because she didn't know what else to do and she was afraid of her, as Brigitte had been afraid. She waited, wringing her hands together, for Michael to get home, but by eight o'clock he had not come. It started to rain. With it thunder. The sky broke. Silver spears flashed through the clouds, electrifying the towers, knifing the air, a dark-grey colour over everything.

Through this sudden storm some time after midnight Michael walked, with a loose whiskey stagger, over the hill past Cobb's Corner, down the high street, expecting the house to be still and at peace, the small breathing of the children from the second room, the meaner breathing of her from the master court. He was alarmed, then, when she was there in the hallway, wearing her cappuccino slip, her shoulders bare, her breastplate bare, a slice of light from the skylight piercing down on her, her hair all wild and unkempt. He had a mind to grab her immediately on seeing her like that, to rush at her and lick at her shores, to capture her, suck her, eat her, fill her up and make her burst in a storm of love all over him, succumb to him the way she used to. But she said, 'Where the fuck have you been?'

And he was smiling nevertheless because he couldn't help it, because of the swirling she was making inside him just by standing there like that, that she could still do this to him, even now, even after everything. 'I went for a drink,' he said, his shoulders wet from the rain.

'Where? With who?'

'With Damian, in Brixton. The Wileys were doing a thing so we passed through afterwards.'

She snorted, looking disgusted and appalled. 'And you couldn't even call to say where you were? I've been trying to call you for hours. You couldn't even answer the phone?'

'It's out of battery,' he yelled.

'Well, why didn't you *call*? Didn't it even occur to you to call? What's *wrong* with you?'

'I'm sorry, OK!' He swayed, and she saw that his mouth was loose from drink. 'Jesus, man, it's Friday night, I went out. What, I'm not even allowed to go out now?'

She kissed her teeth to the highest octave she could manage, which was quite high. Her teeth-kissing had advanced over the years. She had adopted some of his Jamaicanness. It endeared her to him more. The whiskey-haze was awash all over her, in her contours, her curves, her lines. He went towards her with soft eyes.

'Don't be like that,' he said, pulling her into an embrace, 'Come here, my empress. Just come here and tell me you love me.'

His arms were around her, the octopus engulfing her, his smell of booze and dry-cleaned suit. She struggled against it but he was stronger than her. He did not realise quite how strong he was being in that moment, how strongly he was applying that strength. The bulls of the Assyrian Court were stamping. The lions in the Alhambra Court were roaring.

She shouted, 'Get *off* me,' and pushed him with such a force that his grip loosened and he was caught by a strange fury that seemed not quite his, to belong to an older version of himself, one that had been suppressed, by her, by living by her scripture, by the world outside. He retrieved his grip. 'You're *supposed* to be my woman,' he said, 'you're supposed to be my wife, remember? You're playing with me. You're supposed to love me, don't you know that?'

'I am not your woman. I am not anybody's woman.'

She wrenched his arm away and ran into the kitchen. She did not know where she was going. The house was a prison. It was cursed. She did not want to go upstairs because she might wake the children and the night thing that was Lily and that was getting inside Ria was up there and she couldn't bear the sound of the floorboards. She wanted to go outside but it was raining, and even if she could get out back, there was only that mean square of concrete and the barrier of fence to escape to. She was trapped. Michael followed her. He was saying sorry but she kept on walking away from him. Once she reached the passage there was nowhere else to go and she started to weep.

'Look, Mel,' he said, reaching out for her, 'let's just —'

'Don't call me Mel! I hate it when you call me Mel!' She swung round to face him. He said, 'OK,' curtly, putting his hands up, then turned and went to the wine rack. He needed more. He too needed to escape. He found a glass and poured, with a miserable, defeated expression on his face, the beginnings of an old man. The drinking was giving him a paunch.

'Don't you think you've had enough? You're drunk.'

'Yeah, and I have every reason to be, coming home to this shit.'

'*Coming* home to this shit? Try *being* at home, *with* this shit. Do you have any idea what I've been dealing with here today? Oh yes, you don't, because you didn't answer your phone. But if you *had* answered your phone, you would know that Ria is sick now too. She's got Blake's tonsillitis. And there's something . . . oh god, you have to listen to me, Michael. There's something horrible happening. There's something evil in this house. There is. There is. Don't tell me I'm being ridiculous or I'm overthinking it because I'm not. You're not here all day to know what's happening. All I know is that we've got to get out of here. We've got to. I'm scared of what will happen to her if we don't. What if she takes Blake too?'

'Who? What if who takes Blake?' He was looking at her full of derision, like a doctor would look at a patient he has given up on.

She whispered it. '*Lily.*'

He wanted to laugh. He held it back, at least he tried his best to, but a little bit of it came out by itself. It was not that he found it funny, as much as that he didn't know how to respond. He felt speechless, as if she had exited to another world and they had lost their language. His face, then, after the bit of laughter, assumed a calmer look, that first kindness she had loved in him, but with a sharp edge.

'OK,' he said in this calmer, factual tone, moving the bottle to one side on the kitchen counter. 'Don't take this the wrong way, all right? But I think there's something going on with you, Mel – sorry, Melissa – that you need some help with. Lots of women get postnatal depression after having a baby. It's common. Damian was saying Stephanie had it after Summer was born. It's an actual real thing. I've been reading about it online. It can happen to anyone . . . yes, even you. It can cause delusions, breakdowns. I'm serious, man, you need to talk to someone. It's worrying, the way you're carrying on . . .'

Listening to this, a bitter, spiteful determination had taken over Melissa's body, curling her lips inwards, clenching the sinews in her arms, her shoulders. She wanted to hurt him. She wanted to make him feel small and humiliated and dismissed, the way he was making her feel. 'Why, thank you,' she sneered. 'Thank you so much for your concern. Is *that* what you've been doing all evening, huh? Sitting there with Damian talking about your crazy woman, your postnatally-depressed woman who won't fuck you any more? You clueless, insensitive bastard. Did Damian make any other suggestions perhaps? Any other revelations? Did he enlighten you at all on how to get down with this woman? On what to do when there's trouble in Paradise? Did he tell you to go and sleep with someone else's woman instead, like he did?'

'What d'you mean? What are you talking about?'

Melissa glared at him, waiting for it to dawn on him. When it did it cut him right through his heart. It went straight into the blade of light and set him on fire. It was a physical pain. It broke him, like he'd told Perry she would one day, all that time ago in Montego Bay.

'You?' He shrank with the word, afraid of it.

'Yeah, that's right. Me.'

'With Damian? You mean, you . . . and Damian?' He laughed again, only very briefly. He had taken on some of Melissa's habit of laughing in response to something negative. He looked haggard suddenly, his shoulders and torso hanging limp in his suit. 'Are you kidding me?'

'No I am not kidding you.'

Melissa started to feel cold along her arms and chest. A

fear, a different kind of fear, was stealing up on her. She went past him into the living room to get the blanket from the sofa and wrapped it around her, partly just to get away from him for a minute, to not have to behold the expression in his eyes, the hurt, the incredible hurt, the wet shine of it. She did not go back into the kitchen but stayed near the dining table, looking in at him through the doorway, from the shadows.

'When?' he said.

Her voice quietened. 'In Spain.'

'In Spain? *When* in Spain? When we were all there, together?'

He wanted to know everything, every detail, the exact circumstances. He forced her to tell him, the pool, whether she had liked it, what shape, how many times. Then he exploded and kicked over the dustbin. As he did so more sawdust came spilling out on to the paprika from the gash in the wall. The storm shook the house with another blast of thunder. The monkeys in the monkey house were screaming. The parrots in the parrot house were shrieking. The mice under the bath were playing their violins in a frenzy. 'And he was there?' Michael said. 'He was there tonight, *drinking* with me. Chatting with me like nothing's happened?'

'What are you so angry for?' Melissa said. 'You did the same thing, remember? You went there first. I didn't react like this, did I?'

'Oh, so is that why you did it? To get back at me?'

'No!'

'Why, then? Why'd you go there with him, of all people? He's my *friend*. How can you disrespect me like that?'

Melissa could hear the lullaby again, playing from above, drifting down the stairs, *If that mockingbird won't sing, Mama's gonna buy you a diamond ring, if that diamond ring turns brass, Mama's gonna buy you a looking glass* . . . She glanced up towards the halfway landing. An upper floorboard creaked. 'It was . . . I didn't' – but she lost her train of thought.

'I'll tell you why I'm angry,' Michael said. 'Let me tell you why I'm so upset,' and the words of John Legend's Used To Love U were reverberating in his head as he did so. 'It's because I *love* you. That's why. Hear that? At least, I *used* to love you, because I'm not so sure I do any more. So yes, it hurts me that you've shared your body with someone else. That was my temple, my sacred place – it was *mine*, get it? I've been dying here waiting and waiting for you to let me in and you go with someone else, with *Damian*, oh man . . . And do you want to know the reason why I have to explain this to you? Why you can't even work it out for your fucking self, the reason *you* didn't react like this? Well, that's because *you* don't love *me*. You never have, have you? I can see it now. I think I've known it all along but I was too scared to face it. I'm so stupid. I'm so fucking stupid . . .'

He had backed away towards the passage so that the shape of him filled the failed double doorway, the top of his head almost touching the frame. There were tears coming down his face, his mouth was slack and distorted. There was a new, deeper bend in his posture, a caving in, almost immediate, like a plant that has wilted in an instant yet the actual movement is impossible to witness. She watched him, full of compassion, wishing she had not told him. It would have been better if she hadn't told him. It was nothing to her, what the body did or whom it belonged to. It was different from love. Love was a palace and the body was just an object inside it, but he didn't see it that way, to his detriment. How could she explain it to him?

'I do love you,' she said, but it felt like someone else was saying it, not her true self, which was somewhere outside these walls. He was shaking his head, refusing.

'No, you don't. You can't. You're a liar. I've never been enough for you. I've never been what you wanted. I bet you think being with me is the biggest mistake of your life —'

'No, no, it's not true —'

'You think I'm a failure. You think I've put you in a cage the way your dad put you in a cage. That I've forced you to live such a plain and ordinary life, the same as everybody else. Do you think I wanted to be this? Do you think I wanted —'

'Michael, look!'

Behind him, just missing the back of his head, Erykah Badu fell to the floor in her frame. Her glittered sky-blue boots, her raised fist and shimmering dreads, their glass home shattered, sending shards of light across the paprika. Before the picture had fallen, Melissa had seen it slide first to one side on the wall and then the other, making itself crooked like the dancers, before coming fully off its nail at some secret pressure from behind. Now Barack Obama was doing the same thing, his calm and thoughtful face dipped to one side, then the other side, smashing as it landed.

'What's happening?' Michael said.

'I *told* you. See? *She*'s doing it. She's here, all over the house. I have to save her. Help me, Michael, I can't do it on my own.'

The felled dustbin rolled across the floor by itself. More sawdust came spilling out of the wall.

'It's the wind. It's just the wind,' Michael said, closing the window. 'Can't you hear the storm?'

'Come with me.'

She was holding out her hand to him from beneath the blanket, pleading with him, moving from one bare foot to the other on the kitchen step. She was all gone now, that woman she once was, that light creature, that lovely flame. He had lost her and this woman here before him, he did not know her.

Directly above her head, Melissa, the other Melissa, she was no longer sure which one was which, heard the floorboards moaning again, creaking and bending and resounding a terrible pressure. She was coming. She was trailing her white hand along the wavy black line. She was coming down the first three stairs, one step, another, quicker step, one step, another, quicker step. It was almost too late. Melissa ran to the bottom of the stairs and looked up. She would be coming now. Yes, there, turning into the halfway landing, that dreadful crooked gait, to come to a pause underneath the skylight, looking down at them – it was her. Ria was almost all gone. The powdered hands. The shine of the broach. The face was too thin, no light in it, only in the broach. And she was so pale.

'Oh god,' Melissa said, clutching the blanket to her chest. Michael was behind her now.

'Daddy,' the girl said, the voice too deep, and a different accent – Deddy.

'Don't touch her. It's not Ria.'

The girl reached out her white hand to her father and started descending towards him.

'Lily, stop!' Melissa shouted. She thought that if she exercised the courage to address her directly and with force, she would listen. Michael turned to her, feverish with anger and confusion.

'What?' he said.

'She's taken her. She's making her sick!'

'What are you talking about? This is *Ria*. It's *Ria*, your daughter.'

'*Deddy*,' Lily called out, 'I don't feel *well* . . .'

'Get away from her, get away from my daughter!' Mellissa went up and grabbed Lily by the arm, feeling disgusted by her awful white hand, tugging at her as though Lily were a coat that must be taken off. There was the sound of crying, this close, too-deep, ghostly crying, and another, smaller crying, a baby, from further away.

'Hey!' shouted Michael. But he was too late. Lily shook Ria from the inside as Melissa was trying to pull her off, so that Ria stumbled. She came tumbling down the last seven stairs, down the wavy black lines on either side, and rolled to a heap in his arms, her skin burning hot, her pyjamas soaked through with sweat.

There was a horrified silence, in which everything came to stillness, even the storm. The house was holding its breath.

Michael said, his face consumed with hatred, 'Look what you've done.'

And Melissa saw the crumpled girl at the bottom of the stairs. She was shivering. Her face was hidden away. The back of her neck was like Ria's neck, soft, with the dark down. 'Oh,' she said. 'Oh . . .' catching herself in the hallway mirror and not recognising herself. She saw only the creature who Michael hated. There in the glass, she saw the picture from her dream of the two of them in the boat, her wildly rowing, he lying dead, and she understood now that it was his love that was dead, not his body, and hence she was alone, but without herself. She was untraceable, irretrievable. She did not know where she was and so she did not know what to do. All around her there was a sense of things throbbing and vibrating. The leaves of the peace lily by the window twins were gently shaking. The frames of the windows themselves seemed to be bulging outwards. The curve of the ecclesiastical arch was pulsating. The black flecks of the inner trees of the crooked floorboards were rising. The other pictures in the passage of the heroes were sliding, melting, losing their solidity.

'I have to get out,' she said, backing away towards the front door. 'I have to get out of here. Something's – *happened* to me, I've *lost* something . . .' She lifted her arms, looking down at them as if studying some unknown object. 'I have to get out!' she cried again, as the throbbing spread further and further outwards, becoming more violent, it was below her, above her. The dancers in the master court were tumbling. The birds in the Tanzania square were twitching. The raffia at the windows was splitting. The toy figures outside in the play-house were snapping. The yellow teddy bear on the red bench was rocking. All around her the dust was falling, raining down. She swung open the front door and ran out into the street, the blanket still around her shoulders but her feet bare, and as she walked quickly along the damp pavement she could hardly feel its wetness. Down she went to the bottom of Paradise looking for her house, and up she went to the top of Paradise searching for her self, past the block of flats where Pauline's light was still turned off, around the corner where the red-lit peak of the Crystal Palace tower came into view, and there the throbbing grew bigger still, took on a greater, older stature, the sculptures in the Grecian Court were crumbling, the tiles in the Moorish Court were cracking, the frescos on the ceilings of the Renaissance Court were dissolving, the lions in a circle in Alhambra were howling, the bulls of the Assyrian Court were stamping, the tomb of Beni Hassan was opening, the colossi of Abu Simbel were toppling, and the ferro-vitreous edges of the ferro-vitreous arches were loosening, and the heads of the statues of the Greeks in the grasses were rolling, and the dinosaurs made of old science were groaning, the spirals of the spiral staircases were spinning, the mummies in the Egyptian Court were wailing, the echoes in the organ loft were deafening, the big glass panes of the central transept were crashing –

And it was there, in the central transept, that on that cold November night in 1936, the final fire started. It began quietly, as fires often do, with a small, orange flame. It swept through the transept in its fast red gown, taking the spirals, the arches, the inside elms and the crystal walls. Into the aviaries it went, sending the birds flying out into freedom. The manacles and the Welsh gold were taken, the Indian silk and the obelisks were ablaze, the cannons, the lace, the Belgian chiffon, all lost in an inferno of molten glass and iron. The flames were visible from the southern shores of the English Channel, and when the fire was at its highest, a flock of those dark birds was seen circling above it, soaring and lifting, higher and higher, up and out into the relative safety of Pissarro's skies.

14

THE WORST THING

The cemetery at Hither Green is set across a sweeping breadth of green hill at the very southern edge of London, close to places like Eltham and Lee, where many of us have never been. The graves form rows of greyed stone arches along the wider arches of the hill, and their flowers are prey to the moods and extremities of the weather, which today is cool and pressing towards winter, the golds and reds of late October falling in the leaves, an east wind toying with their journeys to the ground, and carried on the wind a distant smell of woodsmoke, marking the entrance to the cold season. Through these loose amber leaves Damian walks on a day off from work, wearing trainers and a black Parka, a light growth of neatened stubble over his jaw, looking for one grave in particular, which according to his map is in the north-west corner of the necropolis, in the third row down. The funeral seems like a lifetime ago yet it is only a year. He cannot remember the direction the hearse took or where exactly it stopped, only the lowering of the coffin into the ground and the shovelling of the earth on top, how much earth it seemed, how deep it went. As he walks he remembers these things more clearly, and it is as if he is attending for the first time, fully present. He is holding flowers. He also has one of his father's carvings from the boxes in the garage, an old man with hunched shoulders and streaks of white hair, which he intends to leave with him to change and erode with the climate.

When he gets there, to the third row in the north-west corner, there is a woman at the foot of the grave, bending down and arranging some flowers. They are wonderful flowers, extreme in their colours, orange roses, gyp, bright yellows, a mass of them. The woman is wearing a purple coat with a yellow scarf. As Damian gets closer, he begins to recognise the movements of her hands, the way she bends strictly at the waist with her spine straight and the backs of her knees pushed out. The colours she has chosen for her offering are the same colours that used to sit on the dining table, and in the pots on the balcony. And her coat, most of all the coat, the exact shade of the purple cardigan she used to wear. The gold of the autumn leaves at her feet are reminiscent of those gold buttons.

She turns and looks at him. The same face, still bright, older.

'Joyce?' he says.

She smiles and opens her arms, gives him the biggest hug he has been given by another adult in a long time.

'Look at you all grown up,' she says in a far-off voice, which resounds deep inside his head. 'You're a man now, and guess what? Everything is going to be fine. Just fine. You watch.'

He sat there with her and they talked, until his flowers blended with hers, and the gold buttons faded away.

A day of reckoning. The writing was finished. A play, this time, about Michael Jackson faking his death in order to experience his glory. Nothing might ever come of it and that was OK, for he would find the way. He would find his path. From Hither Green he went to Blackfriars and took the tube to Embankment. By now it was evening and darkness had fallen on the river. Whenever he came to the South Bank he always got off the tube at Embankment rather than Waterloo so that he could walk across this river, and feel what it meant to be a part of it, containing as it did in its spirit the abundance of the city, the history of it, the souls of its people. He watched the silver of the lights on its ever-moving surface, felt the deep breathing of its tide out towards the ocean. And he beheld the magical sight of the blue-lit trees along the southern bank, which was always festive, always reaching for Christmas. The entire wall of the Royal Festival Hall was covered with a glittering curtain of white lights, cascading down in a diagonal direction. There were crowds of people drinking on the terrace, walking among the trees, waiting at the carousel. He relished it, this power of London to allow an escape from the self, for just a little while, in a munificence of surrounding, an enormous activity and excitement.

He had arranged to meet Michael by the Madiba statue outside the Royal Festival Hall, at the top of the terrace stairs. They had not seen each other since their last drink at the Satay, when Damian had been locked inside the madness of his writing, his feet deep in cold water most evenings and his calves bare. He had been happy, riveted, oblivious to almost everything, despite being on the brink of losing his job, despite Stephanie demanding that he set up a bed for himself downstairs until they decided what to do. He would work late into the night, like the old days, and smoke in the driveway during breaks, feeling connected to the stars as he looked up at them, their exquisite loneliness. When it was finished he had saved it on to a USB, sent it to himself via email so that cyberspace would cushion it, then he had risen, taken his feet out of the water and gone out for a run. Dorking had looked so different during that run, greener, colourful. He even discovered a basketball court down an alley off one of the neighbouring streets, which he had started using with the children.

Michael had not been forthcoming about this meeting, which was understandable. Damian had persisted, though, desiring of some essential punishment, yet standing there in the cold next to Nelson he had no idea what he was going to say to him or what either of them could be expected to get out of seeing each other. Perhaps he should have let it lie. Perhaps he should have forced himself to forget that they had been friends, but the thing was that he missed him, it was partly selfish, he wanted to apologise, but he also wanted to know how he was. So when he saw Michael's head, adorned in a flat cap, appearing on his ascent up the stairs, bent at first then lifting, Damian's first instinct was to go and knock his shoulder and give him dap, he was that pleased to see him. But he didn't. He waited dutifully for the tone to be set. He was looking sharp, he noticed, a thick black coat and a suit, a whole suit, walking the power of it, in full effect. There was no shoulder-knock or shake-hand.

'What you sayin',' Michael said, and Damian replied also with a question, 'What's up,' neither of which were answered strictly and thus do not require question marks. Damian said, 'You look well,' as Michael's face became stern, firmly set against him. Two months ago he had wanted to destroy him. Now he felt a mere disconnection, along with an awkward kind of gratitude.

'Been looking after myself. Been running a lot,' he said.

'Is it? I've been running as well.'

Michael did not reply. He had not come here to chat. There was a prickly silence between them while people went wading by in couples and trios and crews, in their leggings and cowboy boots, their dinner jackets or skinny jeans, or symphony clothes, depending on which level and which building of the South Bank complex they were visiting. There was such an atmosphere of sociability around them but they were not part of it, they couldn't quite drink together, definitely not eat together, and Michael maintained a metre's distance from Damian, facing outwards and away towards the river.

'Shall we walk or something?' Damian said.

They fell into step, and there was a little less bounce in Michael's step. He walked closer to the ground. He could still

feel it, a coolness around his shoulders, the absence of something reassuring. She was no longer with him when he
walked. There was only one dimension now. He was concentrating on strengthening it, and being here wasn't helping.
Did Legend go for a walk with the guy he cheated at? He
shouldn't have come.

'How are the kids?' Damian asked as they reached the
bottom of the stairs, turning towards the bank. It seemed the
safest place to start, yet was tinged with guilt.

'OK . . . considering,' Michael said. 'Ria had that swine
flu, though, back in summer. It was horrid, knocked her out.'

'No. That was bad. I heard about that in the news. Was it
really to do with pigs?'

'Yeah, it was. Something about the farms.'

'Nasty, man.'

'You know say I've given up the pork now.'

They came to the book market and paused, a breather. The
cold was lifting off the river. Boys were making curves in the
skatepark underneath the bridge, boats drifting by with parties
going on inside. Further down along the blue trees there is a
quieter place with some restaurants and bars set in a lane and
they came to that eventually. Michael had left Paradise, he
revealed, and was living in a flat, an 'apartment', he called
it, not far away. He had the children at weekends, Melissa
had them during the week. She would also be moving soon.

'I'm sorry. I'm so sorry,' Damian said. 'I really didn't mean
for it to happen, you have to know that. I was in a mess.'

'Oh please, we're all in a mess. You want to apologise? It's
too late. It's irrelevant.'

'But it's completely wrong. You two should be together.'

'Why?' Michael said angrily.

'Because you work.'

'We haven't worked in a long time.'

'She loves you.'

Michael gave a fierce, condescending look made blue by

the trees and Damian was crushed by it. There would never be another side from this. They would not be able to get there. The water was too deep.

'It wasn't you, you know,' Michael said in the end. 'That wasn't the reason. You were just a device in the machine of our breaking, and we needed to break. It's not so bad, when it finally happens. You think the world is going to collapse around you but it doesn't. You can see yourself clearly again. You realise that the fear was the worst thing.'

They did drink together, for they were thirsty, in a bar down that quiet lane. It would be a last drink, and they spoke of other things, for as long as they lasted.

On the train on the way home Damian thought about this, this idea of seeing yourself clearly again, of the fear being the worst thing. Somewhere in the pit of him he was not quite envious, more watchful, accepting. They had taken that devastating step. Bags had been packed. Schedules had been arranged. The physical reconstruction of domestic life had taken place. He had imagined it so many times, what his life might look like, feel like, in that singular 'apartment', on a narrow London street. But to bring it to fruition was another thing, and he understood now that he did not have that kind of courage. He was a stayer, a settler. He had less spirit, perhaps, less adventure inside him. That difficult, more glorious, complex way was for the others, the people who had enough light inside themselves to bear the loss of some of it. Or so it seemed to him, on this side of the water.

When he got home, Stephanie was sitting at the dining table working on a collage of family photographs to put up on the wall. This was something she did at the end of every year. She gathered all of her favourite pictures, of holidays, days in the park, school plays and moments she wanted to remember at a glance around the house, and spread them out on the table. She surveyed them, the highlights of their lives, looking for a pictorial order, a symmetry of love. Then she made slow and careful selections and placed them in a meaningful arrangement on a piece of card, sticking them down only when the position of each photograph was just so, relating to the ones next to it, the whole thing conjuring an enduring celebration of how they lived. When this was done she framed it and found a place for it – there was one in the kitchen, in a curlicued brass frame, two above the stairs, another in the hallway and one in each of the bedrooms. In this way their lives were caught in moments of rightness. Any chaos or discontent was brought to a point of stillness and calm. It gave hope to the coming year. It gave her faith in their continuance.

She did not look up when he came into the room. He had been trying, since finishing his play, to retrieve her – talking with her, holding her sometimes, being present, engaging in the children's lives again – but some of her coolness remained. The house smelt of warm food recently cooked, lasagne, tomatoes. Usually she did the collage in December, in the days between Christmas and New Year. 'You're early,' he said.

'I know. I just felt like it.'

A photograph of Summer, Avril and Jerry at Stonehenge that spring had been chosen for the centre. 'I don't remember that one.' Damian went closer and peered over her shoulder.

'You weren't there,' she said. 'We had a fight that morning in the driveway? So I took them by myself? We had a lovely time actually.'

As he sat down with her at the table she asked after Michael. He told her. He didn't want to lie about anything any more. He was going to tell her everything she needed to know, because she was strong and good. She was a gateway to peace. He had felt it walking towards the house, walking up the path, opening the door. She was home, a place to stop and just be.

'They broke up? But why?'

How should he explain it? The February snow, the black

tree and the cigarettes, and the Baetic night, the big disappointment of it, a balloon descending, sinking to nothing.

'There was a device, in the machine of their breaking . . . And that device – I think . . .'

Stephanie was looking at him and there was something in her eyes, a mixture of gladness and concern, a surge of pride, of righteousness. She didn't let him finish. 'Are they working it out? They've got to work it out, for the children's sake.' And she thought of the marriage guidance leaflets she'd picked up with the bereavement counselling ones back in January. She had not shown them to Damian. She hadn't wanted to, they'd seemed useless, draining, but she'd kept them just in case. She glanced towards the sideboard, trying to remember which drawer they were in. Then her eyes returned to the photographs, with a renewed sense of vision.

'*That*'s why people get married,' she said. 'When you're married, it's harder to walk away. You're stuck with each other.'

'Is that how you see it?'

'Isn't that how *you* see it?'

'No.'

He picked up one of the photographs. It was of the two of them together, before they got married, taken in London, in Camden by the canal. 'This is so old, man. Look how young we look.'

'Well, I've been having problems finding recent ones of us. There's none from this year, obviously, unless you've got some on your phone. I haven't.'

'It's been a difficult year,' he said.

'You think?'

As they worked on the collage together, Stephanie looked up and out at the garden at one point and placed her hand on her stomach under the table. She was about to say something. It was still early and she had wanted to wait, but perhaps now was the right time. She had already decided that everything would be all right, with or without him.

'What?' he said, noticing her watching him.

Her eyes melted. She smiled, but looked down again. Another time. Soon. Let the life grow, regardless of what was outside.

'Do you have one of your dad?' she said.

Later, when she was getting up from the table, the edge of her slipper got caught in the leg of her chair. He went to free it for her, smelling the gist of her bright hair. She looked so pretty in that instant. He bent down and gently pressed the slipper back on to the heel of her foot.

15

ACROSS THE RIVER

Over the river to the north. River through the heart of this city. River of centuries, of black and white histories. The passage from the south. The river that divides the divide. Driving across in a red Toyota saloon, the spires of Parliament and the great slow eye of London that hardly moves when you are inside it. The quiet arches of the bridges and the water trembling through; and the trees on the bank behind you as you cross, and the birds as they soar.

Onwards to Victoria, along the high Buckingham Palace wall to the roar of Hyde Park Corner and the pricey tip of Knightsbridge, passing there, coming off the roundabout, Park Lane northbound. Melissa was going to see her mother. The children were in the back, Blake on the left, Ria on the right. On the passenger seat were a bag of fruit (mangos, apples and melon) and a bunch of pink roses (Alice liked pink). She took the North Carriage Drive off Marble Arch and they sped past the wild grass and the Sunday runners, the Serpentine lake in the distance and the ghosts of the summer bladers who rolled alongside it, weaving in and out of skittles. Now the cold sun of December glittered across the planes. The trees were so many expired afros and fallen weaves, only the roots left, brown and naked in the austerity of winter. Then out again into the traffic of Bayswater, up westwards, approaching Kilburn, where Alice waited in her pink flat in her house hat and dashiki, her cardigan and her slippers, calling 'Is that you?'

when Melissa buzzed, and coming down to answer the door clutching her walking stick. There she was, a shrunken woman in a foreign land, yet home to her children when they most needed it.

This is where Melissa had come that time, when all the glass had fallen and the Sphinx had lost its nose. She had come alone with a suitcase and stayed for a week. This is where you come when you are lost, when you feel that you are never going to find the place. You go to the first place, the first country, to her net curtains and her singular food, to her safe and open door. You lie down. You eat. You listen to her. And you know that this house will not fall down. This house is sturdy and is made of bricks, and the wolf will not come and blow it down.

'You cut your hair!' Alice said. 'Why you cut your hair? It's too short!'

'It's not that short,' Melissa said, touching the back of it. It was short. She had been to the hairdresser and truncated the fro. She wore it pasted down to her scalp with gel, giving a boyish, 1920s look; a new hair, a new her, with a grey streak. She had also been shopping with Hazel in Carnaby Street last week and dived into the clothes, feeling alive and fabricy again. She had bought a poncho, which she was wearing today.

'You look nice,' Alice smiled, but she did hate the cutting of fros, anyone's, especially the good ones, when so many people struggle. 'Why you didn't dye that grey, though?'

'I like it.'

Alice laughed. 'You cannot walk around with white hair. It's secret of age.' This was a lost argument already and she knew it. 'Go in,' she said. 'Mind the stairs with baby.'

She had come up these stairs, alone, in old clothes and her longer hair carelessly tied back. She had ascended to the pink-ness of paint, the heavily ornamented, hand-cushioned living room, the cluttered kitchen where it was always warm, like a warm, dark womb, where the smell of egusi filled the room and Radio 4 was playing and her mother was heating up some akara for her under the grill.

'Sit down, Omo,' she had said, putting the akara in front of her. 'Eat.'

And she did, because you do not refuse the voice of your mother at a time like this, in fact at any time, unless she is commanding something unreasonable or ludicrous, like 'don't talk to boys' or 'don't go out at night', when you are thirty-eight years old. She ate, neither of them talking much, just being comforted by the sound of Alice swishing and shuffling about the room, stirring the stew, mashing the eba, pouring the tea. The eba was fine eba, even through her tears which came here and there, even through the images that kept passing through her mind of that terrible night, her bare feet on the concrete, coming back to the quiet house and Michael waiting there, his face so drawn and resolute, *Where's Ria? Where's Ria? She's upstairs, she's asleep, leave her be.*

'Her leg is better,' Alice said now, having inspected Ria's climb up the stairs. She went to play with Blake in the living room, where Alice had laid a piece of material over the carpet for them to mess up as they pleased. Blake especially liked the plastic telephone with the old-fashioned cord, which he dragged across the room with him making calls. Ria still liked the animal lorry that flipped down its door so that they all came tumbling out. Her hands were better too, smooth again.

'I'm so glad to finally be out of that house,' Melissa said, sitting in the same chair where she always sat at the kitchen table. Alice was putting the roses in water. The akara was heating under the grill and the eba was already mashed and separated.

'One day you find a better house,' her mother said.

But Melissa did not want another house. She was happier in the flat with the two bedrooms on the fourth floor in Gipsy Hill, high up again, the towers in the distance, which had become a landmark of home, a necessary reminder. She no longer wanted upstairs and downstairs and a view of the houses on the other side of the street. It had been a relief, the mountain of boxes ready for leaving, the packing of the Czech marionette and the Cuban moka pot, the emptying of her wardrobe in the master court, then leaving, up Paradise, left at the top, right at the end, away, away. (Behind the fridge, when she was turning it off for the last time, she had found a dead mouse, its face closed and faded, covered in dust. Someone had scribbled over the word 'Paradise' on the street sign at the top of the road.)

So today it was the four of them sitting down to eat the eba and stew on the plastic checkered tablecloth in the warm kitchen. Alice separated Blake's eba into small pieces. She was adamant that they should eat with their right hands, that any sign of left-handedness in a child should be destroyed as soon as it became apparent. To be left-handed was virtually to be disabled, she maintained, even though Melissa regularly pointed out that Barack Obama was left-handed and it didn't seem to have affected him in a negative way. Alice's answer to this was that Barack's achievements were increased by the fact that he had become president despite his handicap, that if he had been able-bodied, things would have been easier for him and he would have become president sooner.

'How is new job?' she said.

'It's OK.' Melissa had started teaching journalism at an adult education college.

'That's right.'

'Are you still going to your keep-fit classes?'

'It's too expensive,' Alice complained. 'At first it was forty pence. Then they said one pound. After that they say it's two pounds. Now, five pounds!'

'Thieves.'

'Eh-heh!'

'More, please,' Ria said, and Alice got up, satisfied.

After the eba, in her old clothes and her eyes swollen from crying, Melissa had dragged herself next door into the living room, where the pinkness was at its peak. It was a huge Victorian parlour, big enough for a single bed on one side separated off by a curtain, where she had slept during that week. There was a cascade of turquoise butterflies hanging from the curtain rail at the window, and scores of photographs and ornaments, Warren and Lauren when they were little, Melissa and Carol at graduations, Alice and Cornelius on their wedding day, then two ebony elephants, a milkmaid, a sewing machine, various bunches of plastic flowers, crocheted doilies, fans, feathers, several cabinets. There was such a paraphernalia of object in this room that it was impossible not to lose some of the urgency of your own personality when you were inside it, and to let yourself sink into the world of Alice, her unbroken cord with the motherland, her individualness, her private whispering. Here Melissa had lain down on the sofa with its hand-sewn cushions, and even though it was summer then, Alice had put a blanket over her to keep her warm in case she got cold when she was sleeping. Before she went to asleep, Alice had also lent her her stressbuster brick, given to her by a church friend. It was soft and made of rubber. 'You squeeze it in your hand and make you feel better,' she said, and she demonstrated with her wrinkled, chocolate-coloured hand, offering it like a pusher, with the deepest and most sincere faith, as if she had invented it herself rather than appropriated it.

As Melissa had slept, alone in that room, Michael on the other side of the river and the children with him, she had dreamt of him, in dreams made of memories. They were making love on the forest floor on a summer's day, the trees towering above her in the sky. He was sitting by her on the bed at Paradise as she was sleeping, watching over her, the great love, the early man, shining down, the sun coming up in the morning. And now they were walking together across the grass of the University of Greenwich, towards the bank of the Thames, he in a white suit, she in a strapless electric-blue dress. A memory of a possibility, a future that had never happened. A part of her still wanted that blue and white picture to happen. She wanted to see him in that white suit, to wear that electric-blue dress, to hold his hand and walk together towards the water. But the way was unclear now. She could not get there without losing herself, which she had still not found. What she was experiencing was a strange opening out of herself inside, so that she could sense what she truly, harshly was, the core of it, which was dark and empty and cold, waiting to be filled from within, and she must guard and hold on to it to stop it from breaking.

She was woken by the sound from the kitchen of her mother peeling apples. She woke with a purity of thought, blank and calm, the way she always woke in this room. Soon Alice came in with the apples and sat down in the armchair next to her. She offered Melissa a quarter. She had put sugar on it. Everything was still and quiet, the butterflies, the milk-maid, the elephants. There was a single candle burning on the mantelpiece for Alice's stillborn child from long ago.

'Mum, how did you feel when you left Dad?' Melissa asked.

Alice leaned her head back in her armchair and thought. She had never articulated how it had felt.

'It was the right way,' she said eventually. 'After a very long time, I was going in the right way. I couldn't live with him any more.'

'I'm not sure I'm going in the right way,' Melissa said. 'I don't know what the right way is.'

'You find it,' said Alice.

'How do you know?'

But there was no reply. Melissa went on to say, the calmness of a few moments ago disappearing, 'I don't know myself any more. I can't seem to find the way back to who I was . . . before . . .'

'Before the children,' Alice said, nodding her head slowly. 'Children change everything. Family change everything. You must cross the river, to the other side of yourself. After that you find it.'

When Melissa heard this, she became very alert, like a small animal caught by a light. She pictured that day, last year, driving across, their loaded red wings and the peace lily toying with Michael's nostrils. She knew full well her mother meant more than that. 'But I *did* cross the river,' she said, in a higher, childish voice. And she knew also that her mother knew that she knew it was more than that.

'You must cross it properly,' Alice said, offering another piece of unnecessarily sweetened apple.

Alice still believed that Melissa and Michael would get back together one day, this month, this week or next year, just as soon as Melissa had crossed the river properly. She tried a little bit not to go on about it during these visits but she went on about it.

'He is a good man, much better than your daddy.'

'You get better house and live together as you supposed to.'

Today she didn't offer the stress-buster because Melissa didn't seem stressed or unhappy, but as it was winter, and your babies are always your babies even when they are thirty-eight, she did give her a hot-water bottle with a yellow and pink cover that she had crocheted herself, and order her to go and lie down in the living room, which Melissa of course obeyed. The hot-water bottle went behind her back. The blanket went over her. The children were next to her on the floor, extensions of her, separate though physically felt, like veins, like ribs, like cubs.

'No, Mum,' she said. 'I think when I'm older I'd like to live on my own, like you, just like this, where I can be completely myself.'

Yet when she slept, the same image came to her. For it was true, she missed him, his boomerang smile, the light by his heart, the whirl of his mahogany waist. The image kept re-appearing, waiting at the edges of dreams, drifting by the water, unfolding on the shore. That blue and white day. She in the electric dress and he in the white suit with khakis underneath. Out they walked from the vaulted room of the old colonial building of the university. Their families and friends stood and watched as they walked across the green and silver grass. As they approached the black railing that holds back the river, Ria and Blake ran out to join them, and the four of them became the fine silhouettes of the dusk, four black shapes against the water's gleam. Boats went by. Bridges stood strong. Like a glittering evening shawl the river wore the night. There they stayed, until all was dark and all the lights had gone out.

★

On New Year's Eve the Wiley brothers threw their annual NYE bashment. They put the chipboard over the bookshelves, the note on the bathroom mirror telling people that this was someone's house and not a nightclub, and left the Ofili on the centre wall. Melissa and Hazel got ready together in Gipsy Hill. The town was red. They were going to paint it more so. They would shimmer in the notes. They were going to find the perfect meeting of beat and feet. Hazel in four-inch heels and her fingernails in fuchsia. Melissa with her new hair and charcoal jeans.

'Ready,' she said in the mirror.

'Looking good,' said Hazel.

Pete had come to nothing. He had cheated on her with a removal company administrator who went to his gym. She put on her new jacket, a white puffer with a silver zip. She wasn't so sure about it, if it was for a woman of a certain age. 'Is it too hip hop?' she said.

'You know you could wear a pleated skirt made of Tesco carrier bags and still pull a Pete.'

'I don't want to pull a Pete. Petes are prats. I want an ugly man who will be good to me.'

This ugly man turned out to be Bruce Wiley. He was infatuated. They danced together to Busta Rhymes and found the place where the feet met the beat. And while they were making this unexpected electricity Michael turned up, with a woman he had met at the CD shop in Catford. Melissa said hi, he said hey. She saw his eventual beauty and wondered whether it was also eventual to this new woman or whether it was straight away and therefore lesser. And Michael's first instinct was still to smell her neck for chicken even though he knew it wasn't there, but somewhere he permanently believed that it would come back and he wanted to be the one to find it.

'He loves you,' Hazel said.

'It's over,' Melissa said.

'Chocolate is never over.'

Now they were sitting on a wall in Stockwell at 4 a.m. eating chips. While they were sitting there they happened to witness the last lunar eclipse of the year. They saw the whole thing, the darkness, the intensity of that darkness, then the light coming back like a new time.

'Amazing,' Hazel said.

'Like being hugged by the night.'

The salt, the vinegar, the cones were just so.

'These are good chips.'

'Yes. They are.'

ACKNOWLEDGEMENTS

Thank you to Arts Council England (Grants for the Arts, funded by the National Lottery), the Royal Literary Fund and the Authors' Foundation for facilitating the writing of this book. To the Santa Maddalena Foundation for providing time and space to write (fittingly, in a tower). Likewise Omi International Arts Center for a spell in the Hudson River Valley. My agent Clare Alexander, editors Poppy Hampson and Clara Farmer, and the rest of the Chatto & Windus team. Also to Rebecca Carter, Claudia Cruttwell, Diriye Osman, John R. Gordon, Jennifer Kabat and Sarah Ee for readings and revelations when needed.

Thank you most of all to Derek A. Bardowell and the little ones for conversation, music and other fundamentals.

For the playlist for *Ordinary People*, go to diana-evans.com